Tor/Forge books by Richard S. Wheeler

Skye's West: Sun River
Skye's West: Bannack
Skye's West: The Far Tribes
Skye's West: Yellowstone
Skye's West: Bitterroot
Skye's West: Sundance
Skye's West: Wind River
Skye's West: Santa Fe

Badlands
Cashbox
Fool's Coach
Montana Hitch
Where the River Runs

SKYE'S WEST: SANTA FE

RICHARD S. WHEELER

A TOM DOHERTY ASSOCIATES BOOK
NEW YORK

SANTA FE

Copyright © 1994 by Richard S. Wheeler

Cover art by Royo

A Forge Book
Published by Tom Doherty Associates, Inc.
175 Fifth Avenue
New York, N.Y. 10010

Forge® is a registered trademark of Tom Doherty Associates, Inc.

ISBN: 0-812-52144-7

First edition: November 1994

Printed in the United States of America

0 9 8 7 6 5 4 3 2

To Loren and Debi,
Paradigms in Paradise

Chapter 1

Hyacinth Zephyr Peachtree didn't like what he was hearing. The Army was saying no. Professor Peachtree had started life as a child prodigy, and hadn't altered a bit since then except that his voice had baritoned. Prodigies do not listen to naysayers. Not even to Captain Dionysus Dillon, the bewhiskered, saturnine officer of the day at Fort Laramie.

The captain was upsetting Peachtree's plans. Being unavoidably detained in the Nauvoo hoosegow for a month was bad enough. And now it looked like he would not get to the California gold fields at all this year. It appalled him. All that gold, there for the plucking, and he could not get to it.

He had been skeptical at first. The Forty-Niners had roared hellbent across the unknown continent, and he had supposed they were chasing a chimera. But they weren't. There was gold in the Sierras. Giant nuggets could be pried out of gravel; placer gold could fill pouches in a few hours. Hundreds of men were returning to the States rich. Professor Peachtree wished to make amends for his skepticism.

"Look, Mister Peachtree. It's late August. It'll be December by the time you get to the Sierra Nevada. I *promise* you that if you attempt a crossing, you'll perish—you and your party and livestock. Then where'll you be?"

"Oh, the weather might hold. I'm uncommonly lucky."

"The Donner party. Ever heard of them?"

"We all have, Captain."

"That's right. We all have. They ended up snowbound, starving, and eating each other for supper," Dillon said.

"Well, we might try it. There's a woman in the party whose flesh is delectable. Carlotta Krafft-Ebing. Otherwise known as the Potawatomi Princess. A little roast thigh . . ."

Dillon looked offended. "Sir, your jest offends the ear of an officer and gentleman. I can't stop you. The Army can only advise. You are perfectly free to commit suicide; to lead others to their doom; to end up in one of the thousands of graves along this trail. If you wish to donate yourself to history, that's your business. Your options are to turn back and try again next year; winter at Salt Lake with the Mormons—which would get you to California in June or July of next year—or go via one of the southern routes—which would get you there in a few months."

"The Mormons, you say?"

"There are eleven or twelve thousand Saints in the great basin around Salt Lake. You might get permission from Brigham Young to winter there—if you have money enough. They'll fleece you in ways you can't imagine. They tend to let people stay who are willing to convert—but only those—"

"No, no, no. That's like vacationing in Bedlam," said Peachtree.

"Well then, go back and try again next year." The captain surveyed Peachtree. "You're ill dressed for bad weather, sir."

Hyacinth Z. Peachtree smiled. Sooner or later they all got around to his black clawhammer coat, his white shirt with the floppy polka-dot bow tie, and his black silk stovepipe hat. "If a man dresses as befits his high station in life, that doesn't mean he can't negotiate the wilderness, my friend. Now tell me, how does one get to the southern route?"

"One goes back east and then takes the Santa Fe Trail and then the California Trail or the Gila River Route. There are several that stay clement during the cold months."

"All the way back to Missouri?"

"That's right, sir. You couldn't manage a trip directly south from here. There's no road for your wagons. Nothing but horse and lodgetrails. There's constant danger from Arapaho, Utes, Cheyenne, Comanches, and Apaches. And even more danger once you hit the Santa Fe Trail."

"But you say those southern routes stay open?"

"Normally."

"Where does one get a guide, Captain?"

"Why, sir, talk to the post sutler, Colonel Bullock. There's one named Skye who's unemployed just now."

"A wastrel no doubt."

Dillon wheezed like a folding accordion. "Hardly. He's the best man in the West. A Napoleon of the wilds. He and his wives and a brute horse named Jawbone."

"Wives, you say? Is he of the Mormon persuasion?"

"Indian wives, Crow and Shoshone. They make an army, sir, along with that nag, which is an army in itself. They'd get you there—but they'd cost you a pretty penny."

"The sutler, you say? I'll go there."

"Good luck, Peachtree. Just take my advice and don't maroon yourself in the Sierras. It's too late."

Professor Peachtree abandoned the captain and pierced into the sunbaked parade and located the sutler's store at the far corner. His wagons and his troupe waited beside the Laramie River. Even at that distance he could see the ribs corrugating the sides of his mules. There had been almost no grass on the trail; it had all been nipped off by the livestock of the earlier travelers, miles to either side of the road.

Soldiers stared at him. He always made an impression, and that always helped sales. The sun cooked him so he hastened to the sutler's emporium and plunged into a brown gloom. At the rear, in a pool of light, was a railed-off office, so he headed in that direction, past bolts of pungent canvas and calico, sacks of coffee beans and rice, tinware, stove fittings, and a rack of percussion-lock rifles and revolvers.

"Suh?" said a furrowed man from behind a Vandyke beard. The graying gentleman rose from his swivel chair.

"You're Bullock, I presume. I'm H.Z. Peachtree, Professor Peachtree. Looking for a guide. They tell me you—"

"I'm Colonel Augustus Bullock, Retired. You speak of Skye, suh. I'm his agent."

"Well, yes. This Skye. I'm looking for a good man. I suppose you'll tell me he's good no matter what he really is."

Bullock looked him up and down until his sharp glances settled on the professor's stovepipe hat and funereal attire. "Maybe Skye's not for you, suh. He chooses his clients carefully. Out here, fools might get him scalped. I don't think you're the sort that'd fill the bill."

"He turns down clients, Bullock?"

"Most of them. It's not just his life at risk; it's the lives of his wives, Victoria of the Crows, and Mary of the Shoshones—and now they've a new son tucked into Mary's cradleboard. Frankly, suh, your arrival here at this late date speaks against you."

"I was unavoidably detained."

"Where do you wish to go?"

"Santa Fe. The captain says it's too late to assault the Sierras; I want to be taken to the southern route to the California gold fields."

"And who are you, suh? What is your party?"

"I'm a doctor of natural science, Heidelberg, of course, and I purvey remedies for those who suffer. The Peachtree remedies are based on years of study of—"

"A medicine man."

"A vulgar term, sir. I am a man with a sacred mission. I've discovered the means to cure many diseases and relieve the

pain and suffering of all of them. I employ the most modern
formulae to be found in Europe as well as ancient Potawatomi remedies, herbs and roots and spiritual disciplines unknown to white men. I'm as different from a common
medicine huckster as a hawk is from a dove."

"That's entertaining. What's your party, suh?"

"Two wagons drawn by Missouri mules; five persons, one
of them female, another elderly. They are gifted musicians.
They do a little fandango to draw citizens to our wagon, so
that I may bring my blessings to them. Of course they also
tend the mules and drive the wagons."

"A medicine show. Out to mine the miners."

"A vulgar expression, sir. We bring blossoming health and
scientific comfort and release from torment to the toilers in
the gold fields. We bring entertainment, succor, and enlight-
enment, which is worth more than all the gold in the world."

"Hucksters," muttered Colonel Bullock. "Well, suh, much
as I'd like to recommend your sterling entourage to Skye, I
don't think you'd be a suitable party. He lacked a client this
year, but I just don't think—"

"I pay well. The laborer is worthy of the hire."

"Well that's a novelty. No—"

"Colonel Bullock, you've interviewed me; I'd like to interview him. I don't want to employ some worthless border
brigand. I have valuable properties to protect. I've made a
considerable investment; I even have a portable laboratory
with which to decoct new elixirs. No sir, I wouldn't want to
entrust our lives and fortunes to some wastrel who couldn't
survive in civilization, some fool who'd get us shot by the
savages—"

Bullock was laughing politely. It puzzled Peachtree. "You
wouldn't know of Barnaby Skye, suh. Few people from the
East do. But in this country, the name excites attention. Skye
is a former mountain man, as wily as any who walked the
wilderness. For years, since the beaver trade died, he's been
a guide. He was guiding from this fort when it was a fur post

and people were flooding out to Oregon. Let me tell you, he always gets through. He's known among all the northern tribes. They say he has big medicine—power. His horse, his wives, why, suh—"

"Let me interview him. Then I'll decide."

Colonel Bullock peered out the grimy window into the bright August heat. "Very well, Peachtree. I'll send for him. He can decide and you can decide. Bring your whole entourage here in a couple of hours. Everyone. Suh, if he spots one bad apple he'll turn you down."

"Is there another guide here?"

"You could hire any of a dozen border men, suh, and perhaps make it. But there's only one Skye."

"There's only one of me, too," said Hyacinth Zephyr Peachtree.

Chapter 2

Hyacinth Z. Peachtree had never encountered a buck like the one standing on the veranda of the sutler's store. Skye radiated strength and assurance. He was modeled upon a barrel, and what he lacked in height he more than overcame in width. Skye squinted at the world from obscure blue eyes, buried in creased and weathered flesh; assessing eyes that bespoke a keen mind, examining Peachtree and his colleagues, even as the professor was studying Skye and his savage wives.

This he-goat of the wilderness wore a green calico shirt, fringed buckskin leggins, and a medicine necklace of grizzly-bear claws upon his bosom. But Indian attire stopped at his feet, which were encased in practical lace-up brogans. Nor did it reach his head. A battered topper confined his coarse, gray-shot black hair. But it wasn't the man's attire that attracted attention; it was the easy dominion radiating from him; the air of being a lord of all he surveyed.

Between those buried eyes rose a nose such as Peachtree

had never seen: a mountain of a smeller, mauled and swollen and pocked like a hogback; a nose that bespoke years of brawling, hours of happy assault and battery. In all of Peachtree's wide and worldly experience, he had never seen such a nose. It spoke well of Skye to have the lord of all noses rising from his face.

"Professor Peachtree, suh, this is Mister Skye," the sutler said. "And his wives. The elder is Victoria of the Crow, and the younger is Mary of the Shoshone. The tyke in the cradleboard is named Dirk, after Mister Skye's brother in London."

"Delighted, absolutely delighted to meet you, Skye."

"It's Mister Skye, sir."

"Why, Mister Skye it is, then. A man deserves his title."

Peachtree turned to the women. The Crow was as thin as a greyhound, as weatherbeaten as Skye, and she surveyed Peachtree from suspicious black eyes. Definitely the sort who could scalp in thirty seconds and then perform other surgeries upon the victim. The younger Shoshone wife dazzled him. He'd never seen a woman of the red race half so well fleshed. A lovely sweetness suffused her golden face. She smiled cautiously at Peachtree, ready to accept and enjoy new company.

"Ah, ladies, I am honored to meet such esteemed consorts of such an esteemed man. Victoria, indeed." He took her bony hand and grasped it. "And Mary, indeed." He squeezed her soft one, wondering how to induce her to join his medicine troupe. She would be a sensation. "Never have I seen fairer specimens of savage pulchritude."

"Sonofabitch," said Victoria.

Some of Peachtree's troupe whickered. They knew Peachtree's appetites.

"Ah, Colonel Bullock, I am truly impressed. These intrepid souls shall escort us to Sante Fe in perfect security and comfort."

"And who are you?" asked Skye, in a voice that rumbled like distant thunder.

"Why, sir, Professor Peachtree—Hyacinth Zephyr Peachtree, reared in New York City, educated in all the arts and sciences found in the capitals of Europe. A mendicant healer, devoted to the sacred mission of bringing relief and comfort to suffering mortals beset by the weaknesses of the flesh."

"A travelin' medicine man, Mister Skye," added Bullock. "An American institution."

"Why, Mister Skye, my troupe contains the finest talent that I could gather, ladies and gents learned in the healing arts, while at the same time adept at the musical arts, the means by which we entice good yeomen to learn about the most advanced scientific remedies known to the red and white races of mankind."

"Talk English," said Victoria. "I don't want to miss none of this stuff."

"Ah, Mrs. Skye, I am pleased by your attention. Your sachems of the red race have much to teach us about the healing arts. You walkers of forest and plain know the herbs that heal dropsy or ague or catarrh; I must say, before this great journey is accomplished, we shall all be richer and wiser in the healing arts."

"Where do you want us to take you?" Skye asked.

"To Santa Fe, sir. From there we will find passage to California. We plan to bring our healing to the argonauts in the gold fields."

"Santa Fe's a long way from here. There's no regular wagon road. But there's no obstacles either."

"We can pioneer a pike, sir. Now as I was saying, we are a troupe of healers. This glorious raven-haired dumpling beside me is the Potawatomi Princess, a woman who has mastered the herbal arts of the Potawatomi people, an adopted daughter of the legendary chief Old Gourd, and a royal personage among them."

Normally he introduced her as a pureblood Indian princess, but he supposed that wouldn't wash here. Carlotta Krafft-Ebing had been born in Vienna. Her dark hair, buxom form, and prominent facial bones gave her a certain native cast. She had been an operatic contralto once.

"I am utterly overjoyed to meet you; I adore noble savages, untainted by civilized vice," said the princess in dulcet voice.

"Mister Skye, let's get the hell outa here," said Victoria.

The guide ignored his senior consort.

"Why, sir, let me present the rest of my worthy entourage. This gent here"—Peachtree waved at a gray-complected giant—"is Concorde Danton, a New Orleans quadroon I purchased and freed. He's my percussionist, equally at home with drums, cymbals, revolvers, and fowling pieces. He's as lazy as a sloth, but comes to life upon the beginning and end of each day. He drives one of the wagons and is uncanny with the mules. Mister Danton has a keen knowledge of phantasms and dark forces. Some of the supplicants who come to me are possessed, and we encourage Concorde to beat the devil; a worthy act which precedes the application of our tonics and balms.

"And finally, sirs, I would present Hercules to you. This young roustabout takes tender care of our mules. He tells me he was once a coal miner in the Appalachian hills, but his fists were too large for local chins."

"Hercules who?" asked Bullock.

The youth answered. "Just Hercules. When I taken off from home I left my surname behind me, and my given name too, and come out here to be someone else. I taken Hercules because that's the strongest in the world."

"There!" said Peachtree. "You see what a feisty company we are, worldly and yet humble. Now then: I have one more gent to introduce." He gestured toward a shriveled old man in bib overalls, with a corncob pipe drooping from his lips and two days of white stubble on his cheeks. "This is Pontius P. Parsons, a godsent treasure for us all. Without Pontius, we could not reach the souls of all the good citizens who gather at our wagons to witness a better life. Pontius is sixty-eight, and stronger than he looks, though he suffers from gout, slow water, rheumatism, and other ills. But don't let the palsy fool you. He's a man of great moral courage."

"What does the P stand for?" Bullock asked.

"Pilate," the old man replied in a reedy voice. "My dear parents had certain views of organized religion, which, bless their souls, they imparted to their unworthy son before ascending."

"Jaysas," said Skye.

"Now, sirs, we have presented ourselves whole. Will we come to terms?" Peachtree asked. He was anxious to get on the road.

"Let's get outa here, Mister Skye," muttered the elder consort.

"Our fee is considerable, Professor," Skye said. "That's a long trip; the longest we've ever undertaken. We'll have to winter in Taos, which will require cash. We'll take you to Santa Fe for six hundred dollars. My regular rate is five hundred."

"Why, sir, that's an admirable price. I've no objection. The laborer is worthy of his hire. For that amount we get not one but three worthies. Consider it done."

That took Bullock aback. "Suh, I should tell you that Mister Skye hires only for cash in advance. Some people decide at the end of the trail that they didn't need him after all. I'm sure you're not one of those, but we do require that the cash be in his account with me."

"Why, Colonel, I can understand your logic. But from our standpoint, we must resist. We have no experience of the man, and he comes without credentials. The best way to assure faithful service is to pay for it after it is well earned."

"Sorry, mates," Skye said. He looked ready to leave. Obviously there would be no compromise on the point.

"Mister Skye, our purse is temporarily reduced, thanks to ill fortune just before we started. I thought to recoup it all en route, doing a lively trade in Santa Fe and perhaps among the tribes as we go. We're going to the gold fields to mend our fortunes. Now, how about if we make a preliminary offering—say, fifty dollars?"

Skye laughed genially. "Sorry, Peachtree. There's risk in this. We'd all be in constant danger. No, it's cash in advance. I'm indebted to Colonel Bullock and always square that account before we travel."

"There's no possibility of compromise? Would you consider some of my elixirs and nostrums as a barter?"

Skye shook his head. The elder consort looked positively joyous. Peachtree sensed she had no stomach for a trip that would take her so far from her homelands.

"No, it's cash in advance. We learned about that the hard way, sir, from travelers with good intentions and a few with bad intentions."

Peachtree could see that Skye was resolute. He sighed. Something about Skye and his consorts comforted him.

"I grieve that we can't do business, sir. We'll spend the night. Maybe we can come to terms in the morning. . . . Colonel, have the soldiers here been paid recently, by any chance?"

"Yes, suh. The common private gets his eight dollars and spends the whole of it in hours, mostly in my store, on tobacco and sassafras, the rest to pay gamblin' debts. I doubt that you could sell fifty dollars of your swampwater to the whole garrison."

"A pity," said Peachtree. "I have tonics and solaces for them. But perhaps they'll enjoy our entertainment. Yes, indeed. We'll give them melody and see what happens. Music at seven; deliverance from pain, bursitis, gout, scrofula, blackwater, ague, female miseries, melancholia, and migraine at half past the hour."

"I'll spread the word, suh."

"Tell them about the Potawatomi Princess, my fine friend. Tell them she'll appear in her native attire. It'll fever their imaginations."

"And you have the fever remedy, right, Peachtree?"

"Oh, you could say so," said H.Z. Peachtree. "You'll want to stock it before I leave."

Chapter 3

According to the reckoning of H.Z. Peachtree, the finger of the Divine Principle pointed at him around four o'clock. At that hour a large eastbound wagon train from the gold fields of California halted at Fort Laramie, right before his nose. The professor stared in amazement and joy at the sight of a dozen ox-drawn wagons and scores of packmules and burros, led by sixty or seventy people, halting for the night.

He was heading for the gold fields, but now the gold fields had come to him. This company had gold. Every able man carried a rifle or fowling piece, or a brace of Samuel Colt's revolvers. A dozen, armed to the eyebrows, stood around a certain enclosed and padlocked mule-drawn wagon.

Most of these men were afoot, leading pack burros that carried their worldly possessions. A few families were outfitted with covered wagons, refurbished in California for the arduous trip east. One could not even join such an armed company as this without displaying dust or nuggets to the others. These people had forsaken the land of milk and honey to return to their farms and homesteads in the East and live out their lives in luxury.

A vast delight built in the professor. He had been in a petulant mood, thwarted by the obdurate Skye's price. But upon the stroke of four, everything had changed.

All about him, the wayfarers set up their camps, cared for their livestock, and meandered toward the sutler's store at the post to outfit themselves or gossip with the soldiers. But the dozen grim men guarding the gold wagon didn't budge, and eyed Peachtree and his entourage with long, hard stares.

H.Z. Peachtree watched all this bustle with lively interest, noting the half dozen women, the seven or eight children, and the large assortment of males, all in various degrees of health. The long journey had gaunted them all, along with their ribby animals. A few leaned on staffs or used canes.

Fair enough. "We'll drum up company at seven," he said to Carlotta. "There'll be plenty of daylight. Let them rest and eat. With a little beef in their bellies they'll open their fat purses all the more. My juicy little savage, you're going to do the liveliest show you've ever done, and you're going to woo every man in that outfit. You know what to wear. We're going to sell enough to buy Skye. I figure we'll get it back on the road; that man has appetites, unless I miss the mark."

"You stick to your swampwater and I'll stick to singink," she said. "You want some red bosom on display. Maybe I will, maybe I won't. I'm an opera singer and don't you ever forget it."

"You're the Potawatomi Princess, filled with mysterious medicinal wisdom. You will ooze carnal heat for lonely miners."

She laughed. "Little do they know," she added.

He found the sulky Concorde doling out costly baits of oats to the ravenous mules. "We'll start at seven. Dame Fortune has clasped us."

Concorde avoided Peachtree's eye. "You want the all-out,

gut-buster Christy Minstrel act tonight. Ah'm not in that humor."

"It might be worth a nip of Pain Extractor."

"Ah'm your bootlickin' slave," Concorde said.

Peachtree knew the man would come around. The laudanum bribe never failed. He unlocked the cabinet in his wagon and studied his bottled stocks. He had abundant inventory of the Peachtree Pain Extractor, Cordial, Female Pills, Balsam of Life, Catarrh Remedy, Blood Bitters, Liver Medicine, Blood Purifier, and Swamp Root, but he was low on the Egyptian Regulator Tea, the Indian Root Pills, and the Wild Cherry. He might also bottle up some Mandrake Root and Wizard Oil. But he could do that on the road. For tonight, he was in capital shape.

A pair of bearded Forty-Niners hulked into his camp and Peachtree took them to be the captains of the eastbound caravan. Their hard-eyed gazes settled on Hercules, Carlotta, Concorde, and the two wagons.

"Just a neighborly visit," one said. "We like to know who we're campin' next to."

"Why, sirs, I am Professor H.Z. Peachtree. We're bound west. I am a businessman and scientist."

The two armed men didn't introduce themselves but they eyed the lacquered green wagons, and read the gilded legends upon them: Professor H.Z. Peachtree, Doctor of Natural Sciences, University of Hidelburg, Relief for the Suffering.

"You're a medicine man," said the one with the longer beard and a double-barreled Greener in the crook of his arm.

"That painful animadversion unsettles me," Peachtree said in dulcet voice. "I'm no more a tawdry medicine barker than you're packrats. Why, gentlemen, peruse my conveyance. Do you see gaudy colors? Do you see carnival advertisements? Do you see flamboyant posters and sheets? Of course not. You see a serious professional man's equipage, lacquered a subdued olive, with my credentials quietly gilded in gold upon them.

"Do you see some carnival barker in me? Of course not. You see a man who's ransacked the dusty libraries of Europe, looking for every known anodyne for the flesh and spirit. A man who has turned to the herbal remedies of the red race to supplement European science. A man who can heal, comfort, bless, and calm ravaged mortals. That's what you see. There's not another like H.Z. Peachtree on the breast of the earth."

They stared at him, flummoxed. "Well," said one, "when does the racket start? Some of us have a notion to take a gander."

"Why, before seven, and we'll waltz until the soft bosom of twilight enfolds us. We've some fine minstrels."

"And probably some fine confidence men," said the other Forty-Niner. "Here's a friendly warning, Peachtree. Anyone wandering around our camp at night's going to take a load of buckshot that you can't cure."

"Why, sirs, I admire your caution. The world's full of scoundrels. Rest assured that doctors of natural science have no inclination to wander at night, not even to the bushes. What's more, the unblinking eye of the United States Army gazes benignly over us all this fine August evening."

"Just a little warning, Peachtree."

"Why, I admire enterprising men. It fills my bosom with joy that you are returning from the diggings with the means to pleasure the rest of your mortal lives. Now, if bad health doesn't interfere—bilious fevers, or the staggers or ague don't erode your fortunes, you'll live in blessedness until your loved ones pull the pale sheet over your ancient face."

One of them grinned. "Medicine huckster," he said.

"Seven," Peachtree retorted. "Bring your bad spleen and I will make you whole."

The pair scrutinized Concorde, Hercules, and Carlotta, no doubt memorizing faces for future hangings, and then wandered back to their camp like suspicious spaniels. Fortunately, they had not noticed Pontius Pilate Parsons, who leaned upon his knobby walking stick near the river, a doddery old geezer not connected to any party. No one ever noticed him. Professor Peachtree permitted himself a moment of sheer exuberance.

Well before seven all was ready. In the yonder camp, the cookfires were dying. Women scrubbed pots. Men lounged beside their bedrolls or wagons, picked at molars, lit corncob pipes, and rubbed down their oxen. A few blue-shirted infantrymen meandered among the civilians, hearing tall tales and taking the air.

Concorde and Hercules unfolded Peachtree's wagon into a little theater. Its oaken roof formed a stage, behind which were painted panels depicting mountains and waterfalls, and sprightly fairy maidens with gossamer wings.

Peachtree changed the collar and cuffs on his shirt, powdered his newly scraped face, and flapped the alkali dust out of his clawhammer suitcoat. Inside a small canvas leanto off the back side of the wagon, his troupe dressed and painted. Concorde appeared first, a gaudy majordomo in a spangled scarlet uniform with massed gold braid at the cuffs and shoulders, and a visored and ostrich-plumed red hat. He resembled a Hottentot brigadier. He toted his bass drum, cornet, trombone, and banjo to the little deck and arranged his instruments on stands.

Carlotta emerged, gorgeous in whited and fringed buckskins, the skirt daringly high on her shapely calves. The scoop neck bared a joyous amount of Carlotta's bosom. A little greasepaint transformed her into a sullen savage. Her alchemy transmuted her into a ravishing temptress. Lastly, Hercules appeared in a lumpy black suit, his blond hair trapped under a silk topper. He carried an accordion and a shotgun for audience control.

Peachtree plucked his Waltham timepiece from its nest in his waistcoat, noted the hour, and returned it to its little pocket, adjusting the potmetal Phi Beta Kappa key on the fob.

His troupe tuned brass, squeezed bellows, or sang scales. Peachtree climbed the little iron ladder, and nodded.

Concorde began with a thunder of the bass drum, which he operated with a foot pedal, and then tromboned into "Camptown Races," while Hercules picked up the lively tune with his accordion. The music shattered the peace. It started the camp dogs to howling, which was just as Peachtree intended. But it summoned everyone within earshot, and from his perch on the deck, he could see soldiers knotting on the parade and trotting his way, the Forty-Niners drifting toward him, and assorted fort loafers congregating into a cheerful mob. Then, after the rabble had collected, Concorde struck the first note of "Oh! Susannah," and the whole congregation burst into the song that had immortalized the gold rush: the song about themselves.

> "Oh! Susannah, don't you cry for me,
> For I'm off to California with a banjo on my knee."

H.Z. Peachtree smiled, nodded, tapped his shiny patent leather shoe to the rhythm, and observed a great levity among these isolated soldiers and trail-weary sojourners. Tonight he would mint gold. Tomorrow his troupe would be off to Santa Fe.

Chapter 4

Much to his own surprise, Barnaby Skye was disappointed that the medicine man hadn't come up with the money. But Victoria and Mary entertained the opposing view. The man was a slippery-tongued crook, they said. A real medicine healer would give himself to his people, accept only gifts, and regard his calling as sacred.

Skye saw it differently. These were seasoned travelers. They were comfortable among all sorts of people. The wagons—which Skye inspected—were first-rate, fashioned of hickory and ash, and built to last. The mules were gaunted, but once they got onto good grass they would recruit. Skye sensed as well some valuable qualities in Peachtree: the huckster accepted the Skyes. He would not jeopardize their safety. He and his cohorts might be tricky in commerce, but they would be reliable trail companions.

At seven the Skyes ambled down to the Laramie River.

"I want to see the sonofabitch talk," Victoria said. "I never saw a medicine show. This here is going to be fun."

They elbowed through a crowd peppered with blue infantrymen's shirts just as music blatted from the wagon. The dusky Concorde tooted a trombone; the blond Hercules squeezed an accordion as if it were his lady love; the raven-haired Potawatomi Princess, gauded up in a whited doeskin Indian dress, wiggled her hips and snapped her fingers. A lot of calf poked through the fringes, and acres of bosom pushed up from the scoop neck. Skye had never seen an Indian maid dress like that.

"What strange and mighty tribe is she from, Mister Skye?" Victoria asked.

"She's not Indian."

"Well how come her tits are almost out?"

Barnaby Skye smiled. "It's for white men."

"You're all crazy," Victoria said.

The woman began to warble. Skye recognized a well-trained contralto voice and an operatic style. Its intensity quieted people, and they stopped their jostling and whispering to listen.

"Is this white men's religion?" asked Mary.

"No, this is just a show. The medicine man's going to make his pitch—his argument—soon."

"Your witches sure are strange," she said.

For another twenty minutes, the troupe beat out lusty tunes, which blared across the flats. Skye's wives stood enraptured, seeing something beyond their experience, while the crowd listened and sometimes joined in cheerfully when a familiar song lit the evening. Then, after "My Old Kentucky Home," the troupers set down their instruments, and Professor H.Z. Peachtree stepped forward, tugged at his waistcoat, and waited for quiet.

"Good evening, my friends," he began, in one of those subdued voices that somehow pierced far beyond the crowd. "I hope you enjoyed our little concert. There'll be more—lots more—after my message of hope."

That news elicited a happy stir.

"My friends and fellow travelers on the walkway of life, the first thing you should know about me is that I'm not a medical doctor. No, sir. You don't see M.D. after my name; you see Doctor of Natural Sciences, University of Heidelberg. This gives me certain knowledge that's not disseminated in medical academies. And that knowledge is what we're going to think about now."

The spiel fascinated Skye. Peachtree was as comfortable on his little stage as a veteran actor.

"Friends, in my youth I became obsessed with the arts and sciences of healing. I was a sickly, consumptive child. A dozen homeopathic and allopathic physicians despaired of me, and advised my sainted parents to let go of that thread of hope that sustains and comforts us in moments of need; for their son was not long for this beautiful world."

Peachtree gazed at distant hills, as if recollecting that solemn time.

"They had diligently taught me my letters," he went on. "I begged books from doctors and chemists; I read about frail lungs and weak hearts. Much to my everlasting joy, I stumbled across an account of a Shawnee sachem who had healed desperate cases in the Ohio River valley. And there on those yellowed pages were precious herbal formulae that this wondrous red man used to heal frailties of the flesh. According to the account, he never asked anything, but always told white and red men alike that it was his sacred duty to heal all people.

"Well, let me tell you. I hastened to acquire those herbs. Some were hard to find. I was too weak to hunt, but I prevailed on family and friends to comb the woodlands and swamps and fields for the required leaves and roots. These I decocted into medicinal tinctures using my mother's pots and pans. And hesitantly—oh, this was my last and only chance—hesitantly, swallowed my first spoonful. Well—look at me now. I am my own best advertisement. Robust! Sound of mind and flesh! Without pain! Yes, friends, that was the beginning of a sacred calling."

He waited quietly. The crowd had become attentive.

"That was the beginning of a consecrated life. As soon as I was able, I embarked for the learned centers of Europe, there to study every known remedy, some of them long forgotten. When I returned, I couldn't set a broken bone as any doctor could, but I knew more than any living doctor about those potions that heal mortal flesh and ease the soul and spirit."

He paused, letting his words sink home, surveying the quiet crowd.

"But that wasn't enough. For I had not forgotten the Shawnee sachem's healing art. I turned to the wise old medicine givers of this new continent, sat at the feet of the red healers, gave gifts to shamans and imbibed their precious wisdom, for our red brethren knew the healing arts even better than the great doctors of science. Why, I have, right here, the greatest healer of the red race, a fullblood Potawatomi Princess, Sumac Petal, who has joined me to heal all who seek our remedies. Look at her! Is she not the most noble and best-bred woman of her race you've ever seen? She's the youngest daughter of the great chief Rosebud."

"Sonofabitch," muttered Victoria.

"Now, what can I do for you? A lot. Man or woman, young or old, you suffer from diverse ailments. Your head aches. Your teeth hurt. Your back tortures you. Your stomach burns. Your limbs palsy. Your breath is short. Your stout heart flutters and races. You suffer periodic bilious fevers, inflammations, paralysis. You have trouble with regularity. You eat and gain no strength from it. Why, many of you are so weary at the end of a day that your tormented flesh cries for rest, and you wonder why you live on, with life such a flickering, faltering spirit within your bosom. Your hearing fades, and your sight dims, and you feel perpetually cold, even on a fine summer's day like this one. Oh, I know all of these things, my friends. I have seen them countless times, and I've helped countless people."

Skye peered around him into rapt faces.

"Now why do I travel these lonesome roads when I could set up my practice in a great city and wait for my trade to walk in? Why, ladies and gentlemen, because I am infused with a sacred mission, to bring these healing decoctions to all people. It's a holy purpose within me. I could not sit back and help only the rich citizens of opulent cities while my rural brothers and sisters cry out in want and pain."

Peachtree suddenly turned brisk.

"There's a cure for most diseases, but I'll be the first to tell you there's not a cure for everything. I'll tell you what separates me from the quacks; if they try to sell you a single all-purpose tonic that supposedly cures a long list of ailments, from gout to consumption, beware. There's no such medicine, my friends, no such elixir, no such tonic. Each disease has its own magnetic and electrostatic nature and requires its own remedy. You'll not see me offering you some all-purpose magical remedy. I'm going to describe a dozen or so healing remedies, each carefully compounded by me personally in my laboratory, and you'll have to decide which ones you need."

"He's a flannelmouth," said Victoria. "When'll he shut up?"

"Not until he sells out or he loses the crowd," Skye said.

Peachtree held up his products, one by one. "This one, friends, is H.Z. Peachtree's Pain Extractor. It is guaranteed to subdue the wildest ache. And this is the Peachtree Liver Pill, good for bilious conditions. And here is the H.Z. Peachtree Swamp Root, for goiter and cancer. The Wild Cherry here cures indigestion, fever, ague, dyspepsia. The Blood Purifier is a certain remedy for nervous debility, and kidney complaints, while the Magnetic Oil is the exact tonic for despondency, depression, hysteria, numbness, apoplexy, Saint Vitus' dance, and sick headache, all of them a single family of disease. And don't overlook my Quaker Bitters, for female weakness, failure at marital duties, ague, chills, and all affections of the nervous system."

On he went, amazing Skye with his bottles and tablets.

"And all for a dollar. One dollar apiece, a small price for health and comfort, the richest of all treasures. Buy a mixed assortment; arm yourself for every future ill. Buy ten for nine dollars. Oh, that's not cheap, but no price is too much for good health. Now, who will step up and be healed?"

A long pause ensued. Then a quavery voice rose from the rear. "Is it guaranteed? If it don't work, do I git it back?"

"It is, sir. On every bottle is the address of my St. Louis laboratory. Just write if you aren't satisfied. But if you're happy with my products, write me a testimony. I have here a scrapbook of hundreds of testimonial letters. Come up, sir, and have a look. See what people have said about my products."

"Well, I'll think on it. What if she don't work? Then where'll I be, eh?"

"I promise it'll work. I see you have palsy, sir."

"More'n that. Hurt so bad I can't stand to walk, even."

"You come up here, sir, and try my Pain Extractor. You take some right now and see what happens. Tell these good folks whether it works. It's one dollar, and you'll never make a better investment."

Skye watched the man dodder forward and recognition hit him: the gent was Pontius P. Parsons.

Chapter 5

Skye watched Pontius P. Parsons, in his bib britches and frayed straw hat, dodder up to Peachtree, who had descended to the ground before the wagon. The trip, although but a few yards, exhausted Parsons, and he leaned into his cane for support as he parted the silent crowd. He was plainly winded by his exertion, and bent almost double. But he jabbed his gnarled hand into a pocket and extracted a grimy bill.

"I'll try that Pain Extractor. I'm so stove up I could use a barrel of her," he said. "This enough?"

Peachtree examined the currency. "Why, sir, you get some change." Peachtree pulled out a billfold and handed Parsons something, along with the rectangular green bottle.

"Pain Extractor, eh? You think she'll do her?"

"It's so powerful, sir, you'll want just a nip. One half teaspoon is all I recommend. Why, one bottle will last and last. Some people need only a bottle a year, because the dose is so small. You just nip it and tell these fine folk about it."

"I ain't a talker," the old man muttered. He hooked his

cane over his arm and uncorked the bottle. He took a long swig, smacked his lips, and smiled. "Sure don't taste bad, Perfesser. Like wintergreen."

"Well, old fellow, you just let the compound percolate a minute. Now, while we wait, I want to tell you lovely ladies that I have special preparations just for you. The Potawatomi Princess not only speaks perfect English, she is most understanding about female difficulties. She's going to be right beside the wagon, there, and if you wish to consult with her in utmost privacy, she will advise you, and offer several alternatives based on the herbal remedies of the Potawatomi people. I will guarantee you, ladies, a swift cure for weakness of blood and other delicate matters. And my Egyptian Regulator Tea's guaranteed to expand your female attributes."

The princess gathered some bottles and stationed herself next to the doubletree. But no one moved. The crowd waited to hear the verdict from the old man.

"Land sakes," Parsons said. "Maybe I should try another little jolt."

"Sir, you will never need a second dose," Peachtree said. "That decoction will chase pain like hounds after a fox."

"Well, it's tasty. I reckon it's the flavor. There's some as believe the worse she tastes, the better she is for you."

"A myth, disproven by modern science, over and over. All my products are tasty, sir. I'm in the healing business and have utterly no desire to inflict anything repugnant upon anyone."

"Land sakes," Parsons said. He tucked the bottle into his bib, and meandered through the crowd, somehow straightened. The palsy had vanished. He hooked his cane over his arm.

Skye thought that either Parsons was one of the best actors ever to tread the boards or else that bottle was loaded with gin.

"Well, that old gent isn't inclined to testify," Peachtree

said. "It'd help if he would. Some gents don't want to make public speeches."

Old Parsons ambled to the rear of the crowd, obviously transformed, while people watched.

"I'll try that stuff," said an infantry sergeant. He pushed forward.

Peachtree, stationed where he could rake in coins and dish out bottles and pasteboard boxes, took his coin and gave him a bottle of the Pain Extractor. The sergeant pulled the cork and swilled, then corked up his prize and grinned.

"Tastes mighty powerful," he said.

Something seemed to give way, and in moments a clamorous mob pressed money upon Peachtree, shouted for this or that elixir. A few women gathered around the Potawatomi Princess and bought pills from her. Some people toted away a whole carton of bottles. Peachtree serenely doled out medicine and sympathy, listening intently to their organ recitals, and then pressing the proper bottle into eager hands. The pockets of his clawhammer coat began to bulge with bills and coin.

Even as twilight lowered, it occurred to Skye that the next morning he would probably be escorting Peachtree's entourage to Santa Fe.

Skye, Victoria, and Mary strolled to the rear of the crowd, where Parsons stood in the dusk. He was a transformed man.

"Mister Parsons, you're a gifted actor," Skye said.

Parsons eyed Skye sharply. "I don't like the word. Thespian. Call me a thespian, and you'll do me honor. Why, sir, I've trod the boards of every great city, from London to Terre Haute. I've played Hamlet and Macbeth. I've played before the crowned heads of Europe, the Prince of Wales, the Queen of England. Why, sir, the name of Parsons was top-billed on the broadsheets."

"Well, you're as fine a thespian as I've ever seen."

"What's this, a thespian?" Victoria demanded.

"Why, a person who acts a role in a play," Parsons said.

"Now this, of course, wasn't playing a role at all. My body betrays me. It cries with pain and anguish. It drove me off the boards at last, and into grinding merciless poverty. I couldn't even stand up. I was bent like a hairpin. But this—this"—he pointed at his bottle—"this is my daily sacrament, my Communion, my happiness. It's a tincture of opium and a few other items the professor tosses in for flavor and effect. The professor gives me one a day, and I give him a small performance when called upon."

"Your ailments are real, then."

"All too real, sir. But you'll find me sprightly after my dose. By morning the effect's gone and I'm a shipwreck again. But I'll be no trouble on the road. I'm never a burden to anyone."

"You're a valuable man, I see. Look at them, mate."

"Why, I am at that. Peachtree says I'm the most valuable person he's got. The trick is not to overdo it. Now if I launched into a pitchman's harangue, if I leaped up and hollered, if I rushed to buy six more bottles and praised the medicine, I'd be no Pied Piper at all. I'm a true-born, crib-trained thespian, sir, and proud of it."

"A natural-born shill."

He glared. "Why, if you want the respect of Pontius Pilate Parsons, don't ever employ that word, sir. I'm a Pied Piper. My flute lures all children of God. A shill is a nefarious fellow. Peachtree's medicines are the true thing."

"All right, mate. I'll call you Pied Piper Pontius Parsons, and you call me Mister Skye."

By the time the evening star shone in the west, the crowd had dissipated, and Professor Peachtree was tallying up. He had a small gold scale at hand; many of the Forty-Niners had paid in nuggets but a few paid with octagonal fifty-dollar gold slugs minted in California. Most of the soldiers had paid with grubby currency. The professor worked in lantern-light at a small drop-table within his laboratory, surrounded by empty bottles, cartons of powders, and utensils. Skye, Victoria, and Mary waited outside to see whether the man would meet the price.

At last Peachtree emerged into the evening cool.

"Mister Skye, I can spare you three hundred and eighty-seven dollars now, and the rest upon reaching Santa Fe, where we will find markets again. A good offer, sir."

Skye sighed, badly tempted. He could pay off his account with Colonel Bullock and have a hundred fifty to winter on in Taos. But this would be an arduous, dangerous trip, weeks longer than usual. And from all he remembered about the merchants at Taos, he wouldn't have enough.

"It's a little shy, Professor. I can bend some; I'd do it for five hundred rather than six. But not this . . . I tell you what: I can find a man who'd take you for less than my price."

"I may have to resort to that, sir. It's odd, but I've taken a fancy to you and your enchanting ladies. And Carlotta, the princess, is absolutely ravenous to make their acquaintance. She's a disciple of Rousseau, and wants to see noble savages firsthand and study their uncorrupted natures. I rather supposed we'd have a fine time, good company and as much safety and comfort as any border man can devise for us. I'm rather fond of my life and my hair, Mister Skye, and don't want to sacrifice the former, or see the latter decorate some savage's lance. I suppose I could make it four hundred, if I pulled my pockets inside out. The rest in Santa Fe."

"I'll want to think about it, mate. If Bullock would take some of your wares as merchandise for sale in his sutler's store, maybe he could credit my account."

"Well, I can't dip into my stocks, sir. Those are the life-blood of my enterprise."

"Well, let's consult with Bullock in the morning, Professor. . If you and he could work something out, you could meet my price."

"You're a hard man to employ, Mister Skye."

"By design, Professor. You notice I have my hair. Too many coons I knew in the beaver days don't have hair or life.

They went under. It makes this child cautious. If I keep my bloody clients safe, I keep my family safe. Mostly that requires caution, running and hiding, ducking trouble. That's what separates me from some border men. None of us"—he gestured to his wives—"scruple to retreat or hide. Your wagons won't help any if it comes to that. But I bloody well figure we'd get you there with your topknots on."

Peachtree sighed. "You make me all the more determined to employ you, sir. Let's settle this in the morning. Perhaps I can sell a few more bottles then."

"Maybe one for me, Mister Skye?" asked Mary.

He ignored her and steered his ladies back toward the post, where Jawbone and their mares awaited them for the ride out to the Skye lodge up the Platte River.

"Mister Skye, you didn't even buy us a bottle. I want to try all that stuff," Mary said. "Especially that Pain Extractor. I think I'm going to like all those happy-happy syrups."

Chapter 6

Elisha Carmody tied his big mule to the hitch rail at the sutler's store, giving wide berth to a battered blue roan with evil eyes and laid-back ears. The post commander had told him to ask for the sutler, Colonel Bullock, or a man named Skye. He worked his way down an aisle of stove and carriage hardware, barrels of nails, and rolls of duck cloth, toward a knot of people at the rear.

He recognized some of them at once: the medicine man, Professor Peachtree, was standing there, and the one billed as the Potawatomi Princess. He had watched the show last night.

A slim man with a goatee stood behind the office rail. A miscreant with an awesome nose stood there also, along with two squaws.

"I'm looking for Colonel Bullock," Carmody said.

"Yes, suh?" said the man behind the rail.

"They told me—Colonel Hoffman told me you might help me. It seems I'm too late to go to California; I must either turn back or negotiate with a man named Skye for passage to the southern route. Is that the correct information?"

"I'm Mister Skye," said the ruffian. "Maybe I can help."

Carmody beheld a formidable man, burly but not unduly tall, with squinty blue eyes buried in weathered flesh. He was dressed in the manner of the mountain men and the savages, except for a battered top hat clamped over stringy hair. The two squaws, dressed in their customary doeskin garb, eyed him impassively.

"Why, is it true you're taking a party to Santa Fe?"

"It's being considered, sir. Do you wish to join the party?"

"Well, I might."

"You'd have to share Skye's fee," said the medicine man without preamble.

"You're Peachtree. Saw you last night. Is Skye taking you?"

"It's Mister Skye, sir," said the ruffian in a voice that rumbled through the cavernous store.

"Why, I always respect a man's wishes. Mister Skye it is, sir. I'm Elisha Carmody."

"If this gent'll pay a just share of your fee, we'll resolve this impasse," said Peachtree, looking pleased.

But the roughneck didn't seem to be in any rush. "Mister Carmody, you might tell us what you have in mind, and how you're equipped. It's a dangerous journey. There are no roads; only lodgetrails. There are no military posts."

"What Mister Skye's sayin' suh," said the sutler, "is that he's mighty careful about who he deals with. A man not fitted for danger and hardship—he could get the whole shebang into a jackpot."

"Well I like that, Mister Skye," Carmody said. "It heartens me that money's not your only consideration."

Skye grinned. "It's a major one. Now, what've you in mind?"

"I don't want to turn back. I'm eager to get to the gold fields. I'm afoot, leading a sound mule packed with my gear."

"Alone?"

"Yessir."

"A gold seeker, then."

"No, not at all. I'm a reformed politician."

"A what?" asked Bullock, who began to chuckle. "That, suh, is a novelty."

"People find it so. But I'm quite serious about it. I served two terms in the Ohio Legislature and two more terms as an Ohio congressman in Washington City. I wasn't defeated, but declined to run again once I fathomed the nature of my calling. By vocation I am a lecturer. I can think of no greater good than to present my views to the California argonauts."

"Mister Carmody," said Skye, "how are you fixed? If you've walked from Independence, you know that you'll need several pairs of boots, or the means to resole what you have. Have you shelter and food?"

"I'll replenish here, sir. I have an awl and cobbler tools and shoe leather to repair my boots. I took some instruction in it. I'm armed with a carbine for hunting. My needs are simple, and I've endured seven hundred miles with no difficulty. I'm forty-four and in sound health. The mule's thin from the lack of feed on the way but he's a tough brute with the spirit of a veteran sinner."

"Why, Carmody, you can split Skye's fee with us," Peachtree said. "He wants five hundred, which is a fair price, all things considered."

Carmody paused. "I can't begin to afford two hundred fifty, sir. If that's the case, I'll proceed westward at whatever risk of winter I may face and thread my way to California."

"What can you afford, mate?" Skye asked.

"I resolved to set a limit of fifty dollars. I've so governed my affairs to afford myself a small sum each year for five years to lecture. I charge nothing for my lectures but permit donations. It must be fifty or I'll decline."

Peachtree sighed. "Well, Mister Skye? That brings your kitty to four-fifty."

"Mister Skye, suh, that's enough. I can't float you through another winter."

Skye pondered the matter. Carmody felt himself being studied intently by a man who was no doubt a shrewd judge of human nature. "Mister Carmody," the man said at last. "What about these lectures. Are you a missionary?"

"No, Mister Skye. My purpose, while uplifting and ennobling, is entirely secular. I certainly respect the faith of our fathers, but my mission deals with this world, not the next."

Skye grunted. "You're a puzzle to me," he said.

"I've been called worse," Carmody replied.

They laughed.

"The closest I get to religion, Mister Skye, is the belief that faith in politics, and the business of mulcting money out of the public treasury, is idolatry. I argue that each mortal can redeem and transform his life by his own exertions, and nothing else is needed to fulfill ourselves and triumph over our private slavery."

"I don't suppose you're a temperance lecturer," Skye asked, with a certain blandness.

"Why, temperance—the discipline of our bodies and minds against the slavery of intoxicants—is a part of it, but not the whole. Drunks are slaves. But lots of things enslave men and women. No, I'm not associated with any temperance society. I'm quite independent."

"I should like to hear you," said Peachtree. "I wonder how you feel about my calling."

"I am in favor of legitimate commerce," Carmody said, measuring his words.

"I'd like to hear more of your ideas on the trail, mate," said Skye.

"You'll take me, then?"

Skye glanced at the squaws. "These are my ladies. Victoria of the Crow nation, and Mary, of the Shoshones. The tyke in the cradleboard is my son, Dirk. We'll take you."

Carmody had not paid much attention to the squaws. The

older stared at him with flinty eyes and suspicion. The younger—how had her beauty eluded him?—smiled shyly.

"Two consorts. You are an amazing man, Mister Skye."

"Two wives, sir. Not consorts. We're a family. Ourselves and my nag out there. Together, we'll get you to Santa Fe safely and comfortably—so long as you all follow my instruction. Especially when it comes to dealing with Indians. If you can't bind yourself to that, this old mountain child won't escort you for any price. Every life in the party, including yours, depends on it."

"I am pleased to bind myself so long as you never ask me to do anything dishonorable."

"I bloody well won't."

"You have an inflection I can't place, sir."

"Born in London. Pressed into the Royal Navy as a boy and never saw my kin again. A limey slave on men-o'-war for too many years. Jumped into the Columbia at Fort Vancouver in eighteen and twenty-five; trapper and brigade leader for Chouteau's American Fur Company. A guide after the beaver trade died. There's still some Londoner in my voice, and some of the tongue of the trappers, too."

"Ah, that places you."

"All right then," said Skye, with sudden authority. "We'll leave around noon. Colonel Bullock'll accept your payments. He'll provision you. My ladies and I'll break our camp upriver and be back here shortly." He waited a moment. "Colonel, pack the usual kit—no, we'll be out longer. Make it half again as large, and double my medicine."

"I'll be right at it, Mister Skye. You and your charmin' ladies'll be well fixed. And I'll put together some travelin' money for you."

"Some spare Dupont, caps and balls, Colonel. And be sure to double my, ah, refreshments."

"We'll have it ready. And we'll fix up these gents too."

Carmody wandered out of the sutler's store, followed by

the Skyes. The guide walked straight to the wild-eyed blue roan and mounted.

"I noticed that horse, Mister Skye. Are you sure he's sound?"

"He's sound, sir. He's also dangerous. I don't want you to come within fifteen feet of him, not ever. I mean that. Don't come near him and don't let your mule get close to him." Skye's eyes bored into Carmody.

"He sounds dangerous, Mister Skye. Does he kick?"

"No, he kills."

"Amazing," said Carmody. He had no trouble believing it.

With that, Skye turned the horse without visible direction while his ladies settled themselves on their mares.

Elisha Carmody sensed that this wild country held dangers beyond his imagining, and wondered whether he had made a sound choice not only about the trip, but also about the guide.

Chapter 7

That first morning the Skyes took their clients up the Laramie River, which angled southwest from the fort through barren plains. Once they got well away from the California Trail they rolled through good grass, which the hungry mules and horses nipped as they passed.

Carlotta Krafft-Ebing sat on the thumping seat of the show wagon, which Hyacinth Z. Peachtree drove expertly. The rest rode the supply wagon. These solitudes stretching from horizon to horizon filled her with an unfocused dread. She felt hollow so far from anything. Every turn of the wheel took her deeper into a trackless land where no one knew how many years she had studied at the conservatories. That was the saddest fate of all: to go where her glory was unknown. Had any savage ever heard her sing *The Magic Flute*?

She studied the Skyes as if they were her jailers. The older squaw, Victoria, had ridden off. Carlotta gathered that the Crow woman was a scout who probed the surrounding hills looking for trouble. The younger Mrs. Skye took charge of the family's possessions, loaded onto two travois drawn by runty mustangs. She rode a little bay mare and carried the infant in the cradleboard, but sometimes she hung the cradleboard from the horn of her squaw saddle. The child rarely whimpered when it was locked in leather, and Carlotta wondered if that was because of its Indian blood.

Skye himself meandered up and down the caravan. Occasionally he rode far ahead; other times he rode beside the travelers, getting to know them. That strange Mister Carmody trudged along to one side, his face hidden under the broad brim of his felt hat, his packmule on a slack line behind him.

They said scarcely a word that morning, though sometimes Hyacinth pointed to Victoria Skye, who would appear at the base of some knoll far away, hunched over her mare. On those occasions Skye would lift his top hat and screw it down again, apparently some sort of signal that all was well.

This was going to be a two-month bore. At least on the California Trail they were constantly meeting people. What struck her most forcibly was the anonymous sky, as empty and meaningless as her own futile life.

The guide was taking them away from even the remotest outposts of white men. It made her uneasy. The California Road was patrolled by Fort Laramie cavalry. But here they were on their own; their fate, their lives, in the hands of a rough guide and his sluts.

"It's a little ominous, H.Z.," she said. "Do you know what I mean?"

"Colonel Hoffman told me we have the best guide in the West, Carlotta. What else can we do?"

"I wish I had a revolver."

"That's no defense against a few hundred Indians. But the Skyes are."

"I hadn't quite realized what we're gettink into."

"You're the one who wanted to see the noble savages, dear."

"I'm havink second thoughts."

"We'll rely on Skye's medicine. Did you notice that grizzly-claw necklace he wears? That's red men's hoodoo."

"You should know," she said. "We're sittink on a whole wagon load of white men's hoodoo."

He laughed. "That's what I like about you."

The guide called a halt near a grove of majestic cottonwoods that would supply shade. The midday sun roasted them.

"We'll take a long break, mates," he said. "Those mules need it. There's grass aplenty here; that cured bunchgrass on the slopes has more power in it than this grass along the river. I'd like you to unharness and picket the critters out there. Watch out for rattlers. We'll start again midafternoon."

"Unharness?" There was protest in Peachtree's voice.

"Unharness. Santa Fe's nearly seven hundred miles away, and the mountain miles are brutal. You haven't got a spare animal. We'll make these last."

"But unharness? It takes a half hour; another half hour for all of us to harness again."

Skye took it patiently. "They'll eat, roll, sleep and eat again. They'll gain ground."

"You're the guide," H.Z. said, surrendering. He nodded to Concorde and Hercules, who had listened from the other wagon.

"Ah don't picture why . . . ," Concorde complained.

Skye addressed him quietly. "If we should have to outrun a Comanche village—run to a place where we can fort up, mate, you might be glad you kept your mules prime."

Concorde needed no more argument. He swung down from the rear wagon and began to unbuckle harness. Then he tackled the other team, sighing and groaning his martyrdom.

Carlotta clambered to the ground and stretched, enjoying the release from pain. H.Z. would be after her to produce a lunch, but she wouldn't. She was a singer, even if it was for a rotten medicine show. She wasn't paid to cook meals. And there wasn't a thing Peachtree could do about it. She would quit again.

It occurred to her that maybe the Skyes would cook; wasn't that what guides were paid to do? But the older wife had hunkered down beneath a knoll a few hundred yards south; the watch never ceased. Carlotta liked that. The younger wife freed the infant from his cradleboard pouch and packed something that looked like moss into it, while the child wriggled its unbound limbs joyously, cooling in the dappled shade of the quivering cottonwoods.

Skye pulled a light pad saddle from that ugly roan and examined its hooves one by one, feeling its pasterns for heat. He muttered something and ran a weathered hand under the roan's mane. The horse squealed, snapped yellow teeth, nipped Skye's shoulder, and stole Skye's top hat, which it flapped up and down.

"Avast!" Skye yelled, and snatched his topper.

The horse butted Skye in the chest, almost bowling him over, and wandered off to slaughter grass.

"That's the most unmannered saddlehorse I've ever seen," said H.Z. Peachtree. "I suppose it must have some sort of virtue, but I can think of none."

Skye laughed. "That's Jawbone. He's a horse out of hell. He's a bloody army. He's a killer. He's a saint. He's also a medicine horse, a legend to the tribes. Before the end of this trip, you'll be mighty glad he's with us."

"How do you control him, Skye?"

"It's Mister Skye, mate. I started on him the first day of his life and never stopped. When he's mad I can't control him. No mortal can. Remember it and steer clear."

"Sounds like me, darlinks," Carlotta said.

Skye's gaze fixed her a long moment, and she basked in it. He was taking the measure of them all. He studied Concorde and Hercules, who were picketing the mules; examined Pontius Parsons, who groaned theatrically with hurt as he limbered his old muscles. Skye watched Carmody pull a coffee mill from his plunder, grind a few roasted beans, and set a pot full of creekwater over a tiny fire. She could see that the guide liked what he saw of Carmody. But she didn't care for the lecturer: an obvious bluenosed moralizer. He would probably brace her about duty soon, and give her a list of things not to do.

"Well, my dear?" asked Hyacinth.

"I didn't go to three conservatories to study how to cook."

"It's a good thing you didn't," Peachtree retorted. "You'd have spoiled the buffalo soup."

"Will you ever stop that?" She despised H.Z. when he was trying to amuse others at her expense.

Pontius Parsons doddered up. "H.Z., can I lick it now?"

"Not until tonight. Then you'll sleep."

"You lack gratitude. Think what I did for you at the fort. My best performance ever. One little nip."

"Tonight."

"My bones ache like the arrival of Satan."

"Endurance builds character."

"You're a spawn of the Marquis de Sade." Pontius sighed dolefully and creaked toward the supply wagon, groaning with each step. He never stopped acting except when he was alone. She'd seen him head for the bushes at night on springy legs, with nary a whimper. He was at his best portraying pain and martyrdom.

Hyacinth followed him. They would rustle their own lunch. Then H.Z. would either snooze or else bottle up some new potions and paste the florid gummed labels on them.

She watched Skye settle beside his honey-fleshed wife and lift the infant for a moment, something gentle in his weathered face. The boy hiccoughed and babbled. The young Shoshone woman smiled and handed Skye some cold meat. They laughed, and Carlotta felt warmth and love rise from that magical circle. He had fondled that ugly horse with some odd tenderness and now he poured that same affection upon his lady and child. For a man who was reputed to be a one-man army, Skye certainly had a tender side.

Carlotta wished, suddenly, that she could join that circle and receive whatever it was that flowed out of the man. She had known only misery all her futile life; vicious swine like the maestro in Italy who had stolen her pitiful savings from the postal bank or the snobby critic in Stuttgart she had flung herself upon in one foolish moment when she had been starved for just one little compliment. She sometimes wondered how she could endure one more hour, one more day, one more week in a world that enjoyed her rich cello voice, and gave her nothing but bitterness in return.

Chapter 8

Elisha Carmody liked what he saw of the Skyes. They were obviously gifted at the business of taking people through wild country. He suspected that Skye had a roaring weakness or two, but what frontiersman didn't?

Skye obviously wanted to visit with Elisha, but every time the guide steered that menacing horse close enough to talk, Elisha's packmule balked and refused to move until the blue roan edged away.

At last Skye dismounted and fell in beside Carmody. The weird horse, entirely free, simply tagged along twenty or thirty yards to the side, joyously massacring grass as he went. It astonished Carmody.

"I like to get acquainted with all my clients," Skye said. "I know a bit about these show folks, but not about you."

"I'm flattered by your attention, Mister Skye."

"Don't be. What I learn about each of you helps me keep you safe. I didn't quite plumb why you're going to the gold fields, sir."

"Not to get rich, I'll tell you that. My long years in public service bore unexpected fruit. Not wealth or power or fame. No, sir. I had a chance to examine the gods that failed. My two terms as a Whig in Congress turned me into a lecturer."

"Well, mate, lecturing's not so different from being a congressman, is it?"

Carmody chuckled. "Why, there are similarities. What I discovered in Congress is that politics boils down to two things. One is to determine how the public purse'll be spent and who gets it. The other is to get the government to benefit one party at the expense of another. It all boils down to that, the hue and cry, the passions, the debates. Whether it's tariffs or taxes or who gets to collect customs or who gets the public lands, it's all about getting advantage, usually cloaked in high ideals such as patriotism."

They walked around a thicket of hackberries that had rooted beside the Laramie River next to the lodgetrail, while ahead the wagons creaked. Occasionally Skye studied the horizons, his gaze seeking anything out of place.

"Now, that's well understood," Carmody continued, "and I claim no originality. But over the years I noticed something else. The fellows the government helps, the ones who get the tariffs, the clerking jobs, a fancy pension—why, they're worse off than the fellows who get out into the world and grub. It's all for naught, sir. The ones who do it by politics are spiritually impoverished. There's the paradox. They're unhappy eating at the public trough. Once I grasped that, the rest fell swiftly into place. I abandoned Congress and created a reform society." He smiled. "I am its sole member and contributor."

Skye pondered that awhile. "I don't quite grasp the connection between all this and going to the gold fields."

"Why, I haven't even given you the bare bones of it. Once I saw how people are slaves to greed I saw also that people are slaves to other vices. Spirits, opiates, fleshly lust, gluttony, power, fame. Almost any goal that's a virtue in moderation becomes a vice in excess. That's why we hear warnings against blind ambition. Let a passion steal our souls, and we become prisoners, made miserable day by day by the cravings we can never satisfy."

"You can't help the whole human race, mate." Skye sounded skeptical. He glanced backward toward his younger wife and her menagerie. The guide never stopped absorbing and observing the world around him, even when lost in talk.

"No, but I hope my ideas will carry," Carmody said. "I rented lecture halls and posted notices promising an edifying discourse. Many a lamplit night I've addressed the problem of private slavery, surrendering to vices and ending up a prisoner of the vice we embrace. There are men walking the streets who seem paragons of virtue and strength—yet are lost in misery because they can't resist some vice or another. Men who are prisoners of lust, betraying their wives and their own bodies, and hating themselves for it. There, right there, is the nature of unhappiness. I discovered it by observation, like Isaac Newton discovering the laws of gravity."

"You're a temperance lecturer, then."

"Oh, temperance is a part of it. I lecture against all slavery, not just one branch of it. I urge my listeners to live a free life, in command of body and soul, avoiding all vices— avarice, drunkenness, power, fame—and politics."

"But the gold fields. Why the gold fields?"

Carmody chuckled. "I lectured from one end of Ohio to the other and hardly got a hearing. They thought I was daft. I'm no stranger to the world, Mister Skye. Half of Congress thinks the other half's daft. But back there in settled country, people are set in their ways. They've plugged their ears and minds. I yearned to show them what a free man or a free woman could be, but they didn't even listen. They thought I was talking about the absence of public laws. They thought I was promoting anarchy, lawlessness, the untrammeled will, even free love. They thought they were already free—but they are slaves."

Carmody remembered several of his Ohio auditors, big thick-skulled galoots with arms folded, looking ready to tar and feather him and run him out of town for disturbing settled opinion. He chuckled at the flinty skepticism of the American yeoman.

"I'm going to try it out west. Try to reach men with open minds, living in an unsettled land where no city rises and no fields are plowed. They braved the seas or the wild continent to get there. Some were inspired by greed—they thought they could pluck up nuggets and make a quick fortune without labor. Others went there with more realistic designs. Most of them are slaves of one thing or another—spirituous drink, lust, power. But I think they're ripe for my harvest. I'll help them capture the happiness that's the lot of freemen. They'll hear me, even if Easterners won't."

Carmody eyed the guide, wondering how he took all that. The big galoot had spent most of his life in wilderness, naturally beyond the gaffhook of laws and taxes. He might not grasp the vision at all.

"Well, mate, you must be getting something from it."

"Mister Skye, my satisfaction comes from freeing mortals from their dungeons. That's all. I've given my life to a cause, and devoting a life isn't the same as tossing it away. Why, if I should rescue half a dozen from those vices that enslave us, I shall have lived a worthy life."

"You'd walk clear across a continent, brave death from Indians or all the rest, to lecture the gold miners?"

"I would. I have seen a vision and I must share it."

"You're spending your entire substance. What of your family? Your wife?"

"I'm a widower, sir. Cholera took her in forty-nine, and filled me with unquenchable grief. A daughter too. My sons are adults."

"But you kept on."

"I kept on. I found I had the courage of my ideals."

"But what if you get out there and fail? What if miners

heckle you? What if you fail to persuade anyone? Vices are fun, mate. I've a few I enjoy."

"It won't be time lost, Mister Skye. I will have tried. If I didn't try—that would be true loss. I will have lived a finer life for the trying."

Skye became reflective. "After I was pressed into the Royal Navy, I thought my life was done. I was a prisoner of the bloody Queen, sir. But I learned how to knuckle. Had to fight old salts for my gruel, fight for a hammock, fight to be left alone. I thought it was a loss—but it was all a preparation. This North American continent required all that I'd learned. No, it wasn't lost. Took this child a decade to grasp that, though."

Carmody heard a gentle tone in Skye's voice that was new to him, and responded in kind. "I counted my years in public office as a loss, although they probably weren't. I got to see how calculation and power work. It's universal, you know. A poor man can be just as conniving as a rich one, and meaner, too."

They spanned another sunny mile before Skye spoke again. "You're on the road with folks who wouldn't agree with you much."

"Perhaps we should think upon their virtues, Mister Skye. They're braving death and discomfort, just as I am, to take their product to the world. I admire entrepreneurs."

Skye chuckled. "You're still a congressman, Mister Carmody."

"If you mean I'm a worldly man, I wouldn't deny it. One can scarcely serve in public office without seeing the follies—and genius—of mankind. What amazes me more than anything else is the failure of so many to take advantage of a free nation. They can stretch themselves, grow, begin any business, settle any wild, prosper themselves without public hindrance. But they don't. No other nation on earth offers people a chance to start life over in perfect wilderness. But it requires grit. Courage. Grinding labor. Bravery. They have to be as good as their word."

"This is a hard place, Mister Carmody. Harder than it looks." He waved at serene grasslands, waltzing in the breezes.

"Of course. It takes a strong man to subdue it. But what do so many do? They slink to Washington and badger us for clerking jobs. They want to be secure forever, free from risk. Small-spirited men, sir. Why, Mister Skye, they aren't the best Americans; they're slaves to their own cowardice. A wild land requires brave men."

Skye doffed his battered topper and screwed it down again. "Mister Carmody, I'm going to enjoy your company. It'll be a hard trip; we'll go hungry some times; we'll face trouble. But you're a man to side me when trouble finds us—which it will."

Elisha Carmody sensed that he had received a great gift from the rough old border man.

Chapter 9

Victoria saw the horsemen angling down a long draw toward the Laramie River and knew they would intersect Mister Skye's party. There would be visitors in camp this first night out. She sensed they were Sioux. A woman of many winters simply knew those things. She sensed also that this was a war party, even though there had been no war talk at the fort. She counted a lot of them, thirty-four if her old eyes didn't betray her.

She didn't like this. Mister Skye didn't know these clients and hadn't yet fathomed their natures. They were only a dozen miles from the fort, but it might as well be a hundred.

She studied the advancing party from her vantage point in deep shadow, knowing that only the keenest eye would pick her out among the rocky ridges above the river bottoms. She could not tell whether they were painted for war but she could see that they held no weapons. They wore their bows and arrows in quivers slung over their bare shoulders; their rifles were sheathed.

She edged toward the river bottoms, sticking to the deep shadows cast by the low sun, hoping to reach Mister Skye before they did. He would not like the news. He always hoped for a few suns on the trail before trouble met him. Wraithlike, she hunkered low over the mare and guided it down to the bottoms. At last Mister Skye saw her. She signaled with an upraised arm. He nodded, and halted his party right there. It was as good a place as any to camp. She could see her man telling them they would have visitors in a few minutes.

She sighed. So far, Mister Skye's discipline held. But one never knew. She supposed that if trouble began, Peachtree would start it. Or maybe that strange medicine seer named Carmody. She trotted her mare into camp just as the visitors broke out of a draw into the bottoms and beheld the white men. They were painted, hideous streaks of vermilion, ocher, and black decorating their faces and torsos.

"All right, mates. This is touchy. They're wearing war paint but they look peaceable enough. You must mind your manners and you'll keep your topknots."

"Are you quite sure, sir?" asked Peachtree. "We could put up a defense."

"Do you see any bloody weapons in hand? No, just let us handle it. If I ask you to do something, do it."

They were Sioux, the enemies of her Crow people; famous liars, great-hearted fighters, cruel torturers. She choked down her own loathing of them. Mary watched them gravely, poised to hide Skye's infant boy. They paused in knots about an arrow's flight away. A headman rode in when Skye lifted a hand, palm forward, the friendship signal among the peoples. She itched to shoot the Sioux dog.

The headman, a giant with braided hair, eyed the wagons and mules, and then his gaze settled upon Mister Skye, Mary and Victoria, and lastly upon Jawbone, who clacked his teeth and laid his ears back. She thought she knew him; she had seen him at the fort a time or two. An Oglala, like most of the Sioux in this vicinity. She could not read anything in his expressionless face except that he recognized the Skyes. She counted five war wounds on his yellow torso and arms, one of them a new red slash across his ribs. He had painted black coup stripes on his arms and whited his face.

Skye's thick hands flew. He welcomed the headman and his party to the camp and asked who he was honored to speak to.

Blue Heron, came the finger-reply, which Victoria could read. She knew that one by his reputation. A cruel warrior with a vile temper. They were going back to their people, said the headman. They had tried to steal horses from the Shoshones but they had been spotted and driven away. Black Buffalo had died. Blue Heron and two others had been hurt. One badly. They had no horses or scalps to display to their village. There would be no triumphant parade, but only much wailing.

That was bad news. The Shoshones were Mary's people, and she was in mortal danger. These Sioux had been humiliated and might settle for a few scalps and mules to salve the hurt.

But the headman was telling Skye with sign-talk that they would share two does they had killed; they would have a feast and learn about the people in the wagons and why these wagons weren't following the big medicine road of the white men.

Victoria didn't like it.

"All right, mates," Skye said. "These are Oglalas. This is Blue Heron. They've been on a horse-stealing raid and got hurt. That's bad news. He says they'll share a couple of does they killed. That's good news. You just unhitch and put your mules on pickets and stay peaceable. We can avoid trouble if we're careful."

The Sioux poured in, looked about grimly, well aware they were utterly in command. They helped two seriously wounded warriors off exhausted ponies and settled them in blankets on the grass. Concorde, Hercules, and Elisha Carmody nervously watered and picketed the mules on good grass. The warriors eyed the mules sullenly, sizing up booty. The long-eared animals weren't any warrior's ideal steed, but squaws liked them and they were useful for hauling travois. A gaggle of mules would give this horse-stealing party a fine victory.

"Mister Skye, are we in peril?" asked Peachtree. "They certainly outnumber us. I count thirty-four."

"Yes, we're in trouble, mate. They could do anything, including knifing us on the spot."

"I think they're magnificent," said the Potawatomi Princess. "I want to meet every one."

"This isn't the time," Skye replied curtly. "These warriors have just been humiliated. They're as bitter as man can be."

"Oh, I'm so enchanted. These are the first real savages I've met. Completely uncorrupted by white men. I've waited a lifetime for this, darlink. We're so jaded we've lost our way. Someday we'll all have to live like them."

"It's an interesting theory you have there, madam," Skye admitted. "But right now, leave them to me."

"I will sit at their knee and imbibe their purity. They're Natural Man. They'll help me find my true self. My nature was corrupted by all the world's naysayers, beginnink with my mother. These Sioux—oh, I love them."

Victoria decided the woman had a mad underwater spirit, and stalked off to comfort Mary, who knew exactly what this horse-stealing party might do to her. She found Mary secretly preparing for war, gathering the pack animals and readying her bow and quiver.

Warriors picketed their ponies and meandered boldly through camp, pausing at the wagons, plainly curious about what they might contain. Others hung the does from cottonwood limbs, deftly gutted and butchered them, and built several little cookfires in the deepening shadows. Victoria watched them sharply.

Blue Heron approached Skye: *What is in the green wagon,* his fingers asked.

Medicine, Skye replied. *The white men are healers. They cure diseases.*

Astonishment lit the headman's face. *Are they all healers? What about the woman?*

She helps the healer. She sings. She is called the Potawatomi Princess. The man with the black coat is the healer. He is named Hyacinth Z. Peachtree. Skye had to speak the names because there were no signs for them. *The others care for the mules and wagons, and make music.*

Why is she dressed like a squaw? Is she a white woman? asked Blue Heron.

White, Skye signaled.

Is she a witch?

Carlotta knew they were discussing her, and rushed in. "Oh, Skye, darlink, introduce me to this wonderful man." She smiled gorgeously at Blue Heron.

Skye looked nonplussed, but then his hands set to work: *Here is the Princess of the Potawatomi people. She wishes to meet you. She honors you.*

Why does she honor me?

Skye paused. He didn't really know. *She sees your glory.*

"What is he sayink, Mister Skye?"

"He's curious about you."

"Tell him that I am his slave."

Skye tried. Blue Heron stared. Victoria watched the strange hand-dance, knowing Skye was having a bad time of it. Sign language was as crude as drawing pictures. The headman dismissed Carlotta with an impatient wave.

I want the healer. Bring me the healer, Blue Heron demanded.

Skye's hands asked why.

He will heal me. He will heal Wolf Eyes and Running Crane. White men's medicine.

Skye paused, uncertain. Then he nodded. Peachtree lurked at his wagon.

Skye beckoned him. "They've got some injured from that

horse-stealing party. I told them you're a healer. They want you," Skye said.

"Will they buy my wares?"

"No. But you're going to do what you can. Or can you do anything, Peachtree? Is it all spirits and swampwater?"

"But Skye—I can't give away product. Would they trade?"

"Professor, they don't have anything to trade—except one thing: your life."

Peachtree swallowed hard. "I see," he muttered. "All right. I can do something. My Peachtree Pain Extractor has a little opium in it. I can take away pain. It might help them get to their village."

"Do it. Your life depends on it."

"I hope the sonofabitch knows what he's doing," Victoria said, faintly enjoying the white man's terror.

Chapter 10

Skye felt out of control. This party had stumbled into trouble too soon. He didn't know what any of his clients would do. He didn't know whether Peachtree was a total fraud, selling swampwater and hokum, or a semi-fraud, with a few herbs and drugs in his bottles, which he huckstered to rubes for a dollar. He was about to find out.

While Peachtree unlocked his wagon and extracted a rectangular green bottle, Skye eyed Mary and Victoria. They had Jawbone with them, and their mares stayed saddled. They were quietly slipping caps over the nipples of their rifles. Good. They had reacted as they should to a sullen, defeated war party of their enemies.

Blue Heron waited, his body twisted to relieve the pain of his long wound. A score of murderous-looking Oglala watched. They carried no arms but they weren't far from their ponies. Skye had only his belt knife but Blue Heron would feel it rip into his gut if the headman made one false move. They would all die if things fell apart. Carlotta might suffer a terrible fate, all the more because of her fawning on Blue Heron. Sioux warriors tabooed women when they were on the warpath.

Hyacinth Z. Peachtree wobbled toward Skye and the Oglala, making an obvious effort to put one shiny patent leather shoe ahead of the other. But he succeeded.

"You'll have to do it, mate. You've been performing for years. This is your biggest show. I told them you're the healer, and now you're going to be a healer—whether you're a real one or not. You're going to save a lot of lives."

The medicine man slowly brought his quaking under control. Then, almost as if transformed into another mortal, Hyacinth Z. Peachtree turned into the professor of natural science before Skye's eyes. "Translate for me, Mister Skye," he said.

He had his audience. The sullen Sioux gathered around. The two injured warriors lay in the center of the circle, breathing shallowly. One groaned with every breath. The stump of an arrow protruded from his shoulder, its point buried in his collarbone. Brown-dried blood caked his chest. Skye couldn't see the other's wound.

Skye spotted Carlotta Krafft-Ebing among them, utterly oblivious to the mortal danger. He studied his own party. Concorde and Hercules hung around the supply wagon, no doubt with their double-barreled scatterguns at hand. In a fight they would last about thirty seconds. Carmody simply kept his distance, standing among the picketed mules. Good enough.

"Why, my blessed Indian chums, I'm here to soothe and heal," Peachtree began, as suavely as if he were atop his wagon addressing farmers. Skye translated, sometimes with Sioux words, sometimes with sign-talk.

"I am not a doctor. I am not a medicine man. I am not even a healer, though you may have heard otherwise."

Skye translated reluctantly while Peachtree gazed at him, triumph in his face.

"I am a man who collects and sells herbs and powders, that's all. But I happen to have a powerful medicine here that will give this man peace. It will bring sleep. It will hide the pain a while but then the pain will come back. It might hide pain long enough so that you can cut that arrow out of him. He will be asleep and won't feel it. Which of you will take out the arrow?"

If nothing else, Peachtree was a performer. The man might be quaking within, but now he paced like a stallion within the circle of glowering Oglala, occasionally adjusting his clawhammer coat, puffing his twin coattails behind him.

"All right, Blue Heron, will I take your pain away first?" The headman stared back impassively.

"Ah, yes, I think you'll be first. I will make your pain vanish. Not right away, but soon."

If I die, you die, Blue Heron signaled.

"What did he say, Mister Skye?"

"He said you'll die if you kill him."

"Peachtree's Pain Extractor will kill no one when properly used." The professor plucked a tablespoon from his pocket, poured a half measure of a brown liquid, and motioned to the headman.

It was a terrible moment. The headman's gaze bored into Peachtree, who held the spoon aloft, waiting. "Ah, you don't trust me. I will sample it myself."

And he did. Peachtree sipped gingerly, skimming off a bit. "See? I am not yet a carcass. Drink."

This time the headman lifted his fingers to the spoon and guided the fluid down his throat. Peachtree smiled benignly. "Happy dreams," he said.

"Will that put him to sleep, mate? I hope not."

"No, there's not much opium in the compound. It'll make him swoon."

Blue Heron stood stoically, not the slightest change in his features.

Peachtree knelt beside the one with the shoulder wound

and fed him two tablespoons of the elixir. "Tell them he'll go to sleep, and when he does, they can take the arrow out."

Skye translated into distrustful faces, while the medicine man examined the other warrior on the ground.

"Mister Skye, this one's weakened beyond hope. A wound to the abdomen. He's going to croak from peritonitis."

"Then don't give him any. They'll blame you."

"That was my very thought."

Skye translated to the Oglala: *this one is too weakened to receive the medicine. There is nothing the healer can do.*

Peachtree stood, finger-combed his dusty coattails, and waited. The headman smiled, astonishing the Oglala. Then he said something to the other Sioux that Skye was able to pick up: "It is better than firewater, this medicine."

The one with the shoulder wound drifted into sleep even as suspicion clouded the faces of the Oglala. Peachtree knelt again and gently shook the man. But the narcotic had carried him away. Still, he breathed regularly. Warriors stared as his chest rose and fell, obviously waiting for the subtle movement to stop.

"All right. Tell them to have at it," Peachtree said.

Skye gave the word and two old warriors knelt over the fallen one. They tugged at the stump of the arrow, amazed that the drugged man didn't groan. The gore-soaked arrow didn't budge. Extracting it would require some surgery. One of them, an older man with a surly glare, swiftly pricked his knife into the fallen one, got no response, and sat dumfounded.

"Tell him to hurry; don't let him bleed," Peachtree said.

Spurred on, the warriors opened flesh bit by bit, levered the arrow loose, and finally slid it out in a rush of blood and fluids. The injured man groaned. These warriors knew exactly what to do. With an awl, they strung sinew until they had bound the wound, while their patient sighed and muttered. They had removed the arrow but a thundercloud of fear loomed in them.

Blue Heron quietly sat down, benignly examining the tropical world he had entered. He softly ran a finger along his angry rib wound and laughed. The Oglala watched, thunderstruck. They muttered to the headman and he replied, but too fast for Skye to catch any words in that clattering tongue.

"Mister Skye, tell them Professor H.Z. Peachtree is ready and able to mend bodies, heal wounds, and drive away hurts. Let them step forward."

Skye translated it. No one moved. The headman demanded the whole bottle.

"He wants that stuff, Professor."

"No. If he swallows that much he'd kill himself. Tell him that."

Skye did, but Blue Heron wanted it anyway. "He says anything this happy won't kill him, Professor."

Peachtree thought a moment. "Mister Skye, tell the bloke I'll give him a full bottle. I'm going to the wagon and dilute this with spirits. It'll make him buzz like a bumblebee, leap from limb to limb like an ape, and dance on live coals like a fakir, but it won't turn him into a carcass if he guzzles the whole bottle."

Skye promptly informed the headman that he would receive a great gift from the white healer, an entire bottle, with all best wishes and the hope of untold pleasure.

Blue Heron grinned. His eyes seemed unnaturally large. "I'll share it with my war brothers. We will eat now with our white brothers," he said in a peculiar voice. "This is good medicine and I don't hurt. Better than firewater. I am not hungry."

The headman had forgotten to use sign language, but Skye caught the gist of it. He wondered whether they were out of danger—and decided they weren't. Over thirty angry and shamed Sioux warriors stood there looking for an excuse to butcher them.

"We're eating now," Skye said to his party. "These warriors are as unhappy as warriors get. They're going to be proddy. Don't give them an opportunity to start something, or we'll be fighting for our lives."

"The poor darlinks," said Carlotta. "They need hugs."

Skye sighed. "Miss Krafft-Ebing. My warning goes double for you. Steer clear of them. There are Sioux taboos involved here, things I can't explain easily."

The Potawatomi Princess reared like a cobra. "I will have none of your insolence!" she said. "I am free; I will do what I want!"

Oglala stared at her.

"Be glad you're alive," said Skye. She was probably going to cause trouble the whole trip, if not the next instant.

Chapter 11

Skye thought he might die this day, a dozen miles from his home. Death always frightened him, even after facing it countless times. The peace with the Sioux was as fragile as a soap bubble. And these reckless clients might destroy it out of sheer ignorance. Only his two women understood the knife-edged balance of the moment. He watched Victoria slip over to the family gear and quietly gather her bow and quiver, while Mary barricaded herself and Dirk behind the ponies and prepared to die. That was their ancient pact: never surrender.

The Oglala were drifting through the camp like pickpockets, waiting for their three tiny fires to cook the meat. Others clustered around the warrior who had undergone surgery. That one slept under the opiate that Peachtree had given to him. Skye knew they were waiting for him to die—or wake up. And if he didn't wake up soon, the Sioux would murder everyone for the sheer joy of it, beginning with their ancient enemies the Skyes. And they would not forget to murder their old nemesis Jawbone.

But nothing bad happened. Skye's frequent, stern gazes at Peachtree and Carlotta Krafft-Ebing held them in check for the moment. He tried to anticipate what they might do next, but both were unpredictable. They not only had no experience with the Sioux, but had barely any understanding of the Plains tribes and their war customs.

Blue Heron sat quietly, radiating cheer while the other Sioux stared at him, unable to fathom his mood. Once in a while he uncorked the green bottle and sucked some of its juices with relish, licking his tongue around the bottle's neck. He laughed, remembering some secret thing.

Then something stirred the Sioux. Curious, Skye walked boldly among them and found the man who had taken the Shoshone arrow in his shoulder awake and gazing peacefully at his friends. They were asking him questions. Skye knew enough Sioux words to realize he was telling them he didn't hurt; he felt good. He was glad to have had the arrow painlessly removed.

The tension leaked from the camp. Skye felt it, but he knew that those greenhorns never even suspected how much danger they had been in. Victoria emerged from behind the screen of ponies.

"It may not be over," Skye whispered to her. "Anything could start it. That other one could die."

Victoria nodded.

Hyacinth Z. Peachtree pushed through the sulky warriors, beheld the injured man awake and alert, and smiled triumphantly. "There, now. He'll be good as new. You see? My medicine did him no harm." The Sioux stared blankly. "You can give it to that other fellow if you want."

"I don't think it's a good idea, mate," Skye said.

"Why of course it is. That fellow's hurting worse than the others. Tell Blue Heron to lend me the bottle and I'll dose the other one—the half-dead one." Peachtree exuded triumph.

Skye paused, trying to find a way to express a life-and-death proposition to the pilgrim. "Professor Peachtree, trust my counsel. That's why you hired me. I can't help you if you won't listen. You are in mortal danger."

"Oh, fiddle, Skye. The man's hurting. Look at him. He's never stopped groaning. This is charity. They'll thank me."

"Peachtree—we've got thirty unhappy Sioux looking for an excuse to kill us. Any excuse'll do."

"Darlink," said Carlotta, "get me the merchandise. If these Skyes won't do it, I will. They are all noble Indian gentlemen. See how they look at me, with innocent eyes."

"No," rumbled Skye, even as Peachtree trotted off to the show wagon for the elixir.

But Peachtree didn't stop.

"Dammit, Mister Skye, stop him," Victoria cried.

Skye didn't. He lifted his topper and screwed it down, a silent message to her. The Sioux studied them the way butchers study a veal calf, trying to fathom what all this was about. They could see he was being defied, and no doubt wondered whether Skye's famous powers had deserted him.

Carlotta Krafft-Ebing settled to the ground beside Blue Heron, who looked her up and down and smiled. She gestured toward the groaning warrior, and gently plucked the green bottle from his hand.

"No!" roared Skye. "There's taboos—this is a war party. Don't touch him. Don't touch his weapons or his shield. It destroys his medicine. He'll need to purify himself in a sweatlodge. Don't pour a drop of that syrup into him."

But the woman ignored him, headed for the prostrate warrior, and settled herself beside him while the Sioux glared.

"Here, darlink. This'll make you feel better," she said, lifting the warrior's head. He gazed at her from pain-shot eyes, and slowly sipped the stuff in the green bottle.

Victoria muttered savagely under her breath. "Go get her, Skye. Take her away from them."

But Skye stood stock-still, preferring to avoid a scene.

Maybe Carlotta's plain compassion would mollify the warriors. He would have to explain to these greenhorns that the Sioux had their own codes, as sacred to them as Communion was to whites.

The Potawatomi Princess dribbled the brown fluid into the warrior while the whole horse-stealing party watched with crackling hostility anyone could feel.

"I think you'd better stop now," Skye said softly. "You've given him an inch of that stuff."

"You just want him to hurt. I know your type," she retorted, but she pushed the cork back into the bottle and stood. "You are the true savage." The Sioux studied their wounded man, and Carlotta, and the Skyes.

Skye sighed. "Madam, because of you we may all die."

He knew he was going to take this party back to Fort Laramie—if they got out of this trouble alive. He never guided people who defied him.

Carlotta didn't back down. "This man I helped, he's a better man than you. These are innocent children of Nature. Not yet barbarians like us. They have no evil in them." With that she marched back to Blue Heron and returned the bottle.

The dosed warrior slid into peaceful comfort. His groaning abated and his breathing steadied. His face relaxed. The surly Oglala watched him awhile, then turned to their meat and began slicing off steaming pieces. Victoria muttered angrily.

They all ate. Even Blue Heron. An injured Sioux sat up. The man with the shoulder wound sipped broth from a horn spoon held by one of the warriors; the one with the stomach wound accepted some broth.

Victoria hacked loin for herself and Mary and Skye, and they filled themselves in total silence, all of them pondering what to do as darkness overtook them.

"Now, darlinks, we will perform," said Carlotta sweetly. "They will like our music, I think. We will make them happy."

Victoria glanced at Skye, but Skye said nothing. Music, he thought, might not be a bad idea.

The troupe disappeared behind the wagon, and in a few minutes the performers reappeared in all their plumage. The Sioux gasped and murmured among themselves. They had never seen such a sight. Concorde, grinning happily, strutted his gaudy red uniform, knowing how its gold braid glinted and burned in the firelight. Carlotta had added a headdress to her Potawatomi Princess outfit. Hercules looked like an undertaker in his black suit. They climbed to their stage atop the wagon, tuned up, and plunged in, the trombone, bass drum, accordion, and Carlotta's vocal chords shattering the opiated peace. Astonished Sioux warriors gaped, listened, and sometimes peered into the darkness. Between melodies a coyote laughed on the brow of a distant hill, answering the Potawatomi Princess.

For half an hour the performers whooped out lively airs, while Oglala Sioux watched, at first solemnly but then in the spirit of the music, clapping in time with the big drum, laughing, whistling, and even doing a shuffle around the fire, throwing wild shadows into the murderous dark.

Skye could scarcely believe it. The Sioux were entranced with the Potawatomi Princess, hearkening to her every note, watching her as she pitched her whole body into her singing. She had cast a spell on them.

Even Blue Heron rose, ignoring that painful gash along his ribs, and amiably swayed to the lively tunes. The other injured Sioux didn't dance, but both sat up. Even the man with the stomach wound, with brown blood caked upon his breechcloth and loins, sat and watched while the rest stared at him amazed.

Then Hyacinth Z. Peachtree adjusted his black clawhammer coat, and began a mighty talk.

"My noble red friends," he began, "you've been entertained absolutely free and without obligation by H.Z. Peachtree and Company, purveyors of tonics, elixirs, anodynes, and cordials, the finest preparations in all the world to relieve the torments of the flesh and assure the healing of your every part. Now my red brethren, I want you to know all about the H.Z. Peachtree company, devoted to helping mankind overcome its ills . . ."

On and on he went. The Sioux didn't understand a word but they sat politely, watching Peachtree orate, watching his arms fly upward, his finger point, his hands elevate a bottle of his elixir.

In all his years in the wilds, Skye had never seen anything like this. The bamboozler was soothing the wild beast.

Peachtree finally wound down, and turned the show over to his minstrels, who played one final tune into the darkness. Skye wondered what would come next. He was prepared to sit up all night and guard the party, his Hawken across his lap, to keep the Sioux from slitting their throats in the night.

But instead, Blue Heron rose, embraced Peachtree, gave an amulet to the Potawatomi Princess, and then snapped a quiet command. Much to Skye's astonishment, the Sioux swiftly gathered their ponies, helped their wounded up, and rode into the night.

Mister Skye sighed, utterly confounded. The medicine show troupe had made a fool of him.

Chapter 12

Carlotta Krafft-Ebing rolled out of her blankets and embraced a glorious August day with a joy that brimmed over. Wilderness intoxicated her more than strong drink ever could. She sucked the dewy dawn air into her lungs, enjoyed the acrid scent of sagebrush, and then exhaled. The morning zephyrs caressed her plump body, making her feel unusually cheerful.

She trotted down to the Laramie River to perform her ablutions, wearing her chemise and petticoat. She didn't care who saw what. The wilds had freed her at last; she could do whatever she chose, and there would be no one to say nay. If she felt like wandering around in dishabille, that was her absolute privilege.

The Skyes were up, and the elder wife was kindling a fire while that big oaf was scratching himself and yawning. He had already screwed that topper onto his grimy locks. She glared at the guide, knowing she was going to put him in his place. She absolutely refused to let the imbecile impose his rules upon her.

She knelt and scrubbed herself with her ball of lavender-scented soap from England, enjoying the delicious chill of the water, which tingled and goosebumped her flesh. She was such a hedonist that she could relish even the bracing chill of the water she splashed over her legs and arms.

Victoria pushed through the riverbank brush and dipped a leather bucket into the sluggard stream, studying Carlotta with a flinty stare. Carlotta laughed. She stood, lifted her lovely arms to the sky, and meditated for several minutes in that supplicant posture, seeking the eternal wisdom of the sun and wind and meadows and waters. She would have no gods with rules governing her life. She took twenty deep breaths to keep herself in voice, while absorbing the peace of the wilds. This slumbering land was far safer than any city, where she could scarcely walk to the opera house without being accosted by a pickpocket.

She needed to wash some of her linens, but put it off. It absolutely annoyed her to have to perform manual labor. It invaded her untrammeled freedom of will. Duties! Let those learned fools back in the cities talk of them. Carlotta Krafft-Ebing had none, and would never submit to them again. Maybe she could hire one of the Skye women to wash.

Back at the wagon she slithered her nankeen cotton dress over her and buttoned it langorously, making a sumptuous act even of preparing for the day. It needed scrubbing too, but she refused to bow to appearances. What did it matter what others thought? She was her own mistress. And this was not a city.

The others stirred, eyeing her the way men did when they wanted something. But she smiled winsomely at them and sashayed away. They could flip their own flapjacks. Hyacinth scraped his black stubble before a mirror dangling from the wagon, which he did every few days. Men who shaved got to perform a wanton act of self-adoration each morning.

After a meander through the meadows she found some flapjacks waiting for her; Concorde had cooked them. She smiled sweetly at them and ate lustily. Hercules wordlessly scrubbed pots and pans in the river. Carlotta enjoyed the sight. She had escaped female bondage.

The three Skyes approached, and she renovated her distaste for that grotesque plainsman. At his breast hung the ornate bearclaw necklace that was supposed to give him some sort of magical powers. His rolling sailor's gait told her all she needed to know about the idiot.

"We're about ready," Hyacinth said to them.

"Mister Peachtree, we're going back to Fort Laramie," Skye announced without preamble. "I'll have Colonel Bullock refund your money. We're not taking you south."

Carlotta exulted but Hyacinth was amazed. "Why, sir, we employed you; we came to a costly agreement. We—"

"We don't take clients who're likely to get us into deadly trouble, mate. We like our topknots."

"But what have we done?"

"We're lucky we're not lying here butchered, scalped, and robbed, sir. That's how close it was."

"That's absurd."

"That was a humiliated war party, mate."

"Why, darlink, they was just injured people who needed help. They even offered their meat to us," Carlotta retorted. She wasn't going to let this big idiot intimidate them.

"The usual ploy to get into a camp," Skye said.

"Skye," Peachtree said, "you can't renege on a contract. I won't allow it."

"It's Mister Skye."

"It's not mister. You don't deserve the title. This is an infernal and dishonest act."

Skye lifted his topper, looking like he wanted to say something sharp. Instead, he spoke very softly. "We won't risk our lives. That's all there is to it. We'll be leaving for Fort Laramie in a few minutes."

Carlotta boiled. She hadn't been so mad since they wouldn't let her sing *The Marriage of Figaro* in Vienna and she'd walked out on those rotten impresarios. "What do you think you are?" she snarled. "Some idiot backwoodsman. I'm glad we found out your true character the second day out, and not a month from now. You're a coward. That's what. You're all cowards. We should go alone, Hyacinth."

Skye said nothing. Victoria glared. Even the younger one, Mary, didn't flinch under her assault.

Finally the guide replied in a gentle voice. "You, more than anyone, endangered the lives of everyone here, Miss Krafft-Ebing. I warned you, Sioux warriors have certain warpath customs—"

"Don't lecture me, you swine!"

Skye didn't argue. He and his women turned toward their campsite. She watched triumphantly as they dismantled their camp and saddled the horses. She was used to people turning their backs to her. Every opera impresario she'd ever battled had ended up sacking her. Which was why she was now a gypsy chanteuse, singing for a miserable gyppo show. She'd been trained for higher things. Every time she thought of her present condition a wave of shame overwhelmed her. She dreamed of better times. When they reached California, she was going to ditch this vile little outfit and sing like a nightingale in real opera again. Meanwhile, she had to endure barbarians and fools.

"Cowards," she yelled.

Hyacinth sighed. "Was your aria from *The Magic Flute* or was it from *Figaro*? I don't suppose it was *The Abduction from the Seraglio*."

"You brute! I will sing exactly what I please."

"That's fine. I'm going to drop you from the company and hope the Skyes will guide us again."

"You're discharging me?"

H.Z. Peachtree smiled. "Maybe I can employ the Skye women to be my Potawatomi Princesses. They're the real thing. Don't leave without returning your princess outfit. It cost me twelve bottles of tonic."

"I quit! You can't fire me. I quit right here."

"As usual. It's been three days since the last time you quit. You have a whole wilderness to enjoy. There it is." He waved grandiosely toward innocent cottonwoods, hills, and browned bunchgrass.

"But I have to eat."

"Why, pluck berries. Chokecherries, buffalo berries. There might be trout in this poor excuse for a river."

"You're despicable, Professor of Swampwater H.Z. Peachtree. You have no manners. You have no sensitivities."

He shrugged. "I'm partial to *The Magic Flute*, myself."

"You swine!" She threw a rock at him, and stood huffing as he dodged it.

He hailed the Skyes. "Mister Skye—before this goes any farther, I want you to know I've taken certain steps."

Skye paused. He was tying the lodgecover onto a travois.

"I've discharged Miss Krafft-Ebing from the Hyacinth Z. Peachtree Medicine Show. We'd like to continue. We'll abide exactly by your counsel at all times, sir."

"You baboon!" she yelled.

"You figuring to take her back to the fort first?"

"No, she's amazingly fond of wilderness and noble savages. This is her natural home. Her whole life has been devoted to arriving at this exact spot on the face of the earth, latitude and longitude unknown. You see, she's a great devotee of Jean-Jacques Rousseau."

"You have me there, mate."

"A Frenchman, sir, who believed civilization corrupts the innocent soul and turns us all into hypocrites and bounders. Only those who have escaped civilization—such as the noble American savage—are Natural Man, uncorrupted and beautiful, like sweet children."

Skye laughed skeptically, enraging Carlotta Krafft-Ebing.

"You don't know anythink about savages," she said. "They are beautiful and virtuous—unlike you."

"Never supposed I had much virtue, madam," Skye said. "I try for honor, though."

"Carlotta," said Peachtree smoothly. "We're only a dozen miles or so from the fort. You'll be there by midafternoon if you walk fast."

She threw an egg-sized rock at Peachtree, hitting him in the calf. He bawled.

"You owe me two months' wages, darlink."

Peachtree shrugged. "You can sing for your supper at the post. I never knew a soldier whose heart doesn't melt when he hears *The Flying Dutchman*."

"I will find some savages. They'll love me more than you," she cried.

Skye watched all that with worried glances. "Mister Peachtree, I'll talk privately with my women about your offer. I'm not sure this changes anything."

With that he escorted his two ladies out of earshot, where they conversed at length. Then, at long last, Skye approached, looking apologetic.

"We'll take you south. Victoria'll take Miss Krafft-Ebing back to the fort and catch up with us. We'll put her on one of our mares." He eyed her solemnly.

"Oh! You have no heart," she cried, unloosing a flood of tears. It didn't melt any of them, so she bawled harder and threw herself into the hard earth, sobbing and gasping, just as Sergio D'Atilla had taught her to do in *The Abduction from the Seraglio*.

Chapter 13

Elisha Carmody wondered what sort of company he had fallen in with. Miss Krafft-Ebing sprawled on the ground beside the wagons, sobbing, gulping, and hammering the clay with her fists. She was having a tantrum of prima donna proportions.

Around her stood her troupe and the Skyes, mute and horrified.

"Carlotta, get hold of yourself," Peachtree commanded, but it was like directing the wind.

Carmody thought perhaps he too had better head back to Fort Laramie and find another way to get to California. He intuitively trusted the Skyes but not this bizarre party of medicine show minstrels.

"I'll take her back," he said to Skye. "You people go on."

Skye smiled wryly. "Don't blame you, mate."

Carlotta sat up suddenly. "I wont go back. I am stayink here in this beautiful wilderness." Her rage had vanished.

"Miss Krafft-Ebing, Victoria'll take you to the fort with one of our mares," Skye said.

"This is where I am planted. This is where I will stay," she cried.

"I'm afraid you'll go hungry, my dear," said Peachtree.

"I will find savages and live with them. Put my things on the ground. Here I will live forever like an oak."

Something in her tone dared anyone to defy her.

"No," said Skye. "We won't leave you here."

She exploded again, spraying her shrapnel in all directions. "I will not. I am a free woman. I am adult. I will live my life as I see fit. Don't you dare tell me what to do. Idiot."

Carmody thought he'd never seen such an odd impasse.

"Do it!" she bellowed at Concorde. Reluctantly the grinning musician clambered into the supply wagon and dragged out a trunk and a coat. He set them on the grass, where they looked forlorn and doomed.

"It'd be a criminal act to leave her here," Hyacinth Peachtree said to Skye. "Can't you do something?"

Skye looked perplexed. "It'd be a criminal act to haul her back to the post against her will, Professor. She's not my slave. None of us own her."

"I will find a beautiful savage," she said. The tears had evaporated, leaving smudges on her face. "He will be a finer mortal than all of you and I will give him love."

Carmody studied her thoughtfully. She was the very sort of person he believed he could help: people who were prisoners of belief, or emotion, or habit. But he saw no way to help her now.

"All right," said Skye. "We'll be going. Are you coming with us, Mister Carmody?"

"If these people will give me some assurance that your wisdom in these dangerous spots will be heeded—without fail."

Professor Peachtree replied at once: "I assure you, sir,

we've studied the lesson. My troupe'll heed our guide's directions without fail. I didn't realize ..."

"All right, then," Skye said. Concorde and Hercules went for the picketed mules, while Skye's women loaded bundles of lodgepoles onto a travois.

Carmody had already loaded his mule, and waited for the rest. Last evening he had quietly hovered at the outskirts of the camp, watching as a dozen Oglala wandered among the picketed mules, plainly coveting prizes of war, looking for hobbles, examining Elisha's own giant mule. Then the warriors surveyed the Skyes' camp, steering clear of Jawbone, who stood with his ears flattened and fire in his yellow eyes, ready to massacre them if they approached. Eventually the warriors had retreated, but not before they had looked Carmody up and down, measuring him for a scalping.

Carmody had seen death flutter by. It haunted him all night.

The group was ready, and at Skye's nod Peachtree and Hercules cracked whips over the croups of their mule teams, and Skye's younger wife stirred her mares to life. But all of them were staring back at the diminishing figure of Carlotta Krafft-Ebing, who stood defiantly in the grassy bottoms of the Laramie River.

That was when she began singing, in a contralto voice so pure and gracious that it reminded Carmody of the tone of a Stradivarius cello. It raised goose bumps on his arms. But it wasn't only the tone that riveted him: she was singing, at the top of her lungs, the joyous chorus of Beethoven's Ninth Symphony. He recognized it at once, having heard it at several concerts in Washington City. It was her triumphal coda to all that had passed here. The sheer beauty of her voice in the quiet wilderness melted him. The chorus didn't belong there.

He knew at once who she was and how she had arrived at her present estate: an operatic contralto so imprisoned by temperament that she could sing in no opera company on earth. She had demolished her life and was reduced to sleazy medicine shows for a living. She was a prisoner of uncontrolled passion and some fanciful humbug she had gotten from books.

They were soon out of earshot and rattling along through a serene morning, each person lost in thought. Miss Krafft-Ebing was probably committing suicide. What could anyone do with an adult bent on self-destruction? Especially here? Carmody had no answers and no one else did either. Skye had ruled out force, and all had silently agreed with him.

The triumphant strains of Beethoven's Ninth played in his mind. She was singing her chorus of transcendence over a sorry world. It had been an inspired choice. The echoing music made him acutely aware of the silent slurring of the wilderness. Zephyrs hummed softly in his ear. A crow cawed. He heard the rustle of cottonwood leaves.

He knew that this episode would haunt him for years. His time in public service had given him acute insights into every desire of the human will and every weakness and vice that imprisoned mortals. Here, in the midst of a wild without law, a woman craving to be free of every restraint imposed by civilization—statute, religion, custom—had shown herself to be a slave. He wished he could rescue her with his message: we work out our salvation within ourselves by overcoming our imprisoning weaknesses. But he knew that no mere lecturer could transform the ravening heart of Carlotta Krafft-Ebing.

Skye's younger wife, Mary, yelled something and Skye halted the entourage, peering down their backtrail. Carmody turned. There the woman was, running toward them, stumbling along as if the devil's pitchfork were driving her. They were going to have to deal with the opera diva once again. They all waited silently, and some of them looked annoyed.

Miss Krafft-Ebing stumbled toward them, gasping and sweat-soaked, her hair in wild disarray, tears streaking her cheeks. She headed straight for Skye, who held that demonic blue roan in tight control when he turned skittish.

She was panting so hard she couldn't speak, but at last she gulped out what she wanted to say. "Please take me. I'll do what you ask."

That was all. The guide was plainly discomfited.

"Please!"

"Dammit, I'll go get her stuff," Victoria said, deciding the matter. Skye's woman grabbed a halter rope and led one of the family's travois ponies back up the trail while the others watched, distrusting themselves to speak.

Carmody expected Skye to be harsh, and was surprised when the guide simply lifted his topper, screwed it down, and nodded. Peachtree said nothing, but Carmody sensed that Miss Krafft-Ebing had just rejoined the show, probably for the fiftieth time.

Ten minutes later they started down the trail again, this time with the opera singer sitting quietly beside Hercules on the second wagon. Carmody felt better, and from the look of the rest, he supposed they did too. He kept pace with the wagon, his stride matching the mules' gait.

"Miss Krafft-Ebing," he said after a while. "I'd enjoy your company. Would you walk with me a while?"

"You want to discipline me."

"No, I want to learn about your conservatory training. You have the most beautiful voice I've ever heard."

"Ah! It is so," she said. She eyed him doubtfully, but then clambered down from the creaking wagon and let Hercules drive it alone. Carmody made no effort to engage her, knowing that sharing the trail would create its own camaraderie. They trekked through a glorious morning, brimming with the peace of nature.

He let time drift by without much talk, once pointing at a pair of mallards bobbing near some cattails, and again at a hare, and again at a soaring bald eagle.

"I've sung in every great opera house in Europe," she said after a half hour. "Milan, Rome, Paris, Vienna . . . I was fashioned by God to sing Richard Wagner's operas. I have *Lohen-*

grin with me. I bought the libretto and score from a copier just before we started for California. It is breathtakink. He gets better and better. He has feelink."

"You'll sing it some day," he said.

"Ha!" The way she said it sounded like a rifle shot.

"I've never heard of *Lohengrin*," he said.

"Last year was Wagner finishink it. It has never been sung on this continent."

"Why, sing it for me, then. All the parts."

"Sing it for you? Here?"

"Yes, for me."

She eyed him. "Later I will. For an audience of one. Not in front of the others. For them I sing only minstrel songs."

"Miss Krafft-Ebing," he said. "Your voice will transform the wilderness into Paradise."

Her eyes rivered tears, and he wondered what he had done.

Chapter 14

The vast and empty wastes did not pleasure Hyacinth Z. Peachtree. He was turtling across a desert. Not until this Sahara was well populated with white people would it bloom into anything worthy of his attention. He might enjoy this broken prairie country if he knew there would be a town ahead or a ranch nearby. But there was nothing but endless rocky slopes, rising and dipping in giant tides, arid and brown; nothing green except the sagebrush raked by harsh winds.

Skye led them up the Laramie River as far as Chugwater Creek and turned south. At that point they left good water behind them. The sluggish creek ran brackish water, and not a lot of that. Even the mules didn't like it. Peachtree considered bottling and selling it as the Peachtree Saline Purgative.

The guide told them they would soon be following something called the Old North Trail, an Indian turnpike down the front of the Rocky Mountains, well worn by countless travois.

After that frightful first day things had quieted to the point of sheer tedium. Peachtree barely bothered to steer his mule team. They plodded along behind Skye, their tails smacking flies, their attitude one of weary resignation. The guide had insisted on resting and grazing them frequently. Now, after half a month, the mules were showing some flesh.

They had seen no more savages. Indeed, the Skyes had not even found signs of their passage, which Peachtree regretted. He had intended to peddle his elixirs to them in exchange for some valuable pelts and hides. The land was lonelier and windier than ever. Off to the west the Laramie Mountains humped in a long dreary spine. From several prairie hills Skye had shown his clients the snowy tips of the Rockies lost in the autumnal haze of mid-September. Those giants had caught early storms, but out on the prairie the days stayed mild.

Carlotta had taken up with Carmody, which suited Peachtree just fine. The earnest reformer had a laxative effect on the opera diva, and she had scarcely thrown a fit since that first day. She hadn't quit Peachtree's medicine show for two weeks. That amazed him. She usually quit every two or three days. He figured he had rehired her seventy or eighty times since they had crossed the Missouri River. She hated the medicine show, and he didn't doubt that she would bolt it for good in California.

She had formed friendships with Skye's wives, or at least thought she had. Hyacinth suspected that the savage women were merely humoring the witch. At any rate, each evening Carlotta dawdled at the Skye lodge, watching them toil but never helping, gushing over them, admiring what she called their noble natures, while the elder Mrs. Skye cursed cheerfully in a tongue so profane that it wilted the spikes off prickly pear.

Skye often inspected the caravan, but found nothing amiss. Peachtree knew he never would. His party had spent thousands of days on the road; they kept the two wagons in good repair, treated their mules respectfully, and knew how to stay clean and reasonably rested during the long pulls. The H.Z. Peachtree troupe had encountered every sort of trouble known to man and had survived. Peachtree doubted that Skye grasped that.

The big guide often conversed with Carmody, and sometimes with the rest. Peachtree found himself being assessed each time they talked and knew that these encounters compassed more than pleasantries. Why didn't the old mountaineer mind his business, which was to steer them to Santa Fe?

The weather held until the equinox. But on the twenty-first a low gray overcast crawled out of the north, attacking them with vicious winds that penetrated whatever one wore and numbed hands and toes. Skye's women broke out blanket capotes, but Peachtree had trouble staying warm, especially up on his wagon seat where he could get little exercise.

They made early camp near Big Bear Creek under a stone ledge that tamed the savage gale. Peachtree reluctantly admired the choice of locale. Game had been thin. Victoria often rode in without meat slung over the rump of her little mare. He had seen no deer for days. Skye said they were rutting. But even though meat was lacking, the Skye women found food. They knew how to concoct meals from amazing things; brown roots pried from the prairie; buffalo berries, hackberries and chokecherries; wild onions; meaty bulbs chiseled from the clay bottoms of the plains. That night the Skye women made a stew of roots, greens, and two hares chopped into small chunks. It wasn't tasty.

Sleet probed the camp even before they had settled into their bedrolls, so Peachtree and Concorde unfurled a tarpaulin and lashed it on poles as a half-shelter. It flapped and thundered in the knifing wind, but it subdued the sleet and caught an echo of warmth from their fire. Carlotta repaired to the supply wagon, where she burrowed a nest under the tarpaulin, making pillows of bagged flour and coffee beans as was her wont during rainstorms. She envied the Skyes, whose lodge seemed to take the wind easily. They would sleep warm around a cheery fire whose smoke was vented by the earflaps above.

The next morning the prairie lay buried under white slush, which was rapidly gophering into the ground, turning the clay to gumbo. It would be a brutal day for the mules. Wearily the party pushed south with the sleet on their backs, running down their ponchos and soaking their pants and skirts. Every creek had risen. The troupe had to ford them carefully because of quicksand and bogholes. But Peachtree was a skilled driver, and knew exactly how to tackle each stream. Skye always watched, but said nothing. He seemed to approve. Peachtree knew he'd hear about it if he was doing something not to the guide's liking.

The sleet turned into snow for an afternoon, and then retreated into stinging rain that oozed off the mules, dripped down Peachtree's red neck, and puddled on the wagon seat, cooling his privates. The ground had further softened and the iron tires of the wagons were cutting deep ruts. The mules wearied and needed rest every few minutes.

But the troupe endured, hiding from the wind, numbly sucking coffee upon bitter dawns, taciturn because each day was born in misery and died in pain. After three drab days the storm blew east, and summer along with it. They awakened to sharp, clear fall weather. A hard frost whitened the grass. The rising sun illumined an awesome blue wall of mountains to the west, tinting their snowy crests rosy along with the puffy clouds hanging on the peaks. The sun wrought cheer in them all but failed to drive away the razor-edged cold.

That day exhausted the mule teams worse than ever because the gumbo sucked at the wheels. Only Carmody's big mule, picking his way easily over the sodden turf, failed to tire. It dawned on Peachtree why the officers at Fort Laramie had sternly advised him not to attempt a winter crossing of the Sierra, and he was suddenly grateful for their advice. He could only hope that his troupe would reach kinder climates before winter whipped them in earnest.

At noon they reached a swollen river, its muddy water roiling past with sinister swells.

Skye lifted his topper and settled it. "This is the Cache de Poudre, mates," he said. "Right straight out of the highest Rockies. It empties into the South Platte not far from here. I'm not sure we should cross now."

"Why, Mister Skye, we're seasoned wanderers. I spend my life on the road," Peachtree said. "I've tackled worse."

"That may be true, but I think we'll wait. This'll drop in a couple of days. The mules are worn. Not even fresh ones'd get you across that flood."

"If we don't keep going south, we'll face worse, sir," Peachtree replied, feeling testy about the delay.

Skye didn't respond. He turned his blue roan and steered it to the riverbank. The horse screeched, pawed at the muddy banks, and refused to step in. The guide slid a hand under the ugly horse's mane and spoke something to him. The horse sighed, as if in surrender, and gingerly eased into the boiling water, dropping suddenly to his hocks.

Jawbone plainly didn't like it. The flood piled against his legs, pushing it downstream, threatening to topple horse and man into the water. But Skye urged the horse on, and Jawbone edged into the main flow, which pushed against his flanks so mightily that the horse staggered. The horse edged farther out and then seemed to drop off a cliff. Water boiled around his belly, wetting Skye's boots and leggins. Jawbone had enough: he shrieked and bounded back in giant leaps, scrambling up to grass and shaking off water in violent convulsions that almost threw Skye.

"It's a devil's crossing," Victoria muttered.

"There's your answer, mate," Skye said.

"It's a bad one," Peachtree conceded.

"That water'll push your wagon clear around—if it doesn't tip you over. It'll pull your team around with it. We'll wait."

"It's a matter of speed, Mister Skye. I've handled streams like that several times. You've got to whip up the mules and hit it so fast that you're carried across by momentum."

"We'll camp here, Professor. Let the mules recruit. Good grassy bottoms and cottonwoods all along here."

"Why, we can't delay, Mister Skye. We'll be months late in California."

Skye squinted at him. "You've no appointment in California, have you?"

Peachtree laughed. He sat alone on the olive-lacquered show wagon bearing his gilded name. "If you don't take risks, you don't succeed," he said. With that he cracked his whip over the mules, smacking them into a wild plunge toward the river. Peachtree smiled, feeling the muscle of six Missouri giants yank his bouncing wagon down the muddy bank and into the deluge. But the mules lost momentum instantly. The flood hammered through the spoked wheels, which turned more and more slowly and then stopped when the mules hit the main channel. They went under and fought for their lives while the flood swung the wagon around.

Chapter 15

Skye stared, aghast, at Peachtree's impetuous assault of the boiling Cache de Poudre River. There had been no warning; the medicine man had cracked his whip over the rumps of the reluctant mules and bulled into the muddy deluge.

The mule team floundered, thrashed, and found bottom. Even so, the force of the current was steadily shoving the team downstream and threatening to drown the mules whenever water broke over their heads. The medicine show wagon careened under the hammering on its upstream side. Peachtree rocked with it, barely keeping his seat.

But the wagon didn't twist sideways, which meant that its iron tires rolled on hard bottom. The team stalled. The wagon teetered terribly on two wheels, slowly righting itself. Another wall of water smacked its upstream side, tilting it, but Peachtree threw himself to the high side of the wagon, hung over it, his weight balancing it against the deluge.

From behind him, Skye heard the Potawatomi Princess screaming and the rest of the troupe shouting. They were all perched on the second wagon. Nearby, Carmody watched silently while standing beside his mule.

Slowly Peachtree's wagon teetered back, and the mules, now quartering downstream with the flow, found footing and help from the current. Little by little they dragged the bobbing wagon forward into the center of the stream. Another wave battered the wagon, and this time two locked cabinet doors on the downstream side sprang open. Slowly, Peachtree's laboratory slid out, carboys, canisters, an oak cask, pasteboard boxes, a scale, funnels, beakers, and tray after tray of rectangular green bottles, all of them corked and labeled. The river gulped them all, and whirled them away.

Victoria muttered something angrily and spurred her little mare downstream to a brush-choked bend where she might snare a few things. Her sudden departure unfroze Skye, who had watched with mounting horror. He heeled Jawbone toward the water, preparing to go after Peachtree, who still hung over the upstream side of the wagon, balancing it against the roaring flood as the mules clawed their way to shallower water downstream, dragging the wagon behind them.

Then it ended. Much to Skye's astonishment, Peachtree had made it. The mules lurched up the muddy slope, losing footing on the muck, but soon they stood on the far bank, rivering water, their heads low, their flanks heaving. Peachtree stood in his seat, whooped, and began squeezing water from the clawhammer tails of his coat.

"No trouble at all, Skye," he yelled.

Skye pointed at the wagon, and only then did Peachtree discover the loss. He clambered down, still dripping water, and poked his head into the empty cabinet, and then examined the brass lock that had failed.

Downstream, Victoria was gingerly snatching things out of the flood. She nabbed the oaken cask, some floating bottles, and various pasteboard boxes and a stoppered glass bottle full of some sort of herb.

Across the boiling river, Peachtree stared dumfounded at his empty shelves. Then he unlocked the second set of cabinet doors and revealed trays of corked but empty green bottles, along with sundry items for the show, including the costumes, drums, brass instruments, and accordion.

Skye thought Peachtree looked uncommonly cheerful for a man who had just lost his stock in trade and the means of manufacturing it. All he had left was his green bottles.

Peachtree approached the far bank and shouted. "Nothing lost I can't live without. Come along now. You can make it, you dusky scaredy-cat. Just steer your mules downstream and let the flood do it. Don't go straight across—that was a mistake."

Concorde didn't reply. None of the troupe on the second wagon seemed eager to tackle that river.

"You'd better wait a day, mates," Skye said. "High water won't last long."

But Peachtree had other plans. "Come on across just as I said. Solid bottom. It'll be no trouble, Concorde."

Victoria returned, her lap filled with a cask and other salvage as she sat her mare.

"Ah, you got the grain spirits!" Peachtree yelled. "Now I'm back in business."

"Dammit, I should let it all go," she said.

"Come on across," Peachtree yelled. He sounded ebullient.

"Ah'd like to repent fust, boss."

Concorde was certainly scared, Skye thought, watching him and Hercules summon up the courage to try. He turned to Victoria. "I'm thinking maybe to camp here until it goes down."

She nodded, her weathered face full of agreement. Swiftly she herded the travois ponies toward some sheltering cottonwoods. That made up Carmody's mind, too. He tugged on his lead rope and led his mule toward the new campground.

"Mister Skye, kindly bring them across," Peachtree yelled from across the flood.

Skye lifted his topper and settled it. His responsibility as guide always gnawed at him. The river wasn't really negotiable, and had anyone less skilled than Peachtree tackled it, the wagon would have overturned and the mules drowned. Carmody, on foot, had no way across. The packhorses might make it if the packs didn't unbalance them, but not the travois horses. They'd be twisted and flipped over by those long levers. Most of what Skye owned would be lost.

"We'll wait until it goes down," Skye yelled back. "I won't take people across that bloody river. You're not in that much of a hurry, Professor. There's no reason to attempt it."

"Skye, I'm alone here. I'm wet. I haven't a change of clothing. I haven't a match for a fire."

Skye said nothing. The man had gotten into his dilemma by defying Skye's trail wisdom.

"Boss, Ah'm a-coming like hellfire," Concorde yelled.

"I don't want to!" Carlotta howled. "I'll get wet. Why didn't they build a bridge?"

"Carlotta, Ah need you to lean off the upstream side, just like he done, all yoah three hundred pounds of white flesh."

"You beast!"

"You too, ol' Hercules and Master Pontius P. Like the man says, heading downrivah it'll be a cakewalk."

"It'll throw me off," Pontius warned. "Drown me. I'll need a good dose of Pain Extractor first."

"That's stuff's floating down the river, old man," said Hercules with malice. "You'll just have to stop shaking long enough to git on over. Then you can shake until you rattle."

"Whoa, mates. We'll camp here. I'll get some vittles and a steel and flint and his bedroll across to the professor. Jawbone's faced worse rivers than this."

"Skye," yelled Peachtree, "I didn't hire a guide to slow me down. All you need is courage."

"It's Mister Skye, sir."

"Come across, Concorde. Just as I say—heading downstream."

Skye watched unhappily as the troupe readied itself. Even P.P. Parsons clamped his palsied hands onto the bench.

Concorde winked at Skye from a jaundiced eye, whooped, and coaxed his mule team toward the swirling water. The mules balked.

"Whip 'em, Concorde," Peachtree yelled.

Concorde did, but with a lot less enthusiasm than Peachtree. The tassel smacked one rump after another, stinging the mules, jolting them into a wild prancing that plunged them into the brown flood. Concorde popped the mules along, blooding them with the tassel. He steered them downstream so that they quartered with the flow from the beginning. The wagon followed, with Carlotta, Hercules, and Parsons hanging over the upstream side. The flood buffeted and rocked it, and at one point lifted it up on two wheels while Carlotta shrieked, but Concorde's team had an easier time of it, driven by the flow. After a few tense minutes, the team and wagon reached the far side safely. The medicine people all hoorawed.

Skye sighed. He was glad not to be plucking drowning people out of that torrent; glad not to be trying to drag out an overturned wagon.

And worried about something ominous. Twice the medicine troupe had defied his trail wisdom and gotten away with it. If they succeeded twice, they would try again. In their minds, they had proved him wrong. But Peachtree had gained nothing. Skye didn't intend to put his family or Elisha Carmody at risk, which meant that the medicine troupe would either wait on the far shore for him—or strike out on its own.

That, indeed, was exactly what was on Peachtree's mind. "Come on over, Carmody," he called. "The Skyes can catch up to us when they please. The day's half over, the lodgetrail south is plain to the eye."

Carmody refused. "You'd best wait there and let the mules graze," he yelled back.

"Well, we'll see you in Santa Fe," Peachtree bawled over the babble of the water.

"They don't know what's waiting for them," Victoria said.

The Skyes and Carmody stood on the riverbank, watching Peachtree's dripping medicine show roll through cottonwood bottoms and vanish.

"Mister Carmody, I'm glad you haven't the itch to reach California tomorrow," Skye said wryly.

"Self-discipline, sir, is the key to life. Those who lack it suffer for it. That's one of the messages in my lectures."

Victoria squinted at him. "You're the first white man I've met who ain't in a crazy hurry."

But Skye wasn't listening. The two wagons reappeared briefly as they climbed the southern bluffs, and then vanished over the top. The Peachtree Medicine Show was on its own, and Skye wondered what its fate might be.

Chapter 16

Hyacinth Z. Peachtree led his medicine show ever southward, exulting at his good fortune. He didn't need the guide. In fact, Skye would only slow him up. The lodgetrail they traveled was so plain a cretin could follow it. And how could one get lost with the Rocky Mountain Front Range vaulting up on the west? This Indian artery would eventually intersect the mountain branch of the Santa Fe Trail, and after that it'd be like driving a four-in-hand through uptown Kansas City.

He regretted wasting all that lucre on Skye. What could a guide teach him? Peachtree had been on the road for years. He and Concorde and Hercules could resurrect wagons, reseat iron tires on wheels, negotiate any sort of river, doctor the mules, repair harness, shift for grub, live off the land, cozy plain women, and jolly the yokels. He had skunked several angry mobs, converted a sheriff into a pacifist, quoted Scripture to irate ministers, and redeemed tar-and-feather mobs from sin.

That Skye! A walking quagmire of caution. The man who

was reputed to be the lion of the wilderness was afraid to cross a river. Peachtree felt downright jovial about ditching the Skyes, and just as happy to jettison addle-brained Carmody.

Except for the gusty winds, the warm afternoon felt as delicious to him as it would to a boy playing hooky. Not even the calamity of losing most of his laboratory and bottled elixirs bothered him much.

He called a halt at a friendly copse of cottonwoods, whose leaves were starting to turn.

"You gonna wait heah for Grandmothah Skye?" asked Concorde.

"Heavens no; we don't need him. He's as useful as a snapping turtle. Look at this trail. It goes clear down the Front Range of the Rockies, as plain as a pike."

"Getting lost ain't what I'm fretting about. It's dealing with them pesky savages. We don't none of us know the tongue, or even the finger-talk."

"They are all noble people," Carlotta replied. "All we must do is be kind to them, darlink."

"Besides," Peachtree added, "do you see any? We haven't even seen a sign of them. Not a feather. That's how it is out here. We'll probably go clear to Santa Fe without raising a redskin."

"We should wait," said Hercules. "We're pretty thin agin' any big bunch, like two hundred mean devils lookin' for hair."

From up on the supply wagon, old Pontius P. Parsons wheezed his delight. "Wait till they lift my toupee. Say, Peachtree, you got some juice for me?"

"Not now, Pontius." Peachtree wondered if he had any Pain Extractor left. He'd better check. That stuff was Parsons's pay, and Parsons was the most valuable man in the outfit. There'd be the devil to pay if the Cache de Poudre had washed it away, too.

"If them saintly redskins ain't happy with a topknot, they

have a refined taste for pinky fingers, one itty-bitty joint at a time, whiles a body still lives to enjoy the butchering," said Concorde. "Ah heard it somewheres."

"Darlink, you don't know what you're talking about."

Concorde looked sullen. "We'd better just expire here until them Skyes catch up. It won't take Skye long. Tomorrow maybe. Mules need it anyway."

"Concorde," said Peachtree with benign patience. "Hasn't it occurred to you that Skye'll find us when he wants to? He doesn't have wagons to slow him. He can move fast. Let him go at our pace for a change."

"Ah sorta liked having that Skye woman out each day poking around, boss. Keeping an eye out for trouble. Gave us a chance to hide or fort up."

"What is this? Hide or fort up?" Carlotta swelled with indignation.

Peachtree decided there had been enough debate. He ran the show, after all. "We aren't likely to have trouble. But if you see savages, break out your horns. We'll give 'em a few airs. They love shows. Music soothes the savage beast. They'll laugh and jig around, and I'll donate a plug of tobacco. Those are my instructions. You see redskins, you jump into the glad-rags, tune up, and start honking. And you, my dear, warble your bleeding heart out. I think any savage'd swoon over you."

Peachtree thought Concorde and Hercules looked a little sulky. But they didn't have any place to go, so he needn't humor them. He set them to staking out the mules in fat grass for a spell while he dug into the wagon to see just what was left. He needed to inventory his worldly goods.

He found little. It shocked him. The rocking wagon had jettisoned his bottling works into the river, along with all his canisters and carboys of herbs and chemicals. Gone also were his wooden flats of the bottled Peachtree product; elixirs, tonics, catarrh medicine, bitters, swamp root, regulator tea, and wild cherry. Worst of all, he had lost a gross of the Peachtree

Pain Extractor, the wage of P.P. Parsons. Frantically he poked around for a canister of raw opium with which to manufacture his painkiller. But it too was lost, no doubt relieving old-age pain in crayfish.

Even his gummed labels were gone, save for one water-damaged pasteboard box of the Peachtree Potawatomi Indian Cure, the specific for Nervousness, Debility, General Weakness, Poor Blood, Kidney and Liver Complaints, Rheumatism, Neuralgia, Female Weakness, Malaria, Chills and Fever, Exhausted Vitality, Nervous Prostration, Sleeplessness, Despondency, Mental Depression, Hysteria, Paralysis, Numbness, Trembling, Apoplexy, Epileptic Fits, Saint Vitus' Dance, Palpitation, Sick Headache, Dyspepsia, Indigestion, Loss of Appetite, Constipation, and all afflictions of the Nervous System.

The one label would have to do, he thought grimly. At least it covered all known complaints. The losses from the rough crossing had been far more brutal than he had supposed at first glance. Worse, the Skyes had his cask of 200-proof grain spirits, the liquid vehicle for most of his herbal products.

But all was not lost. In the supply wagon was the company's store of ardent spirits, mostly whiskey, recently purchased from the Laramie sutler, Bullock, in exchange for a gross of Pain Extractor. That would do for tinctures. And in the supply wagon was the company kitchen, which could double as his bottling works. Plenty of pots and pans and spoons.

He would have to manufacture the Potawatomi Indian Cure from whatever lay at hand. That would be an entertainment. The proposition behind all proprietary medicines was that the worse they tasted, the more potent the medical properties. And here was an entire wilderness chocked full of nasty leaves, bitter roots, and sour berries, just waiting to be compounded into a fine, foul sludge and decanted into those rows of virgin green bottles.

The crossing had been a blow, but not a fatal one for the likes of H.Z. Peachtree. He closed the lacquered doors, feeling melancholic about the five hundred dollars' worth of valuables rolling along the mud of the Cache de Poudre and terrifying trout. He dug into the supply wagon and extracted the half dozen jugs of whiskey he permitted the company to sample on special occasions, such as a three-hundred-dollar stand. These he carried to the medicine wagon and locked them inside. They comprised his whole pharmacopoeia.

"You got some joy juice for me, Hyacinth?" asked Pontius.

"Later," said the impresario.

"You lose my comfort in the crossing?"

"I'll have to dilute it some, Pontius."

"I'll quit, by gawd."

"We'll see what the Mexicans have for sale along those lines. They have a famous weed called Mary something."

"And what am I going to do until then?"

"Suffer, Pontius P. Without suffering, there's no understanding of the strenuous life. Be stoic."

"That's all I do is suffer. My joints ache. It'll ruin my performances. It'll wreck your box office. My name was top-billed once."

"You'll be world-famous in New Mexico, my friend."

"That's a long, long way from here, Peachtree."

"Well, I intend to apply my chemistry to it."

Peachtree summoned his troupe. "I, ah, have a little dilemma. The crossing cost most of my simples and compounds, including my cask of grain spirits," he began. "I'll have to use our Fort Laramie refreshments instead. We'll replenish in Santa Fe. They must have some powders, although you never know about the backward Spanish. Meanwhile, we'll collect the bounties of nature. Pontius, you'll drive the medicine wagon. Hercules, you'll drive the supply wagon. The rest of us'll gather every herb in sight. I want juniper berries, chokecherries, buffalo berries, hackberries, henbane, jimson, any roots you can find."

"I won't. It is not this for I am beink paid, darlink."

"Yes you will, sweetheart. I'm creating a new Potawatomi Indian Cure. You're going to find the most awful roots and berries ever to fry the gullet of man."

"Ach, nein!" She whirled away.

Peachtree didn't try to stop her. "All right, Concorde, it's up to you and me. Get one of those Harvest Queen sacks and a knife."

"You don' need all that stuff, boss. Injun whiskey, it's just forty-rod booze, muddy water, twist of tobacco for flavor, and some cayenne pepper for bite. We got all that sittin' right theah under canvas."

"We're going to collect every bounty this country offers, Concorde. I'll dry it, compound it, tincture it, and create an elixir. Then you'll sample it. If it makes you gag I'll bottle a few. If it makes you crow like a rooster, it'll make me a fortune. If you croak, I'll sell it for rat poison. If it makes Carlotta docile, I'll patent it and sell it to clergymen."

Concorde grinned, exposing a row of pearly teeth. "It do beat pickin' cotton," he said.

Chapter 17

When Elisha Carmody awakened, he lay in his bedroll enjoying the hushed peace. Nature was benign most of the time, he thought. But he knew that the wilds that yielded the blossoms underfoot also produced blizzards, or murderous assaults upon innocent wayfarers by savages. He enjoyed the wilds but did not romanticize them.

He swung out of his bedroll and stretched, enjoying the bite of the dawn wind. The Skyes lay quietly in their lodge while the horse stood guard over them, their sentry through the bleak passage of the night. Carmody felt a sudden gratitude toward the horse. He was like having a constable station next door.

The horse eyed him malevolently, his ears flattened, his narrow-set eyes wild as jokers. Jawbone took the prize for ugliness, but Carmody had already discerned that Jawbone was the grandest horse ever fashioned. That beast had displayed the keenest intelligence Carmody had ever witnessed in horseflesh.

Carmody padded quietly through the dawn hush to the Cache de Poudre, and studied it. It pleased him to note that the river had dropped in the night and its angry hum had settled into a softer gurgle.

Skye padded up, startling Carmody. The guide was barefoot, but wearing his black topper. "Looks better, doesn't it, mate?"

"I think it's negotiable, Mister Skye."

"I imagine. I'll run Jawbone out there; get the feel of it."

"It didn't take long to go down."

"It doesn't in the fall. It's the runoff from one storm. That's what I wanted to get across to Peachtree."

"Mister Skye, where do you suppose our companions are?"

"They had daylight enough to put a dozen miles on their mules after the crossing. What do you think, Mister Carmody? Was it worth the risk?"

"Why, sir, I admire audacity. It conquers the world. The timid fall by the wayside for the want of trying. Peachtree's a bold man. He risked his outfit and won."

"Except for whatever tumbled out of the cabinets."

"Yes, that was a loss, and I suppose he's regretting it."

Even as they stood at the riverbank watching the sullen water, Jawbone sidled up behind and poked his nose into Carmody's neck. It terrorized him.

"Easy, mate. Jawbone's just getting a whiff of you. He does that once he's decided he likes you."

Carmody felt the wet muzzle sniff up and down his neck and ears, and then felt the sloppy scrape of Jawbone's tongue. "I suppose a lick from his tongue is better than one from his hooves, Mister Skye. It's not the most tranquil moment of my life."

Skye laughed. "He's just getting a whiff. If my bare feet weren't around he could smell you a rod away." Skye laughed at some private knowledge within himself.

Behind them, Skye's women were stirring. Victoria vanished into the brush while Mary cleaned the infant.

Skye stared across the milky water, contemplating the empty land beyond the river. "They gained half a day. Is that what you mean by audacity, Mister Carmody?"

"Not at all, sir. Peachtree doesn't have to be anywhere on any date. He took a risk without any reward for it. That's not audacity. It's recklessness. Audacity's only for the great prize. Audacity is the bold charge that turns the tide of battle when all seems lost. Risk, sir, must be proportioned to the prize."

"I lean that direction myself, Mister Carmody. Back when I was a trapper with the fur brigades we learned caution. We called life out here the Rocky Mountain College. If we failed, we went under. There's some romantic notion back in your East that mountain men were reckless. I'll tell you how it was. We lived in constant danger; we were burdened by cautions. For every rule one finds in civilization, we imposed ten on ourselves."

It amazed Carmody. "You're saying, sir, that men beyond the reach of public law impose heavier law on themselves?"

"Oh, you could call it law, mate. It sure governed what we did. But I'd just call it self-control. It kept this child alive, but a lot of the old coons went under. Wilderness doesn't forgive an impetuous man, but civilization does. Things haven't changed, either. Right here, right now, we might be a few hundred yards from a bunch of armed men itching to put us under."

"Are we, sir?"

Skye shrugged. "Who knows? Too much wind for Jawbone to pick up a scent from any other direction."

"He's like a militia."

"More than that, mate."

"Mister Skye, we haven't even had a drop of coffee and I'm addled until I have it. But I want to talk some more. Why, you're the very model of the man I lecture about. The man who's free because he's not a slave to his own weaknesses."

"Avast! I'm no man's model," Skye said. "You'll bloody

well learn that soon enough." He wheeled abruptly toward his camp and began collecting the picketed horses.

Carmody regretted offending the guide. He saw to his toilet, scraping his beard off beside the river, using a small hand mirror he dangled in the willow brush. It took him only minutes to shake out his bedroll and anchor his packsaddle on the back of his big mule. He left his shoes off, knowing he would soon get a cold soaking and would change his britches over there.

At Victoria's curt nod, he helped himself to some scalding Skye coffee and munched some of his own hardtack. He wandered over to the herd and found Skye hard at work loading the lodgecover atop a mare.

"We'll take everything across on horseback, mate," Skye said. "Travois load'd get soaked."

"I'll help, Mister Skye," Carmody said. "I'll hook up these empty travois." He found a surcingle and buckled it around a mare, and then backed the mare between the travois poles while Skye stared.

"Am I doing something amiss, sir?" Carmody asked.

"No, friend. But you're the first person in all my years of guiding that's lent me a hand."

"Many hands make light work. And we'll be off sooner."

It was Victoria and Mary's turn to stare. The elder woman gaped and muttered and squinted, and finally blistered his ears with the longest string of oaths Carmody had ever heard.

"I fear I'm doing something inexcusable, Mister Skye."

"Haw!" Skye doubled over and roared. "Haw!"

Such undisciplined effusions erupting from the guide shattered Carmody's composure. He stopped his labor and fled to the fire, wondering how to repair the damage he'd done. Three Skyes grinned at him as if he were a naughty boy.

No one said another word while they broke camp and gathered their horses and the mule on the bank of the river. Carmody wasn't relishing the swim across, but he said not a word about it. He watched Skye, on Jawbone, test the bottom, and then lead the laden mares over, unload them, and return. The Skye women rode their mares across, handling their ponies deftly under the heavy thrust of water, which never quite rose above the mares' bellies. Skye guided a mare pulling a travois, leading the mare upstream so that the bucking travois, loaded with lodgepoles, wouldn't twist over and take the mare with it. At last Skye led Carmody's mule over without trouble, leaving Carmody alone.

They all stood on the far side, grinning, while Carmody edged toward the icy water, bracing himself for the worst.

"Whoa up, mate," Skye said. The next thing Carmody knew, Skye had crossed back to him, leading a tough little mare. Gratefully, Carmody stuck his bare feet into the squaw saddle's leather loops, and let himself be led across.

"Squaws get to be carried over," Skye said. Carmody's indignation blossomed, but Skye was heehawing like a mule, and his women were tittering.

Carmody intended to get to the bottom of all this. He had become the butt of some joke they shared.

But Skye enlightened him at once: "Mister Carmody, the Plains tribes divide up all the work between the sexes. No self-respecting Crow warrior would dream of helping his lady."

Carmody enjoyed the joke on himself, and thought he'd keep on helping anyway because it was a kindness.

Chapter 18

Hyacinth Z. Peachtree rued the moment he had tackled the flood without first tying his cabinet doors shut. The Cache de Poudre had cost him his morphia and his raw opium, the powders he needed most. As he drove along the Front Range of the Rocky Mountains, he pondered what to do about a mounting crisis.

Pontius P. Parsons was desperate for the Pain Extractor. He was not only an addict but also suffered acutely from an arthritic condition. With every jolt of the wagon, Pontius Parsons groaned.

"Let me off, Hyacinth. Let me off to die, I say," Parsons said. The old thespian had folded into a quivering ball on the wooden seat beside Peachtree, shrunken into a shadow of his former self.

"I can't do that, Pontius. There's no one here."

"Let me off. I can't endure it."

"We'll get to someplace soon," Peachtree said, unable to think of any. The nearest city where powders might be available would be Santa Fe, at the end of this leg of the journey.

"Hyacinth, I won't last," Parsons said. He groaned pitifully. "I'm gone. And if I somehow survive this torture, I'll quit the first instant I can. You cretin. You empty-brained ticket-puncher. You knew what I need, yet you didn't care. You didn't even think of this tormented old tragedian, once a prince of the boards, bowing to cheering multitudes, picking up roses off the stage thrown by dazzling ladies—why, Peachtree, your callousness will cost you my company."

As the hours went by, Pontius Parsons grew steadily worse. Either that or he was able to depict excruciating pain more convincingly than any other ham on earth. Whatever the case, Peachtree feared he was about to lose his ace of spades. Without Parsons, the shambling genius who won customers by rejuvenating himself before their eyes, he might as well shut down and do something sedentary, like faro dealing.

"All right, Pontius. I haven't studied every simple known to mankind for nothing. Give me a day or two and with a little luck I'll concoct your bliss out of the bounty of Mother Nature."

"I can't last a day or two, you one-line bit part. You lack the brain of an usher. Let me off. It's better for an old thespian to die by the side of the road than to ache away his final days in dire misery."

That persuaded Peachtree. He halted the wagon and clambered to earth. "Concorde, drive this. I'm going to do some wayside scientific research."

"Yoah gonna brew up some witchery, is what."

"I'm going to see what Nature Bountiful has in stock for poor Pontius—and any other customers I might meet, including the slinking savages."

During the next days he stalked the wild simple, halting at every patch of greenery he could find along the lodgetrail, while his troupe continued to drive southward along the Front Range of the Rockies.

Each morning he turned the wagons over to the rest and walked alone, sometimes pausing to snatch up leaf, stem, berry, or root and drop it into one or another of his sacks. With every rest break, he sallied up slopes and down river bottoms, his eye peeled for the known and unknown, things to nip before frost ruined his chances.

Each evening he fended off Pontius Pilate with skinny promises. The old man's groaning had begun to rattle his entire troupe, and it plunged them all into melancholia and irritation. Something had to be done, and fast. Parsons begged to be abandoned like a superannuated Pawnee so that he could croak by the wayside in peace. One bad evening Pontius sobbed so pitifully that Carlotta scolded Peachtree for ignoring such suffering.

"But Carlotta," he replied, "I haven't found what I need. I can't conjure balm and bliss out of thistle."

"Excuses," she retorted.

In the space of two days he nabbed a number of species with known medicinal properties, including goldenrod, yarrow, sweet flag, pennyroyal, mustard, dogwood, gentian, laurel, and the wicked but valuable *Datura stramonium*, or jimson weed, an anodyne and antispasmodic in small doses but a lethal poison in larger ones. He had even found a little henbane. But those were the only ones he recognized.

He had found other possible simples, including a widespread little plant with a purple or pinkish corolla. He had watched a mule nibble on one, after which the mule acted peculiarly, and finally bucked and snorted, entirely discombobulated. That was something wondrous to look into, along with a scraggly plant that Concorde called buffalo burr, which looked to be a variant of nightshade.

His search also yielded edible buffalo berries, which seemed to be in the height of their season, as well as wild plums and crabapples. At Peachtree's word, his troupe halted and stripped thickets of their berries, scaring off raucous magpies. None of them was a hunter but they scarcely needed meat at all, so fecund was the natural world they were traveling. They couldn't do better in the Garden of Eden.

One day Hercules shot a doe with his revolver. The creature had simply stood watching, so Hercules deprived it of life and liberty with a thirty-six-caliber ball. The troupe had no rifle, but as long as game came within pistolshot there would be occasional meat. Among them only Hercules had ever gutted, skinned, and butchered an animal. He was no expert at it but eventually he tugged away the hide, cut off the legs at the joints, and slowly sawed his prize into cookable meat.

Peachtree watched approvingly, but Carlotta fairly bubbled with happiness. The bountiful wilds would provide; she need never corrupt her blossoming soul in the precincts of civilization again. "This is how life is to be lived, darlinks. We are free at last."

That evening he opened the cabinet doors of his wagon and joyously beheld the arrayed bundles of simples there. In this amiable twilight he would begin to formulate a new elixir that might relieve poor Pontius. He had already fastened upon a delightful name: it would be Peachtree's Nepenthe. What civilized mortal, acquainted with the grandeur of ancient civilizations, would ever forget the name of the potion the ancients concocted to release suffering people from pain and sorrow, and bring on blessed forgetfulness? Ah, Nepenthe. The potion would sell itself. He had only to come up with a reasonable imitation of the original.

He had lost his mortar and pestle, but an iron pot and a river-rounded stone would do. He began with leaves of the *Datura stramonium* and added a few more from some henbane he had found on a single slope. He added some leaves and stems of the nightshade, and some of the fruit, stem, and leaf of the buffalo burr. He debated whether to add any more simples, and finally decided to reinforce the effect with dogwood bark, a tonic good for intermittent fevers. As a final fillip, he added a plug of tobacco. On this occasion he would merely guess at the ratios of the simples, but eventually he would work it all out and record the formula in his pharmaceutical notebook.

Patiently, he mashed the leaves and twigs until he had made a soft green pulp, an ideal consistency for infusions. Then he added a plug of tobacco and creekwater, and let his Nepenthe percolate gently over Hercules's dying cookfire until the liquid had turned a satisfying murky brown. This he let cool, and then decanted into twenty of his bottles and corked them.

"All right, Pontius Pilate. Tonight I have an elixir for you," he announced. "It should give you peace."

"Ah, it's about time, you heartless devil. I am in the direst need," Pontius said. "Sir, you've ignored my wants for endless days and I was thinking pestilence and brimstone would be the fitting reward."

"Ah, no, Pontius. I've had you in mind all along. Now this is a new elixir I'll call Nepenthe, inspired by the legendary ancient remedy for pain and sorrow. Why, imagine it. No pain, and every sorrow washed away. There are three anodynes in it and six simples and a joker. Are you ready for the veriest trip to bliss?"

"Professor, I've never been so ready in all my sorrowful life and times. My grief exceeds even that bitter moment when I was hooted off the boards at New Haven by vulgar, squalid Yale academics, the blackest abyss of my life."

"Very well then. We'll experiment with doses. Two tablespoons should about equal the two drams I have in mind. I think you'll find it's sublime."

He handed Parsons the bottle and a spoon, and let the old gent do it himself. Parsons poured, sipped, and sighed. "This is vile stuff, Peachtree. You've outdone yourself. A skunk would be insulted. A dog would roll in it." Then he gulped down the two doses and waited skeptically.

Nothing much happened. Parsons studied him from mean

eyes, bright as agates. Peachtree waited anxiously, supposing he had given too small a dose. Minutes passed.

"Nepenthe, is this?"

"The legendary potion that heals pain and sorrow, my beloved friend."

"Nepenthe it is," he said. "Powerful stuff. I'll be damned. Oh, my gracious. I am seeing the footlights of London."

With that, old Pontius P. Parsons tumbled to the earth, senseless.

Chapter 19

Aghast, Hyacinth Z. Peachtree knelt beside Parsons, seeking vital signs. They were abundant. Pontius breathed rapidly, oozed sweat, twitched, and muttered. But then he slid into coma.

"A little bit much, a little bit much," Hyacinth muttered. "The sorrows of medical pioneering."

"He ain't meat, yet," said Concorde.

"We must vigil. If he succumbs, Hercules, you must pump his lungs like your accordion," Hyacinth announced. "I'll take the first watch."

"I don't like to be around dead people, darlinks," said Carlotta. "Drag him to the bushes."

"What'd you give him?" asked Hercules.

"Uh, some narcotics, anodynes and antispasmodics, and one experimental item—a saucy little blossom that addled a mule a few days ago. I think I've struck upon something. If he croaks, that's the price of progress, I'm afraid. But what an array of simples! Why, I made history this day. Nepenthe will be the toast of civilization. We'll all be rich. Every lady in the republic will take a dose of Nepenthe at bedtime."

"Not if her mastah has any say about it," Concorde muttered.

The state of Pontius Pilate Parsons remained unchanged. He lay like a stiff in a coffin, except for an occasional shudder, exuding a strange odor.

"I don't want to sleep next to a body," said Carlotta.

"No, no, this very hour we'll know the fruits of my labors, my dear."

He proved to be right. After a while, Pontius P. Parsons opened both eyes, which were slightly crossed, and focused them upon his colleagues. He still breathed shallowly but was plainly coming around. Five minutes after that, Parsons sat up and gazed benignly at the rest.

"Gimme some more of that stuff," he said.

"Eureka!" bawled Professor Peachtree. "I am history."

"It was a bit rambunctious, Hyacinth. You might cut her down a notch."

"Just a tad, Pontius. I wouldn't want to deprive people of the fruits of my genius. How do you feel?"

"I don't."

"You don't feel?"

"That's it, to cut it right to a fine point. You've given me the carcass of a boy. I feel fifty years younger."

"Truly?"

"And the mind of one, too. I forgot my lines."

"Your lines?"

"Never mind. I can relearn them. I'm very good at improvising. It sort of cleaned out my skull, Hyacinth."

"It's truly Nepenthe."

"Whatever it is, it's better than Pain Extractor."

Peachtree straightened. "I feel touched by the Archangel Michael," he whispered. "I must go to work."

He reached the wagon, lit a lamp, and began compounding a larger batch, wishing he had kept notes. The rest grumbled at him and spread their bedrolls far away from his labors. Feverishly he dumped leaves and stems, bark and berries into his kettle, consuming his supply of the simples he had used in the first batch.

Then he set it to percolate over the fire, which cast odd shadows into a restless night. An hour later he corked forty warm bottles of Nepenthe, this time slightly more dilute than the first batch, but with undoubted Promethean prowess if one guzzled enough of it. He lacked labels for the Nepenthe, which saddened him. He would have some glorious ones printed in Santa Fe, if the Mexicans knew that art. Nepenthe labels would feature crossed swords or eagles holding snakes in their beaks or something heroic.

He didn't feel like sleeping so he concocted some Potawatomi tonic out of whiskey, water, tobacco leaves, and some juniper berries for a little astringence. It tasted formidable; it'd make a True Believer of anyone sampling a drop. He filled twenty green bottles of that, slapped the gummed Potawatomi Indian Cure labels on them, and felt fulfilled at last. He'd done a noble day's work. Sixty-nine bottles stood on trays, ready to hawk to dusky savages, mountain men, gold seekers, and greasers. He locked the cabinet doors and climbed into his bedroll, feeling the humbleness that came upon great men when they contemplated the wonders of their creation.

The next morning he allowed Parsons a lip-smacking breakfast nip of Nepenthe. They were all in a mood. Concorde attached the jingle bells to the mule-team harness, as a way of defying Skye, who preferred silent travel. They didn't need the old goat and his squaws. Jingling merrily, they drove south along a heavily used trail, while Peachtree hastened along beside, plucking up simples like a man demented. The whole entourage had absorbed Peachtree's ebullience, and were having a fine old time—even Carlotta, who was warbling arias from something she called *Lohengrin*, terrorizing gophers and magpies. Parsons smiled amiably from the wagon seat, his gaze upon distant horizons, remembering his trip to Mars.

They topped a bluff and wound down toward a turgid river, where a dozen coppery savages sat their ponies and watched. Their presence astonished Peachtree and he wished suddenly that he had kept his revolver at hand. But they seemed more curious than hostile. He saw no signs of war: no paint, no drawn bows, no leveled rifles. They just sat there, as astonished as the medicine entourage.

"Concorde, these dusky gents look just fine, just fine. Don't exhibit warlike intent," Peachtree yelled.

" 'Don't exhibit warlike intent,' " Concorde mocked. "Ah declare, you talk like you've just dosed yourself."

"Oh, they're beautiful! See how noble they are, darlinks. They are princes. We are honored by their presence."

Professor Peachtree didn't much like the drift of all that, but he didn't have time for heresies. He adjusted his black clawhammer coat and made sure its long tails hung properly. He straightened his floppy bow tie and wiped a smudge of grime from his white cuffs. Then he polished his dusty patent leather boots, using the back of his gray trousers, and walked boldly toward the magnificent children of nature.

"How. You speakum heap big English?" he asked, raising his hand palm forward.

The noble savages stared.

"Me big medicine chief. Ugh. Me gottum wagons full of good things you-bet. Me trade you good stuff, Big Injun stuff, makum you heap big bucks. Ugh."

Finally the headman, who wore a notched eagle feather in his hair, held in place by a red headband, motioned the medicine entourage upstream. A well-worn trail ran beside the little river.

"They're taking us to their village," Peachtree said. "We'll trade for some pelts. Why, this is a godsend."

He clambered aboard the medicine wagon and nudged Concorde, who reluctantly turned the wagon upstream. The bare-chested noble savages silently turned their ponies and followed alongside, staring at the two wagons and their occupants.

"You sure we're safe?" whispered Concorde. "Ah got the sweetest little two-barrel scattergun right down at mah boots."

"Patience, my friend. These are knights templar of the red race," Peachtree said, but not entirely to his own satisfaction.

They broke out of woods and much to their astonishment found themselves riding toward a towering adobe fortress, complete with bastions, double gates, and a fluttering ensign. Dozens of lodges stood in loose array around the post. Men, women, and children paused, and then crowded forward to see the sights.

"Why, it's a trading post. Our friendly escorts have become our honor guard." Hyacinth's spirits bloomed. "An island of civilization right here in the wilds," he said.

"Darlink, it's pollution. It's white men's darkness in the middle of innocence."

"Whatever it is, we'll be meeting people we can sell to. You get ready to perform."

A slim middle-aged man with assessing eyes waited for them at the gate along with a few underlings. Peachtree stared down from his wagon seat, feeling himself being weighed, top to bottom.

"It says you're Peachtree," the man said. "I'm Bent."

"Bent? The Bent on the Arkansas?"

"William Bent, yes. My post here, too. Built years ago by my partner, St. Vrain."

"Why, sir, I never imagined I'd meet you here. I'm Hyacinth Z. Peachtree, a purveyor of fine tonics and elixirs. We're en route to the gold fields, southern way of course. Meet my performers—we do a little minstrel act—Concorde Danton, Hercules—ah, he owns but one name. Pontius P. Parsons, and our lovely warbler, direct from Grand Rapids, Carlotta Krafft-Ebing."

Bent didn't smile and didn't seem very glad to see them. He glanced at the entourage briefly, and nodded. "You're traveling alone."

"To Santa Fe. We're in a party guided by one Barnaby Skye."

Bent came alive. "Skye? Old Skye? Where is he?"

"Ah, back a way, sir. Struggling along with one of our party who's a bit slower—on foot, you see. Bunions."

"Skye! How is the old boy?"

"In fine fettle, Mister Bent."

"He'll be along—when?"

"Why, we don't know. We got a bit ahead. But right smartly."

Bent smiled at last. "We go back a way. Never a better man. We've some catching up to do. Does he have Victoria with him?"

"Victoria and Mary, his young Shoshone."

Bent smiled. "I heard about Mary. You drive right on in and we'll wait. If you want to do some trading the store's open for business."

"Why, sir, we'll stock up on flour, coffee, sugar, and a few items. I trust we can barter?"

"Barter what?"

"The finest elixirs known to mankind. The world-famous ancient elixir Nepenthe, the secret recovered from an ancient papyrus found in a Babylonian cave and sold to me at great price, or the Potawatomi Indian Cure—"

"Sorry. I only barter for something of value."

"But Mister Bent, there's nothing finer in the universe than the Peachtree line of alternatives for various ills."

Bent shook his head.

Peachtree didn't surrender. "Well, sir, we thought we'd put on a little show for the savages. What fine red specimens are these?"

"Cheyenne. My wife's people."

"I see. Well, Mister Bent, tell them that we'll entertain

them directly. It won't cost them a dime. Absolutely free. We'll rest our weary bones a bit and then make music. Miss Krafft-Ebing will sing arias and airs. She is revered by every critic on the Continent, and especially loves noble savages. Do you suppose you could translate?"

Bent stared. "Why not?" he said.

Chapter 20

All was ready. Concorde strutted his gaudiest red plumage. Carlotta had donned her Potawatomi Princess outfit. Hercules sported his silk top hat and tuxedo. And Peachtree had switched to a fresh gray swallowtail coat and had buttoned a stiff new collar into place, and added fresh cuffs.

Peachtree watched Pontius limp into the savage throng, leaning heavily on his cane and toting a mangy coyote pelt he used for a pillow. Old Parsons always knew exactly what to do.

In the middle of the chill afternoon, Concorde summoned the world with a snappy roll of his snare drum, and the medicine show ensemble began a medley of Stephen Foster tunes. Concorde tooted his cornet and banged the bass drum with his foot; Hercules mauled his accordion and the Potawatomi Princess warbled. This offended a flock of grackles, which retreated to nether limbs and discussed the insult, but it attracted a fine gaggle of noble savages.

Peachtree watched amiably as the Pied Piper music emptied the fort of its Mexican laborers and a dozen squinty white men, including Bent, who stood with his arms crossed and said nothing. Peachtree hoped Bent would translate, but if not, he and Pontius had worked out a little drama for the dumb and mute savages. It wouldn't matter a bit that Parsons had ridden in with the show.

His musicians switched to venerable airs and medleys, and then opera arias which the princess belted out lustily, mesmerizing brown Cheyenne children who put their fingers in their ears. The women clapped their hands to their mouths and gaped. Even the red warriors, in Peachtree's estimation, seemed entranced, but perhaps that was because the princess was making her doeskin fringes swirl, and her ample bosom bobble.

This blissful, sunny afternoon had brought them perhaps two hundred redskins and greasers. There weren't more than a few dimes and a few grubby shinplasters in the whole lot. Even so, this afternoon would enrich the Peachtree coffers. Thank heaven his burst of industry last night had yielded him some product.

They concluded with "The Star Spangled Banner," which the princess belted out in teutonic swells while Peachtree saluted and stood at attention. Then at last they set down their hardware and waited. Hyacinth Peachtree knew this afternoon's pitch would require special skills.

He adjusted his silk topper and smoothed his swallowtails, and began.

"Welcome, welcome my dear friends to the Peachtree Healing and Health Brotherhood. I see so many handsome faces out there."

He peered over at William Bent to see whether the factor would translate. But Bent stood silently. Very well then.

"My friends, I have here elixirs and tonics, anodynes and antispasmodics for your comfort. I have here the most advanced products known to science, the fruits of years of toil at the great universities of Europe, where I diligently studied the pharmaceutical arts, rediscovering lost secrets, preparing myself to bring to this sorry and afflicted world the benefactions of a sincere and altruistic desire to heal."

No one among the redskins understood a word. The Cheyenne chief stood as quietly as the variety in front of cigar stores, but he wasn't as handsome.

"Me gottum heap big medicine. Me makum you feel mighty good. Ugh," he bawled, but no one stirred. A crow responded with an insulting caw. He decided that savages didn't know how to talk.

"Very well then, I'm going to tell you about the finest medicine the world has ever known. Yes, Nepenthe is its name. Why, only last night I bottled a fresh batch, using a secret formula smuggled to me by a sister in a convent in Rome who yearned to free the world from pain, a formula once used by the recently canonized St. Hilarious the Lesser of Padua. Now, dear friends, I have never seen such an effective and benevolent compound. Is there no one who'll volunteer to sip a small sample? Do I see anyone in this mighty assemblage willing to drive pain straight out of his body with one thrust of God's liquid brown sword?"

That was the cue, and Parsons hadn't missed it. Slowly the old gobbler teetered forward, gray as a ghost, looking ready to topple into the earth, his bones creaking, his legs wobbling, his breathing labored, his hands a-tremble as they clutched a walking stick. Gad, the man was a thespian to top all thespians!

The Cheyennes and Mexicans watched his progress solemnly. Even the impish Cheyenne boys stopped their mockery long enough to let old Parsons shuffle through their midst. The squaws studied the feeble man's progress with horror and pity, whispering to one another with sadness. But Parsons paid them no heed, and proceeded toward the medicine wagon like Moses parting the Red Sea.

At last he stood before Peachtree. "Reckon I'll try a swig. Nothing else works. Stove up so bad I can't gad about."

"Why, sir, I believe Nepenthe will help you. Are you willing to try?"

"Nothing to lose, fellow. You sure it's the right thing?"

"Nothing better, my friend. Now, this product costs only one dollar the bottle, but I'm going to give you a free sip. You just let her percolate a minute, and then make up your mind. Be prepared for a miracle."

"Well, I dunno. Hurt so much and so long I've plumb gave up."

Peachtree uncorked a shiny green bottle of Nepenthe and eyed the crowd. They hung on to every word, even though scarcely a dozen understood English. The savages crowded closer and closer, eager to see this white man's miracle.

"All right then, sir. You just take a little swig. Not very much. Just a tongue-wetter. Nepenthe's so powerful and long-lasting that a tad'll do you."

He handed the bottle to Parsons, who wiped his mouth, and lifted the bottle with trembling hand, and swilled. In fact, he guzzled a lot more than Peachtree had bargained for, and it alarmed him. Parsons dribbled a bit, wiped his chin, and handed the Nepenthe back to Peachtree.

The crowd waited silently. Peachtree saw that even Bent had edged in for a closer look.

"Whew!" said Parsons. "Ahhhh."

The old actor sat down suddenly, and the crowd murmured. "Whew! Egad," he said, sitting comfortably on the ground. Cheyenne women clapped hands to mouths, afraid of what was to come.

Parsons began panting, wheezing, coughing, and sputtering, and then, with awesome dignity, he seemed to clamp his bewildered carcass in the grip of his will, and slowly stood up, staring benignly at the world.

"Sprightly stuff," he said. "Knocked the wear and tear right outa me." He eyed the Cheyenne one by one, smiling gently. He surveyed the silent Mexican workers who waited grimly. He spotted a few white traders. "That's some juice."

He let his walking stick drop. He stretched. The tremors ceased. "Aeeya!" he said.

He did a little jig. He pirouetted, hornpiped, and waltzed. He ran a tight circle, touched his toes, pushed through the crowds and broke into a trot, and then returned, panting hard but otherwise no worse for wear.

"I ain't got a dollar. You takin' pelts?"

"I'd consider it. What's that over your shoulder?"

"Dead coyote. You gimme the bottle and I'll give you one coyote."

"Done!" cried Peachtree. He snatched the mangy thing and tossed it to Hercules, who hid it in the wagon.

"Who next? Step right up."

A lovely squaw with flesh the color of honey tugged at his sleeve. "Ah, you want some?"

But she didn't. Instead, she led Peachtree out to the lodges, the whole mob following, and paused before an ancient Cheyenne woman, gray and seamed, lying in a reed backrest, too far gone to get up. The squaw pointed at Parsons's bottle, and then at the old crone.

Hyacinth Z. Peachtree suddenly realized he had arrived at the edge of a cliff. He stared at the gaunt woman, seeing that life barely fluttered in her chest. The old Cheyenne peered up at him solemnly, too weary to speak. Around him, Cheyenne crowded in, barely giving him room. The chief edged close and watched, his face blank.

Trapped. Peachtree sighed, wondering if he would be wearing his hair in the next hour. He signaled the lady of the lodge for a horn spoon and received it. He poured a few drops of the stuff, hardly enough to addle a bumblebee, into the horn and lowered it to the mouth of the ancient woman. She slowly licked it.

"Ladies and gents, we have to adjust the dosage," he explained to the blank-faced listeners.

He waited for what seemed an interminable time, until he was sure that the dose had had no effect. Then he tried a similar dose and waited. He had given, in all, not half a teaspoon of Nepenthe. The old one closed her eyes, alarming Peachtree, and for the next minutes time halted on the hushed flat. Then the old lady opened her eyes and smiled. A minute later she stood, and gravely shook hands with Peachtree, saying something or other.

"She says she hasn't stood on her two feet for a moon," Bent translated quietly. "She's thanking you for all the strange things happening in her body."

Cheyenne hissed their awe.

The ancient woman walked feebly to her family, smiling and clucking.

"Mister Bent, please tell them that my medicine is dangerous in large amounts. It could even kill them. If they'll promise to take only the smallest nips, I'll trade it for peltries."

"You'd better be careful, Peachtree," Bent said. But he explained the warning to the mesmerized Cheyenne.

A half hour later Peachtree had traded his last bottle of Nepenthe except for Pontius's supply, and all the Potawatomi Cure. An hour later the buffalo robes and peltries rested in Bent's warehouse, and Peachtree's supply wagon groaned under fat bags of flour, sacks of coffee beans and sugar, and sundry other items.

Three hours later the whole Cheyenne village staggered around berserk, having sucked up the Potawatomi Cure along with nips of Nepenthe. Warriors whooped and swung battle-axes. Some began a scalp dance. Prostrate bodies littered the ground, dead or alive Hyacinth couldn't say. The Potawatomi Princess had joined them, careening from one lodgefire to another, whooping at the new moon and bellowing arias.

Bent watched silently, and finally turned to Peachtree. "You'd better bring your wagons inside the fort and get your people in too," he said. "If you've killed any, you'll not get away alive. I can't help you with anything like that."

Chapter 21

At least there were no corpses lying around. Peachtree received that welcome news in a frosty dawn, within the walls of Fort St. Vrain. Bent's men had climbed to the parapets at first light and peered out upon the slumbering Cheyenne village, discovering none of the bodies that had sprawled on the clay during last night's debauch.

Bent, dressed in a buffalo coat against the cold, eyed Peachtree somberly. "That doesn't mean you're out of this scot-free," he said. "Wait here."

The factor opened one of the gates, which shuddered on its iron hinge, and vanished outside. His engagés stood at the gate ready for trouble. Peachtree's entourage waited in the yard, the wagons loaded and the mules harnessed. Daylight had arrived only a short while ago and Peachtree meant to consume all of it during this season of shortening days.

A while later Bent quietly returned, and men closed the gates behind him.

"No one died," he said. "You're lucky. Half a dozen were

in a stupor. Whatever swill you're peddling, it's dangerous. Not something to sell to Indians."

"Why, Mister Bent, they had a fine old riot. A swell party. A real fandango. They downed my entire stock of the Potawatomi Cure, and even the Nepenthe."

Bent smiled faintly. "Indians do. They don't stop. It makes them crazy."

"You're married to one," Peachtree said.

"Yellow Woman, and before that, Owl Woman. My boys, George and Charles, are half native. They'll soon be totally native if I don't ship them east. The red men have virtues I admire. But they want moderation in these things." He stared at the entourage. "It's safe to leave. No one'll scalp you."

"We'll be on our way, then."

"You'd best wait for Skye. Things won't be the same ahead. These are friendly people. The Comanches won't be."

"Skye, sir, dawdles along, won't challenge a high river, and is an annoyance. Good riddance."

Bent frowned. "You're innocents. Pilgrims. What you've passed through is nothing compared to what you'll face. I'm talking about Comanches and Jicarilla Apaches. Also about Utes. Comanches are the best torturers in the world. These people out here, Cheyenne, are no mean hands at it, either. Comanches'll keep you alive long after you wish you weren't. I can't stop you from forfeiting your life. I can tell you that's what'll happen unless you wait for Skye. How far behind did you say he is?"

"I didn't say. A day or two maybe. He was stumped by a pawky little trickle back a way."

"The difference between living and dying down around the Santa Fe Trail, Mister Peachtree, is a knowledge of the Indians. You'll want the Skyes with you from now on."

From her wagon seat, Carlotta objected. "Always we hear this. Always we are findink friendly savages. Whites are the true savages."

Bent's solemn gaze flicked up to her. "You'll want the

Skyes along to translate. Misunderstandings lead to trouble. Skye's younger wife is Shoshone. She'll understand the Comanche tongue. You'd do well to wait for Skye."

Peachtree grew impatient. "My dear Bent, I appreciate your caution, but we've traveled tens of thousands of miles, this fine troupe, and we've encountered troubles such as you can't imagine. We've dealt with mobs, fought off armed posses who supposed we had sticky fingers. People take notions about strangers. Concorde, there, isn't just a musician; he's a Hannibal. Now, the road's plain; we don't need a guide, and we'll be off."

‡ "I'm not stopping you."

Hyacinth smiled genially. "Why, sir, we've been honored by your hospitality. You've let traveling missioners, out to heal the world, into the bosom of your life. If I had any stock of elixirs left, I'd give you and your splendid traders here a bottle apiece with my compliments, knowing that each lick would comfort your bones. But sir, you have our everlasting gratitude. We'll all be able to say we've really met and enjoyed the distinguished trader of the southern Plains. Remember Peachtree. You may find a case of my elixir in your freight, some fine day."

Bent nodded and yawned. At his signal, the gates of Fort St. Vrain creaked open, Concorde and Hercules cracked whips over the mules, and the two wagons lumbered out.

Peachtree chose to hike again, a sack dangling from his shoulder. He had to replenish his simples. They rattled into the awakening Cheyenne village. Everywhere people waved and grinned. An ancient crone beamed toothlessly. It dawned on Peachtree he was some sort of magician to them; they were plainly enchanted with the entourage, the music, the elixirs.

Yesterday the Cheyenne had gulped down his bottles of doctored whiskey and then had settled into circles and solemnly passed the Nepenthe around, each taking one small nip until they had stupefied themselves. In small doses it was an anodyne and brought upon them a vast cheeriness. In larger doses it stupefied. Somehow they had all escaped the Reaper.

He spotted his bottles scattered everywhere. "Whoa up," he cried. "Let's get these."

"Dead soldiers," Pontius said. "Humdinger of a party. Never saw such a quaint circus, not even in Beloit."

In minutes they had recovered a dozen of the precious green bottles and stowed them in the wagon. From the gates of the fort, Bent's traders watched silently. A trail branched southward to the St. Vrain River, and Peachtree took it. They forded a mucky bottom that sucked the feet of the mules, broke through skim ice on the far bank, and angled across a flat until they reconnected with the lodgetrail well south of the post. They were on their way again.

"Ah'm thinkin' we should wait for dat ol' Mister Skye," Concorde said. "Can't say that we haven't been warned."

Maybe they should indeed wait for Skye. Peachtree had worried it for a considerable while. He had always made snap decisions and never regretted them. He had a good intuition and his quick decisions always worked out. But this time he worried.

"We might wait for Skye at Raton Pass," he said suddenly.

"We've lost him, darlink. He is days behind us. He is a jailer. I don't know how his wives stand him."

"I'm thinking about the Comanches," Peachtree said. "They're not ones to be trifled with."

"I will sing lullabies and they will smile."

"Bent doesn't think Comanches smile much, Carlotta."

"Ah got wild hair-raisin' Comanche stories," said Concorde. "They like to dig a hole and stuff you in it facing the sun. Then they sew yoah eyelids open. That's some little trick. They got anothah. They stakes you down ovah a big old hill with ten thousand fire ants so mean they eat boot leather for breakfast. Then they smear you with a bit of honey. Them fire ants, they don't respect yoah private property. They crawl right into the mouth, into the nose, right down yoah gullet to yoah lungs and have lunch down there until yoah deader than you evah been before. They crawl up yoah pants and enjoy a feast right where it hurts you. They're a bunch, them savage Comanche. They got more tricks than that, too. It's gonna make this heah jaunt entertaining."

Carlotta had nothing to say after that.

Concorde slackened the pace of the mules. He obviously didn't want to escape Skye altogether.

"You just keep up the pace, Concorde. We have to get over Raton Pass before filthy weather stops us," Peachtree said.

He turned to the important business of collecting simples, but soon found that the country was changing, and frost had demolished most of the leaves. But he found a fine patch of jimson weed, and lustily chopped vines out of the clay and stuffed them into his sack. Here and there he spotted some more of that purple-flowered little plant that had addled the mule. Bent had called it locoweed. He got a whole armload of buffalo burr that had eluded the frosts, and more golden-rod. He found no more henbane, and feared he'd have to alter the formula for Nepenthe when he brewed the next batch. He thought he might add more tobacco to make up for the losses.

They stopped to rest the mules in the broad trough of a creek hurrying out of the southwest. The wind had chapped them all, so Hercules built a fire in the lee of a rim of shale and made tea while they stood about trying to stay warm.

It proved to Peachtree that he had been right: the sooner they got south, the sooner they'd escape the deepening cold. Let Skye dawdle at his own pace. There was more to con- sider than the savages. Northern weather could trap them or even kill them just as surely as a heathen arrow. And always, just over the horizon, lay California with its mountains of gold.

They were resting, letting the mules graze on the well- cured bunchgrass, sipping scalding tea, and then they were surrounded.

Chapter 22

Mister Skye halted in a broad coulee to get out of the nippy wind. Elisha Carmody needed to rest. The lecturer had to get off his paws now and then, as any man would who was walking across a continent.

Skye didn't mind. The frequent breaks allowed the horses to recruit on good summer-cured grass. Jawbone and the mustang mares were in better flesh than usual after weeks of travel.

While Carmody unlaced his boots and rubbed his feet, Mary released the whimpering infant from his cradleboard, cleaned him, and repacked it with moss. Skye's son was usually a quiet soldier on the trail. Skye could hardly wait to enjoy a son old enough to be a companion.

"Your feet all right, mate?"

"Oh, they complain now and then. But they're callused up now. I had real trouble when I left St. Joseph—blisters, calluses, tough shoe leather that tortured me. I thought I wouldn't make it. But I didn't wish to buy a horse. I endured.

That's how to tackle life sometimes. Just endure it. I was walking in blood for a while."

"If you get into trouble we could shift our kit around some and mount you on a pony."

"No, thanks, I'll be all right. I'm sorry I'm delaying you. That does trouble me."

"We're not on a schedule."

"Mister Skye, I know you'd like to catch up with the rest, and I'm preventing it."

"I'm not so sure I would," Skye mused. "I think I've been sacked. If they want a guide, all they have to do is wait for me. They're a day ahead by Victoria's reckoning. She's spotted a smudge of smoke about a day's ride up the trail a couple of times. You can see it at dawn and dusk."

"It could be Indians."

"Oh, it could. There's a lot around here. She's cut fresh trails almost every day. Probably Utes coming out of the mountains for some fall buffalo hunting. One was a whole village, she figured."

"A whole village—we're close to a Ute village?"

"Yesterday. We crossed right over it. Lot of travois tracks, moccasin prints, horse prints."

"I must've walked over it. Why didn't I see it?"

"You're not trained to see it. We see it. She's a sight better'n me, too. It keeps our hair on."

"Keeps you from being scalped?"

"She sees things. We take to hiding, mostly. Best way to avoid trouble is to get out of sight. That's the first rule out here—just hide. But sometimes we can't. We leave tracks too."

"Someone could follow our trail?"

"It's as plain as iron rails, mate. They can tell how many horses. They'll know from the cut of moccasin prints that we've a Crow and a Shoshone with us. They'll read our boot prints and know there's a pair of white men. They'll know we have a mule. They'll know some of the horses wear white men's iron shoes. They'll also know a party with two wagons and mule teams passed by a day earlier. They can read that, too."

"Are we in danger?"

"Always. Especially with the Ute bands wandering out of the mountains. They make meat before the snows and get themselves some haired-up robes."

"But it's too early for the buffalo to hair up."

"Not too early for the Utes to come out here and devil the Plains tribes for horses, do some trading, or have some fun. It takes time to find a herd anyway. Sometimes weeks."

"Are they friendly?"

"Not often."

"We ought to catch up with the rest. There'd be more safety in it."

Skye sighed. "I wonder about that. I can't count on them. They're likely to start trouble—get us into a box we can't get out of. The truth of it is, I'm not unhappy they've scuttled me, if that's what happened."

"They paid you to guide them, Mister Skye."

"That's right, mate. And I'm going to Santa Fe. It's a bloody puzzle, isn't it?" He lifted his topper and screwed it down. "I've got the idea that they want to travel alone but want me just over the hill to bail 'em out. That way they can do whatever they take a notion to do, but still get themselves rescued."

"My children were like that, Mister Skye."

Carmody tugged his heavily darned stockings over his feet and laced up his boots. Skye clambered aboard Jawbone, who snatched one final mouthful of grass. Mary started the packmares and travois ponies.

That afternoon they crossed open plain with scarcely a hollow or a hill to hide them until they reached the St. Vrain River. Victoria waited on the far bank, her horse below the skyline, as always. She nodded to Skye, and he lifted his topper in response.

He turned to Carmody. "Used to be a big 'dobe post near here, couple miles up this creek. My friend Ceran St. Vrain started it in the thirties for Bent, St. Vrain Company—that's the big fur outfit on the Arkansas," Skye said. "Likely to be some unfriendly sorts hanging around the old place."

"Let's be on our way, then."

"Afraid not, Mister Carmody." He pointed at the disturbed earth. The tire tracks of two wagons turned west. There had been a lot of horse traffic, too. "They went over there. We'd better go after them."

"You think it's occupied?"

"Last I knew it was abandoned. But these are a lot of tracks."

Victoria rode down the far slope, urged her mare across the placid creek, and drew up before Skye. "That fort got more people around it than a dog has fleas," she said.

"Lodges?"

"Cheyenne dogs."

It didn't surprise Skye. "Bent's people came up to trade with Forty-Niners last year. If those lodges are Cheyenne, it's probably William Bent."

"I don't follow you, Mister Skye," said Carmody.

"William Bent's married to a Southern Cheyenne. His fort's how come the Cheyenne split into northern and southern. The southern trade with him and hang around down there, close to Comanche country. If there's Cheyenne lodges around this old place, Bent's probably fixing it for business."

"What if it's not what you think, Mister Skye?"

"I live on the proposition that nothing's what I think it is, sir."

Victoria stared grimly, barely containing her thoughts. The Cheyenne were ancient enemies of the Crows, and he knew she wanted nothing from them other than their scalps.

"You willin'?" he asked her.

"I go where you go." She spat.

Skye laughed. "Let's go find out. Peachtree's either separated from his topknot by now or he's hawking swampwater to everyone in sight—if he has any left."

"I don't know why the hell we gotta go in there, dammit. We could lose our hair."

"Mary?" he asked.

"We've done many things, Mister Skye," she said softly. "Your medicine is good."

Victoria glared at the younger wife as she might glare at a traitor. Wordlessly she steered her quiet little mare out of the river brush and up the gentle bluff, where she could keep a weather eye on the hostile world.

"Mister Carmody, there's probably traders at that post. We'll just mosey in. Might be a chance to do some trading if you need to. They'll have vittles if you need some. Last time I saw this outfit, the walls were cracked clear through, the big gates were lying on the grass, and no one lived there but packrats."

"Mister Skye, I trust your judgment."

With that, Skye steered his family up the creek on a heavily used trail that mired occasionally in mud puddles from the recent rains.

Jawbone smelled the throng ahead, walked on stilts, his ears laid back and his mood murderous. Skye ran a gnarled hand under the mane of the great horse, an ancient sign to cool down. The horse quieted under him.

They emerged onto a broad flat where the low bluffs widened, and beheld Fort St. Vrain, in good repair, with an American flag flying over it, brass cannon in the weathered adobe bastions, and several hundred tawny Cheyenne lodges leaking smoke into autumnal skies. Its gates were wide open.

But there was no sign of Peachtree's wagons.

Chapter 23

Skye stared over Jawbone's ears, astounded. Old Fort St. Vrain had been refurbished. The massive gates hung on their iron hinges. The crumbling adobe walls had been patched with fresh mud. A large village surrounded the place.

"Cheyenne, all right," Skye said.

"How do you know that, sir?" Carmody asked.

"It's a three-pole lodge. Basic structure's a tripod—three poles roped together. The rest of the poles are laid in. Gives the poles a spiral look from the smoke hole. Lots of tribes use a four-pole method. These could also be Sioux or Arapaho. But the smoke holes are Cheyenne."

"You amaze me, Mister Skye."

"Damned no-good dogs," Victoria said. "I'd like a few scalps."

Skye grinned, lifted his topper, and screwed it home again. "They're not friends of the Crows," he said to Carmody. "Well, let's get on and find out who's keeping house."

"Is it safe, sir? We'll go right through that village."

"Traders impose a peace around the fort, mate. Any fighting and they shut the trading window to all sides."

"I see. Well, let's brave it."

"Nothing to brave, Mister Carmody." He steered Jawbone through the village while solemn Cheyenne children ran along beside, the little boys shooting their toy arrows from toy bows, and the berry-eyed girls shyly studying the strangers. Angry squaws gathered the children and hustled them away.

They passed a surly warrior, bare-chested in spite of the cold. His hair had been roached. The huge man eyed them with calculating black eyes.

"Dog soldier. Probably headman. That's their elite warrior society. See that necklace?"

"It looks like your bearclaw necklace, Mister Skye."

"Human fingers. Dried up and strung on a cord. Big medicine. Every finger taken from an enemy he's butchered. Another way of counting coup. Dog soldiers are the toughest outfit on the Plains. Be glad we haven't run into them."

Carmody sighed. "There are times, sir, I wonder why I am making my way west or why my hair remains on my skull."

They pierced the gates and rode into the yard, where engagés working the robe press eyed them. Most were swart Mexicans, but Skye spotted a scattering of Anglos in loose cottons, and what probably were some Creoles, decked in bright woolens. A well stood in the middle, protection against a siege. The musky smell of buffalo hides filled the air, along with the acrid odors of horses, manure, and roasting meat.

"Well, Mister Skye, you haven't changed much," said a slim, graying man at one side.

Skye turned and beheld an old friend from the beaver days. "William! Haw! I should've guessed."

Bent eyed him intently, and then the horse. "I've heard about that horse for years. I heard he had horns, fangs, a few extra hooves, armor, and was twice as large as he is. Things grow in the telling." Bent smiled.

Skye ran a hand under Jawbone's mane. "I trained him up from the day he was born, William. He's like a brother. Don't come close. He's inclined to murder. Now, there's another you haven't met. This is my Mary of the Snakes. And you remember Victoria."

Bent smiled, delight in his eyes. "My pleasure, Mary Skye. You and that little tyke brighten this old post."

Mary smiled as she usually did. She scarcely knew what to think of white men's compliments.

"And this is Mister Carmody, a client of mine."

"You have others. The Peachtree outfit. They passed through."

"Ah, William, I was coming to that. We thought we'd catch them here."

"They left at dawn."

"Dawn? Why didn't Victoria see their tire tracks across the river?"

"They cut across the angle. You'd have picked them up a mile south. Well, don't just sit on that ugly brute, Skye. Come in. Meet Yellow Woman."

"Maybe we should catch up with Peachtree, William. He's half a day ahead."

"Mister Skye, I'm not going to let you out of here until we share some meat and some history."

That did it. Skye slid off Jawbone. "He doesn't tie, William. You'd better tell your Creoles and Mexicans not to get close." As if to emphasize Skye's point, Jawbone laid his ears back and snorted like a bull.

Bent stared at the blue roan with respect. "I'll do it," he said. He spoke quietly to a burly *jefe* of the Mexicans.

Moments later, Bent escorted them into the post's mess hall, where they settled on massive split cottonwood benches.

"What're you doing here, William?" Skye said. "My gawd, what a bloody good treat to see you."

"It's the gold rush, Mister Skye. We've got two thousand oxen fattening along the South Platte. We wagoned up to the

Oregon Trail last year thinking we could sell sundries. That didn't work. The Forty-Niners were well supplied. But they wanted fresh oxen. They offered most any price. There's not a blade of grass along that trail, ten miles either side. Their oxen were down to bones. So we went into business. Opened this up."

"Whose village is this?"

"Yellow Wolf's. He's family for me."

"So I reckon."

"They trade a little. Came up here with me for the fall weather. But we're mostly peddling oxen. I've got Lucas Murray up on the Oregon Road now, trading with the east-bound miners. Lots of them coming back now. Ever seen one of these?" He dug into his britches and extracted an octagonal gold slug with "50" stamped in it. "Fifty-dollar slugs, two and a half ounces. That's how they're bringing the gold east." He smiled. "We're diverting a few in my direction."

"You have the knack, mate."

Bent sighed. "It's not the same. Not since they killed Charles. Something changed. Whole West died."

Skye nodded somberly. Taos Indians and Mexican patriots had killed William's brother and partner, Governor Charles Bent, at his home in Taos in 1847. His wife, Ignacia, and the Bent children had barely escaped by clawing through an adobe wall. After that, Skye had heard, William changed. His spirit darkened. He blew up his old post and built a smaller one downstream. Skye could see a weariness in William's face.

"I understand, mate."

Bent seemed grateful not to have to talk about it. "We entertained your clients," he said briskly. "I've never met the likes of Peachtree," he said, caution in his tone. "A force of nature."

Skye scratched his head. "I'm not sure they're my clients, William. They paid me, all right. And I'm on my way to Santa Fe, which they hired me to do. But they took to thinking I'm too slow for 'em, and they took to disagreeing with my counsel. Almost got us into a jackpot with some Sioux, and tackled the Cache de Poudre when it was running over its banks. They didn't wait for us on the other side, either . . ."

"I don't think they want you along."

"Well, that's the puzzle. Maybe you can steer me out of this bloody mess. If I let them run ahead, they're likely to get themselves killed. If I do catch up with them, they're likely to get us all killed, my family, Mister Carmody here. I can't make any sense of it."

Bent stared at the wall. "I got the impression that they've been on the road a lot; they've gotten out of some tough corners back east. They're armed with shotguns and revolvers, and that's not going to keep them an arrow-length from trouble. Let 'em run, Mister Skye. That kind won't heed you, no matter what you do. Better to keep your hair on."

"You reckon I owe 'em to be right there?"

"They didn't wait for you. Isn't that answer enough?"

"It's a bloody puzzle," Skye said. "I don't feel right about it. This keeps clawing at me."

William told the Skyes about the medicine show, the sale of the potent elixirs, and the debauch. "I told him if he'd killed off those Cheyenne he'd never get out of here alive. But he didn't kill 'em. The bodies were all alive and laughing the next morning." Bent smiled wryly. "Fact is, Peachtree's sort of a god to that village. They're asking me when he's going to return with more of that juice."

"Where'd he get the stuff? Most of his equipment got tossed into the Cache de Poudre."

"He said he'd been collecting it. He's got a lot of jimson, and some locoweed, and God knows what else." Bent sighed. "He took those Cheyenne to the brink. I'd have paid hell if one had died. I was glad to get Peachtree out of here, if you want to know the truth of it." He eyed Carmody. "Sorry, sir. The Indian West's no place for people on a lark."

"I understand that, Mister Bent."

Skye relaxed. "Why, William, you've made up my mind for me. I've no further obligation to Peachtree. We'll stay the night. We're eager to meet Yellow Woman. My ladies might even cotton to a Cheyenne, long as she's tame."

"Speak for yourself, Skye, dammit," Victoria said. "The only thing Cheyenne dogs are good for is a scalplock shirt."

Bent chuckled. "We've got a night of catching up to do, Barnaby Skye. We'll have some buffalo hump on the table about sundown. And you'll join us too, Mister Carmody. I'm always interested in what people think."

"Haw! William," Skye bawled. "We'll see how the stick floats."

Bent nodded, obviously enjoying the reunion.

But Skye didn't feel right about staying. Peachtree was out there, probably getting himself into more trouble than he could imagine.

Chapter 24

Terror clamped the throat of the Potawatomi Princess. The savages poured out of nowhere and surrounded the two wagons. One moment the Peachtree troupe had been rolling through an empty plain; the next moment wild Indians with drawn bows circled them. At first she thought there were ten or fifteen; then they seemed like twenty; then fifty; and finally she realized she was seeing over a hundred of them.

They had smeared paint over themselves. One giant had painted half his face black and half red. Some had daubed white or blue or vermilion on their arms and chests in mad patterns, chevrons, circles, jagged streaks. Most wore only leggins and breechclouts, even in the sharp chill.

They aimed their arrows at everyone in the troupe. She could almost feel the black metal arrow points piercing her with one hot, lethal burst of pain. Beside her, Hercules started to reach for the scattergun on the floorboard but a savage snarled something and Hercules thought better of it. Several savages grabbed the bridles of the mule teams.

"Oh! Ah! Now, my fine feathered friends," said Peachtree in an oily tone of voice, "what's the meaning of this? We are happy vagabonds, merely sojourning in your fine country, meaning no harm."

No savage indicated he understood. Carlotta peered at one who seemed to be the headman, a sullen, bowlegged giant whose blue-black hair fell in twin braids. He wore a red headband with two eagle feathers. Horrible scars chasmed his ribs and both arms. His face, daubed with vermilion, was as expressionless as a block of wood and his black eyes had no more animation than those of a rattlesnake.

"Maybe you are not a noble savage," she said. "If you are not noble, darlink, you don't deserve my company."

He ignored her. With an authoritative wave of his hand, he directed several of them to pry open the cabinet doors of the medicine show wagon. Professor Peachtree clucked unhappily. They rattled the olive lacquered doors, tried the brass locks, and discovered the doors wouldn't yield. A giant savage lifted a hatchet and cracked it into a brass lock. It gave. The doors to Peachtree's little laboratory sprang open.

"Stop that, you varmint," Peachtree said. "My good man, I'll compound whatever you wish. I scarcely have a thing to give you now, but I want you to know that the Peachtree Elixirs are all guaranteed to yield peace of mind, yes, peace of mind, and sublime happiness. My friends, if you'll just let me do a little compounding, in one hour I'll have a little treat for you—"

Hyacinth Z. Peachtree shut up when the headman loosed an arrow that thudded into the wagon just one inch from Peachtree's armpit. Peachtree jumped. The arrow shivered. Peachtree gaped at the headman, who was quietly nocking another.

Warriors pawed around in the cabinet, obviously disappointed. They lifted a few green bottles and pitched them to the grass. Other warriors began unhitching the mule teams.

"But you can't—" cried Peachtree.

For an answer the headman motioned them down to the ground.

"But I'm a true and sincere friend of the entire red race," Peachtree croaked. "My brothers . . ."

He and Concorde and Pontius P. Parsons clambered down from the seat and stood shivering and subdued in the grass. The headman waved at the other wagon. Hercules slowly lowered himself to earth while Carlotta shivered and stared on the seat. The headman motioned her down but she couldn't bring herself to do it. She felt safer up there; on the ground her life would run red into the dun clay.

"Darlink, you have it all wrong. We must talk. I will draw little pictures. I will show you—"

His thick arm leaped upward; his hand clamped her wrist so hard that it hurt, and with one tug he yanked her clear off the seat. She smacked the ground, bruising her shoulder, knocking her head, and twisting her wrist. She screamed. "I will report you," she snapped. "I will see that you never work again. Not even as a ticket-seller. I will never set foot on this place again, that's what I think of you."

He grabbed her hair and lifted her to her feet. This time a faint, mean amusement filled his face.

She shrank under the gaze and wished he would let go of her hair. She was getting irritated. She slugged him in the gut and boxed his ear. "You are an imbecile. No one treats Krafft-Ebing like that!" she screamed.

Her screech halted every warrior.

Carlotta Krafft-Ebing, the terror of every opera company in Europe and the United States, was having a tantrum. She was being treated worse than any impresario or director or orchestra conductor or critic had ever treated her. She felt volcanic lava boil in her bosom, rise red-hot up her esophagus, and erupt from her well-trained throat.

"You will stop!"

He stared at her, a certain respect in his face. She stomped on his moccasin. He winced.

"You will let go of my hair. You will not touch me with your fingers or I will claw your eyes out. You are a swine." She snarled and writhed, while he held her by her hair. She booted him, banged his shins, and finally bit his arm, drawing blood. He clobbered her and she tumbled to the ground.

She leapt up again, raking him with her manicured fingernails. She felt them slice his flesh. He danced backward, but she threw herself at him, her teeth, fingernails, and feet all weapons. But he held her off and finally knocked her with a war club. She felt the blow glance off her head, slumped dazed, and then got madder still.

"I have sung in more opera houses than you can count, you beast!" she shrieked. "I will have you strung by your toes. I will cut your heart out and eat it. I will make you a soprano."

He held her at arm's length, amazed. Blood oozed from a dozen lacerations of his brown torso.

"You are goink to suffer," she added. She spat at him. Her spit hit his forehead and dribbled down his face. His eyes dilated and he tossed her to the ground again like a sack of grain and kicked her.

She rolled up, but he shoved her down. She grabbed his legs, almost toppling him, and pounded on his moccasin. She bit his leg. Then she slowly got to her knees and onto her feet. And much to her amazement, he let her.

"Not for nothink am I a leadink lady in the opera," she said. "You are no different than seventeen directors I have dealt with. Oink, oink! Do you know what I do with idiot directors? I break their baton." With that she snatched the headman's coup feathers from his head, crushed them, and threw them to the ground.

They lay in the grass, crumpled, innocuous, the remains of a bald eagle. He stared, a terrible heat building in his face. She laughed, softly at first, then wildly, better than she'd ever laughed through a mad scene, of which she had mastered several. Up and down octaves she laughed, staccato, then marchtime, and then a waltz. She slapped him.

Not even that despicable Renata D'Amore had ever done it better, except maybe once in Milan, and that was because she slept with the critics. But anyway, D'Amore didn't have a voice. Only Carlotta Krafft-Ebing had a voice big enough to laugh like that, and the critics said so, too. Even Leopold Luftwig in Salzburg admitted it, swine that he was.

She grew aware that she was the cynosure of all their gazes. Time had stopped. The lava had slid back down her throat. She smiled sweetly at them. "You make a big mistake, darlink," she announced to the headman. "You shouldn't fight me. I'm your friend. Besides, you don't know anythink about making war." She patted the headman on the arm and poked the massacred coup feathers back into his hairknot.

A hundred-odd savages stared at her. Hyacinth Z. Peachtree blinked and adjusted his clawhammer tails.

She swept grass and dirt off her skirts and stood, tapping her dainty foot, knowing she had won. "Now, darlink, you will be noble savage and I will be your friend."

Blood still oozed from his lacerations.

She turned to Concorde, who gaped like an idiot. "We will play for our friends," she announced. "We will make music. We will fill them with love and happiness."

"Heah? Now?"

"Concorde, you behave."

Numbly, Concorde extracted his cornet, snare drum, and bass drum from the wagon while Hercules slid the accordion straps over his shoulders. The accordion sighed like a dying animal, startling a dozen warriors.

She glared at Peachtree. "You get us into trouble and I get us out," she snapped.

Hyacinth Z. Peachtree's facial muscles twitched.

A vast quiet had settled over the creek bottom. Not a bird flew. The wind barely soughed in the leafless limbs of the cottonwoods.

Concorde licked his lips and tooted tentatively, while

Carlotta warbled warm-up scales. Peachtree fiddled with the broken lock on his cabinet.

Around them, scores of painted warriors collected, their bowstrings slack. She wondered who they were. It didn't matter. They were no better than directors and critics.

"You may begin, my dear Concorde," she said.

Yellow-eyed, Concorde rattled a fine roll of his snare drum, which galvanized the attention of the mute tribesmen. Then he tucked his drumsticks into his belt and began Stephen Foster's "Camptown Races" on his cornet, while Hercules squeezed his accordion like a newfound lover and Carlotta warbled sweetly. A few warriors clapped hands to mouths.

It was better than a matinee.

An hour later, having exhausted their airs before the mesmerized warriors, they quit.

She clasped the headman's hand and pumped it.

"Now, darlink, you go kill your enemies," she said. "Eat their hearts." She tried to kiss his vermilioned cheek, but he recoiled as if struck by a rattler.

"Uh, Carlotta, I think Skye was saying there's a certain taboo about being touched by a woman while they're on the warpath," Peachtree said.

"They don't know what warpath is, darlink," she replied cheerfully. "But Carlotta Krafft-Ebing will teach them. I will touch anyone I feel like touching." She wandered among them, touching each one just for the joy of it. They let her.

Warily, Concorde stored the instruments while Peachtree tied the broken cabinet doors shut. The warriors watched mutely, and then began doing something strange: they started a fire, and next to it they began to build a framework of saplings.

"I think it's going to be a sweatlodge," Hyacinth said. "They probably think you've put the hex on 'em, and they've got to sweat you out."

"They'll never sweat me out, darlink," she said.

Chapter 25

Mister Skye had never felt so itchy. It was as if a thousand graybacks were crawling through his hair and clothing. But he knew he had no cooties on him and he knew these were lice of the soul. No, this itchiness came from within and was making him frantic.

He, Elisha Carmody, and William Bent sat around the Bents' table in the glow of a wavering lamp. The ladies had retired. Yellow Woman, decked in a woolen dress, had gravely served choice buffalo hump and greens to them all, saying little to these hereditary enemies of her people. Mary and Victoria had said just as little. But as the evening progressed, their reserve vanished. They could all communicate in English, and soon tried it out on each other. In time, the three women retired to an adobe guest room, there to care for Skye's babbling boy and gossip.

Skye eyed William's crockery jug of whiskey but didn't touch it although he felt like pouring a gill of it down his gullet. Carmody intimidated him with all his talk of personal sovereignty. So Skye suffered, itched, squirmed, fought his raging need.

He did not join the palaver. Bent and Carmody had struck common ground so Skye merely listened. He could not remember a time when he had felt so pent up and crazy inside.

"Mister Carmody, you didn't tell me why you're going to lecture in California," Bent said.

"Why, sir, a prophet is without honor in his own country. I lectured from Lake Erie to Kentucky and got nowhere. Some nights I talked only to an empty hall. I failed to excite the press. They're settled people there, smug in their comfort. I simply need to find an unsettled place where men are willing to listen, to try out new ideas the way they try out hats."

"But why the Forty-Niners?"

"Without personal dominion, they'll struggle for naught. They'll toil until they have some dust, and then squander it all in brawls, boozing, or—other vices. Why, sir, I'm taking a message of hope to those who are most at risk."

Bent eyed him skeptically. "You're going to tell them to behave themselves, is that it?"

"Oh, much more. Telling them to behave themselves won't accomplish a thing. They've got to see what they can do with their mortal clay. Self-restraint is the tip of the iceberg. Self-government is the only way to be free, sir. Let a man control his passions, and he'll be free. Temper's one of the worst. Let a man lose his temper and he's already lost his life."

Skye had heard that too many times from Carmody. "Mister Carmody, are you sovereign? You've conquered yourself?" he asked harshly.

The reformer eyed him patiently. "I wrestle with pain. I wish I could be stalwart when my body hurts. Other than that, I think I'm holding my weaknesses at bay."

Skye sat suffering. "I have more'n I can count," he said. "I'm glad to meet a man who's conquered 'em. I never met such a critter before."

Carmody smiled. "Your response isn't new to me. When I

talk about self-dominion, people look at me to see whether I measure up. No, of course I don't. It's only an ideal. Practically, we all fall short—including myself."

Skye had to admire an amiable reply like that.

William Bent stared into the gloom. "It doesn't matter how upright a man," he said. "Evil strikes blindly."

Skye knew he was thinking of Charles's murder.

"Yes," Carmody agreed, quietly. "But it doesn't alter the reality. The person in command of his own appetites has the better chance."

Skye decided he'd had enough of talk. He rose, feeling scratchier than ever. "I'll see you in the morning, William. The fat buffalo times are gone, aren't they."

"I'm afraid so, Mister Skye."

Barnaby Skye slipped into the blackness of the yard and stared at the stars. Somewhere out there, Peachtree's bloody troupe was riding into the jaws of death. Somewhere out there, some pilgrims made cocky by their experience with white men were blundering into a world they knew nothing about.

Jawbone butted him. He ran a hand along the old warrior.

Barnaby Skye knew suddenly why he squirmed. It was simple. They had paid him to watch over them. He was shirking his duty. It didn't matter that they had fled him. Skye knew only that he had a task to do. And that he had to catch up.

The insight brought him swift peace, and all the restlessness vanished from his soul. There had been mountain men like the Peachtree troupe: boisterous youths who had defied the wisdom of the old coons, who had rejected everything that Jim Bridger or Kit Carson or William Sublette had suggested. They had all gone beaver.

He contemplated the slumbering post, knowing he was about to irritate half its denizens along with Mary and Victoria. But a man had to do what he had to do.

He returned to the Bents' door and let himself in. The two

of them were still trading ideas. William Bent was cherishing the kind of serious talk he didn't get much of out in this land.

"Mister Carmody, I'm sorry to interrupt. I'm leaving in a few minutes if William'll let us out. I can't bear the thought of Peachtree's people alone while I'm being paid to protect them. I'm going to waken my ladies, load up, and start out right now."

"Why, Mister Skye, that's rather precipitous—"

"You can join me or not, Mister Carmody. Your life'll be at risk. They won't heed my cautions. They could get us killed. I'm going because I have to. If you prefer, I'll refund your fifty dollars and see to it that William's people get you somewhere safe. But I'm going, now, before it's too late—if it's not already too late."

William said, "Sleep on it, you old coon. You'll think differently in the morning."

But Skye shook his head. He had never been more certain.

He whirled into the frosty night, dreading to impart his news to his family, who were warm and asleep in their buffalo robes. But he couldn't help himself.

He entered into blackness and sat down beside them, trying to gather his wits.

"You been sipping stuff?" Victoria whispered.

"Not a bit. It's something else."

"I knew it, dammit. All right. You been crazy for days." She rose and threw open a shutter, letting faint light bathe the room. "We'll go after the sonsofbitches." She suddenly hugged him. "You're one hell of a man, Mister Skye."

Mary sighed, unhappily. Skye sensed that this was something his wives had talked about this very night. How well they knew him. He watched Mary pluck his unhappy son from his warm nest, wrap him in a small blanket that could be folded over his head, and bind him into the cradleboard, all in a darkness almost impenetrable. Only his soul seemed filled with light.

A while later, Skye's family sat their ponies in the starlit, quiet yard. The horses were loaded. Carmody, good soldier that he was, stood beside them, holding the lead line of his mule. Skye admired the man more than ever. The Skyes' fate would be his fate. Skye's terrible need to protect fools had become Carmody's need also.

"You're crazy, Barnaby," William Bent said softly. "But there's no man on earth I'd rather have beside me. *Vaya con Dios.*" He turned to Carmody. "And to you sir, *vaya con Dios.* You have a vision. I hope it inflames the world and keeps men free."

"Why, William, I'll tell the world you're the living example of what I believe makes a true man."

"I am only a man alone, like all men," William said.

Skye felt a lump collect in his throat. He had known this great trader and Santa Fe supplier for almost as long as he had wandered the lonely reaches of the New World. He might never see him again. He fought back his own tears, and clasped the hand of his host. Then he climbed onto Jawbone, who yawned listlessly, while Bent opened the creaking gates and let them ride into midnight.

Then the towering doors squeaked and chattered shut behind them, the dropping bolt echoed in the icy night, and they rode alone through the silent lodges of Yellow Wolf's village, awakening a few dogs, and out into the big and lonely wild.

Chapter 26

After their fearsome encounter with the savages, the Peachtree troupe split into feuding factions. One party, consisting of Concorde, Hercules, and Pontius Pilate Parsons, wanted to halt and wait for Skye. The other party, consisting of Peachtree and Carlotta, insisted on heading south just as fast as they could go.

From that time onward, Peachtree and the Potawatomi Princess shared a wagon seat while the rest perched on the supply wagon. Peachtree maintained a pellmell pace, careening along the lodgetrail, making time by leaps, abandoning the usual rest breaks for the teams, pushing ahead to escape the bite of winter and the bite of savages.

The mules thinned; their ribs showed. They grew reluctant to pull the heavy wagons and required the whip, but Peachtree didn't relent, except that he made Carlotta walk whenever they tackled a steep grade. As far as he was concerned, the Skyes and Carmody were well forgotten. They were probably leagues behind, slowed by Carmody's foot passage and Skye's plodding caution.

They forded what probably was the South Platte, finding a dangerous sucking bottom and little water. After that the trail ran along a south-flowing stream that paralleled the Front Range and supplied water, grass, and level travel mile after mile. So excellent was their progress along the river that Peachtree paused to let the mules snatch the dried grass now and then.

The country grew more arid, and the lush foliage gave way to juniper and aromatic shrubs of a kind Peachtree had never seen. He took a few samples for medicinal purposes, but in the main he preferred to make time. The October weather stayed mild, but the dry winds sandpapered their faces.

Occasionally, during brief breaks, they climbed to high points and reconnoitered, but saw no sign of any mortal. One thing Peachtree had learned: he intended never again to be caught flatfooted by savages. He instructed his colleagues to keep their double-barreled fowling pieces in hand and make sure the caps were on the nipples. While he drove, Carlotta carried the piece across her lap. She chided him for it but kept it handy anyway.

They hardly needed to bother. They saw neither savage nor sign of passage as they hastened toward Santa Fe.

"I want a savage," she said to him one sunny afternoon.

"Uh, how do you mean that, my dear?"

"How do you think I am meanink it, idiot?"

"We all like exotic friends."

"Friends! I want a savage lover. I want a wild man, a beast. I am so sick of pale, poetical lovers, like oatmeal."

"Uh, that's what I thought you meant," Peachtree said. "You might find that savages aren't very good lovers."

"I want a mad, berserk lover. I want a wild man."

"This wilderness is affecting your appetites. What if your wild man has graybacks?"

"What is this, graybacks?"

"Lice."

"There you go again. Always, prejudices against the savages. Show me a savage with bedbugs. Everywhere in hotels are bedbugs. So why should you feel so superior? I try French, German, Italian, American lovers sometimes. They are like orchids, wilting all the time. Give me a mad savage, that's what I am thinkink."

"I'll be your savage lover, my dear."

"Hah! You? How many times you try, eh? You think someday I will have you. You think someday you get to enjoy Carlotta Krafft-Ebing, who sings in every opera house in Europe, the intimate friend of kings and princes and cardinals. You are an idiot, H.Z. I will not unbutton one little button for you."

Peachtree sighed. He had heard this a dozen times but it didn't keep him from trying now and then. She always managed to insult him in the process, but he didn't mind. Most every performance of his medicine troupe had won him a few insults, along with jeers and maybe a rotten egg or two.

"I have twenty-seven lovers so far, skinny idiots who wave skinny batons or sing bad music; once a madman in the second row who sends me ten thousand red roses. Ah, that was a mistake, that madman. He didn't know how to please a lady. He should send me gold, not roses. Old and unsatisfyink, he was. I am the toast of Europe, darlink, and don't ever forget it. You! You want to take me to bed, along with a hundred dukes and earls and a thousand millionaires. But I will have none of you. Now I want a real savage, ten times more man than you—willful, frightening, and a lunatiç. If I take a lover from this troupe, it will be Pontius P. Parsons immediately after you have given him his nightly dose of Nepenthe. I think maybe he would entertain me the way I like to be entertained. I am a woman with appetites."

Peachtree thought the conversation was progressing in odd and scintillating directions, and it had novelty to recommend it. Being on the road with someone always resulted in boredom.

They arrived at the confluence of the river they followed with another much larger one that flowed eastward and carried cold water out of the western mountains. And much to Peachtree's astonishment, they found themselves approaching a settlement.

Ahead were adobe hovels thrown up in rude disarray, surrounded by milk cows, burros, mustangs, dogs, and small vegetable plots alive with chickens. Even more astonishing, his wagons were attracting wiry greasers and a few bearded trappers in dirt-blackened buckskins, who squinted suspiciously at the Peachtree Medicine Show as it rolled into town. The whole lot of them looked to be as murderous as a jail population.

He reined the mules to a halt and the wagon stopped in its own dust.

"Where are we?" he asked from his seat above them.

"The seventh level of Hell," a flint-faced son of nature replied.

"What river is this?"

"If you don't know, you don't belong hyar, pork-eater." He spat something brown and slimy at the tawny clay.

"My friend, we don't belong here, that's for sure. We're passing through, from the Oregon Trail to the Santa Fe Trail. I'm Professor H.Z. Peachtree, and I sell elixirs, tonics, and anodynes for the pains of body and soul. Who might you be?"

"Nobody you ever met before, Peachtree."

Peachtree bridled. "Well, sir, we've a river to cross. Is there a good bottom for a wagon?"

"Wouldn't know; never tried. It wets the belly of my hoss this time o' year. This child can get acrost. Now them Mex, they cross their *carretas*, them big old wooden-wheeled carts, right yonder above the rill. That's a rock ledge under the water."

Peachtree studied the place where the ruts vanished into blue water and erupted from the far bank. He could see no obstacle in the ford.

"That's a fine piece of advice, sir," Peachtree said. "We'll follow it. Now I don't suppose any of you are ailing. I just happen to have a few of my bottled Nepenthe, the famous Peachtree herbal remedy for pain and sorrow; and I've some Potawatomi Indian Cure also, fine tonic that'll cure whatever ails you."

The gritty man laughed crazily, baring gaps in his teeth. "Nothing cures my gizzard but a gill of *aguardiente*."

"What's that, may I ask?"

"Taos Lightning. Whiskey so raw she slits your throat and hangs your tongue out to dry."

By now the crowd of sullen ruffians had expanded to fifty or so, and Peachtree made a decision. "Why, sir, before we tackle that nameless river there, we'll provide you with a little levity, absolutely free of charge. And then I'll introduce you to my patented products, the fruits of many years of university study in the capitals of Europe."

Another ruffian in a sun-faded shirt that once had been green laughed mercilessly. "That's the Arkansas River, pilgrim. She flows clear to the Mississippi. This hyar place is Pueblo, as she's called by greasers."

"The Arkansas. Really? Why, my stars and garters, we've come a mighty piece," Peachtree said. "You know, gents, I'm the greenest pilgrim all right. A scholar, actually. We're just passing through, hoping to keep our topknots. I don't suppose you've had any trouble with the savages lately?"

The rubes laughed raucously. "Not a bit. We kill the buggers when they come skulkin' around. Had us a few Lipan for breakfast other day, but mostly it's the Comanch. We feed 'em to the hogs."

"You are criminals," said Carlotta. "You should be taken to the justice of the peace."

"Carlotta, you just go fix yourself up, and we'll do a diddly little musicale for these friendly gents and ladies."

"Where are the gentlemen and ladies, eh? I don't see any in this—this yellow place."

"She's got a right smart tongue to her, Peachtree."

"Why, sir, she's the finest canary west of the Atlantic."

"You monster; I am best both sides of Atlantic. Maybe I won't sing now. I quit."

"Carlotta, you go change. I see Concorde's getting ready."

She huffed off the seat and scurried to the supply wagon. "I don't suppose you folks do any trading," he said.

"We don't have a damn thing to trade, Peachtree, except a few squaws and a stray cayuse or two. Mebbe some acorn squash."

"How do you live?"

"We don't. We hoe them squash gardens and shoot buffler now and then, rob tourists like you and float their carcasses down the old river. We butcher redskins for sport on fiesta days."

Peachtree paused, absorbing that. "You must have robes and hides then. I trade for peltries."

"You jist give us that free show, Peachtree, and be gitting off. You hang around here overnight and we'll be missing dogs, children, and mules by the mawning. You're a caution. Maybe you'll be missing whatever you got in them wagons, along with your heartbeat."

Peachtree admired the man's bluster. He thought of hiring the fellow for the show but decided against it. It pleased him to observe old Pontius creaking and groaning out into the middle of the mob, where he posted himself among the greasers.

Peachtree had put up a few more bottles of Nepenthe. It wasn't quite the same juice, since he found no more henbane, but it knocked the old actor on his gizzard as usual, because it contained a tad more locoweed. That was the name Bent had given to the mysterious little plant that had addled his mule. Fine stuff, Nepenthe: jimson, a dash of locoweed for sport, tobacco, buffalo burr, dogwood, and whatever came to mind.

His troupe clattered up to the deck of the medicine wagon, set up their act while Carlotta somehow clawed at stratocumulus notes with her contralto tonsils. Peachtree had in mind to pacify these cutthroats with melody, but all they seemed interested in was the Elysian fields of Carlotta's bosom she had bared to them by wearing her Potawatomi Princess outfit.

Twenty minutes later, after scarifying chickens with Wagnerian arias and Stephen Foster, Hyacinth Z. Peachtree adjusted his clawhammer coat, straightened his bow tie, and prepared for his sermon.

"I reckon that was a right pretty show," said the gaptoothed old codger. "You give us some friendly doses of that parsnip juice now, and we'll let you git away alive."

Chapter 27

The whole settlement probably didn't have a cash dollar, but that had never stopped Hyacinth Z. Peachtree. He surveyed the scurvy lot cluttering the plaza and decided they needed his tonics and elixirs anyway. He flapped alkali out of his clawhammer tails, massaged an ear with his finger and thumb, which signaled Concorde and Hercules to be ready with the fowling pieces, and climbed to the deck of the wagon.

"My dear friends and neighbors in progressive Pueblo," he began in sonorous voice. A few buckskin-clad degenerates hoohawed at that. "I am H.Z. Peachtree, formulater of balms, elixirs, tonics, and secret Indian cures guaranteed to comfort your aching bodies and soothe your sorrowful minds. At this advanced stage of my life, I have seen the terrors of disease and injury that afflict most of mankind. Why, I've seen the halt, the blind, the deaf, the maimed, the grieving widow, the starving orphan, the colicky child, the bedridden victim of rickets or scurvy or diphtheria. Yes, and I've seen the cruel work of the ague, the bilious fever, the ruin wrought by consumption, and the tragic face of the leper and syphilitic. Oh, yes, dear neighbors, I've seen them. Oh, how can I forget?"

A platoon of sheep meandered through the plaza, blatting at the world. H.Z. Peachtree had never suffered competition well, and waited impatiently until the woolies vanished.

"It's been my lifetime ambition to bring healing to all the world's sufferers; you are all my brothers and sisters, my mothers and fathers, my blessed little children. Ah, I see you out there listening intently. Surely a healer comes infrequently to this exquisite Pueblo on the Arkansas. But here we are, pressing to the farthest reaches of the wilderness so that no suffering mortal will be neglected."

He eyed the Mexicans carefully, wondering if they fathomed English. From the blank looks on their faces he suspected they didn't. He was really selling to the dozen or so Yanks leering at him out there.

"Git on with it, Peachtree. You sound like you et too much beans," a ruffian bellowed.

"Why, sir, my sympathies to you. For I have a tonic for flatulence, and for several other ailments, called the Potawatomi Indian Cure. The secret of this amazing elixir came from the lovely lady who sang just minutes ago, a true Potawatomi Princess, of purple blood among her noble people. She is a sachem of her tribe, and conveyed the secret remedy to me some while ago because she pities suffering white men."

Carlotta smiled and bowed low, exposing the Grand Canyon of bosoms. Some *señoritas* giggled.

"Now, dearly beloved, I have also an anodyne and narcotic tonic called Nepenthe. It is the exact formula the ancients used to drive away pain and induce blessed peace and forgetfulness. I found it upon a dusty parchment stuffed into a clay jar near the Delphic Oracle in Greece and had it translated by a distinguished professor of Biblical Greek at the Brooklyn Theological Seminary, Adjunct Professor Win Bullwinkle."

He lifted a rectangular bottle of the murky juice high above him. "My friends, I wish I could just give this magnificent elixir away to you all. That's what my heart cries out to do. But even though the Peachtree entourage is a charitable endeavor, we must pay our expenses. And so I charge a nominal dollar a bottle for this, and for the famous Potawatomi cure. Just one dollar. Do I see any takers? Do I see any suffering people in dire need?"

That was the line that triggered Pontius.

"Aghh! Hold up there," Pontius cried, from among a thicket of Mexicans. "I might try 'er." Pontius Pilate Parsons limped his way forward, creaking with every step, leaning into his walking stick, trembling like an aspen leaf in a gale.

"Ain't he one of them suckers on that wagon?" asked a cretin in blackened buckskins.

"Pretty fair actor, looks like," said another.

P.P. Parsons stopped and eyed the culprit. "I happen to be P.P. Parsons, the thespian," he said with vast dignity. "I am more than a pretty fair actor. Ask any reviewer. My name was once written large upon the broadsheets." With that, he wobbled forward. "I'll try 'er," he said. "Only got two bits though."

"I'm sorry, sir, a dollar is our price—the necessary recompense for our industry and learned skills."

"I got this here pelt. You trade?" Parsons cast the mangy coyote skin at Peachtree's feet. That coyote skin had caught more sheep than a pack of wolves.

Peachtree picked it up, examined it, and nodded. "I'll give you one bottle of Nepenthe for it, sir," he said, handing Pontius the bottle. "Take it light. One little sip'll do for you. Two sips'll last a week. Take a wee little swig, sir, and let us all know how it feels."

The old boy whooped, uncorked the bottle with trembling hands, and guzzled. Then he rocked, sighed, sat down suddenly, and began breathing rapidly. "Pretty feisty stuff," he said. Then he convulsed like a trout lying in grass.

Peachtree hoped it wasn't too feisty. Parsons neared oblivion, but stopped an inch short of the comatose.

"You done him in, Peachtree," said a one-eyed villain with a waist-length beard. "Looks like Taos Lightning."

They watched Parsons, who sat stupefied, hiccoughing and dizzy. But then Parsons stood up like an accordion playing out, a little dazed but bright-eyed. "Hot tamales," he bawled, and whooped. "By gawd." He began a little jig, and switched to a hornpipe, and then began hugging greaser women and patting their bottoms. They shrieked and laughed.

"Sir," asked Peachtree, "would you say Nepenthe took your pain away?"

"Hoohar!"

"There, ladies and gents, *señors* and *señoras*, there you see it with your own eyes. A miracle. A man with two legs in his grave, prancing like a stud horse."

Peachtree frowned. Pontius P. Parsons's hands were taking assorted liberties with half the *señoras* of Pueblo, a situation that could result in all of the troupe dangling from a cottonwood limb.

"I say there, sir, it's fine to be young, but don't get too frisky. A smaller dose is recommended."

P.P. Parsons ignored him.

Various of the upright citizens of Pueblo watched Parsons closely as the old goat began a private fandango with several giggling ladies. And then several swart gents emerged from the mob bearing fleeces.

One of them thrust a thick, creamy fleece toward Peachtree, who proceeded to examine it, finding the leather velvety and well tanned, and the fleece so thick it felt like a pillow. He supposed it might fetch a pretty price in Santa Fe. "Why, sir, I will spare you a bottle for this. What'll it be?"

"Nepenthe," the man said, pointing to an unlabeled bottle.

Peachtree smiled benignly. "Ah, take a little bit, itty-bitty bit. Ah"—he turned to one of the buckskinned varmints—"tell him just a nip unless he's planning to croak."

"*Poco*, Paco," the varmint said.

Paco tittered and vanished into the throng.

Ten minutes later Hyacinth Z. Peachtree possessed thirty-two fleeces, a sack of pinto beans, some squash, some chilies, and a breathy invitation from a fiery-looking *señorita* to vamoose into the bushes. He gave her his last bottle of Potawatomi juice.

An altogether satisfying outcome. A tide of satisfaction washed through him. He wondered if something in the new batch of Nepenthe stimulated the base senses. Around him, the denizens of Pueblo were heading toward a bacchanal. Concorde and Hercules sat on the wagons looking sullen and cheated, but Peachtree didn't intend to release them from their guard duty. Carlotta, however, sashayed into the whoopdedo and commandeered a sip from a gigantic greaser who wore a volcanic cone-shaped hat and whose monster hands swiftly explored her.

Peachtree watched quietly. He never permitted himself the slightest emotion, and he supposed emotions were the root cause of inferior intellects.

More and more bodies littered the barren clay of the plaza. Some of his customers sat stupefied. Others convulsed. A few lay as still as corpses, and these Peachtree fretted about. Three women sprawled on the caliche, skirts akimbo, looking powerfully dead. Peachtree didn't like the look of this at all. He'd warned them. Just a little. *Poco* . . .

One of the ruffians slid close to him, and Peachtree suddenly felt a sharp sting under his ribcage.

"Peachtree, this heah's an Arkansas toothpick."

Hyacinth stared down upon a wicked-looking blade which pressed hard upon the tender and vulnerable flesh of his belly.

"This here toothpick, it's cut a lot of meat in its time. I stuck a shoat with 'er just the other day. You see that *señora* over thar? She's mine. She took a few swigs of that stuff and it like to flattened her. I'm some partial to her; she been a good-timer for a few seasons now, keeping a man happy. I'd hate to lose her, Peachtree. She looks some dead, don't she. I reckon maybe she is. But lemme give you the lay of 'er. If she don't git up in a few minutes, you don't git up ever again, because this here sticker's going to separate your throat from your gut."

"Ah, I trust you told her a little sip . . . ah. I think we can come to terms." Peachtree broke into a sweat. He glanced up at Hercules, who was studying the arts and sciences of Mexican seduction.

The bodies lay almighty still out there. It pained Peachtree to suppose that people might abuse his friendly products. He had no murder in him; not even a smidgen of it. "I am dreadfully sorry. Perhaps I can revive her. Let me fire up some coffee, eh?"

"She's gonna revive herself while this hyar evenin's young, or she ain't. You better say some prayers if yoah believing type. Me, I believe singularly in my toadsticker heah."

The woman never stirred, and Peachtree began to understand that the sands of time were running out.

Chapter 28

The Skyes and Carmody tunneled through a night so dark they could not see the lodgetrail. Skye lifted the collar of his elkskin coat against the sharp north wind and let Jawbone pick the way. Victoria rode ahead, as usual, somehow keeping to the road, even when massed clouds plunged them into pure blackness. In those moments Skye couldn't see stars, and all he registered was the clop of hoofs, the occasional thump of Carmody's boots, and Jawbone's yawns.

"Mister Skye, sir, I fear I'll ruin my feet if I don't rest them soon," Carmody said with apology in his voice.

"You're right, mate. If we hobble you, we'll be stuck."

"I will walk awhile," Mary said out of the blackness. "I'm cold and need to walk."

"There you are, Elisha. You get on that mare."

"I'm grateful to you, madam."

"Maybe I will sit on a travois and take care of Dirk."

In moments they were off again, piercing through a night increasingly bitter. Skye had inured himself to most weather, as any man must who lived out of doors. But he knew that cold and weariness were taking a toll on the lecturer.

He felt Jawbone sidle sideways as Carmody heeled the mare closer, and soon sensed the presence of the man riding beside him.

"It's a mean night, Elisha. I'm sorry to put you to the test."

"I'd rather be sleeping in a comfortable room at Fort St. Vrain," Carmody replied. "I'm not sure I understand your hurry. At least to my way of thinking, the Peachtree party made its own choice. They're adults, and the consequences of their acts belong entirely on their shoulders. I think that frees you from any obligation. I admire your zeal, even while doubting the wisdom of all this."

Skye pondered that a moment. "I don't cut it so fine," he said. "I hired out to do a job, and I'll do it."

"We shouldn't be protected from our follies, sir. They teach us life's lessons. You've a mighty heart, Mister Skye. It's like a father's love, but every child has to cut loose or he remains a child forever."

A faint annoyance built in Skye. He wasn't much for arguing. If he had ever had much faculty for words, he'd lost it long ago in a wilderness where there weren't any words.

"It's my goal to help adults be adults, sir," Carmody continued.

"Look, mate, out here mistakes mean death."

"Nonetheless, Mister Skye, you've no responsibility."

Skye remembered how it was in the mountains with the trapping brigades. Without it ever being put into words, every one of them looked out for the others because every minute in the wilds was fraught with death. Word that some child was in trouble leagues away would send them all rushing to help out—and once in a while that help became some man's salvation.

"I've made them my responsibility, Mister Carmody."

"But that's paternalism. That's like saying that those adults are really children."

"I think they bloody well are children here. They've been on the road for years; they've got more experience than any outfit I've ever guided. They've been in more jams than anyone I've met. They're tough and ready for anything. They think they can get out of any scrape. But, mate, all their scrapes were back in settled country. There are other rules out here."

"Ah, Mister Skye, you make my point for me. They're adults. They're smart enough to know they know nothing about surviving out here. I wouldn't think of wandering here myself without someone of your experience beside me."

Skye didn't feel like replying to the man. He rode silently through the blackness. The cloudmass passed and the emerging stars gave him a sense of direction again. He couldn't see the mountains on his right but he knew they were there.

Victoria loomed out of the night ahead of them. She hunched over her pony, waiting for them. "Big damned river ahead," she said. "Pretty quick now."

She meant an hour off. Victoria had trouble with white men's time and distances, hours and miles.

"South Platte. We'll rest there until daylight," Skye said. "Horses need it and so do we."

Skye felt plenty tired and Jawbone was lagging under him. He watched Victoria vanish into the gloom ahead, and knew she would pick out a campsite, check it for safety, and break off some squaw wood for a little fire.

"I'll walk the rest of the way," Carmody said. "I'm grateful for the rest." He dismounted, even as Mary materialized out of the darkness.

A while later Victoria silently led them into a protected river bottom where cottonwood limbs erupted into the stars and the lee of a rocky escarpment tamed the wintry winds. Skye reckoned it was three in the morning. But the women swiftly erected the lodge, setting up the four-pole base, laying in the lodgepoles and then raising the small eleven-hide cover and fastening it with willow pegs. It would be a haven for a few hours. Skye let the horses water and then picketed them on good grass close to the lodge.

He eyed Carmody unhappily. This night, for the first time, the lecturer had struck him as being a man with too much opinion for his own good. But in spite of that, Carmody had been a good soldier the whole trip.

"Elisha, we've a small lodge but there's room for one. Air's freezing now."

"But someone should be on guard, sir. You can't see out of a lodge."

"We have a sentry every night. Jawbone's been trained to it since he was small enough for me to carry in my arms."

"This one night, then, if you're certain I won't be a nuisance."

As swiftly as the lodgecover had been pinned together and a few rocks had anchored it to the clay, Victoria built a tiny fire in its center, striking sparks on flint with her steel until the tiny ball of dry inner bark caught and glowed. She blew softly on it until it flared to life, and then added sticks. When she had a little blaze she adjusted the wind ears to draw the smoke away.

Skye crawled in, carrying his kit and his battered Hawken. The warmth caught him instantly and he knew he'd sleep well for the few hours he allotted. His women vanished for a moment and then returned, each bearing a curly-haired buffalo robe made from half a buffalo hide. Silently they cleaned the pawing child and wrapped him in a soft old blanket, while Skye unlaced his boots.

"You gonna drive Carmody out, taking off them damn boots?" Victoria asked.

"He's an adult. He can choose to sleep outside if he wants," Skye said edgily.

Mary giggled.

In another moment, Carmody crawled in, having watered and picketed his mule. He seemed faintly embarrassed as he glanced from Skye to the women and the babbling boy in the flickering light of a tiny fire. "Where do you want me?" he asked.

"Near the flap there, mate."

"Are you sure it's safe here?"

"It's never safe, Elisha. But we're half a mile off the lodgetrail, and Jawbone's never failed us."

"Is there something rotten here, sir? I believe I smell a skunk."

Victoria coughed. Mary convulsed, and finally wheezed amusement.

"I fear I've given offense," Carmody said.

Victoria couldn't contain herself. "Mister Skye, he's got two stinking damned skunks with him all the time, and they follow him into the lodge every night."

"You really have skunks, Mister Skye?"

Skye sighed unhappily. "I am cursed with offensive feet, Mister Carmody."

"Oh. Now that I look at them, Mister Skye, I can see the white streaks down the back, and the blackness of them. You have truly remarkable feet, sir. I have never seen such dirty feet on a white man. Why, they're like tar itself."

"I reckon it's bloody well near dawn, Carmody."

The women were enjoying themselves all too much, Skye thought. He threw his topper at them.

The fire ebbed into nothing but orange coals.

"This is the first time in years—many years—that I have been in the bosom of a family, Mister Skye," Carmody said from his bedroll. "I lost my beloved wife and soul mate, Deborah, and my dear daughter, Abigail, to typhus in Washington City my second term. I have grown sons, but I've really been alone since then.

"That awful tragedy changed me, sir. I left politics at the end of the term. You know, there's something I can't explain about myself. The typhus that took my darling from me, my darlings I should say, was an act of God, and yet it burdened me in strange ways. I've lectured the world since then, driven by something I can't describe. I felt guilty, sir, that I'd even entered Whig politics and taken my family to that hot Southern city with its foul miasmas. If I hadn't gone to Washington City, I wouldn't have lost them."

Skye found himself listening intently in the darkness. When a man needed to tell something of himself, Skye always understood the importance of listening.

"For the next year, my life was bleak. I returned to Ohio—and our homestead farm—and lived alone, thinking about why mortals are set on earth and what makes a man higher than a beast. And when I emerged, Mister Skye, I was not the same man. I don't know what I am now, but I beg your forgiveness for anything that doesn't set right with you."

"You get some rest, mate. You're welcome in our lodge," Skye said gently. "It's a humble place, but we're happy as we are. I am richer than the world."

Chapter 29

The woman sprawled on the earth, firelight playing on her inert form. Her chest didn't rise and fall. She was either dead or in a coma. And she wasn't alone, either. Peachtree counted five other bodies strewn across the plaza. Still other people sat or knelt, obviously stupefied.

He felt the cold steel prick his belly and knew terror. He hadn't meant to kill anyone. That had never happened before. He was opposed on principle to assassinating his customers. If only he hadn't lost his regular simples and powders he wouldn't be in this awful fix.

"I don't see no life in her, Peachtree. If she goes to hell, you'll be hot on her heels," the ruffian said, twisting the knife slightly for emphasis.

"She took a tad too much," Peachtree croaked. "I warned you all; just a nip."

"Don't matter none. If she's headin' for the Pearly Gates, yoah headin' for the brimstone."

"I'm sure she was a beloved wife and companion, my friend."

The man cackled. "She warn't no wife. But she war a comfort, that's spoken true. I got right partial to her Mexican charms. She was pretty perky where it counts."

"If she goes, I'll grieve right beside you, my friend. We'll bury her properly and say some powerful prayers for her sweet and virtuous soul."

The fellow cackled. "You won't be around to say nothing. I don't take to diggin'. You're gonna do the diggin' and it'll be a hole for two."

Peachtree stealthily peered about him looking for succor. He could usually count on rescue by Concorde or Hercules in moments like this. Even old Parsons would brandish a pair of revolvers in his trembling hands if he had to. Once Carlotta had aimed a piece at a mad bull of a customer, getting Peachtree out of a corner.

But none of them seemed to notice Peachtree's extremity. Nepenthe and booze had plainly loosened all restraints and the whole pueblo was cavorting. Concorde and Carlotta were off somewhere. Hercules was studying the nightlife with awe from atop the supply wagon, unaware of the steel pricking his employer's belly. Peachtree realized he was on his own this time.

"What's your beautiful lady's name, eh?" he asked.

"Concepción."

"Well, I think we ought to slip a blanket over her. It's a tad chilly."

"She'll rare up or she won't, Peachtree."

"But I think a little warmth and some tea—"

"She'll live or croak, Peachtree. If she croaks . . ."

"Say, friend, I have a little Nepenthe I held back. One of my colleagues is partial to it. It's a nippy night and I'm thinking to swill a tad. You interested? We'll nip it while we wait. It'll be easier for both of us."

"You gonna sell me something. First you whonk my woman, and then charge me for the juice."

"No, no, it'll be on the house. This'll be my treat. Say, what did you say your monicker is?"

"I didn't."

Peachtree waited for a name but never got one. He eyed the scraggle-bearded man cautiously, smiled, and edged toward the cabinets. The man let him go. With trembling hands Peachtree untied the knot that pinned the cabinet doors and extracted one of the bottles he kept for Pontius.

"Here. Just a nip now."

"You first, Peachtree. Iffen you croak it'll save me cleaning the blood off this toothpick."

Peachtree popped the cork and allowed himself one little sip.

"That ain't enough to wet your tonsils, Peachtree. Now you take a manly swig or feel some steel."

Peachtree took another nip.

"That ain't enough to soak your gizzard, Peachtree. Shows what kind of man you are." He plucked the bottle from Peachtree and sampled it. "Jaysas," he muttered. "It's puke."

"Have some more, friend," Peachtree said. "Nepenthe drives away pain and sorrow. Nepenthe's the very thing for grieving. If your heart's heavy, why, just a tad'll make a new man of you."

He was feeling queasy. This locoweed version of Nepenthe was about as friendly as arsenic. If he survived the next hour he would revamp the formula a smidgen.

"I ought to poke this toadstabber right to the hilt in your gut, Peachtree."

"Ah, what did you say your name is?"

"Cutter Bill."

"Cutter, you say. Have some more, old Cutter." Peachtree thrust the Nepenthe at the ruffian.

"Nope. Jist wanted one sip to see what kind of varnish it is. She's the foulest brew ever to visit my liver."

"Cutter Bill, let's go sit down beside your sweetheart. I think she deserves your respect while she sails across the heavens. We'll admire her together."

Cutter Bill eyed Concepción, and parked himself beside her. Peachtree settled himself across the carcass from Bill after flipping his clawhammers out behind him. Concepción didn't move.

The need to flee overwhelmed him. He couldn't spot any of his people. He could hear occasional sighing, and sensed movement in the night. The fire smoked sullenly, covering the flat with choking fumes as if this were a layer of hell. Its orange coals threw just enough light to illumine dark bodies sprawled everywhere. He had the sensation that he'd massacred a whole settlement.

Cutter Bill sat with his blade in hand, running a thumb along the whetted edge. "Don't take notions of running off, Peachtree. She throws true and I can put her in real fine."

Peachtree didn't doubt it. He stared at Concepción, yearning for something, anything, to happen. But it didn't. Her mouth had opened like a carp's.

An hour elapsed though it seemed like ten to Peachtree. The night grew still. His tailbone hurt. The bodies didn't twitch. Someone threw some sticks on the fire and it flared, then died again. A slender moon rose, and Peachtree eyed it as a traitor. He needed absolute darkness to escape that deadly knife.

A gent materialized out of the gloom and settled on his heels beside him. Peachtree realized it was Concorde. "Ah been lookin' for you-all," he said gently.

"Uh, Concorde, this fine specimen is Cutter Bill. We're keeping an eye on his lady, Concepción here. She had a tad too much."

"They all did," Concorde said. "Stiffs."

"Uh, Concorde—where are the others?"

"To the wagon. We're wondering what you've in mind. Fixing to stay heah tonight?"

"If she croaks, you all gonna camp heah about six feet under, fella," Cutter Bill said softly. "She was some woman."

"Well, Ah'll go tell 'em," Concorde said, rising.

"No, you gonna stay and vigil. This hyar toothpick sails plumb center up to fifty feet."

"We reckon we oughta be gitting along," said Concorde. "We don't much cotton to camping in a graveyard."

"You stayen put, darkie."

Concorde eyed the long, glinting Arkansas toothpick and settled back on his heels again. Then the devil took him and he poked at Concepción with a skinny finger. Nothing happened. He poked harder and she groaned.

"There you are, Cutter Bill," he said, standing.

"She ain't kissing me yet," Bill said. He poked her himself, and she muttered something in the greaser tongue.

"Well, we'll check in a while. Ah'm gitting itchy just settin'. Come on, Hyacinth."

Peachtree rose cautiously, ready to drop to earth if the knife hand twitched. It didn't.

"Don't you git farther than I can throw," Cutter Bill muttered. "She ain't come around yet."

But they ignored Cutter Bill and hurried gingerly to the wagons. Peachtree saw moonlight glinting off double barrels.

"They ain't friendly," said Hercules. "Now we got us together. Soon as the moon came up I gandered at the river, and got the ford picked out."

"You want to run for it?"

"Best time I can think of."

"How are the mules?"

"Chewin' on leather. We'll have to stop and let 'em grass up."

"You think those peckerwoods'll come after us?"

"I don't think. I just wanna git, Hyacinth."

"Darlinks, it was good party. I haff a new friend. Very, very fine gentleman."

"Get on up there, Carlotta," Peachtree said. He helped her

climb to the seat, and followed. The moon silvered the whole plaza now, and he could see bodies humped like white gravestones.

Quietly, Hercules jarred his team and the supply wagon rumbled ahead, while Concorde and Pontius held shotguns at the ready. Peachtree gently popped his whip over his weary mules and felt his wagon creak forward. Nothing happened. Cutter Bill didn't move.

They rolled down a long slope into the river, fearful of being ambushed, but Pueblo didn't stir. The crossing seemed to take forever; the Arkansas was a mighty stream. But they rattled over water-smoothed rock the whole distance, and slowly mounted the south bank and into a frosty moonlit night.

Peachtree hoped no one had croaked. It wouldn't help the show any.

Chapter 30

The Skyes and Elisha Carmody hurried south along a creek east of the Rockies. But they didn't seem to be gaining ground and never caught a glimpse of the Peachtree troupe. Carmody knew he was the reason. His aching feet could stand only so much pounding each day. But the Skyes' travois ponies were slow, too. They dragged heavy lodgepoles and the lodgecover behind them, and resisted the younger Mrs. Skye's discipline.

Often Carmody could see the ribbons in the dust left by the iron tires of the Peachtree wagons. The perpetual wind hadn't yet dusted them over. They looked so fresh that he swore the medicine show was just ahead. But Skye told him the troupe was probably a day and a half to the south and gaining ground.

"I'm willing to walk into the night, sir," Carmody said, as he rode beside Skye for a spell on Mary's pony.

"That's good of you, mate. But we're hurting the horses.

I've learned to keep my horses fresh no matter what. That's saved our lives once or twice."

"I wish my feet would stay fresh."

"If we need to run we'll cache a pack and put you on the horse," Skye said.

Skye called the languid stream they followed Fountain Creek. The Front Range of the Rockies surrendered, and they entered arid bunchgrass country with juniper blackening the slopes. From high points Carmody spotted snow-tipped, isolated mountains off to the west and south.

"Not far to Pueblo now," Skye said one afternoon. "Peachtree might be there."

"Why, if we catch up, sir, they'll simply abandon us again."

"They're greenhorns."

"I'm not following your logic."

"They're stuck with me. I'm paid to protect them, even if they don't want me." He lifted his battered top hat and twisted it down. Carmody never ceased to marvel that the wind didn't sail it away.

They pushed as fast as their tired stock would permit, but Skye kept his horses fresh with frequent short breaks. Mary took to walking much of the time. The Skyes rotated the packloads on the horses and watched for saddle galls.

They descended one yellow afternoon into the valley of the Arkansas River and followed the rutted road into a hodge-podge settlement of adobe houses with rain-eroded walls, rude pole fences, and squash gardens, all of it blasted by wind. A ribby cur rose, its neck hair bristling, and then sat watching like a household god.

They entered a plaza and terrorized a squad of crows feasting on manure bugs. An ancient Mexican the color of dried tobacco slouched against a sunny wall, but when they hailed him he turned out to be deaf and blind. Victoria squinted around the sullen plaza, not liking it, while Skye tried to make sense of the silence. Then Victoria spotted a crowd at a graveyard on a far slope. The whole *placita* was burying someone. A whirlwind drove sour-smelling dust into Carmody's face. Life here was hard.

Victoria pointed to the ribbons that continued toward a rippling ford in the surly river. So the Peachtree show was still ahead.

."May as well rest our nags," Skye said. Jawbone sighed happily, bared his yellow teeth at some nearby burros. "We'll find out how far ahead they are."

Someone's dust-tanned laundry flapped behind an eroded adobe.

"I don't like this none," Victoria said. "I got bad feelings."

Skye stared at her. "I've learned to rely on my women's instincts," he said.

"Surely we're safe here among white men," Carmody said.

Victoria glanced at him sharply and Carmody knew he had offended her.

The plaza hummed with biting black flies that tormented the horses and angered Jawbone. He clacked his teeth imperiously at Skye. Carmody marveled at the communication between the guide and his half-berserk horse.

Even as the crowd up at the cemetery on the slope dispersed, rough men in grease-blackened buckskins slid into the plaza, all of them armed with a variety of pieces. It disturbed Carmody that these ruffians spread into an arc, as if to defend the settlement—or butcher the travelers. Carmody felt his pulse lift, and he eased back to his packmule, where he kept a carbine sheathed.

But Skye sat Jawbone easily, surveying the brigands.

At last a gap-toothed mountaineer who looked even more murderous than the rest walked partway toward the Skyes. The man squinted at the guide, studying the bearclaw necklace. "Who you be, and what's your business?"

"I'm Mister Skye. These are my wives and my son. The gentleman is a client of mine, Elisha Carmody. We're traveling downwind."

"Nobody I know. We don't take kindly to strangers. Git."

"All right," said Skye amiably. "Thought you might tell us when the rest of our party came through here. Couple of wagons, man named Peachtree."

The sudden hatred that smacked Carmody seemed terrible. The ruffian's face darkened. "Peachtree, eh? By gawd, Peachtree," he said at last.

"Clients. I'm a guide. They got ahead."

The man squinted. "Who's that one?"

"Mister Carmody's a lecturer."

"A lecturer! One of 'em, then. By God, we'll let him lecture the devil."

"No," said Skye. He lifted his topper and settled it again.

His women prepared for trouble. Victoria let her little bay mare amble a way off. No one paid attention to her. Mary frowned and stepped behind a packhorse.

Carmody realized he was in danger. "I have no connection with that show, sir. I advocate certain private disciplines—"

"We just buried a man and a woman. Plumb dead they was this morning. Samplin' that pizen Peachtree peddles. Let go o' that mule. I reckon we'll deal two for two. You and that silk-hatter there for Manuelita and Emilio. Feed you to the vultures."

The other ruffians lowered their rifles until a dozen black bores pointed at the Skyes and Carmody.

"Git down offen that ugly nag, top-hatter."

"It's Mister Skye, mate."

"I don't care iffen it's Napoleon. You step down peaceable."

"Not much point in that if you're planning to kill me, is there?" Skye asked.

"Just shoot 'im," someone yelled.

The plaza was filling fast with the rest of the settlement. Most were Mexicans. Urchins crowded forward; women stared from behind funeral mantillas. Dust raked their skirts.

"I think a man ought to hear the charges," Skye said. "Just

so he knows what he's dying for—in case he hasn't any notion."

"You taken two lives; we're taken two lives."

"You mind telling me about it, mate?"

The ruffian spat. A brown gob raised dust at Jawbone's hoof. The horse laid back his ears, half berserk. Skye touched Jawbone on the neck and the horse quieted.

"Your outfit come in here yestiddy and peddled some brown pizen. It kilt a woman and a man. That's all there be to her. Now git down or we'll blow you down."

Skye didn't move.

Two burly, bearded border men circled toward Carmody, and sprang. They wrestled him away from his mule. His pulse climbed his throat. "Sirs—I'd like to explain."

"No explaining. We'll show you what we do to outfits like yours."

"I'm a former congressman lecturing on self-discipline—"

One cackled. "Yeah, what're you selling?"

"I'm selling good character and private liberty."

The ruffian wheezed and then spat some tobacco chaw at Carmody's boots. "That's a new one on Cutter Bill. Sellin' good character. He's gonna preach about conduct. We'll show you what a good lecturer is. The only good lecturer is a dead lecturer, ain't it so, boys?"

They laughed.

Carmody's captors threw him to the clay. He hit hard. A boot bashed his ribs. It shot pain up his chest and out his arm.

"That's how your pizen felt. Shot pain right into the heart."

Carmody shrank, knowing he had no time left. He sagged to the clay, his face streaked with tears, his suit soaked with manure, his mind whirling. He despaired. They would butcher him for some terrible thing Peachtree had done.

He heard Skye addressing them tautly. "You in the habit of killing strangers?"

"We're in the habit of killin' anyone we don't like, Skye. Like you."

"Carmody there has no connection with that show. He joined the party at the last moment."

"Git off that nag, Skye. I'm not going to ask you again."

Carmody felt a terrible ache in his soul—and something finer. He could be a man. Slowly he stood. His whole side ached.

"All right," he whispered. "Do what you will. I will show you how a man should die. And what a man can be if he has heart. Take me, and let Skye go. He was simply someone we hired."

"Carmody, no!" Skye roared. "Let me deal."

Carmody stared at them all. He forced himself to stand tall. He saw sudden respect in their faces. "Let's go," he said.

Cutter Bill grinned and motioned him toward the nearest adobe wall. It was pocked.

Chapter 31

Victoria had faced death many times, and had meted it out too. Now she faced it again. No one was watching her; they never paid any attention to a wizened little squaw. She crouched behind her slat-ribbed mare and eased the quiver and bow case from her back. Mary could do nothing for the moment. Her beauty hadn't escaped the white men who spread across the filthy plaza, their rifles jabbing at Mister Skye.

Victoria strung her bow and nocked an arrow almost without motion, and waited. Her man would talk as long as he could. Talking often saved blood. She had seen him talk his way out of grave trouble several times. But the gritty wind stole his words.

She watched sharply, knowing her arrow would find the heart of any of them who cocked a hammer. She would kill maybe two before their bullets found her.

Carmody walked without being prodded toward a cancerous wall of a *cantina*, herded by two white men in buckskins.

She suddenly admired him even if his path wasn't the Absaroka path. An Absaroka warrior would fight, taking as many enemies as he could before dying. But this man wasn't a warrior, and she understood his courage. It took another kind of honor to accept his execution bravely, and it touched her.

"All right, Skye. Git ye over to that wall."

"You figure that's justice?"

"It ain't anything but blood revenge, Skye."

"It's Mister Skye, friend. That's a courtesy I ask."

"You want courtesy." Cutter Bill wheezed. Then he flicked a knife out of its belt sheath. "Git!" he snarled.

"You might not want to do that," Skye said quietly. "You're tired of burying your people. It's a day for grieving. You'll not want to bury any more, especially a congressman from Ohio."

"Git on with it," one of the ruffians yelled.

Skye addressed that one. "With killing a congressman? Your officials wouldn't like that, would they? Neither will the Army. They'd be inclined to hang the killers of a congressman."

"Skye, if he's a real congressman, we been neglectful. We shoulda shot him on sight," Cutter Bill said. "He's a pizen-peddler for sure." Men laughed. Cutter edged closer, getting into knife-throwing range.

Victoria knew time was running out. Cutter Bill was about to flip that deadly knife into Skye's chest. She tensed, knowing that her arrow would find him first.

Beyond, Carmody stood quietly at the scabrous wall while his executioners paced away from him. He looked strangely beautiful. The light seemed to gather around him. The village women noticed it and clapped their hands to their mouths.

"*Santo, santo, santo,*" wailed one.

"Tell you what, mate," said Skye, warily. "Let's you and me settle it ourselves. Leave Elisha Carmody out of it. Give me a knife and we'll see."

Victoria squinted. Skye's belt knife rested at his waist.

Cutter Bill grinned. She could see the blood-lust in him now, and knew he would try to kill.

"You're too late, Skye," he said cheerfully. His arm cocked back.

She lifted her bow and drove an arrow into him. He stared at the shaft in his chest. She nocked another. He stood, amazed, and the knife slid from his hands. Disbelief filled his face.

The others shouted. Skye dropped to earth in one snaking move and flattened himself. Jawbone screeched, terrorizing horses and burros, which began rearing and plunging. Jawbone thundered into the riflemen, his yellow eyes berserk. They tumbled away from his path as he wheeled and pawed and sliced and bit. They screamed, toppled to earth, crawled away, took murderous blows from his hoofs that sounded like popcorn popping.

He whirled madly around the plaza, screeching hell and fire and repentance. One cool white man retreated, lifted his piece to shoot the horse. Victoria's arrow found his shoulder; his piece discharged into the dust. He screamed, clutching his bloody shirt. A cur licked his gouting blood from the dust.

Skye sprang up, raced toward Carmody, knife in hand. The two remaining mountaineers fired at Skye, wide of the mark. A ball spanged into the clay near Victoria, plowing a wormtrack. Mary shot a mountaineer who was trying a shot at Jawbone. The ball drove the man backward into the filth. He choked and sobbed and vomited. Somewhere, a woman began wailing, her sobs ratcheting sorrow up the adobe walls.

Jawbone cleaned out the whole square. Women, children bolted for safety, screaming their terror. Men vanished. Cutter Bill sat down suddenly and died. Two of the ruffians lay on the plaza, their limbs twisted grotesquely.

"Carmody!" Skye yelled.

The lecturer slowly returned to the living and stared about him. Victoria admired him; he had given himself to death in the bravest way. Carmody was a man.

"But Mister Skye," Carmody said. "They're dead."

"Come on, before they start sniping. We could be too."

Carmody didn't move. Skye lifted him bodily and carried him toward his packmule.

Jawbone screeched and raced around the plaza, a gray horror, finding no more enemies to massacre.

Skye hurried them all to the river crossing. He whistled Jawbone in. The reluctant horse finally surrendered and raced to Skye, who slid his old Hawken from its sheath and covered their retreat. Victoria climbed aboard her mare. Mary hurried past, with Dirk in his cradleboard on her back.

A shot from the settlement spanged off of Carmody's mulepack. The mule bucked. Carmody plunged into the river on foot, dragging his mule behind him. More shots erupted from shadowed corners of the settlement, some buzzing close. Skye whirled and dodged. A shot seared Jawbone's croup. This time Skye paused, aimed, and shot back. A wild scream echoed in the *placita*, followed by sobs that tortured the silence. Skye mounted Jawbone, unstoppered his horn and poured a small handful of powder down the octagonal barrel, stuffed a wadded ball into it, and rammed it home with his wiping stick. He clawed in his pocket for a cap, and armed the heavy Hawken again.

They staggered up the south bank of the Arkansas and raced eastward until they were out of rifleshot, rivering icy water off their legs and flanks. Then Skye halted them.

"Who's hurt?" he asked roughly.

They stared at each other and their mounts. None of them bled. Not even Jawbone. The ball had seared hair off the rump, without cutting flesh. The wild-eyed horse bit at his wound.

"You saved my life, sir," said Carmody.

"Not over yet, mate. They might come."

"You saved me."

Skye sighed. "Hated to do it. They wouldn't listen. I always hate it." Skye stared at his client. "You're a man, Carmody."

Victoria knew how much her man hated killing. She could see the sadness etch his face now. He had prepared for war not so that he might hurt others, but so that he could protect himself and those he loved. It was odd how white men regretted killing enemies. Her Absaroka warriors would have danced with joy, taken scalps, held a victory feast.

Sometimes after he had fought and killed, Skye found his crock of whiskey and blotted out the memory. She hoped he wouldn't now. Mister Skye might leave them for one of his long dark journeys. He sat Jawbone, his spirit wrenched from his body, hating himself. She wished she could nurture him, but she couldn't. She had learned long ago that she could do nothing until he wrestled his demons into their caves again.

But Mister Carmody, who didn't know Mister Skye well, tried.

"Sir, you gave them every chance to back away."

"It doesn't change anything," he said. "Dead is dead." They had rested enough so he motioned them toward the beetling river bluff, which they ascended slowly.

"Mister Skye, Cutter Bill wasn't a bit interested in justice. I've never seen murder in a man's face before, but now I have. It was the face of the Prince of Evil himself. I am utterly indebted to you and your horse and your valiant women."

Mister Skye growled something at him, and heeled Jawbone ahead, not wanting to talk about it.

Mister Carmody walked patiently. "I'm very tired, you know," he said to Victoria. "There's something about facing death. I have no energy left."

"We gotta move, dammit," she snarled.

"I know that. I tremble with each step. You can't imagine . . ." She watched him put each foot forward and walk. She watched him glance fearfully to the rear, as if expecting death to follow them. But it didn't. Mary rode with her long rifle across her lap, guarding their rear.

"You some brave sonofabitch," Victoria said, squinting at him. "How come?"

He shook his head. "I've never been so afraid. If I faced death well, it wasn't me; it was the belief I subscribe to, and which I take to others." He seemed to gather courage from talking to her. "They didn't have to kill us. It was the lust boiling in their blood. It all fits my beliefs."

She could see that Mister Carmody was rehashing the whole thing. She never did. If she thought about the dead, she only invited their spirits to torment her. She didn't want any spirit sonsofbitches to come visiting.

Mister Skye led them through an empty afternoon as hollow as a politician's promise, each of them trapped with their own dark thoughts. Victoria knew that this would torment her man a long time. She pitied him and all white men. She lifted her arms to the Above One, and thanked him for their salvation, and then rode on ahead, needing to be alone, too.

Chapter 32

The Skyes and Carmody toiled southward under a scowling heaven, all of them caught in their private worlds. Carmody found no friendliness in the naked steppes. He had come from the bountiful East, with lush vegetation and abundant water. Here the grass thinned to fragile brown bunches, sagebrush silvered slopes, and stunted juniper choked the gulches. But the dry air gave him vast perspectives reaching to sullen horizons some infinity away, as bleak as the future. The mountains crept back like vagrants returning home, but they lacked the grandeur of the Front Range, and seemed hard-bitten. He supposed only savages could thrive in such wastes. Surely this desert wasn't intended for human habitation.

Even as they fled Pueblo, gloom chased them all. He peered behind him fifty times an hour, expecting the Horseman of the Apocalypse to ride him down and plunge a lance through him. The memory of his brush with death haunted him, as real now as when it happened. But as the hours passed, his questing mind shaped these events until they meshed with his own philosophy.

That wind-chafed afternoon he caught up to Jawbone and walked beside the guide even though he dreaded that murderous horse more than ever. Skye rode silently, his topper pulled down over his hooded eyes, his face as bleak as sleet.

"I believe, sir, that those fellows in Pueblo were entirely responsible for their own misfortunes," Carmody began.

Skye didn't reply.

"You see, they had the chance to act in an adult manner, but rejected it. All they had to do was listen. They would've learned we really aren't connected with the Peachtree show."

Skye glanced at Carmody with smoldering eyes, but kept his silence. Carmody could see the guide's suffering and thought to relieve it.

"No, sir, the real problem was those white savages. They lost control of themselves. Self-control is the key: that's all there is to it. I use a dozen examples in my lectures. All they had to do was contain their blood-lusts and they would be among us now, enjoying the afternoon. I want to assure you, sir; you had every blessed right to defend yourself. We all did. We were completely innocent. I am frightened of death, sir. But the certitude of my own innocence gave me a dab of courage when I needed it. I didn't offer those wretches toxic brews or skin them of their lucre. Why, if I'm alive, it's because my innocence is plain to all, that's why."

"Let it lie, Carmody," Skye growled.

"It all needs to be factored out. We'll feel better knowing that the tragedy wasn't our fault."

"Let it lie."

"No, it needs addressing. They obviously imbibed too much of Peachtree's elixirs. That was overindulgence, one of the things I dwell on in my lectures. You can't blame Peachtree for that. Now, as the direct result of their excess, two of them died. You can't blame Peachtree for that, either. This is all of a piece with my philosophy. I'll use this episode in my lectures because it perfectly illustrates my point: we aren't free until we discipline our own souls."

"Carmody, let it lie."

"I can't, Mister Skye. I want you to know that nothing you or Jawbone or your wives did to save us was blameful. You must understand that."

"I killed."

"No, Jawbone did."

Skye spoke intensely. "Mister Carmody, I did. Jawbone's a bloody weapon. When I tell Jawbone to do that, I'm firing my weapon."

"Well, you had a perfect right."

"Carmody, they lost a man and a woman before we got there. They had reason. They were grieving. They thought they were doing justice. That's the most important thing in the world, Mister Carmody: justice."

"Why, it's a minor matter. What counts is self-mastery. Even grief gets beyond control. We must always control our excesses, or we become prisoners to them. You see, Mister Skye—"

But Skye wheeled Jawbone away. Carmody watched the guide steer his horse back to the knot of pack animals. Skye slid off Jawbone and pawed around in a parfleche. He extracted a gray crockery jug and then clambered heavily onto Jawbone. The horse laid back his ears and clacked his teeth, not liking whatever was happening. Skye kicked the horse into a canter and reined him about twenty yards ahead of Carmody and Mary.

"Now he will drink," Mary said.

"He'll what?"

"He's got bad feelings. You give him bad feelings."

"I did just the opposite. I told him his conduct was entirely proper. Those fellows in Pueblo succumbed to their own excesses."

"He doesn't like to kill. He doesn't like Jawbone to kill."

"Why, he saved my life, Mrs. Skye. And yours."

Mary stared sourly at him with compressed lips, and withdrew into herself.

Carmody found himself alone. His bunions hurt. He wished Skye would slow the relentless pace. But Skye didn't. Victoria rode far ahead, somehow radiating her anger even at great distances. They hadn't even glimpsed the Peachtree caravan ahead.

Ahead, Skye was lifting that jug regularly, gasping at the sting in the raw whiskey. With each swallow Jawbone snarled at him and snapped at flies. But Skye ignored Jawbone. He rode through the gloomy sun with the jug clutched to his lap, rhythmically sipping, sputtering, coughing the wild spirits down his throat, and weeping.

Carmody absorbed the spectacle silently. So, then. The guide had his excesses. It came as no surprise. The lecturer wondered whether to give Skye a little talking-to. But something warned him not to do it. He hoped Skye would swiftly recover and return to being the powerful knight Carmody had come to admire.

But as the heavy day wore on, it became apparent that Skye's debauch wasn't going to end so swiftly. Eventually Skye cast the empty jug away, wove back to the packhorse, and extracted a second jug. The guide teetered in the saddle, now to the left, then to the right, while Jawbone minced along under him waiting for a chance to strike.

Through all that afternoon Skye drank. By subtle degrees his women took over; Carmody realized they had done this before. Twice Victoria halted them for a rest and set the horses on thin frost-cured grass that wouldn't founder them. He unlaced his boots and released his aching feet from their torment. But the women no longer offered him a pony to ride on now and then. Mary used hers to study their backtrail as restlessly as Victoria probed ahead. From time to time they studied Skye, who only sank deeper into his private world. Carmody heard not a cross word spoken about their man, although Victoria had become even testier than usual.

Once in a while Skye sang some sailor's ditty in a whiskey voice, or mumbled a tuneless dirge, or babbled about Piccadilly. Twice he tumbled off Jawbone to relieve himself. Once the angry horse bit him on the shoulder, and Skye pawed helplessly at the yellow-eyed monster. Never had Carmody witnessed such a bitter transaction between man and horse.

Once Skye meandered up to Carmody. The man's topper tilted like the Leaning Tower of Pisa. "Prisoner of the bloody Queen," he muttered. "Three men-o'-war, one frigate. Never got out of the brig. Not like you, Carmody. You were born free."

"But, Skye—you can be as free as you want to be."

"Mister Skye, mate." Skye cackled nastily and clambered aboard Jawbone again. The horse snapped at a horsefly and sidestepped.

Carmody found himself alone in a wild place, with only a drunken guide and two savage women for company.

"Mrs. Skye," he said to Victoria, "does this happen much?"

She didn't reply but her mouth turned down.

"It's so unnecessary. There's no reason for it. He had every right to defend us all."

The lithe little woman paused. "You ever kill anyone?" she asked.

"Never."

"Then leave him alone."

"But, madam, I'm not judging. I'm saying—"

"He's drinking because he killed. White men feel like that. He feels damn bad."

"But the horse did it."

She walked off.

That evening Victoria and Mary erected their lodge back in some juniper thickets near a soda spring. Under the overcast sky, a sharp wind sliced out of the mountains. Carmody picketed his mule and crawled into Skye's warm lodge, where he had been welcomed each evening.

Skye slumped in the rear, jug in hand. "Not good enough for you, Carmody. Common bloody seaman. Bloody drunk," he muttered.

"Sir—"

"Out of my house," Skye rumbled.

He turned to the silent women and found no succor there.

Carmody crawled into the stabbing wind, feeling utterly abandoned, and tried to make a comfortable bed in the brush. But it would be a hard cold night that would test his soul.

Deep in the restless night he felt a presence, and peered up in terror. Jawbone loomed over him, his ugly snout inches from Carmody's face. The horse was about to kill him. Carmody shrank to earth, frozen. The horse sniffed Carmody's breath, nickered softly, and licked Carmody's ear. Elisha Carmody wept. He had a staunch friend in these wilds after all.

Chapter 33

The close call at Pueblo put Hyacinth Zephyr Peachtree into a mood. He and Carlotta Krafft-Ebing rode for hours without speaking to each other. Behind them, Concorde, Hercules, and Pontius rode the second wagon. They had ceased objecting to Peachtree's pellmell speed; they all wanted to put leagues between themselves and the howling residents of Pueblo.

They passed through open arid country marked by distant buttes and conical mounds. Far ahead lay a pair of snowy peaks. Hyacinth looked in vain for simples but the dry land didn't yield anything he knew.

He wanted more jimson or henbane. The more he thought about Nepenthe, the more he thought he had a bonanza. Why, it couldn't miss. A familiar name rising out of the mists of history, a promise of sweet things, and some powerful ingredients would be irresistible to suffering people everywhere. But where, in October, would he find the leaf and seed of the jimson weed, or the rare henbane?

He would hunt with hawk's eyes. His supply of simples had been reduced to almost nothing. If he intended to bottle his way to the gold fields, he would have to put something fancy in his green empties. He had a whole troupe to support and Pontius to keep supplied.

That had been a scrape in Pueblo. He thought the woman had croaked. She looked comatose. He had been measuring the last yards of his own bolt of life when Concorde finally poked her. Never had he heard a more welcome sound than her groan. The locoweed had felled her. That was a Western simple he knew nothing about. Jimson weed, tobacco, and henbane posed no mysteries to him. But it had always been in him to experiment, to add and subtract, to switch from decoctions to effusions, and from effusions to concentrates or tinctures, seeking the one perky formula that would line up the customers at the back of his lacquered wagon. So he had added more than a tad of the weed.

He merely wanted to give suffering people a sweet little trip out upon the ether and bring them safely home. Let them sample a true and virtuous Nepenthe, and they'd clamor for more. Nepenthe! Better than gold.

They pushed ever southward under gloomy autumnal skies, although the temperatures remained mild. The creeks were well spaced for travel, and the troupe rarely lacked water even in a dry land. The wagon wheels squeaked on dry axles. The mules looked worse than ever and he knew he should stop and let them recruit. Ahead somewhere lay the Santa Fe Trail, Raton Pass, and days of heavy mountain travel that would kill his team unless he let up. But somehow he couldn't: he pressed recklessly onward, ignoring the baleful glares of Concorde and Hercules.

Even the voluble Carlotta had scarcely said a word since fleeing Pueblo. She had not quit the troupe for days. He had not rehired her for a week. He suspected she had given her favors to some mountaineer, or maybe he had simply taken them with or without her lower-register adagios. Whatever the case, her secrets remained locked within her.

She did sigh now and then, and several times she gazed at gray horizons and opined that it was a wild land, so unlike the barbarous East where everything was too polite and people were too considerate. Hyacinth choked down the worm of envy that kept crawling up his throat. Had she preferred some mountain brute to his own civilized, polished self? Impossible. But nothing sensible ever came from opera divas.

He thought he ought to fire her in Sante Fe and hire the Skyes. Mary Skye would be a sensation onstage, and the real article too. It wouldn't matter what she said; all she had to do was stand there and look gorgeous. Oh, it would be delicious to fire Carlotta Krafft-Ebing for good. She would erupt like a Vesuvius. She had always thought she was too good for a medicine act, and that would make it all the more fun.

"You ought to quit. You're a famous opera star, too good for us," he said.

"Darlink, as soon as I get somewhere I quit. I was not made for this unworthy life. Maybe soon they will be applaudink and throwink snapdragons at my feet."

"You could quit now. I'll stop. Castor and Pollux are about done in anyway. They could lunch on some grass while we get your trunk out."

"Don't tempt me, darlink. You think I am maybe your captive? I'm goink to show you what I am. I am a wild savage. I will make the Indians look civilized. I will sing to the trees and the grasses."

"You're a romantic."

"I am gifted woman. You won't have me forever. You couldn't pay me enough to keep me. I make savages put down their lances and weep."

"I think you made that big oaf in Pueblo raise his lance."

"You are vulgar. It shows what a swine you are, darlink. If you talk like that I will quit for good."

"I think you made him your one hundred fifty-ninth conquest, and he didn't enjoy it."

"I quit."

Hyacinth reined the mules to a halt. They took no persuading and stood with heads lowered, their breathing heavy.

"You resting, boss?" yelled Concorde.

"No, Carlotta quit. We have to get her trunk out."

"Yassuh," Concorde yelled. He jumped to the clay and began untying the grommeted canvas cover.

"You wouldn't dare."

"I just did. I can't afford you anymore, sweetheart."

"I will complain to authorities."

"You never stopped."

"I will have you arrested."

"Fine, there's a constable around here somewhere."

Behind them, Concorde and Hercules lifted her black steamer trunk off the wagon and gently set it on the naked earth between the ruts of the trail. It sat there reproachfully, an abandoned box of comforts.

Concorde was grinning like a lynx. Hercules chewed on a stem of grass and looked at distant horizons.

"Oh true apothecary! Thy drugs are quick," said Pontius. "The Bard, of course."

"How did this happen?" Concorde asked.

"Rare opportunity," Hyacinth said. "We had a swift meeting of the minds. I thought she should, and she thought so too."

"I will get succor from the savages."

"That sounds like a fine idea. Try the Comanches first."

"You owe me money, darlink."

"I'll leave some in Santa Fe."

"I want two fleece right now."

Hyacinth thought that was amazingly cheap, all things considered. He nodded. Moments later, Carlotta clutched two of the soft, thick fleeces to her heaving bosom.

"You can take me to Santa Fe; then I quit forever. I never

say the name Peachtree again. I will forget the name. You are dead in my memory."

Peachtree shook his head. "No, by my count you've quit a hundred nineteen times since Missouri. That's the Pikes Peak of quitting. I'm not taking you to Santa Fe."

"I will wait for Skyes. They are not civilized and corrupt like you. They have savage virtues."

Peachtree laughed. "Come join me, Pontius. I lack company."

Parsons doddered to the seat beside Hyacinth. "You gonna gimme a sip now?" he whispered.

"Not for a while, my fine friend."

"Glad to git rid o' that titillator. She thought she should have top billing. The very idea offends my dignity."

"You're the most valuable man I have, Pontius. I can do without the Potawatomi Princess, but I can't do without the True Thespian."

"I like compliments but they never go far enough," Parsons said. "All compliments are inherently flawed."

Hyacinth cracked the lines over the croups of the weary mules, and they lumbered heavily southward. Behind him he heard Concorde cracking his whip.

"I will see you in Sacramento," screeched Carlotta.

"You quit, sweetheart."

"You really gonna doodle her this time, Hyacinth?"

"Absolutely. She's unbearable."

Peachtree turned to see what the Potawatomi Princess would do. She stood there warbling, her tune running from contralto ranges to screeching. It reminded him of steam calliopes.

"Feels better already," he said.

"Why, bless me, it does, Professor. I could never abide women who wanted top billing. You going to give me some Nepenthe now?"

"Oh, not for a while. My simples are nigh used up."

"Well, you get some together mighty quick, or I'll quit too. Then where'll you be, medicine man?"

"With two less mouths to feed, Parsons."

"I knew spear-carriers who had larger brains than you, Hyacinth."

Peachtree sighed. Being a student of experimental medicine always seemed to invite insults from those with less vision.

That evening they camped on a stream the omniscient Concorde called the Huerfano, and Carlotta didn't show up.

Chapter 34

Carlotta watched the wagons shrink to dots and vanish. A chill dry wind plucked at her coat. A deep silence enshrouded her. She stood upon a clear trail, marked by the scraping of lodgepoles and travois. It was not a white man's road. Open prairie stretched in all directions, with grasses so thin that the earth seemed naked. Patches of sagebrush silvered the gentle inclines. On the horizons, she saw buttes and hazy mountains. She was far from help.

She sat on her leather trunk wondering what to do. It would be a two-day walk back to Pueblo. Ahead somewhere lay the Santa Fe Trail. Peachtree had been wicked. He had goaded her into quitting. He knew how to rile her any time he chose, making her jump like a marionette on a string. She could not imagine an act more callous and cruel than depositing her in this wasteland. Soon she would thirst; then she would starve. What sort of beast was he? She hated him.

She knew he was counting on the Skyes to come along and rescue her. They couldn't be far behind; a day or two, dawdling at their own speed. But how long? By this evening she would be ravenous. By tomorrow she would be perishing of thirst. What if they were late?

Nothing stirred. She saw not even a bird soaring through the silent heavens. The thin October light warmed her a little, but this night would be cold and mean. She hugged the two fleeces gratefully. If the weather held, she would at least not freeze to death. She eyed the large trunk, wondering how to hide it. She could not drag it far. But at least it contained some clothing and spare shoes. She opened it and rummaged for useful things. If she was going to walk to Pueblo, she would need clothes. But she found little of use: an ostrich-plumed hat, a shawl, spangled dresses, some toiletries, combs and powders, lisle stockings. She selected carefully, knowing that weight would slow her, and then closed the trunk. She doubted she would see it again.

That beast! He was sitting on his wagon, no doubt amused. She would come along with the Skyes a few days behind and he would hire her again. Oh, that's what he had in mind, all right. But she would fool him. Nothing on earth would induce her to join that miserable, poverty-stricken quack show again. She would sing where she was loved and admired, and not with some gypsy caravan. They were all scum.

She sat on her trunk changing shoes. She hated practical shoes. Comfortable, ungainly shoes did nothing for her big feet, so she wore the tightest little slippers she could squeeze her feet into in spite of the corns. She didn't have much to walk in, and regretted her vanity. She would have to walk a long way for two days. But at least she did have one pair of winter shoes, high, white, and pinched, with raised heels to give her a spare inch of height.

She stood on these, feeling the pain in her feet, and gathered her nerve to leave her vulnerable wardrobe to the mercies of this wild universe. Standing there, she spied two horsemen. They weren't following the trail, but riding toward it from the east, apparently heading into the western moun-

tains. Succor! She sat down on the trunk and waited for the
distant dots to grow into something larger. They spotted her
and rode easily toward her. She realized that they were Indians, and that the ponies they rode were lithe little mustangs.

Good! These simple souls, uncorrupted by the vices of the
civilized world and filled with childlike decency, would help
a lady in distress. She refused to let herself doubt that; all the
best philosophers of Europe had noted the innocence of these
North American natives who had never tasted the lies and vi-
ciousness of Christian Civilization.

She stood and waved, welcoming them as they rode down
upon her. At last they sat their ponies before her, studying her
from expressionless black eyes. Then they surveyed the surrounding country, looking for those who left her there.

"I'm alone," she said. "Those beasts left me, and besides
I quit."

These two were the color of copper, short and thick. They
wore breechclouts and leggins with elaborate fringes, but
their chests remained bare. Even their moccasins trailed
fringes off the heel. She admired them. These swart and powerful men would comfort her. Their raptor gazes reminded her
of eagles, and it delighted her. These were lords of the southern Plains, radiating power and kindness and innate virtue.

"Ah, darlinks, I'm so glad you've come," she said, smiling
gaily. "I don't know the finger signs but I want to go to Santa
Fe. You are so good to rescue me from those beasts!" She
waved a languid white hand southward.

"I sing opera, you know. I am the best contralto in the
world, but I have bad times now."

They seemed perfectly harmless. Each carried a quiver and
bowcase over his back, a sheathed knife at his belt, and a
stone-headed club of some sort dangling from his waist. Both
wore their straight blue-black hair loose and long, but one
had pinioned it under a headband of red cloth. She saw no
ensigns of office; no feathers, no war paint. But both horses

had been painted. One little gray had black handprints on its croup. The other, a dun, had black stripes on its withers.

One spoke something to the other and slid easily off his horse, which stood perfectly still. Why, the pony had manners, unlike that monstrous horse of Skye's. The warrior was bandylegged and scarcely taller than she. He was obviously the elder of the two, with a few strands of gray salting his hair. He approached, stared, and then cuffed her head hard enough to hurt.

"Why did you do that?" she asked, offended.

He didn't reply. He opened the trunk and pawed through it, throwing dresses and skirts and linens onto the clay. He spotted the picture hat with the peach ostrich plume and exclaimed. He ran his fingers softly over the plume, obviously amazed by it. Then he put it on his head.

"Darlink, you look beautiful," she said. Then she giggled. He stared at her with unkind eyes. "But darlink, it's for women. Now be good and put it back."

But he didn't. He settled it on his black hair and tied the hatstrings under his chin. The peachy plume horsetailed out behind him.

The other gentleman eyed the trail warily, studying its empty reaches north and south, as the gentleman on the ground continued to ransack her wardrobe. He found an ivory comb and hand mirror much to his liking, and examined himself solemnly in the mirror. Then he handed up various items to the one who sat his pony, who stuffed them into a sack of some sort that lay behind his saddle seat.

Then the one on the ground examined her again, and barked some command she didn't understand.

"Do you speak Spanish, my dear?" she asked. *"Español?"*

That got no response either. She had thought maybe these southern Plains fellows might understand the barbaric tongue of Seville.

"Santa Fe?" she said, pointing south.

This time the older one paused intently. But then he returned to his pillaging. He jammed virtually everything that remained into a bundle made of a crinoline petticoat, and tied it together. This he anchored behind his rawhide saddle while his ungroomed pony sidestepped.

He pointed at her white shoes and said something. She hadn't the faintest idea what he was requiring.

He growled at her and pointed again. Why, he wanted to examine her shoes. They were splendid Parisian ones made of softest kid. "You have good taste, darlink," she said. She smiled, settled herself on the trunk, and began working her laces until she could pull them off. Then she handed them to him. He studied the shoes, grunted, and pitched them into the grass.

Then he commanded something. She hadn't the faintest idea what. He grew agitated. She stood. He clasped her wrist and pulled her violently. She scarcely knew what to do. He got a braided rawhide rope from his pony and dropped its noose over her neck. It had some sort of slipknot.

"But darlink—" She tried to lift the noose off but he batted her hands away. With a thong he tied her hands behind her.

"But you don't need to—I'm your friend!" she said. *"Amiga!"*

He ignored her, clambered into his saddle still holding the other end of the braided rope, and kicked his horse.

A terrible, strangling jolt yanked her forward. She could barely breathe; she couldn't claw at the noose with her hands to get air.

"But darlinks," she whimpered.

He set his pony into a smart jog, and she staggered behind. In seconds, she had bloodied her bare feet in prickly pear, then on a rock, until each step seared her feet. Even when she trotted, she couldn't keep up, and every time she staggered, the noose clamped tighter.

"But I'm your friend," she cried into the nothingness.

Chapter 35

Carlotta Krafft-Ebing trotted for her life. Her legs ached but she made them pump onward. Her feet radiated pain up her legs and bled into the sand, but she ignored the white-hot hurt. She lacked balance because her hands were bound behind her, but she dared not stumble; the noose would tear her head off. Her lungs pumped air desperately; her shoulders ached. She saw her captors only in a blur.

She would die. She refused to die. But she was coming to the absolute end of her strength. When she fell the man would keep on, dragging her by the noose around her neck. She hated him; ruining her vocal cords, wrecking her lungs, destroying an instrument she had spent years perfecting in two academies under the best maestros. She felt a sagging helplessness. She lacked even the strength to shout at them.

They jogged eastward across open grasslands, heading toward a distant gray line that looked to be a creekbed. But she would never get that far. The harder she ran, the farther away it seemed to be. Terror washed through her like acid; and then rage. The beasts! She didn't know what tribe they came from but she cursed it. If these were Comanches, as she suspected, then she would curse Comanches with her last breath.

Her only salvation lay in keeping the braided rope slack. But when she did that, her captor deliberately speeded up. He was killing her and enjoying the sight of her desperation when he occasionally glanced backward with an expressionless gaze.

She spent the last of her strength, and a great temptation washed through her to sit down and let her head be yanked off. But she would try one more thing. She had a weapon after all, in fact four weapons; her teeth, her two feet, and her will. She gathered the last of her energies and burst toward him. She kept on, stumbling forward until she ran beside him. He gazed down upon her serenely. Then she veered to his pony and clamped her teeth on his leggin, staggering as she did, knowing she was falling. With one powerful thrust he kicked her aside and she tumbled to earth, hitting hard because she had no arms to cushion her fall.

She braced for the fatal yank on her neck. Instead, he stopped. She lay too stunned to do anything but stare up at him as he loomed over her. Then she mustered some final strength and kicked with her bare feet; a harmless blow, but at least a blow.

"You are a beast," she said.

He had that stone club in hand and she knew he would split her head in two. But he didn't. He bantered in some strange tongue to the other one. Then he bent over her and loosened the taut noose that half-choked her. She gulped air and summoned saliva from her parched throat. She spat. It hit his face. Slowly he wiped it off and eyed her. She spat again, missing.

The two warriors talked.

"Barbarians," she gasped between gulps of air. "You have no decency. You don't know how to treat another person. I curse you all; I bring the wrath of God down upon you. I tell you, you're not fit to walk the earth."

It poured out of her like lava. She tried to kick him again but he just eyed her calmly, as if she were a bug.

"I am a person too. I am a woman. I make friends but you do this. I want respect. We have laws for people like you. We try you in courts. We put you in dungeons."

He kicked her. She felt the blunt toe of his moccasin thump her ribs. It hurt. She screamed, demented. She tugged her arms, but the bindings bit into her wrists. She wanted to scratch his eyes out, and couldn't. Finally her weariness overpowered her, and she lay inert, too tired and hurt to care.

They talked.

Then her captor, still wearing her ostrich-feathered hat, lifted her easily and settled her into his saddle, hiking her skirts so she could sit. Her white thighs intrigued him. He ran a hand over her pale flesh but she didn't care. She slumped in the rawhide seat, her feet dripping blood into the stirrups.

He led her toward her fate. She felt a little calmer on the pony although she was so dizzy she could barely sit upright. Her heart slowed. Thirst devoured her; she was frantic with need to gulp cool water. Surely when they reached that distant line of leafless trees they would let her drink.

They plodded quietly through a solemn, sunny afternoon, and in a bit she recovered her senses enough to ponder her fate. She knew almost nothing of the Comanches—if that's what these warriors were—but the others had said that they would be found south of the Arkansas River. She ransacked her memories for what she did know, and the prospects were not heartening. They might torture her and eventually kill her. They might make her a captive and treat her terribly. Or they might sell her to Mexicans as a slave for some plantation there.

Concorde had told hair-raising tales about the Comanches' prowess at torturing. They were skilled at keeping a victim alive long after the victim wished he were dead. And the Co-

manche women were even more fiendish than the men. . . .
But what did Concorde know? He couldn't even read. And he
had lived out his days in New Orleans. How could a darkie
know anything? Still, the prospect of such a slow, maddening
death haunted her.

She studied her captors for the first time. She could see
only the back of the one who led her horse, but it was the
muscular back of a powerful man. He padded ahead of her
easily, obviously capable of trotting for long stretches. The
other, riding beside her, was younger, maybe thirty though it
was hard to tell. He had a wide face and wide nose; a keen
squint under beetling brows. From time to time he eyed her
with his soft brown eyes, his gaze as inscrutable as the other's. She could not fathom from their faces what either of
them had in mind. She desperately wished they could speak
Spanish. Everything she said was nothing but the sighing
west wind to them.

Could she kill them and escape? She knew the answer to
that. She felt a helplessness she had never felt in the cities of
the East or on the road with Peachtree. She had nowhere to
turn; no constable to go to, no passerby to plead with, no
moral law to appeal to, no religious belief to remind them of,
no rights, no powers. They didn't understand the protections
accorded to womanhood, either. She did not even seem to be
a person to them, someone who could speak, think, love, and
hurt. They were treating her as if she were a captured sheep.

Finally they descended a gentle grade into a shallow bottom filled with leafless trees. She had wondered whether others of these people would be there, but she saw none. She
intuited that these two had traveled far from their band. She
wished she had paid more attention to what Mister Skye had
been teaching them those first days. They halted in a grassy
park beside a thin stream even as the sun was setting.

Now they would be kind to her. Now she would have water. They would give her something warm to sleep on. At
least they would give her the fleeces. She sat on one; the

younger warrior sat on the other. The older one motioned her down. She dreaded to step down because her bleeding feet would scream again. She smiled, and waggled her bound wrists behind her to let him know he must help her.

He yanked and she tumbled off, hitting the dry grasses hard. The jolt shot pain up her shoulder. Why didn't they treat her decently? Is this how they treated their own women? She swung up, and then stumbled to her feet, which was difficult without the use of her arms. It would be just as hard to drink but she would manage it.

"You could let me wash now," she said.

But they were tending their ponies.

She stepped gingerly toward the murky river, rejoicing to end her parched desperation. She reached the gravelly bank and lowered herself to her knees, wondering just how to manage this. The water laughed and burbled and invited. But a man's hand slid around her bosom and dragged her bodily back from the river.

"Water!" she screamed. *"Agua!"*

Burly arms and hands as hard as stone lifted her body and dragged her toward a rough-barked tree. There at last he undid her wrists. She rejoiced at the freedom given her arms, but then he yanked them behind the small trunk and tied her wrists tightly again. Her hands tingled with life a moment and then vanished from her senses. She slumped into the tree, her freedom gone and her life ebbing away. The act of keeping her from water stole her spirit from her. She sagged until her lashing held her up, too weary to care about the renewed pain.

She slid into a world beyond her grasp. She knew the warriors drank and washed themselves, then talked quietly. But theirs was a separate world. Her world had reduced to pain and thirst and confusion.

The twilight matched her own twilight. The men built no fire, but chewed on something they had taken from their saddle kits. Darkness settled, and with it their renewed interest in her.

She felt their hands probe her and touch her familiarly. Then one of them unbound her wrists. She could not support herself and fell into the tree roots. They knelt over her, tugging at her clothing; her coat, her skirt, her petticoat, her drawers and chemise, until the cold autumnal breezes bit her vulnerable flesh. She supposed they would take her, but she had drifted into a fog so thick that it didn't matter. She hoped it would soon be over.

But it wasn't.

Chapter 36

Victoria sat her little mare, staring at an empty leather trunk that lay in the middle of the lodgetrail. It was unfamiliar to her, but the two white shoes lying nearby she knew. She squinted carefully at horizons, looking for the faintest clue, and saw none. Then, cursing softly, she slid off her pony and stood, trying to read tracks before she walked over them.

She couldn't read the sign. The hardpan there bore little witness. She discerned the familiar tracks of iron wagon wheels. She found a few faint mule prints in the dust, their elongated hooves different from the circular hoofprints of horses. But in this windswept spot not enough dust clung to the hardpan to tell a story. This could mean nothing more than some argument. But that isn't what she felt within herself. She always respected her hunches. Her suspicions were screaming at her now.

Carefully she walked a loop around this place, making sure her own Crow moccasins landed on nothing. To the east, in softer ground, she found the prints of two unshod ponies heading west; and nearby, the same prints heading east. Two riders had come here and left. Their unshod ponies suggested they would be one or another of the Peoples. She followed the prints eastward until she found the thing she feared to find—the barefoot prints of a not-large person. She followed them a while more, and read hurry in them. Then she found small brown blood spots on the clay beyond a prickly pear. She followed a while, finding more blood, and places where the barefoot person had staggered.

The Potawatomi Princess had been left here—probably she had quit once again—and had been picked up and taken away. Victoria grunted. Maybe the damn fool woman deserved her fate. But if her fate was captivity or torture in the hands of the Comanches it would be a fate that no person deserved.

She had learned that from Mister Skye. Like all the Plains people, her Absaroka had considered themselves the Real People, and the other tribes inferior. Mister Skye, with his white man's views, had told her that all the Peoples had the same right to subsist. She had acknowledged it grudgingly, especially when white men themselves treated the red people as if they had no rights at all. But as much as she begrudged the ideal, she admitted it was a good Way.

She needed a moccasin print to tell her the rest, and knew she wouldn't find it on this bloody path marked by hoofprints and a barefoot captive. She returned to the trunk and studied the barren clay around it until she discerned a single print, barely visible in the thinnest skim of dust. But it was all she needed: the print revealed a soled blunt-toed moccasin with fringes trailing off its heel. The news couldn't be worse for the Potawatomi Princess.

She climbed onto her little mare again and turned it back toward Mister Skye and Mary and the travois, not far behind her. She rode to a hilltop where she could see them toiling along, and also study the entire country. She waited there, absorbing the silent vastnesses, quite certain she was alone.

She waited until Mary spotted her. Mister Skye still clutched his jug and was worth nothing now. Then Victoria wheeled her pony back to the trunk and the white shoes. In a while Mary and Carmody joined her and eyed the debris while Mister Skye lifted his jug to his flushed face, oblivious of the world.

"Damn Comanches," she said.

"What happened? What is this?" Carmody asked.

"Fringed heel. Two ponies. They dragged her barefoot. She started bleeding over that way." She pointed.

"Who?" asked Carmody.

"Carlotta. They'll use her. Torture her to death," Mister Skye said, a sudden sobriety in his slurred voice.

"Carlotta? Comanches have Carlotta?" Carmody asked.

"Damned no-good bastards," Victoria said.

"How long ago?" Mister Skye asked.

She shrugged. "I can't tell; no dust here. But she'll not last the night."

He lifted his topper and screwed it down, canting it against the wind. "We'll go get her," he mumbled.

"You ain't going nowhere. You'll get yourself killed. I'm going myself."

A gray line of leafless trees melted into the haze about half a day's ride to the east. That's where she had to ride.

"I'll go," Mister Skye said. "Keep an eye on things." He meant Carmody.

"You're not going, dammit. You're not even all here. Go suck your jug."

He smiled wryly. "I'll go."

"I'm not gonna take care of you, fight off two Comanches, and keep them from killing the white woman."

"I'll help," Carmody said.

"No, dammit! You and Mary take him and Jawbone over

there." She pointed to a slope of junipers to the south. "Wait for me there."

"I'll come, Victoria," Mary said.

"No! You take care of the boy."

"I'm coming," Mister Skye said. He leered at her.

"You get the hell outa here," Victoria said. But she knew he was going to come and get himself killed.

Mister Skye sighed and scratched his ear. At least he didn't suck any more from that sinister gray crock. He handed the jug to Mary and belched. Then he withdrew his Hawken and checked the cap. He pulled his old dragoon revolver and examined each nipple. He slipped out his throwing knife and slid it into a special sheath dangling down his back. "Let's get her," Mister Skye said. He belched again, and yawned. "We'll fetch ol' Carlotta."

His drunken resolution worried her. "Damn you," she cried.

Mister Skye avalanched off of Jawbone and staggered. But he lifted the trunk and anchored it onto a travois.

"You're not fit to help, Skye," Carmody said.

"Just stick with Mary," Mister Skye replied. "She'll take you to that timber. Wait for us there. We won't be back until after dark."

"But, sir, you're not fit—"

Mister Skye stared at him. "Two Comanches picked up Miss Krafft-Ebing. She won't live the night unless we get her."

"You don't know that for sure."

"No, we don't, Mister Carmody. But my woman is the best tracker I've ever known."

"Why, I see nothing at all."

"Go to hell," Victoria said to him. She nodded to Mister Skye, surrendering at last. "Git your drunken ass on Jawbone."

"Wait—what'll you do?" Carmody asked.

Skye replied in measured words. "Whatever we must do."

"But she made her own choices. I admire your charity but you have no obligation. Obviously this is a dangerous thing."

Mister Skye sighed. "Stay with Mary," he muttered.

"Mister Skye," said Mary. He turned, and she leaned over her mare and touched his cheek. He clasped her small hand quietly. Then she nodded to Carmody.

Mister Skye and Victoria rode hard, following the trail while they had daylight, fearing they would run out of light before they reached that line of trees. They put their horses in an easy canter, punctuated by restful walks. She could see the increasing patches of blood.

Then suddenly the bloody barefoot prints stopped in a jumble of moccasin prints and disturbed ground. After that the Comanche had led the horse that carried Carlotta. She lived.

The gray row of trees loomed larger and larger, and suddenly Victoria wanted dusk to hide her. The first thing the Comanches would do, when attacked, would be to kill the white woman. She paused to let Mister Skye catch up and eyed him covertly. The ride had sobered him some.

"If we follow them damn prints, they'll see us and kill her," she said.

He nodded. She swung north, taking advantage of a slight swell of land to help hide their passage from eyes in that strip of brush. They rode quietly, letting the evening thicken before turning eastward again. Jawbone seemed charged with energy, but her little mare had wearied from the extra toil this day. Both horses sensed water ahead and pressed eagerly toward it.

Maybe there would be more than two. She could deal with one or two if she could surprise them. But she would have to look after that drunken bum too. The knowledge lay like lead in her.

Comanches could saddle the whirlwind, shoot accurately from under the necks of their ponies while concealing themselves from enemy bullets, get more out of their ponies than any other tribe. From childhood onward, they lived in their saddles until each Comanche had become one with his horses.

Victoria felt the familiar chill of death race through her thin frame. She eyed her man, loving him, glad that he was a caring man who would try to rescue this foolish woman. But he was drunk.

They struck the creek well north of the trail by her reckoning, and moved softly along it. She feared the horses would scent each other and whinny their welcomes. The wind was behind them, carrying their scent forward, which was very bad.

They eased ahead in that bleak dust that muddied the world just before blackness, and paused suddenly. A shriek rose from the gloom ahead. It set teeth on edge and started her pulse racing. The woman! The shriek rose higher and higher, never subsiding.

She nocked an arrow with a three-inch metal point set loosely in the haft so that it would remain buried in an enemy when he tried to pull it out. The screaming and sobs of the woman somewhere ahead raked the darkness with red. She, and they, were running out of time.

Chapter 37

A horse nickered. Jawbone replied. Victoria's mare whickered greetings. An arrow whipped in, yanking Skye's top hat from his head. Another hissed by as he dove off Jawbone. From somewhere in the dark he heard Victoria cursing.

Skye hit the earth hard, jamming pain up his shoulder. Jawbone screeched and wheeled away. Skye dizzily tried to rise, but the booze stupefied him. Victoria had been right. He would get himself killed. Something loomed against the starlight filtering through the branches. He rolled. An ax stabbed the ground like the devil's pitchfork.

A heavy warrior landed on Skye, his knife arm rising high and then plunging down. Skye gasped, rolled, and felt the knife sear his ribs, cutting through his buckskin shirt. The knife rose again. Skye bucked, loosening the man above him; rolled as the knife landed. Skye heard quiet breathing. The warrior wasn't even exerting himself. Skye's boozy sweat burst from every pore. He was fighting by instinct, not skill.

The warrior crushed Skye and chopped down with his

knife. Skye caught the wrist, deflecting the blow from his
heart. The edge burned along his neck. The warrior yanked,
but Skye held on. The warrior plunged and bit Skye's hand.
Skye screamed. His mauled hand released the warrior's wrist.
The warrior's other fist smacked Skye's jaw, knocking him
back, while the knife arm cocked. Skye felt himself sliding
into oblivion. He kneed upward as his senses left him. The
warrior grunted. Skye didn't know what happened next. The
blade seared his arm and his cheek, and he felt his own hot
blood.

He heard a woman's scream. He wished he weren't so
drunk. It was too late. He writhed under the warrior. The man
had lost his knife. He was trying to strangle Skye. The Comanche's iron hands clamped Skye's windpipe and squeezed
life out of him. Skye gasped. He heard a shriek and a heavy
thump. Above him, the warrior bucked and shivered, and
slumped.

Jawbone screeched in Skye's ear.

Skye lay on his back, sobbing the whiskey out of his eyes.
Jawbone snorted. The body atop Skye quivered and then lay
inert. Skye felt more blood, but not his own.

He lay panting, his senses awhirl, unable to move. Jawbone pushed his ugly nose under Skye and rolled him. The
warrior slid off. Skye breathed, his windpipe hot, his neck
hurting where fingers had clamped it. Blood leaked from razored flesh.

He heard snarling. Victoria. He sat up, shook himself like
a downed boxer, and listened. Jawbone screeched. Skye rose,
trying to fathom where he was and where Victoria was. He
staggered toward noise. He heard hard thumps and Victoria's
desperate sobs. Someone was killing her. He plunged through
crackling brush, feeling branches whip his face. He sounded
like an elephant. He landed on some hulking form and
pushed. Victoria lay underneath, gasping. Skye raised a massive fist and clobbered the scrambling warrior. He was re-

warded with a whoof of air, and gasping. Jawbone thundered through the brush, clacking his teeth, berserk.

"I gonna get his scalp," Victoria muttered.

But the warrior bolted. Jawbone reared up and plunged after him. Skye peered about keenly, seeing nothing. He couldn't see his own nose, and his eyes were blurred anyway.

"Victoria," he muttered.

"Damn you," she cried. "Drunken bum."

He didn't know what that meant. Probably she was dying. But he saw her crawl to her feet.

"Why aren't you helping the woman?"

Skye shook his head. He had forgotten Carlotta. He had gone to war stinking and stupid.

He heard the sound of a running horse. The other warrior was getting away. A pony whickered. It didn't sound like Victoria's little mare.

"You all right?" Skye asked between gulps of air.

"You sit. I'm gonna take care of her," Victoria said, wiping her tears away.

She was all right. He stood shakily, his body bleeding and hurting. He walked on trembling legs back to where he thought he had fought the warrior. He stumbled over the body. He knelt for a closer look. Jawbone had kicked in his head. He heard wild sobbing nearby, but it wasn't Victoria's voice. Carlotta lived—but in what condition? It didn't take much Comanche toying to drive a victim mad.

Jawbone materialized out of the night like some prehistoric monster, crashed through the brush, stopped before Skye, smelled Skye's breath and then butted his head into Skye's chest. Skye stood, dizzy, and ran a hurting hand along Jawbone's neck. The horse nickered, then vanished into the blackness. When he returned he bore Skye's hat in his teeth. Skye felt the brim strike his hand, and took it from Jawbone. An arrow dangled from it. He yanked it out and settled the hat over his aching skull.

The horse wheeled and vanished again, and Skye heard

whinnying. Skye recovered his wits enough to go help Victoria. He wove through branches that lashed his face, not knowing where to look, and burst into a grassy spot beside the creek. In the bleak and murky starlight he saw a white form, Carlotta, naked and spread-eagled, her arms and legs anchored to earth with stakes. Carlotta sobbed, and Victoria cursed, a curse so tender and gentle and melancholy that it prickled Skye's hair.

"Get out of here!" Victoria snarled at him as she cut Carlotta's bonds.

Skye stared helplessly. "But—"

"Git out, damn you. This ain't for no man."

Skye reeled backward as if struck by a warclub. He had glimpsed something so terrible in that starlight that he couldn't come to grips with it. He retreated from the agony of Carlotta's sobbing and Victoria's muttering.

He fled to cleaner air, to a place that had never witnessed a thing so foul that it polluted the world around it. He felt his gut churning and his throat starting to burn as convulsions rode up his esophagus. He fell to all fours and loosed the slime that erupted out of him, sour and acid, into the prickly grass. It erupted again, the fruits of his drinking and bile and terror, fouling the earth. Then, when his gut had quit spasming, he wiped his mouth and staggered to the creek. He lowered his whole head into it until the water cleaned him, and then drank a little.

Behind him he heard awful sobs, and something more: Victoria's crooning, a kind of cursing so tender that she turned white men's oaths into lullabies. Then Carlotta screamed.

"Almost, almost," Victoria was saying. "I gotta do it. You gonna be okay."

"No, no, no!" Carlotta whispered between broken sobs.

"Just one more," Victoria said softly.

Skye couldn't stand it. He wanted to be out upon the clean grass, not in this brush and terror-choked bottom.

Carlotta screamed and broke into wild sobs again.

"Dammit dammit dammit," Victoria was muttering.

Then silence. He thought Carlotta might be dead.

"You bleeding some," Victoria said. "Not too bad. Lie quiet."

Silence again. Skye fought his impulse to get help, go look, go kneel before her and sob. Victoria hastened past him to the creek, dipped something into it, and hurried past bearing a wet cloth.

"Go git the horses, you big drunk. Go watch out for trouble. Maybe that one come back. You lose your mind?"

"Is Carlotta—"

"How should I know. She hurt plenty. All torn up."

"I mean what—"

"Big stick, chopped to a point. Comanches! I'm gonna scalp them bastards. I never seen this."

Skye had heard of this and worse. The Comanches were the worst torturers the world had ever known, a terror to red men and whites from time immemorial. The Comanches were kinder to dogs than to strangers. Because of the Comanches, every wise traveler on the southern Plains saved a loaded barrel for himself.

He struggled out of the bottoms and found Jawbone silhouetted by the night sky, along with Victoria's mare and another horse. The dead man's pony. Skye wanted it. They would need it. Rig up a litter to carry Carlotta back. He approached the Comanche pony, but it reared back. Jawbone snarled and the pony stopped dead. Skye found a dragging picket line and took it.

Skye waited, helpless against a woman's special hell. He felt the cool night breezes dry his sweat, and felt his sodden brain throw off the last of the whiskey. He didn't know why he drank. He simply couldn't stop at times. He had survived this one. Someday he wouldn't.

Victoria materialized beside him. Skye suddenly felt awash with guilt, not just for his drinking but for all of the cruelty that men had ever visited upon women. "Victoria—I'm sorry," he whispered. "How—is she?"

"Bad."

"Can we move her?"

"How should I know?" she said. She found him and drew her arms around him and wept into his chest, her tears mingled with his sweat and blood. "How should I know?" she demanded.

His Crow wife returned to Carlotta again and Skye waited a long time. Then at last she came to him. "All right," she said. "She's dressed. We'll ride."

"Dressed? She can ride?"

"I'm gonna sit her sideways in my saddle and lead her."

"Is she bleeding? Will she make it?"

"She'll make it. Them skunks just got started."

A load lifted from Skye.

"You ride ahead. She don't want no man looking at her," Victoria said.

Skye nodded. He checked his kit. Everything was together; his Hawken in its sheath, his revolver at his waist, his knife back at his belt. He clambered clumsily into the saddle while Jawbone sidestepped, and hung on dizzily, feeling the caked blood on his body. His sliced flesh tortured him. He grabbed the broken picket string of the Comanche pony, and led it away in clean sagebrush-scented air.

At some distance he turned back to look. The moon had risen, whitening the land with floury light. He saw Victoria help Carlotta up and settle her sideways on Victoria's mare. Then he saw his woman clasp Carlotta's hands between her brown ones for a long moment. Victoria let go, took up the rein of her little mare, and led the burdened horse toward Skye. Something in the scene reminded him of an engraving he had seen as a boy, in which the pregnant Virgin was being softly led, sitting sideways on an ass, into Bethlehem.

Chapter 38

Elisha Carmody waited impatiently through the night. Mary had led him into some juniper that choked a dry watercourse, and there they settled. She disappeared a while at dusk and then he saw her far off, walking a great circle to satisfy herself that nothing would harm them. Then she and her infant retired behind a screen of black branches, leaving Carmody alone with his somber thoughts.

He spread his bedroll but slept only fitfully, wondering where Skye and Victoria were, and whether they had caught up with the Comanches and Carlotta Krafft-Ebing.

He watched the Big Dipper rotate around the North Star until at last he heard the soft clop of horses. Mary hastened through the night to guide her family in. Carmody laced up his boots.

They rode quietly into view, ghostly in the light of a horned moon, Skye, Victoria, and the opera singer sitting sideways on a strange pony. They got her! Skye turned Jawbone loose. Wordlessly Mary gathered the rein of the captured pony and led Carlotta away from him. Something in that disturbed him; he couldn't quite fathom what was happening.

Victoria slid off her mare. "Go away," she said to him.

"I—what—"

"Go away."

Skye intervened. "Come along, mate. We'll talk."

Carmody walked upslope beside Skye.

"I don't understand any of this, sir," Elisha said. "Have I given offense?"

"No, of course not. This is woman business, that's all. Miss Krafft-Ebing was . . . hurt."

Carmody began to grasp something in this. "She was tortured?"

"Yes. Two bloody Comanche," Skye said. "Jawbone killed one that almost got me. I got sliced up bad. Look at this." He pulled his topper off and waggled a finger through a fresh hole. "Shouldn't make war when I'm not fit," he said.

"You came close."

"I'm lucky."

"Were there more around?"

"No, just two. Comanches come in any number. Bands run from one family to big bunches."

"What about Miss Krafft-Ebing?"

Skye didn't say anything for a while, and Carmody concluded that the guide didn't want to talk. "They tortured her."

"Good lord."

"We got there before—the worst."

"Will she be all right?"

Skye sighed. "You and I may never know. Maybe Victoria'll tell me. I don't know. Victoria cleaned her up and got her here. It's not our business, Carmody."

"No, it isn't. Morbid curiosity, I confess. Why, why, would human beings do that to others?"

Skye lifted his topper, and studied the moonlit slopes. "Comanche aren't like other tribes. Less ceremony. Fewer rules.

Fewer dances. Less religion. Not so many big-medicine stories. They're cut pretty close to nature, I take it: few customs, fewer restraints. All outsiders are enemies. But that doesn't answer you, does it. For them, the rest of us aren't people. I don't know, Elisha. Maybe we're going to find out. In this country save a load for yourself."

Carmody felt a chill. "They would torture me?"

"Worse than her. Maybe a pole up your gut clear to your neck. Or bury you to your chin, facing the sun, your eyelids sewn open. That's a favorite. Or stake you over a hill of fire ants, which eat out your lungs and crawl up your nose while you live. That's another favorite. Then there's chopping fingers off joint by joint. Stripping your flesh off. Burning you with brands. Cutting off your privates. Oh, they have their ways."

"How do you know that? You've lived in the North."

"I've been here two, three times. Border men trade information. Got a lot of mine from Kit Carson, William Bent, old Bill Williams, Ceran St. Vrain—lots of others. When they tell you to watch out, they mean *watch out*."

"I believe you, sir."

"One thing more, Carmody. They're the best horsemen in the world. They got Spanish horses first; a single warrior owns dozens of them, sometimes hundreds. If Comanches on horse find us, say your prayers. They'll outride us every time and have fresh mounts alongside."

A faint indignation built in Carmody. "You could've told us that before we started."

Skye shrugged. "Thought you knew. Everyone knows it."

"Did you ask her why she left Peachtree?"

"Mister Carmody—some things are important and some things aren't."

"Of course, of course. I'm sorry. My philosophy contends with my emotions. My ideals about what makes a sovereign human being tell me she's not blameless. But my pity reaches out to her."

The moonlight caught Skye's face, and his flinty stare at Carmody wasn't friendly.

Victoria padded up. "All right, dammit," she said.

"Is she comfortable, Mrs. Skye?"

"Keep outa this." She turned to the guide. "We'll go to water. She needs water and sleep."

He nodded and they returned to the horses. Carmody discovered Carlotta mummy-wrapped on a travois, and the captured Comanche pony packing the Skyes' kit. The poor woman seemed asleep. A travois ride would be rougher than horseback but at least Carlotta didn't have to sit.

They drove slowly through the powdery light, the buttes ghostly and the distant mountains sinister. Every step took them deeper into Comancheria. Mary and Victoria rode beside the bitter-burdened travois, while Skye rode just ahead through sharp cold. The Skyes had turned dour, almost hostile to Carmody, as if he were at fault. He had to remind himself that he wasn't; that he was conducting himself as honorably as anyone could.

As night and separation gripped him, his mind turned to Krafft-Ebing's tragedy, carefully fitting it into his beliefs. The episode would illustrate his lectures and he intended to use it. Only strong, sovereign people avoided life's terrible tragedies.

They shuffled through a stillness that clawed at him. But at last Skye slowed Jawbone and fell in beside Carmody. "Few minutes, we'll be on a creek, sir. We'll pull off the trail half a mile or so, and sleep into the day."

"I'm ready for it, Mister Skye."

"It's for her. Don't know how much she can take, but we want to be close to water."

"I've been thinking about it. I don't want you to think me uncharitable or without sympathy. I have utmost pity for the poor woman. But it perfectly illustrates my entire philosophy of human conduct, and I intend to use the episode to illustrate my ideas. It'll surely move my listeners."

Skye didn't reply for a long while. Then, "You've worked it into a bloody accusation."

"Why, I certainly don't accuse her of anything."

"I've a weakness might kill me. Almost did tonight. I'm hurting because of it. I like my jug now and then. And I know I can't change. You could lecture me all the way to hell and I wouldn't change. I just about landed there tonight; bloody Comanche's blade ripped my ribs. I've lost a quart of blood. But that won't change me. She can't change either, Carmody. She's like me. Locked in. You can lecture all you want but we'll never be anything else. I was born the way I am."

"Well, sir, that's not likely. I think any rational man or woman can overcome weakness, especially after hearing my case. There's no such thing as being born to weakness."

"How about forgiveness, mate? I just want that, not perfection. I expect Carlotta wants that too. Just accepting her as she is. Do you accept her as she is? A flawed mortal?"

"Why, I prefer to see what she could be if she were to reform. There's a better world waiting for each of you."

"You don't. You don't accept any of us as we are."

"Mister Skye, I esteem you all. I esteem Miss Krafft-Ebing. I pity her."

"And me."

"Why, yes, I do. I know why you're a border man. Your weakness for spirits imprisons you in this empty, dull wild. Wouldn't you say that's the stark truth?"

"I don't rightly know, Mister Carmody. I only know that none of us—not me, not my ladies, not Peachtree or Parsons or Hercules or Concorde or Carlotta—none of us'll ever measure up."

They reached a steep grade into a creek bottom but Skye turned them to the right, and his wives followed with the horses and travois.

"Mister Skye, I'm not unaware of what's in your thoughts.

Your tone of voice tells me. I fear I've alienated you. Please know that I care deeply about it."

"I know that, mate. You're a man I'd want to stand beside me in trouble. You're a hero of mine."

Elisha Carmody felt a rush of gratitude for Skye's unexpected compliment, and wondered why.

Chapter 39

Hyacinth Z. Peachtree peered exultantly at the mountain branch of the Santa Fe Trail. He could hardly be mistaken. The multiple wagon ruts lay in a trough ten yards wide along the Purgatoire River. Why, travelers would pass here if he waited awhile.

His entourage had reached an ell in the arid mountains, which catapulted upward to the west and south. Ahead of him rose a peculiar flat-topped red mountain dotted with juniper and glossy-leaved shrubs he didn't know. But this was arid country, the home of greasers.

He had come clear down the Rockies on his own, and now this broad trail would take him directly to Santa Fe. He hadn't needed that blamed guide after all. What a waste of coin.

"Well, Concorde, all your worries were for naught," he said.

"You look at them ribby mules lately, Perfessor? You look at them wheels?"

"The wheels?"

"This heah dry climate puckered up the wood so the tires are loose. Some look like they'll roll right off the felloes."

The mules he knew about, and they were worrying him. They required more and more of the lash. But he had paid no attention to the wheels. They were the finest that lucre could buy in Kansas City. He clambered off his seat and examined them one by one. The iron tires were so loose it shocked him. The flanges that held them to the felloes, which composed the wooden wheel rim, barely held the tires in place. It angered him: he had paid a plutocrat's price for these wagons. They had been built of stoutest hickory and ash, dry and well seasoned.

"It's the Western air," Concorde said. "Ah heard it just shrinks 'em down. It's so dry it'll turn spit to powder before it hits the ground."

Peachtree sighed. Bent's fort and a forge lay two or three days to the east by his reckoning. "Can we drive in some shims that'll get us to Santa Fe?" he asked.

"Naw, there's an easier way Ah heard of. We'll just pull these heah wobbledy wheels and soak 'em in the rivah for a day or two and let the wood swell up again. Maybe we'll have to soak 'em again down the road."

"That works?"

"Ah heah tell it does, boss. Ah never tried it though."

Peachtree knew he had no choice. He was in imminent danger of losing his wagons. He looked around for grass and found none. Every blade had been gnawed away by passing outfits. In October there was precious little of it left.

"Find some grass," he said. "It'll recruit the mules."

Concorde studied it. "Ah'll walk yondah up that gulch," he said at last. "We got to pull these big wheels right beside the rivah, which means we gotta stick close. But Ah can take the wore-out mules up them slopes somewhere."

"Well, let's drive a little farther into this corner. It looks like the trail starts climbing over there. We should find a place we can defend, too. There won't be trouble, but who knows?"

They drove the wagons a mile or so westward along the swift little river, and decided to camp in a thicket of cedar close enough to water that they could roll the heavy wheels into it.

"Maybe old Skye'll catch up," Concorde said as he and Hercules began blocking up the wagons.

"That'd be an annoyance," Peachtree said. He was thinking not only about the Skyes, but also about Carlotta. He didn't wish to face her. Second thoughts had gnawed at him, which he relieved by reminding himself she could walk back to Pueblo. Or else the Skyes had picked her up. He had intended to teach her a lesson once and for all, but maybe it had been too much of one.

Concorde led one mule team toward a ravine that looked promising while Hercules jacked up the front of the medicine wagon and slid blocks of pine they carried for just such purposes under the axle until the wheel was free. He had no trouble pulling the small front wheels; the huge rear wheels would be another matter. Peachtree feared he would have to help, although he detested sweat-labor. Old Parsons wouldn't be worth a lick at this.

Hercules pulled the pin and slid a hub off its iron axle. The tire wobbled alarmingly. Peachtree realized they had stopped in the nick of time. The youth carefully rolled the wheel toward the Purgatoire and wrestled it into the water.

"She won't go nowhere," he said. "Not with that iron tire."

"I think it should be tied to shore."

"Well, we'll watch 'er."

Peachtree didn't like to be defied. They all knew he avoided heavy labor, and they took advantage of him.

But the wheel didn't budge. And neither did the seven others. Peachtree stood at the bank for an hour, watching the swift current purl through the spokes, pouring life into the desiccated hickory.

Concorde found upland pasture within a mile, and picketed the mules. Now they would wait and hope the mules would gain some ground before they tackled several days of uphill hauling. Peachtree rebuked himself for not adhering to his own discipline, which was to keep his stock in good condition. Something about getting to the gold fields had driven him to abandon his usual prudence. Gold! It wasn't so far away now. And dodging winter had been a splendid maneuver, even if it meant going much farther. Gold! The best medicine of all.

Which reminded him that his supply of simples had dwindled to almost nothing and he could expect to find little growing in October and November. Still, there might be roots, barks, and seeds to gather. He ought not to forget the cactus and the yucca either. He knew nothing about the flora of this country, but it impressed him as being harsh, pungent, resinous, maybe laxative or cathartic.

It didn't matter to him what he sold, so long as he could brew up something with a kick in it. He could hawk a cathartic for milady's digestive problems just as easily as he could hawk Nepenthe. But oh, he loved the idea of selling more of that elixir.

That day and evening he hunted for simples along the river where things still grew, and wandered up mountain gulches. He collected various roots and stalks, scarcely knowing their medical properties or even the names of the plants. He sliced off yucca leaves, intending to experiment with them. That evening he gave Pontius P. Parsons a small dose of Nepenthe to keep the old ham happy. He didn't have enough to last until Santa Fe, and it worried him. Parsons might quit, and that would be the worst calamity of all. He could manage without Carlotta; he would sink like a rock without Pontius. In Santa Fe there would be laudanum or something as good, such as that Mary Jane leaf or Indian hemp the greasers loved. It might drive the old man's haunting pain away.

The next day Concorde pulled a wheel out of the cold river

and studied it. The tire remained loose. Another wheel yielded the same result. They would have to wait. Impatiently, Peachtree gathered more roots and barks and began steeping them in hot water, trying out the results himself. All he achieved, he thought, was some nasty stuff that tasted like creosote.

That afternoon, around the time Hercules was boiling the last of the squash they had gotten at Pueblo, the Skyes rode in.

Peachtree wasn't surprised. He had known the lout would bumble in sooner or later. Concorde spotted them first, the riders and travois ponies toiling up the Santa Fe Trail along the river. There was Carmody leading his mule, and there was Carlotta on a horse. Skye's old hag, Victoria, rode down from a bluff above him, surprising him. He had forgotten that she roamed far ahead. She reined her slat-ribbed mare, eyed the camp, studied the blocked-up wagons, and said nothing.

Skye, Mary, Carmody, and Carlotta rode in moments later.

The guide lifted his topper, read the meaning of the wheelless wagons, and settled his hat again.

"We brought her back. You shouldn't have left her."

"Why, Skye, is that how you greet us? With a lecture? We get along just famously without your advice."

Skye stared down at Peachtree from atop that wild-eyed blue roan, and accused once again: "You left a woman to die."

"Skye, she quit."

"It's Mister Skye."

"Skye, she had one of her tantrums and asked to be dropped off. This time we accommodated her."

"You left a woman to die."

Peachtree gazed at Carlotta, shocked at what radiated from her face. This was not the same woman he had left behind. She seemed fragile. She said not a word, which was utterly unlike her. She should be storming and raving, as usual. But he saw darkness under her eyes, and pain in them.

"I grant she had a long walk to Pueblo, but that was her choice, Skye."

"She didn't walk to Pueblo."

"Well, I'll take her to Santa Fe. But not on salary. Maybe I'll hire her, maybe I won't. I'll think about it."

Oddly enough, no one responded. Carlotta didn't shriek. It puzzled Peachtree. The woman's evil temper had abandoned her back on the lodgetrail somewhere.

"I'm paid to take you to Santa Fe," Skye said. "And I'll do it even if you get us all killed. That's how I do things."

Something as cold as a glacier in Skye's tone caught Peachtree, and he had sense enough not to reply. He stared at Victoria's flinty face, and into Mary's angry glare, and at Carmody's solemn disapproval. And at last into Carlotta Krafft-Ebing's ravaged beauty. She turned away. The next weeks weren't going to be fun with the grim Skyes along. The last thing he wanted was lectures and moral superiority.

Chapter 40

Carlotta hurt. She could not look men in the face, except for Mister Skye. Somehow she could look at him. She found a gentleness in that border ruffian that nurtured her. He had arrived in time.

She was not blessed with forgetfulness. Every moment of it remained as stark and terrible as when it had happened. She remembered the impassive faces of her captors. She had detected a faint eagerness in them, almost amusement, as they prepared to make sport of her. She had barely grasped what they might do until it was happening, and then her mind utterly refused to believe it. Not the opera contralto Carlotta Krafft-Ebing. She had felt so helpless when they stripped her and staked her spread-eagled. She writhed against her bindings and knew that her last memory was going to be mortal agony.

Even now she could not imagine why they had chosen to torture her. Why they didn't respect her womanhood as any civilized man would. The first pain had rocked her. Then came worse, much worse, unbearably worse until she had screamed into the heedless night, berserk with hurt and terror.

They had enjoyed her terror. The one thing that burned like embers through her memory was their pleasure in her agony. The smallest touch would set her to screaming, and she saw the delight in their eyes. They toyed with her, preferring to save the mortal thrust until later so they might enjoy her madness. How could any decent person . . . How could any honorable man . . . Mister Skye had told her their women could be even worse. Why, why, why?

She had no answers. Only the smarting lacerations within her, which the Skye women had cleansed with gentle hands. Only the memory of the iron smell of her own blood, and the vomitous terror locking her throat, and two men murdering her as slowly and brutally as possible.

She chose to stay with the Skyes. Victoria and Mary had become her sisters and mothers, sharing her suffering with her and protecting her from others.

That night Hyacinth approached. "I still don't know what happened, Carlotta," he said.

She couldn't reply.

"Dammit, she'll tell you when she feels like it. You go away," Victoria replied.

She knew she would never tell him. And the Skyes would never tell. Neither would Elisha. It comforted her. Let Peachtree never know. Let him wonder forever.

"Ah, well, nothing too serious, I gather," Peachtree said, eyeing Carlotta, who bore no external sign of her ordeal.

"Let it rest, mate," said Skye in that soft voice of his that somehow was command rather than suggestion.

"Skye: if you want to go back, I'm letting you go. You're dismissed. Here's the Santa Fe Trail big as life. This is New Mexico. We'll find villages along the way where we can get vittles. Give us a refund of some sort—half maybe—and be off."

Carlotta knew she would stay with the Skyes, no matter what.

"We're taking Miss Krafft-Ebing and Elisha Carmody to Santa Fe," Skye said.

"Out here I can't even sack an ape," Peachtree said. He turned away, annoyed.

She slept on a soft bed the Skye women prepared for her, river reeds and coarse grasses somehow matted into a yielding layer under a buffalo robe. She hadn't known such luxury for a long time. She had never gotten used to sleeping on hard ground, which lamed her hip and shoulder, and sucked heat from her. Hard nights with the Peachtree entourage had often left her aching and irritable. It comforted her that the women stayed right beside her; that Skye hovered close; that Jawbone stood guard over them.

The next dawn, Peachtree's frenzy to be off drove Concorde and Hercules to drag the wheels out of the Purgatoire. Concorde pronounced them adequately swollen, and the two rolled the cumbersome, slippery wheels to the wagons and lifted them onto the axles, with a lot of muffled cursing. It took several hours to do that, fetch the mules, harness them, and break camp.

She didn't help them. She listlessly tried to help the Skye women but they shooed her away.

"You rest, dammit. You got a long ride," Victoria said.

That relieved her. She didn't want to sit on the wagons. Not beside Hyacinth; not even beside Concorde, her amiable friend. The Skyes were putting her on the captured pony.

Skye inspected Peachtree's teams, saying nothing. The mules shocked him. They had been sweated down to their bones, and the brief rest hadn't helped much.

"Yoah not likin' the looks of them," Concorde said.

Skye shook his head. "I don't know how you'll get over the pass."

"There you go again, Skye," said Hyacinth.

"It's Mister Skye, sir. We'll be climbing for five or six

days. Usually not much grass there. We'll be crossing Raton Creek forty or fifty times. In some places we'll be driving up the creek because it's the only way. In other places you'll be winching your wagons out of the creekbed. Some days you'll be lucky to make two miles—with good mules."

"There's no way around?"

"Only way, Professor. Mountain branch of the trail. Then a worse trip down the other side; the other creek, Willow Creek—drains into the Canadian."

"We'll manage," said Peachtree. He smiled at Concorde and Hercules. "I have two spare mules."

"You'd be better off waiting while your stock recovers."

That was all Skye said, but Carlotta thought it was enough.

They forded the river on rocky bottom and began toiling uphill almost at once. Within a half a mile Peachtree's mules were winded. Unhappily the impresario let them rest. Skye watched, saying nothing. Peachtree would have to learn the hard way because he was the sort who couldn't be told much.

They made only four miles that day. The mules played out every few hundred yards. In some places all the men including Skye had to get behind the wagons and push. As usual, Victoria roamed far ahead, seeking out trouble before it found them. Sometimes they could see her, a tiny equestrian statue on some redrock ridge or promontory. Skye never missed those moments, and always lifted his top hat to her.

Carlotta rode quietly beside Mary, who seemed so much a sister now. She loved Skye's younger wife. Carmody stayed with them, discreetly minding his own counsel. Carlotta realized that the lecturer had been the soul of kindness every day, bringing her cups of cool water, smiling quietly, helping her off her pony, asking nothing but giving all that he could.

"You are a good man," she said to him while they rested the wheezing livestock.

He looked up, startled, and she realized she hadn't spoken to him since—the trouble. "You are a brave woman," he replied. "I admire you."

"You do?"

"You are beautiful."

"Oh, no." Why did he say that? Didn't he know that she had nothing but scars?

He looked stricken. "I'm sorry, Miss Krafft-Ebing; I've wounded you."

She couldn't respond, but she touched Carmody's shoulder. He stared at her hand, and finally smiled.

She no longer felt beautiful. Something more than her body had been smashed. She scarcely knew who she was or what to believe now. Everything had been shattered. She had been an opera singer, a follower of Heinrich Heine and the Romantics; a student of Rousseau, a blazing star in the salons of Europe and America. Now she was nothing. She lacked the strength even to consider her future. She was being carried along to a conquered Mexican capital called Holy Faith, like a shattered porcelain doll. And beyond that the future had become a blank. She didn't even want to think about what lay ahead, but just to endure the trip, minute by minute.

Both Carmody and Mary sensed she needed to be alone, and she felt grateful. She wasn't ready to talk. Not for a long time.

The upward climb, hour after hour, drained the strength from Carlotta's little horse, and he became more and more unruly until she stepped off and led him, the way Carmody led his mule. But she soon wearied of being afoot.

Ahead, the wagons stopped more and more frequently. Not even whips and Hercules' well-honed curses could drive the mules for longer than a few rods.

She waited gratefully, her lungs heaving in the thin air.

Skye halted them early. A sharp cold had already settled in the yawning canyon they ascended.

"But Skye," Peachtree objected, "there's another hour of light."

Skye pointed at the exhausted teams, their flanks heaving

in and out, their heads lowered. "You'll never make it to the top if you don't rest them, Peachtree."

"But there's no grass."

"There's no grass anywhere above, mate. We'll make a meal for your mules."

Skye led them off the trail to the bright little creek tumbling down the red canyon, and into a grove of cottonwoods whose turning leaves hung like thousands of gold coins.

Reluctantly the rest followed, and then sat waiting. How could they camp at a place with no grass?

Skye slid off Jawbone, took the ax Mary handed him, and began chopping the younger green-barked cottonwood limbs. These he dragged to Jawbone and the Skye horses, which began gnawing at the bark furiously, peeling it as well as beavers.

"Ah, I see," said Peachtree. "You have ways, Skye."

"It's Mister Skye, mate."

"Well, you're wasting daylight."

Carlotta saw what it was boiling down to: a clash of wills.

Chapter 41

For several days they toiled up a redrock canyon peppered with cedars and piñon pine. But Peachtree's mules would haul only a few minutes before stopping dead. No whipping would induce them to go farther until they got their wind.

Skye watched somberly, marveling at what greed for gold could do to otherwise sensible mortals. Often they camped at a place without fodder, and on those occasions he and Victoria headed for the nearest cottonwood saplings, chopped them down, and dragged them to the camp. Peachtree's mules devoured all the tender green bark that the Skyes brought them as ravenously as they had nipped and yanked buffalo grass below.

Victoria's hunting yielded nothing. The piñon-dotted slopes offered no game. The gravelly creek bottom produced few greens so late in the season, but Skye's women managed treacly stews of pemmican and buffalo backfat from their parfleches. The Peachtree entourage did no better, having exhausted the squash and beans acquired at Pueblo. Mary fed

Carlotta well and skimped on chow for the rest. Hunger was nothing new to Barnaby Skye. He had bloodied his fists and pulped his nose for his porridge on men-o'-war flying the Union Jack; his long winters in the mountains had been punctuated by starvin' times.

Carmody bore his hunger well, Skye thought. The trail-gaunt lecturer had taken to poking up roots with a fire-hardened stick as he walked, and contributed those and berries to the cookpot each day. But Peachtree grumbled steadily, Pontius Parsons declaimed hotly against the Skyes for neglecting the larder, and Concorde and Hercules had turned sullen.

One snow-flecked day when a mean wind chapped their flesh, Victoria put an arrow through a raven. Peachtree wanted to stop and roast it, but Victoria turned the bird over to Mary. Its few spoonfuls of meat would season another watery stew. The next day she pierced a stupid marmot that was probably hours from hibernation. It yielded a bite or two of tasteless meat for everyone.

Skye fought his hungers, chewed on rose hips growing along the creek, and endured.

Even slowed down by the halfhearted struggles of the mule teams, the Peachtree caravan gradually conquered Raton Pass. Victoria reported one evening that the next day they would reach the summit. After chopping cottonwood saplings and making sure Jawbone and his packhorses had their fill, Skye squatted beside Peachtree's campfire. For days there had been walled silence between the two parties: Peachtree plainly didn't want the Skyes around, and his increasing dependency upon the Skyes for fodder made him all the more irritable.

"We'll reach the summit tomorrow, Professor," Skye said. "Rougher trip down the other side. With your mules so worn, you could lose a wagon. You might want to rest them here a few days. We've got saplings enough to build them up."

"Absolutely not. Mules are tough beasts, Skye. Nothing beats a good big Missouri mule for hard going. We can take care of ourselves. We always have—even before we met you. I was on the road when you were still trapping beaver."

"You better listen to the man, boss," said Hercules. "They taught us how to keep our mules fed. Them squaws scraped vittles together outa nothing a white man would call chow. They fetched Carlotta back, so the whole company's here."

"Yes indeed. And now she'll want to be hired again, and then quit when I look at her the wrong way. It's a tribulation."

"She's part of the outfit," Hercules insisted. "You start peelin' off pieces of the Peachtree Medicine Show and she all goes to hell. You peel off Carlotta, next thing you can't pay Pontius, and next thing you can't pay us. You're owin' three months right now, and it's starting to itch me."

"Well, go ahead and itch then. We're two hundred miles from a paying crowd." Peachtree turned to Skye again. "What happened to her? You act as if it's some sort of secret."

"Nothing you need to know."

"Well, she'll get over it. I've been through weeklong Krafft-Ebing freezes. Tell her she's on board again." He examined Skye dourly. "Look, Skye, I'm cashiering you. What I want is a refund. We'll make our way to Santa Fe. We'll take Carmody. You can go home. Let's settle up. I'm sacking you. Get that through your whiskey-fried brain. Go away. Beat it. Vamoose."

Skye grinned. "You go ahead. We'll follow along with Elisha. I agreed to take him to Santa Fe."

Peachtree threw up his hands. "You're worse than Carlotta. She won't stay hired, and you won't stay fired."

Around noon they rode up a narrowing redrock defile. The gravelly creek itself was the road. Rough country catapulted upward. The trail left the creek on a shelved ramp of rocks, and ascended a grade that would challenge a fresh team.

An overcast scraped the surrounding ridges, and spat pea snow at them. Peachtree halted his mules in the rippling water and stared. Skye rode ahead, feeling the chafe of sleet on his neck, and studied the obstacle. He said nothing. He'd learned not to advise Peachtree.

Behind Peachtree's wagon stood the supply wagon, its team cooling its pasterns in the water. Mary pulled up behind the wagons, her travois and packhorses all standing in water. Carmody had bravely walked up the creek in soaked boots, leading his mule. There wasn't any place to turn around.

"Catching catarrh. Gimme some Nepenthe, Hyacinth," said Pontius.

Skye wondered what was going through Peachtree's mind now, as the man drew his coat collar higher against the stinging sleet and pondered his dilemma. Slowly, Hyacinth Z. Peachtree came to some sort of resolve.

"Concorde, bring your mules. We'll double-team," he said.

"You want me to get mah toes wet."

"That's the general idea."

"But not yoah toes."

"I employ you; that's something for you to cope with."

Sighing, Concorde and Hercules descended into the creek and unhooked the traces. They managed to scrape by the medicine wagon and double-hitch the teams. Skye rode ahead until he reached the crest of the fifty-foot incline. He doubted that even two worn teams could drag those wagons up stairs. The mules stood slumped in their traces, too tired even to scavenge greens from the creekbanks.

"You might unload the wagons, mate," he said.

"Skye, we've been on the road for years," Peachtree replied.

Peachtree cracked his whip, and hawed at the teams. Slowly they gathered their strength and tackled the shelved grade, while Hercules and Concorde pushed, along with Carmody. The medicine wagon lumbered slowly forward, hit the first rock stair, paused, climbed it, struck the second, and stopped. Peachtree cracked the whip, and the mules lunged into their collars, yanking the wagon up two stairs and onto the grade. The wagon careened sideways and righted itself as Peachtree and Parsons scrambled to counterbalance.

Much to Skye's amazement, the medicine wagon topped the grade a few minutes later. The medicine show troupe unhitched the heaving teams and hooked them to the lighter wagon and ascended the stairs and grade with less difficulty. Peachtree's teams had come through.

The rest of the party followed; Mary and Carlotta on horseback, Carmody, and assorted packhorses.

When the party had assembled again, Peachtree puffed himself up. "I keep telling you, Skye, we don't need you or your wives or your horse. If we'd rested the mules back there, we'd be buried in snow."

Skye knew there was no sense in arguing with a man determined to find fault. "Hope you're right, Professor," he replied, amiably. On the other side of the summit lay a vast plain, the home of Jicarilla Apaches and Comanches. A traveler would want fresh teams crossing country like that.

Chapter 42

Victoria urged her weary pony out upon a great promontory that overlooked an ocean of grass. The sinister plain stretched toward a horizon so many sleeps ahead she could scarcely imagine the distances. On her left a gigantic butte interrupted the foothill skyline. The mounting blue ridges of the Raton Range rose behind her, wave upon wave.

She stared at this terrible panorama, sensing its evil. She ought to rejoice because winter had not yet arrived on these southern steppes, and the mules would fatten. But those giant grasslands, as wide as the sky, filled her with the deepest dread she had ever known. They looked innocent, as guileless as a child, but they weren't. She looked for signs of life, knowing that a terrible race lived on those empty prairies. But no smoke intensified the autumnal haze. No dust marked the passage of living things.

But the Comanches were there. She knew they were, from some ancient knowledge that no white man would ever understand. Yes, the Comanche were there, even if she didn't see them. She felt an icy foreboding wash through her. Compared to the Comanches, the Lakota and Siksika were boys at play. The Absaroka had no enemies like these who possessed this grassland by spilling endless blood.

Mister Skye's medicine might fail here; even Jawbone's medicine might be nothing compared to the blood medicine of the Comanches. Soon her scalp would dangle from the lance of a Comanche. Soon Peachtree's and Carlotta's scalps would blow in the cold wind.

Peachtree had big medicine. She had marveled at the man who blithely ignored all warnings, who possessed powers even larger than Mister Skye's powers. Maybe his medicine lay in those long tails of his clawhammer coat, so like crow feathers. Maybe his medicine was something secret that white healers possessed. Whatever it was, harm could not touch him. He paid no price for foolishness.

She rather liked him. He wasn't bad for a white man. She read a certain audacity in him, a fine arrogant willfulness that commanded respect. He had tried to rid himself of Mister Skye, and she secretly admired that in him. He didn't need Mister Skye. His medicine could take him to Santa Fe unscathed—if it was as good as Comanche medicine.

Hyacinth Z. Peachtree. She had never heard of a name like that. Surely that was his secret medicine. He had a medicine-name more potent than Mister Skye's top hat or his grizzly-claw necklace. Mister Skye had told her that a hyacinth was a plant with a spiky blue flower. Victoria knew at once that hyacinth medicine was the greatest of all powers. Someday she would see a hyacinth and be made new. She would take a hyacinth to her people and plant it next to the tobacco gardens, and it would give the people its awesome powers.

She sat awhile longer, savoring the sun's coy warmth. It was time to go back to the white men. They were starving, but now she would feed them. She had found roots and berries on this south slope, still alive and nurtured by the sun in this Moon of the Flying Geese.

She had passed groves of a stunted oak that had dropped thousands of acorns. She had ridden along sloping ravines laden with serviceberries, whose blue fruit had been plucked by her people from ancient times. Many clusters remained. She had seen skunkbush, whose tart berries were edible. The white men wanted meat, and she probably couldn't give them that. She had seen not one print of a mule deer but she would feed them acorns and berries, and these would fill their empty bellies and keep them strong enough to reach the Comanche lands and die there. When they reached the grasslands below she would find antelope for them, and maybe even the sacred buffalo, whose meat would make all of them strong again.

She stared uneasily at the endless garden of grass below, as rich as a white man's plantation: food for horses, mules, buffalo, deer, antelope, rabbits, and men. With an imperceptible nudge she turned her pony, an ugly, eager creature with long hair sprouting under its jaw, back up the chaparral slopes toward the garden places.

She rode up and down slopes, topped ridges, slid softly as a spirit through a hushed land waiting for the Cold Maker to throw his fatal lance. She thought this land of low, dark junipers and pungent piñon pines and scrubby oak was a sweet land, like her own country far north. She paused now and then, feeling Sun warm her, and feeling the pungent breath of the sagebrush, the acrid resinous breath of the needled trees. She rode down to a long bottom crowded with the little oaks, and slid off her pony in a carpet of acorns. In a while there would be none because the squirrels would carry them away. She would need a great many: it was a heavy burden on a little Crow woman to feed nine persons twice each sun.

She filled her skirts with one load and deposited the acorns into her saddlebag. Then she gathered another load. Then she filled her calf-high moccasins and tied them to her saddle. Barefoot, she trod along the moist bottom, and then froze. Under the oak trees a flock of black turkeys pecked at the feast, fattening their big carcasses against the cold. Her heart lifted. She eased back to get her pony. The turkeys could flee faster than she could run. She needed mobility.

She slid barefoot into her light saddle and turned the mare toward the flock, nocking an arrow. She said a small blessing to her arrow and bow, and to the Givers of Food, and knee-reined the pony over downy grasses toward the flock. She edged close enough for an easy kill, and selected a fat bird pecking greedily at the earth. Her arrow plunged home. The turkey exploded upward and collapsed, flapping its wings and singing its deathsong. The others squawked and fled, half-flying, half-running upslope. She kneed her pony, feeling its boundless energy. It seemed almost like running the buffalo, that great white hour of madness that hunters loved.

The birds scattered in every direction. Some flapped straight toward the highest limbs. She chose one that had paused in a low limb, and put an arrow through it. She reached into her quiver, nocked another, and drew her bow upon a bird that raced overland, its wings out. She loosed her arrow but the bird careened ahead, limping. She rode it down and clubbed it with her bow while it flapped and shuddered in the grass.

Satisfied, she collected her three heavy birds and tied them by their feet to her saddle. Hot, sweet meat this night! Her mare turned its head, not liking the scent of blood even after all the times she had borne dead animals. Victoria retrieved her precious arrows and wiped the blood from them. Then she turned toward the white men's road, knowing her family and the medicine show people would have all they could eat tonight.

She waited at a flat where they would probably camp that night, but they didn't come, even as Sun fled behind the layered ridges and icy air bit her lungs. Irritably she rode her weary mare upslope, a tiny woman piercing into the unknown. She found them not far away, clustered around the team. They scarcely noticed her. Only Mister Skye and Mary watched her come, their gazes surveying the burdens anchored to her saddle.

The off lead mule lay in the trail, his lungs heaving in and out, while the white men tried to bring him to his feet. One grasped his tail and twisted it. But the mule simply endured the pain, blatting whenever the cruelty tormented him. He wasn't going to get up, not for all the white men in the world.

Mister Skye sat on Jawbone, looking like he wanted to say something to Peachtree. But he held his peace. He quietly saluted his sits-beside-him wife and her fat burdens. Mary did too, a smile breaking across her worried face.

The men couldn't make the mule get up. The mule had decided to die.

"All right. Unbuckle it and get the wagons around. We'll shoot it," Peachtree said, some exasperation in his voice.

"Why shoot it, mate?"

"Mind your business, Skye."

"Why shoot it? Free it and it'll likely recover in a while. Join your string tonight."

"We can't use this mule, Skye. It's all but dead."

"Don't use it. Tie it on to the wagon. We're five miles from some of the strongest grass in the world."

Carmody elbowed in and looked at the mule. "I'll buy it for cash, Peachtree," he said. "Would two dollars do?"

"Cash money—for that?"

"My risk," Carmody said.

Peachtree looked offended. "We'll shoot it," he said.

Hercules and Concorde freed the downed mule and led the team around him. A few minutes later both teams and wagons stood below the mule, which lay in the dirt, lungs heaving.

"All right, Hercules," Peachtree said.

The blond young man extracted a heavy revolver, walked back to the laboring mule, pressed the muzzle to the mule's neck, and pulled the trigger.

Victoria wondered if the bullet killed Peachtree's medicine too.

Chapter 43

The country south of Raton Pass seemed somehow different to Elisha Carmody. It was as if they had passed from one world into another, like crossing the equator. North of the pass lay endless grasslands stretching east. Here the grassland raced south to hazy obscurity. To look at a horizon was to look a fortnight into the future. But that wasn't the thing he felt in his bones. This grass had been Mexico's until 1846. He had crossed into a different nation.

Peachtree wanted to camp beside the sparkling creek that had tumbled out of Raton Pass, but Skye motioned him westward toward a lonely copse of cottonwoods, well off the trail.

"We want to see, without being seen, mate," Skye said. "This is a hard land."

"My mules are done in, Skye. First you blame me for using them hard and now you want to use them harder."

Skye smiled. His women filled skin bags with creekwater and rode toward the campsite.

Irritably Peachtree followed, his mules barely able to drag

the wagons that last quarter mile. The wagon tires cut glossy stripes into the clay, and Carmody wondered why Skye was trying to hide what couldn't be hidden.

They made camp in a protected hollow, their wagons below the surrounding flats and out of sight. Carmody admired Skye's choice. The yellowing leaves would filter and dissipate their smoke; the stock could fatten on the lush flats by night, but could be hidden by day if trouble came. They were out of the chafing wind and near water. They had turkey enough for a feast, and tomorrow Victoria might down an antelope or mule deer roving this paradise.

He picketed his mule and watched it tackle the thick grass. His mule had scarcely even thinned, so carefully had he looked after it. But the others were close to ruin, even some of the Skye ponies. For once Peachtree didn't object to a halt and set about seeing to the succor of each of his big mules.

It seemed an idyllic place, yet Carmody felt something sinister about it. Restlessly he plucked up his carbine and stalked out upon the sweeping grass, wanting to think. To his surprise Hyacinth Peachtree hastened after him and they walked through a chill twilight together.

"I pushed too hard," Peachtree said. "The gold fever does that to a man. I never believed it could derange me. I've always put the welfare of my stock first—for obvious reasons. But here I am, rebuking myself for a month of follies."

That surprised Carmody. "We need to fatten them for a week at least," he said.

"Well, I don't know about that. We'll have snow on us before we know it."

"I see the gold fever still burns, Hyacinth."

"Oh, we'll pause in Santa Fe; grain the mules, fill our purses. Until then I mean to press hard, Skye or no Skye. That brings me to a proposition, my friend."

"I suspected you had one in mind."

"I'd like to borrow your mule. It's fat. We'd put your kit on our wagon and you could ride beside Hercules. You'd be spared a couple of hundred miles of walking, my dear friend. And of course I plan to slow down. The mules'll be treated better than Queen Victoria. Why, this grass'll strengthen them in a few days."

"I'm afraid not, Hyacinth."

"I understand your hesitancy. That one's all you have. But, my fine colleague, bear in mind that I'm reformed. That poor dead mule up there brought me around. Why, I let my appetite for gold get the better of me for a while."

"Hyacinth, I simply prefer to keep my own few things under my own thumb. But I appreciate your offer."

"You'd save a lot of walking, my friend."

· "Walking across the continent has helped me to understand two or three virtues—endurance, perseverance, and the triumph of soul over body. When my feet ache, soul keeps me going. I'd walk, even if I were to lend you the mule, which I won't."

Peachtree sighed. "Very well, then. We'll nurse my mules along. Say, while I have you here out of earshot"—he waved at the empty grasslands far from the camp—"would you mind telling me what happened to Carlotta? The Skyes don't say a word. She's a bit daft, I'd say. As silent as a ghost for weeks."

"It's up to her to tell you, Hyacinth."

"Ah. You, too. It's a conspiracy."

"But I'll tell you something you wouldn't know. Two people—a man and woman—died in Pueblo of your elixir. It bought grave trouble for us."

"Died, you say? Died?"

"That's what they told us. We arrived just after the funeral."

"Well, you know, I warned them—always do. Warned them to take only a nip, a proper dose. I'm sorry they died, but I don't hold myself accountable. They probably died of a drunk, not my elixirs. As you keep lecturing us, Carmody, people do it to themselves. It's like spirits—there are always those who'll drink themselves to death. The distiller isn't at fault because he sold them spirits."

Carmody pondered that. "You know, Hyacinth, that's close to my thinking but not quite. Those people in Pueblo had no grasp of self-discipline. They were simple peons living for the moment. Now, if they'd heard my course of lectures about the governance of their appetites, why, they'd be armed against excess. But these were ordinary souls, you know, innocents. You might wisely have declined to sell to them; at least watered down your elixirs—which seem to be poisonous at some level."

"You're saying I'm culpable. I'm not. You tell me I'm to blame for their excess. I'll not have it from you."

Carmody listened to Peachtree's voice climb an octave. They reached the clear creek that tumbled out of Raton Pass, and he stooped to wash in it.

"My Nepenthe elixir is a sublime blessing out of ancient history. I intend to benefit the whole race. It keeps poor Parsons, who's all stove up, from maddening pain. That's his salary, you know. A little Nepenthe. And before that, some laudanum in a tonic. If some cretinous undisciplined, doodlehead gulps—"

"Hyacinth, let it rest."

Done with his evening toilet, Carmody hiked back toward the encampment in thickening gloom, with Peachtree at his side and still agitated.

"You're all scornful. You and the Skyes. Brimming with your lofty moral judgments. I'm a man of road and byway, taking my healing willy-nilly to the heedless world; you take me for a charlatan. If I'm a bamboozler, sir, how is it that my elixirs and tonics have such effect, eh?"

"Hyacinth—"

"The truth is, you stare down your noble noses at those who have a little vagabond blood coursing their veins. You think we're engaged in rapine. The truth is, sir, that none of you'll even grant me the dignity of being proper company for your unsullied selves. I'll tell you something: I was reared in luxurious circumstances—a fine merchant family. My parents poured out their substance upon tutors and masters: violin and pianoforte; geographers, scientists, chemists, philosophers; instructors of rhetoric.

"I'm probably the most educated mortal in all of North America. I might have held a chair at some great university, made myself famous, endowed the Peachtree family escutcheon with laurels. I'm a Doctor of Philosophy a dozen times over. I've mastered more apothecary science than any dozen medical quacks. But I chose a mendicant life; it didn't choose me. I consider myself a St. Francis of Apothecary Arts. If you don't like my company, then don't associate with me."

Carmody laughed. "I'm associating with you right now."

"No, sir, I'm associating with you. I sought you out for a favor you chose not to grant. No, I'm quite unsuitable; that's obvious. You go lecture the world about virtues no one can ever live up to, and I'll do the humbler thing, and sell some herbal effusions or tinctures that comfort body and soul."

Peachtree glared at the empty prairie, as agitated as Carmody had ever seen him.

"I know what you think of me: a man with a sly tongue who can lure suckers to part with their hard-won dollars. I have that gift. And I use Pontius Parsons to help it along. But if that were my bent, sir, I'd fill those bottles with swampwater and beguile the world with their healing prowess. Oh, it'd be easy. A little whiskey with something tart or resinous mixed with it—strong medicine, they'd say—and I'd coin gold.

"That's who I am. But you'll never separate me in your mind from those unscrupulous bounders. Oh, no. Let a man acquire the gift of selling, and he's a bounder. I've been driven out of towns by sheriffs and mobs; by constables and judges. I've had a hemp noose around my neck. For what? For offering comforts to the world. Your attitude is nothing new to Hyacinth Z. Peachtree."

"You're reading things into my conduct, Hyacinth. I'm not walking the earth to condemn others, but to show them a path toward happiness."

"Then there's not one iota of difference between us. Our missions are to heal the world."

Carmody kept his silence. He had learned, in his years in public life, that the world's most compelling mountebanks are those who believe in their own nostrums. The guileful Professor Peachtree seemed to have a spoiled child's perception of those he might exploit.

It was Carmody's habit to examine himself regularly, and ask searching questions about his own conduct and goals. In the cold discomfort of his own bedroll, spread upon the cast-iron earth, he pondered Peachtree's nettle: was there an iota of difference between them? He knew there was.

Chapter 44

By the third day, the protected little hollow that sheltered them seemed like home to Carlotta Krafft-Ebing. She dreaded to leave it. Not since Hyacinth's thirty-day sentence for peddling without a license in Nauvoo had she been in one place so long.

The mules and horses mowed the lush bunchgrass, yawned, rolled, bit at their flanks, dozed, and grazed again. Victoria and sometimes Skye restlessly rode out to hunt or study the surrounding oceans of grass from promontories that would let them peer into tomorrow. Skye carried a small spyglass, and with it he patiently surveyed horizons as if he were studying birds.

Between them they brought in meat: an antelope one day, a big buck so heavy they had to drag it the next day. Hercules and Concorde soaked wheels again, two at a time, in the creek. No one came down the trail, not even local Mexicans driving their *carretas*. The weather remained mild by day, but the nights put frost on the troupe's bedrolls. She yearned for the comforts of a featherbed in a warm hostelry. She dreaded icy rain above all; and sometimes great slabs of dark cloud robbed the day of the heat of a coy and low sun.

She had fended off Hyacinth several times. The man's insatiable curiosity demanded an answer she would not give him. Let him wonder. More than her body had been torn that terrible hour, and she felt adrift and uncertain. She wondered what they said about her behind her back, whether the Skyes or Carmody had let slip what happened.

She had started this wilderness journey a person she knew, and now she was a stranger to herself. All her certitudes lay on the clay like potsherds. Her vision of the American savage as an innocent uncorrupted by civilized life had been merely the figment of a romantic European imagination. The thinkers she had loved seemed to be nothing more than pale fevered fools.

She had slid into solitude, and yearned to find a friend. She pondered them all, one by one. Not Hyacinth, spoiled boy wonder in man's clothing. Not Hercules, Pontius, or Concorde, though Concorde would at least accept her without judging. Not Elisha Carmody either. She feared his judgment. Somewhere inside of that man was a jury ready with a verdict. Not the Skye women, dear as they were. They simply were too different and lacked her European roots. But maybe Skye . . .

She eyed the guide shyly for days, just wanting to talk, but afraid to. He studied her amiably now and then, plainly concerned about her spirits and her recovery from an ordeal her mind was unable to blot from memory. No. It would be better if she held her emptiness within her. She slept her days away, hid her occasional tears from them all, and slid into total isolation.

Until one chill eve with ice in the sharp wind, when he hunkered down beside her. "Thought I'd take a stroll to the creek, Miss Krafft-Ebing. Not a pleasant night, but stirring up the blood helps. Would you join me?"

She peered into his amiable face, afraid, but saw no harm in his squinty eyes. Wordlessly she rose from her fireside seat, pulled a thick blanket about her for a shawl, and they set off into the gloom. He said nothing for a while, adjusting his pace to her slower one. When they reached the creek he didn't stop, but continued southward until she eyed him nervously.

"Good to walk," he said. "Hard to camp for long. Requires patience. How can anyone sit still for days? But the stock needed it. Looking almost frisky now."

"Yes, it is slow," she said, surprising herself because she spoke at all.

"Not easy for you. You probably grew up in comfort."

"Salzburg. Not comfort, but we were never cold. My father was a chamber musician, a cellist. A poor livink. My mother took in needlework besides."

"Well, that's how you got started in music."

"He was a fanatic; he was makink me a singer before I had a will of my own."

"You're a long way from Salzburg."

"Oh!" she cried, not knowing why. Tears welled up unbidden. She was a long way from anything, especially the safety and comfort of a placid Austrian city rich with civilized arts. She was a long way from her handwringing mother and dead father, the *meister*, Herr Reinhardt Krafft-Ebing, bald as an egg and inflammable; from her sisters and the maestros and academicians. A long way from the Alps and the Salzach River and Capuzinerberg and Monchsberg and its old fortress.

"Hard place and hard time for you. I admire you, Miss Krafft-Ebing. You've got more courage than you know."

"I do? Ah. Now I understand. You flatter me but I will not have you, darlink."

He laughed. "I love my wives," he said, and they walked quietly into a wind-whipped gloom. She realized that Jawbone was ghosting along behind them, a loyal sentry and friend of this rough man.

"I am a long way, yes," she said. "I'm thinkink I will die here, and no one will know. If I die, will you write to—"

"These are hard doin's, but I imagine you'll keep your hair."

"This mountain tongue of yours, it makes no logic."

"I'm just saying you're a brave woman and we'll get you to Santa Fe. How came you to join up with Peachtree?"

There it was. She had been asked this many times before. Her stock answer was that opera bored her and she wanted some adventure.

"No one else would hire me," she said softly. "I am a terror to them all. I am a terror because that is how my father was. He was a terror. I am a terror. I stamp my foot at him, and he knew I was like him. But he's dead now."

"I'm sorry. Hard to go on all alone. Being a terror's been a lifelong rip of mine. What'll you do next?"

"Go to California. Where else. Work. Sing in cafés maybe. Do dirty dishes maybe. Maybe I'll end up a whore, yes?"

"No. You have a voice that brings tears to the eyes of angels, Carlotta."

"Oh!" She felt wetness well in her eyes again, and hated him for it.

"I'm thinking," he said, "you'll become what you deserve to be, queen of the gold fields. Faster than they can raise an opera house, you'll be singing your heart out in one."

She felt her tears slide down her cheeks and fall to the hard earth, and was glad it had become too dark for him to see her. "No. I will have more bad temper and will walk out on them, and they will find someone else to sing," she said.

"I reckon it's possible. I don't believe it, though, Miss Krafft-Ebing. I'm thinking you'll reach Sacramento and you'll think that you've faced the worst a woman can face, and done it bravely, and nothing'll ever bother you again. Those Comanches were harder on you than anyone else will ever be."

She could not respond to that at first. A lump hurt her

throat so much she couldn't swallow. "Please . . . ," she whispered.

"I've seen lots of fire-eaters come out here. It puts them to a test sometimes. They're not the same afterward. You've been reborn in pain. I was reborn in pain myself. I was pressed into the Queen's Navy, a bloody powder monkey thirteen years old, and almost died of starvation until I learned to fight for my porridge. Got myself pounded to a pulp—but I won my porridge. I've never stopped fighting. You'll never stop fighting either. You're not helpless."

She could not endure that. "We must be turnink back now," she said. "I am cold."

He swung around at once, and they traced the creek north in silent companionship, walking into bitter wind.

"Do you know what helpless is, Mister Skye? It's a woman with her modesty stolen, nothing covering her flesh, staked to the ground. There is a leather cord around each of my wrists, biting in. It goes to a stake. There are leather cords around my ankles. They pull my legs apart and I cannot move. I am all alone; there is no help, not even a thousand miles away. I beg God and angels to help me, but they have wax in their ears. There are savages above me, looking down at me. I scream and no one hears, I pull and yank and only I hurt my wrists and my ankles. I am lyink on a hard rock that jabs my back, and a root that stabs me. And I can do nothink. That is helpless."

"I can't imagine worse."

"I hate savages. They are all evil."

"No!" he said. "They're like us, sometimes good, sometimes evil. I know what you've been through—but don't hate them. Find something kinder if you can."

She walked, feeling comfortable in his presence. "I'm glad I can talk to you. I wanted to talk to him—to Elisha Carmody. He's a good man. But I just can't."

"Well, I'm the same way. I've got too bloody many vices to cure. I'll never get that kind of grip on myself. I admire him, though. You see him these days? Cutting wood. Helping Mary smoke jerky. Moving the stock to new grass. But I just can't face him. He's right; we've got to master ourselves before we're free. He's triumphed over himself. But I'm not very bloody free. I can't be like him. I'll be what I am now all my days, and no lecture's going to change a thing."

"I will never be the same," she said.

They reached Skye's warm lodge, and she let him go in ahead. She needed to rub away her tears before she faced its firelight and climbed into the bedroll they offered her within its safe circle.

Chapter 45

Victoria paused in the dry riverbed that concealed her from the surrounding world. Something on a distant grassy knoll caught her attention. She steered her mare under the cutbank that hid her, and cautiously studied the little knob poking up from the knoll like a boulder. Her keen eyes limned the shape, and she knew she was seeing the upper torso of a man. She watched quietly, letting her senses tell her more. The man might be a Mexican but he wore no sombrero. No, this was a warrior and he was studying Victoria's own camp.

She continued to watch him, but now she surveyed the other hills and horizons. She saw only the lone warrior. When they rode alone like that they probably were scouts. It worried her. The leather-shirted upper torso disappeared suddenly, hidden by the knoll. Immediately she eased her pony out of the watercourse and raced toward the knoll, an arrow nocked in her bowstring. Before she reached its crest she halted, slid off the pony, and crawled the rest of the way up until she could see beyond it. There indeed, a horse bearing a man raced eastward, carrying his news.

Victoria squinted at the surrounding country, seeing nothing more. For days they had toiled south through a comatose land gathering itself for winter's first blows. They had angled closer and closer to a noble range of mountains the Mexicans called Blood of Christ. Now the Santa Fe Trail paralleled them and intersected the various creeks and rivers flowing out of the high country. They had passed a place where the trails divided, one of them going to San Fernando de Taos, a village where her man said they would winter after they took their clients to Santa Fe.

She climbed upon her pony and steered it north, taking advantage of whatever cover she could find, always avoiding skylines that would reveal her to unfriendly eyes. In all those peaceful days of travel, they had encountered only one party, three Mexican men with little burro-drawn, wooden-wheeled *carretas* filled with hay. Carlotta had questioned them in Spanish and found that no, there had been no sign of *los Indios* to the south. The Comanches never come after All Saints' Day, they told her. Not until the Feast Day of San José would they come again.

But they were here.

She passed a group of mule deer but ignored them, and found her people resting the livestock beside a cottonwood-lined creek the Mexicans called the Ocate. A nod of her head brought Mister Skye to her, out of earshot of the rest.

"They are coming," she said.

He listened quietly, rubbing his unshaven jaw. "Bent told me there's some dragoons building a post down on the Mora," he said. "Right on this trail. We'd better run for it. If you didn't see the rest, they're plenty far off."

"They're damn fast. They'll catch up."

He sighed. "We haven't much bloody choice. I don't know how far it is, but we'd better make tracks."

"It might be just a few. It might be some other People."

"All right. Let me know, fast as you get wind of 'em." She nodded. He turned to the rest. "Victoria's spotted a warrior. We'd better get out of here. We'll be running for the Mora River. With some luck we'll find some soldiers there."

"How do you know it's a warrior? What tribe?" asked Peachtree.

Annoyance swept through Victoria. This white medicine giver was going to resist Mister Skye to assert himself again. But Mister Skye didn't answer directly. "We'll know more soon," he said simply.

"Comanches?"

"Or Apaches or Utes."

"We should dig in here. We've got water, some cotton-woods for barricades, and our scatterguns."

Even as he spoke, Mary pulled a bull-scrotum bag from her household kit and filled it with creekwater. Hercules raced to hitch the mules, while Concorde pulled a small cask from the wagon and filled it through the bung.

"Concorde," Peachtree said, "my instructions are to stay here and fort up."

"Ah'm going with Skye, boss."

"What?"

"You done heard me. Tell you the truth, Ah never did fig-ure them scatterguns and revolvers was much against a big bunch of redskins. They'll have arrows in mah yeller hide be-fore we get the range."

"The Skyes have rifles. Carmody has a carbine. We're equipped long-range and short-range. It couldn't be better."

"Four rifles, boss? Against what?"

Victoria liked Concorde's common sense.

Mister Skye dug in his saddlebag and extracted a small brass spyglass. "Here," he said to Victoria. She had always scorned it. White men had weak eyes. But now she took the come-closer gratefully. "If you find them south of us, we're in big trouble," he muttered. "But you won't. He ran east, eh?"

She nodded.

"They're on the Canadian River somewhere. We've got a chance." He studied her a long moment. "Be careful," he said.

It was the same as saying he loved her. "Damned no-good bean-eating bad-eyed Comanches," she said. "I'll take a scalp before I die." She eyed Mary dourly. Once, in the grandfathers' time, these terrors of the southern Plains had been Shoshones.

She watched the rest hasten through their tasks. Hyacinth Peachtree, realizing he was going to be left alone with his medicine wagon if he didn't follow Mister Skye's counsel, finally clambered to his wagon seat beside Pontius and hawed his mules to life. Mary finished cleaning Dirk's cradleboard and laced the whimpering infant into it. Mister Skye checked the caps on his big dragoon Colt, and spoke quietly to Jawbone, who laid back his ears and screeched.

Victoria trotted her mare east, concealing herself along the creek bottom for a while. Her senses were as razored as a new Green River knife, and as piercing as a steel awl. She wove like a ghost through cottonwood flats, and then set her pony toward a distant hogback where she would be able to see the future with her come-closer. At its greatest range, it could see what would arrive after one sleep. On the rising slope a mean wintry wind probed through her buckskin coat, finding her flesh around the neck and wrists, and driving up her back like icewater. Any day it could snow; the great mountains to the west were already buried in white. She ignored the cold. Soft white men feared it; her stronger Absaroka people knew how to scorn the Cold Maker's arrows.

She picked a drainage to follow, peering over its banks once in a while. She never let herself be surprised. In all her years with Mr. Skye, she had seen others before they saw her because of her ancient habits. But someday when her magpie medicine was no good she would be surprised. She knew that, but knew it wasn't going to happen this time, not with each of her senses so alive.

She dismounted, tied the pony with a wrap of the rein around a juniper, and edged upward until she could look east. She squinted at the grasslands, missing nothing. She took a segment at a time, looking especially for the thin blue lines that indicated watercourses where armies might dwell. But the giant land looked empty. Maybe the scout had circled west, instead of east, to avoid being seen by his prey on the Santa Fe Trail, and she cursed softly, wondering whether to turn in that direction.

The wind numbed her fingers, and she pressed them under the armpits of her leather coat. Then she pulled the telescope from her pocket. She snapped it open, making a long brass tube out of a short one, and leveled it. For many heartbeats she studied the country through the bobbing lens, seeing nothing but frost-cured brown grasses, and some standing water from autumnal rains. She cursed the rains; there would be no columns of golden dust to tell her the things she needed to know.

Then the round white image slid past something. She halted her sweep and found the movement again, almost at the hazed horizon. There a thousand locusts crawled the grasses, dark dots and nothing more, but they crawled southwest, at an angle that would intersect the white man's road. More of them than she ever had seen in one band. Something cold filtered through her. She studied the dots, but they were beyond counting, and the image bobbed too much, the smallest puff of wind deranging her view.

She explored the grasslands between herself and the moving village, and found what she was looking for: the one who had found her party, racing east with his news. In what Skye might call three or four hours, the village would know, and come for the kill.

She was not done. She prided herself in looking a second and third time. She glassed the empty grasslands and found three more scouts west of the village, all of them converging on the one who raced east with news. One would take the news to the People; the others would come this way to stalk Peachtree like skulking wolves around buffalo; watch, harass, try to steal mules, and kill silently with well-aimed arrows while they waited for the rest. Put an arrow in a few of Peachtree's mules, and the medicine man would limp like a lame deer.

She studied the crawling, wind-shivered grasses again, and then hastened back to Mister Skye, her heart heavy. She knew what Mister Skye would do: he and Jawbone and Victoria would hunt the scouts before the scouts hunted them.

The mean wind bit her nose and brought tears to her eyes, but she ignored it and rode her dutiful mare back to the white man's road, with bad news bitter on her tongue.

Chapter 46

Skye listened to Victoria while the wagons passed him by.

"How many are there?"

"As many as the stars."

"When'll they get to us?"

She pondered it. "Some will come soon. Maybe even before the sun hides."

"An advance party to pin us down?"

"A few scouts. The rest will meet us when Sun comes back. Tomorrow will be the day to die."

He rode along on Jawbone, Victoria beside him. "Those soldiers on the Mora are all we have—if William Bent was right and they're there. We may be alone."

"I will take a scalp first."

Skye felt a foreboding slide through him. The news came like a sleet storm in a place of no shelter. "How many scouts did you see?"

"The one that found us, and three more. They'll stalk us like wolves following the buffalo. Soon they'll wait for us in a hiding place, shoot arrows into the mules and flee. They'll slow us to a crawl, the way the wolf hamstrings the buffalo."

"They're our first problem, then. I suppose you'n I are it, Victoria. You up to hunting the hunters?"

"I am a small woman, not a warrior. But you've taught me well. My Absaroka arrows fly true. They kill Comanche as well as deer. Now I will sing my victory song. Then we will go out to kill or die."

"They may not be Comanche, Victoria. Could be Southern Cheyenne, Bent's people. Utes, Apaches . . ."

She squinted at him. "Which of these are friends of us, dammit?"

"All I'm saying is, any other tribe would be better than Comanches."

They steered their horses toward Mary and the baby. Skye explained what Victoria had seen and where safety might lie.

"I don't even know where this new post's going in. But Bent said it's right on this road. Don't know how far ahead it is, either. A day and night, I reckon. That's your task, Mary. Get them there. Peachtree's gonna want to run. You've got to keep him from doing that."

"Mister Skye, what if they don't obey me?"

"You and Carmody keep a proper pace. Fall back if you must. I can't help them if they wind-break the teams. I'm reckoning we'll ride all night before we get to that post. Talk to Carmody. He's got a level head and a carbine."

She registered that somberly. "I will send four devils to the spirit lands, two for Dirk and two for me. That is my word."

"Mary, Mary . . ."

She turned to him, her sweet brown face filled with anguish. "Goodbye, Mister Skye," she said. "Goodbye, Victoria."

"Mary—it won't be like that."

"They are bad. The Snake people know them better than anyone. They are like wolves. I will talk their tongue when they come. I will confuse them with Comanche words. They will be surprised by my words, and I will kill them as they listen."

"Dammit, I'll cut them open and eat their hearts," Victoria said. "My medicine is good."

Skye swung Jawbone toward the head of the procession and steered close to Peachtree.

"Mary's taking you to the Mora River; there's supposed to be a new Army post around there. Probably a day and a night away. Follow her pace. If your teams are wind-broken, you'll end up a pincushion."

"What're you talking about, Skye?"

"Comanche."

"Comanche? When?"

"The first in a few hours; in force by dawn."

"Where're you going?"

"They've got some scouts not far from here. Victoria spotted them. We're going out there to deal with them. Peachtree, just don't put a bullet into us when we return. If it's night we'll hail you. Don't shoot friends. Listen to Mary."

"Skye, don't leave us—not with just the squaw."

"It's Mrs. Skye, mate. Give her a name." He rode off, choking back his seething anger.

"You gonna make meat?" asked Concorde from the second wagon.

"You listen to Mary while we're gone."

"She's pretty enough to listen to," he said.

Skye and Victoria cut east, heading into a rolling grassland riven by occasional dry gulches that could hide enemies. He felt his pulse rise, as it always did when death loomed over him. Victoria rode beside him, as lethal as a grizzly and meaner than a badger when she wanted to be. She was crooning to herself, and he knew she was making medicine, stripping her soul for death, pleading with her spirit-helper the magpie, and nerving herself to kill. Sometimes she wept over meat, her tears watering a doe or an antelope whose life ebbed away before her eyes. But she did what she must.

He let her lead; she knew where to find the scouts. He could only hope that she found the Comanche before they found her. She rode quietly along a gulch, occasionally pausing to survey the country above. On those occasions she left her mare with him, and crawled toward a nearby swell or low hogback, carrying Skye's come-closer with her. They covered several miles that way, drifting farther and farther from the Santa Fe Trail as the weary autumnal sun rolled across the southern heavens.

She never said a word when she returned. She simply mounted and continued east by south across lands without feature or landmark. Only the snow-tipped Sangre de Cristos on the west offered direction. Skye felt the country around him change, grow still and charged, like an arsenal about to explode. He checked the cap on his old Hawken again, wishing he had a modern breechloader instead of his venerable mountain rifle. But at least it would drive a ball farther than the reach of any arrow. He carried a powder horn, and in the pockets of his leather shirt lay lead balls and wadding and a lot of little copper caps. He had his Dragoon Colt for close work, and his knife; she had her arrows, swift and silent and deadly. Her long rifle remained sheathed. The two of them would take some killing.

She rode awhile, paused and ascended a slope again, returning with a mouth filled with curses.

"Them evil-eyed sons of the underworld, they're nowhere I can see," she said.

"They've seen us, Victoria."

She snarled something at him, hating what he said.

"We'd better cut south, don't you think?" he asked.

"No, we got no protection until the next creekbed."

He didn't like it. Jawbone chafed under him, absorbing Skye's mood. He ran a hand under the roan's mane, the ancient signal to calm down. But the horse didn't. He swung his ugly snout around, lifted his head as if to trumpet, and then sulked when Skye checked him.

"He's got wind of them," she said. "Dammit! They're around here laying for us. What way's the wind?"

She licked a finger and lifted it into the air, testing the soft breeze, but it told her nothing.

"They got us in here," he muttered. "I'm thinking we should back out, Victoria."

She hissed softly for an answer.

He rode forward, skin prickling, his gaze sliding along hilly horizons, examining each sagebrush. Sweat built upon his chest and rolled down his belly.

The lance hurtled down like a black shadow, burying itself at Jawbone's feet. The horse screeched and reared, which saved Skye's life as an arrow whirred past Skye's chest. He swung his Hawken up but couldn't see anyone. Victoria cursed, and he heard the whip of her bowstring.

He jammed the Hawken into its scabbard and pulled out his Dragoon. He spotted a blur and fired, the muzzle of his revolver ballooning powder smoke into the dancing air. He whirled, looking for another and saw not one, not two, but eight of them surrounding him, some blocking retreat, some ahead, the rest on their flanks above the little drainage. So this day he and Victoria would die. They held nocked arrows upon him and Victoria but didn't release them. He eyed them sourly, feeling sweat build under his topper and slide down his forehead.

"Savin' us for some fun," he muttered to her.

"I kill one first!"

"I'd best get off Jawbone," he said, knowing what it would signal to the horse.

She stared at him, tears building in her weathered brown face, saying goodbye to him. He met her anguished eyes with his own, and slid off the horse slowly, while the Comanches watched. They had painted for this occasion; white, ocher, black grease, vermilion, each according to his medicine.

He saw two wearing bonnets, the ensigns of those who had won fame in battle. The rest wore nothing on their heads.

They stared at him with expressionless dark eyes set wide on wide faces. One, who seemed to be a leader, barked a one-word command. Skye waited, unsure of what they wanted, his revolver still in hand. Then the other bonnet-wearer slid down a grassy slope, bearing a lance. He was going to count coup on live enemies. After that, the jaws of hell would open wide.

Chapter 47

Mary signaled to Peachtree it was time to rest the mules, but he drove on. She heeled her pony, raced beside the medicine wagon, and yelled up at him to stop.

He ignored her. A fear-madness burned in his eyes.

She kicked her pony again, spurting forward until she was well ahead. Then she turned her pony sideways, blocking the path, and waited. Her heaving pony watched the onrushing mule team and began to sidle and prance, resisting her rein. But she held the pony still.

Peachtree tried to swerve, but Mary checked his progress. At last Peachtree reined in his team a few yards from Mary.

"I should run you down," he yelled.

She did not rebuke him. Fear had crazed the white men. "We will rest now," she said.

Sweat blackened the necks and withers of the mules. White foam had built around the oiled harness. Their chests heaved in and out. Peachtree had driven them at a hard trot for miles, until the trail-wearied mules began to falter. She had tried to stop him several times. Her own pack and travois horses had raced along behind, bouncing their loads and suffering.

"But we can't stop here," Peachtree said. "There's no place to hide. Look around you. We're utterly naked."

They had stopped on barren bunch-grass prairie. Gently folded steppes rose on the west, sliding into foothills of the Sangre de Cristos. To the east the land dropped slightly and pancaked into a vast plain scarcely bisected by drainages.

Mary felt her mare's lungs slow down. The mule teams drooped in their harness, sucking air. "It is the safest place," she said.

"But they can see us."

"We are known to them. It does not matter. We must save the mules. It is best to have fresh horses."

"But—the farther we go, the farther we'll be from the Comanches."

She wondered what to say: did he really believe that mules dragging heavy wagons, travois ponies and packhorses, could outrun Comanche warriors? "We will rest them a long time now," she said. "This is the safest place."

"She's right, boss," Concorde yelled from the second wagon. "Looks to me like this heah place buys time. Anything we see crawlin' around, it'll be coming tomorrow."

She glanced gratefully at Concorde, who was already clambering off his wagon, followed by Hercules and Elisha Carmody. Off among the packhorses, Carlotta sat her captured pony, skirts hiked high, her face pinched with terror.

Concorde and Hercules each unhitched a mule team and walked it slowly in a circle, cooling down the animals. Mary walked to the rear, feeling her legs work after their imprisonment in the stirrups. The cradleboard pinched her shoulders. She studied the Skye horses. She hated to unburden them but they would rest better without their loads. So she began to loosen cinches and lift off the packsaddles.

"I'll help you, Mrs. Skye," said Carmody. He began to free a packsaddle. "I never thought of open space as a safe place."

"It is the scouts we must worry about now," she said. "The ones close enough to put an arrow into a mule, or a bullet into us. Here is the best place; we will see anyone coming."

Peachtree watched aghast. "Mrs. Skye—you should keep your outfit ready to run."

She ignored him, and settled next to Carlotta, who sat in the grass holding the rein of her pony. "Help me with my boy," Mary said, sliding the heavy cradleboard off her shoulders. The child of her loins stared solemnly as she loosened the ties. A cradleboard bound an infant so tightly that it quieted the child. Now, freed, he waved his arms, and whimpered. The scent of his wastes smote the air. She lifted the naked boy to the grass, and wiped him with grasses, feeling their coarseness scrape his silky skin while Carlotta watched silently. Then she scooped the foul mosses out of the leather compartment, and tossed them downwind. She had no more moss to repack the cradleboard, so she used the dry grasses that grew at hand. Carlotta lifted the pawing child to her lap. He whimpered in the harsh wind that chafed them all.

Mary pulled her leather shirt upward under her coat, and drew the child to her heavy breast, feeling its mouth suck. The simple act of nurture gave her sudden peace. But her thoughts turned to Mister Skye and Victoria, out on that blue-hazed expanse of emptiness, trying to ward off the first murderous blows upon this little group of wayfarers.

Peachtree paced like a man unable to sit, and squinted at horizons in every direction, but the rest settled into the grass, backs to the raw wind. Let him search. Even if he finally spotted something it would mean nothing. Night would hide them before distant horsemen could reach them. That is what anyone who knew the grasslands would understand. Peachtree didn't grasp it, and was being foolish with his mules because of that.

"Will they torture us?" Carlotta asked.

"We will try to reach the soldiers," Mary said.

"You speak their tongue?"

"Yes. In the grandfather times the Comanche were part of my Snake people."

"Are you the same? Are you like them?" Carlotta's dread infused her face.

"It is said we are much the same. This I am told. I have never met the southern People."

"Do—your people welcome others?"

Mary smiled. "We are very friendly. Our home is in the foothills of the mountains. We welcome visitors and give them feasts. I've never heard of a Snake hurting visitors."

"How do you mean, the same?"

Mary thought a bit, and drew Dirk closer to her warmth because the wind robbed them of heat. Within her hands lay her own son, small and smooth, half her blood and half Mister Skye's blood.

"Each Shoshone and each Comanche seeks his own medicine," she said. "My Shoshone people and the Comanche people have no great chief over us. We do what we will. We are different from other Peoples. Not even chiefs or medicine givers can tell us what we must do, although we respect them. A Shoshone will do what his spirit-helpers tell him. We have no laws like those of white men, and only a few ancient ways to follow. But we love each other and are very happy."

The white woman stared at her a long time, until Mary felt uneasy. But the woman said nothing. Mary returned Dirk to the little prison of his cradleboard, and drew the leather flap over it to keep the icy wind off the child's head. The sun didn't warm her in this open place. She felt the numbing power of the winter wind, but it was not time to go.

"I don't want to die," Carlotta said. "But I'm goink to die. I see I did not get away."

Mary touched her arm. "Don't give up. Mister Skye never gives up. Do you see anything bad out there? There is nothing."

Carlotta suddenly grasped Mary's arm. "Shoot me. Please shoot me. Please."

Mary shook her head. "No, that is not a good way," she said.

Peachtree approached, the wind whipping at the tails of his clawhammer coat making them flap like black flags. "I'm leaving. We've rested the mules."

She shook her head.

"I want to get out of here. We can hide, that's what we'll do. We'll find a place off the trail, a crevice, a gully, and we'll hide. They'll never see us."

"No place to hide, Mister Peachtree. The wheel tracks will bring them to your hiding place like badgers. This is their home; they know every place a rabbit can hide. No mouse escapes them."

"I can't stand it. The wind's blown the heat out of me."

"Rest the mules," she said. "Then they won't fail you when you need them."

"We could be two miles closer to the soldiers on the Mora by now. I'm leaving."

"You will go without me. See how the ponies rest, heads low. See how they suck air. Stay. Maybe we will go when the Comanches come."

"You're trapping me here. Comanches are Shoshones. That's what this is all about." He eyed Carlotta. "Get on the wagon. We'll harness your horse. He'll learn to pull fast enough."

Slowly Carlotta shook her head. Mary thought the woman was inside a dream. Something terrible was flowing through her soul.

"You, Carmody," Peachtree said. "I'm leaving. We can harness your mule; you can ride a wagon. We'll make it. I won't exhaust the stock. Believe me, my life depends—"

Elisha Carmody pondered it. "My deepest instinct, sir, is to place my fate in the hands of the Skyes. Somehow, I find myself believing that if I am still drawing breath tomorrow, it'll be because the Skyes have preserved us. We've not spent twenty minutes resting the horses. It's far from enough. Look at them."

But Peachtree was staring at the eastern horizon, mesmerized by something. "It's them," he whispered. "It's them. I saw them."

Carmody squinted in the direction that Peachtree pointed. "I see nothing, sir."

"I saw them. I swear it. The light caught them a moment. Like a swarm of ants."

They all stared. Carmody professed to see nothing. Peachtree swore there were thousands. Concorde saw them and then lost them in tricky light. Hercules saw absolutely nothing, and laughed.

"It's your overheated mind, Hyacinth," said Concorde. "You'll be seeing them jump out of the grass at you."

Mary stood up. She had keen eyes and she could read the blurred distances better than these white people. For a long while she saw nothing, but then she saw the faintest shadow of movement, a column of them as long as two white men's miles, and a great knot of them in advance, riding her way. Riding where Victoria and Mister Skye must be.

Chapter 48

Skye saw death coming. If he were even to lift his revolver he would be pierced by a half dozen arrows, and he would see his lights go out. He and Victoria would die here in a nameless gulch in the southern Plains, trying to defend an outfit that didn't want help. Their flesh would feed coyotes, and no one would remember them. His son, if he lived, would not remember him. Mary, if she lived, would weep, and return to her people.

The two bonnet-wearers descended the grassy slope to count coup. Skye thought that the only thing that kept life in him now was the peculiar Comanche lust to torture anyone who was not one of the People. Skye thought to kill himself. All he had to do was lift his revolver to his mouth. Victoria would find her own means. Death would surely be more merciful than being slowly dismembered, burned, bled, gutted, emasculated, blinded, or left to parch in the sun.

But that was not in him. "Jawbone," he said to her.

She nodded, and let the tension out of her bowstring. Skye

carefully slid his revolver into its nest at his hip, disarming himself for the sake of living a while longer. This was not the moment to fight and die.

He stared at Jawbone, who stood shivering, flat-eared, wild-eyed, mad. These southern Comanches would not know of him or his medicine. He would be only another prize of war for them to take and use. But soon they would find out that Jawbone was much more than a captured horse.

The short, stocky bonnet-wearers reached Skye and Victoria. One studied Skye's bearclaw necklace, big medicine, and smiled faintly. He lifted a powerful arm to count coup, and Skye judged that the moment to live or die had come.

"Go!" he said.

Jawbone screeched, a demented scream that raised the hackles of the warriors. He whirled madly, his rear hooves cutting an arc that caught one bonnet-wearer and then the next, the brutal thud of hoof against brown flesh spinning both warriors to the ground. Skye dove to earth, Victoria too, squarely into the dying, shuddering bonnet-wearers, whose bodies lay broken.

Jawbone lunged madly at the nearest Comanche, who tumbled backward to escape. Jawbone bowled into him, sent him sprawling, and kicked the downed man even while springing at the next. That one fell back. Jawbone missed, whirled, butted the falling warrior. The terrible blue horse catapulted into a knot of three warriors running for their lives. One Comanche, coming to his senses, hurled a lance at the horse. It scraped by his belly, leaving a thin welt of blood in its wake.

Skye grabbed his revolver and shot a warrior through the chest just as the warrior drew his bowstring. The ball drove the warrior backward into the ground. He trembled and then all motion stopped.

Jawbone screeched, pawed air, and ran down a warrior who had lifted his bow. He hit the warrior with his chest, knocking him twenty feet. The warrior collapsed with a crack of broken bone, shivered, and lay still.

The last two Comanches fled, but Jawbone sprang upon them as they scrambled up a grassy slope. He caught one's arm in his teeth, whirled the man to earth, and ran over him toward the other. He butted the fleeing man with his brute head, sending him flying. An arrow from Victoria caught the warrior in midflight, and he tumbled to earth dead. The berserk horse screeched, ran from body to body, and finally stood, atremble, before Skye and Victoria.

Skye could barely endure the sight of such carnage. Some lay still as death. Others spasmed and groaned, their limbs poking out in grotesque angles. One lay on his belly, his back broken, trying to lift himself. The bonnet-wearer beside him lay dying, his eyes searching Skye's face, his torso convulsing. The one near Victoria lay inert, his head split open by a whirling hoof. Skye saw little blood; the berserk horse had broken bones and skulls, pulverized the innards, while scarcely opening flesh.

Nauseated, Skye sat up and stared at the carnage around him. Eight dead or dying Comanches. He trembled. So much death. He stood slowly, sickened by the whole business. His legs trembled under him.

He saw Victoria alive, muttering to herself. She had weathered the horror better, and stood angrily, her bow poised and ready to punch an arrow into anything that threatened.

Jawbone pawed the earth. The horse scarcely breathed hard. Slowly the madness left his yellow eyes, and he lowered his ugly snout into Skye and pushed.

"Avast," Skye muttered.

He hated death. He asked no more of life than to enjoy it. He spat the foulness from his mouth and studied the dying, alert for trouble.

He saw Victoria's pinched face. The carnage had been too much for her, too. She studied one dead or dying Comanche after another, her eyes blinking back tears. She eyed Jawbone, cursing him, unhappy with the medicine horse even though Jawbone had just saved her life.

Skye felt parched. His body refused to function. He wobbled to each Comanche, his revolver wavering before him. Five lay dead; three lived. One live one was paralyzed from the waist down. Another had a fractured shinbone and a gouting wound that was slowly pumping out his lifeblood. The third showed no sign of injury, but lay on his back breathing raggedly, his gaze alert.

Victoria padded from one to the other, counting coup with a sharp blow of her hand. She had counted more coup in her life than Skye could remember.

Victoria muttered something and climbed the grassy slope to look around. She vanished over its brow, leaving Skye alone with the dead and dying and his grisly mission of mercy. He knew they would have tortured and killed him, yet the simple act of putting them out of their misery filled him with dread.

He knew that killing two of them would be an act of mercy. The broken-backed one had little to look forward to. But that was the difference between him and them. He valued human life, even the lives of enemies; they valued only their own. He supposed it was because he had been born an Englishman, girded by law and simple Christian belief in treating others as he would want to be treated.

He had never liked to kill. For all his years in the wilds he had been forced to it now and then, to defend himself or his loved ones, or his allies and friends. But he had found no glory in it; he didn't rejoice, as tribesmen did, upon the taking of life. It had always left him hollow and diminished, as if this darkest of human acts had robbed him of his claim to be a worthy mortal. He had never taken a scalp; had never felt anything but pity for the dead and those who loved them. That was true even back in his trapping days, when he had to deal with the lethal Blackfeet. Some of the free trappers rejoiced in murder, and turned themselves into savages as bloody as those around them. He never had. He didn't now. He never would.

Wearily, he lowered the barrel of his Hawken to the neck of the broken-backed one, who watched him impassively. But he didn't pull the trigger. It was one thing to fire at a warrior racing down on him with a lance or drawn bow, a rifle or warclub; another to kill a helpless husk of mortality. He found a knife and handed it to the warrior. Let him choose. The man clutched it, his fingers clamping and unclamping, his eyes unblinking.

He found a knife on a dead warrior and handed it to the one with the leg fracture. Let him choose, too. That one lifted himself up and hurled it at Skye. It wobbled by and skidded along the grass. The man fell back gasping. Jawbone screeched. Skye pulled a bandanna from his pocket, ran it around the warrior's thigh, found a stick for leverage and twisted it into a tourniquet while the man gnashed his teeth. Skye placed the man's hand on the stick. The warrior held it, hating Skye for giving him life. By Comanche standards, it was the ultimate shaming to be deprived of a heroic death against the enemy.

Skye cut open the man's leggin and eyed the fracture. The broken bone bulged the lacerated flesh of the man's calf. He was going to have to pull. He sat down opposite the man's moccasin, grasped it, and yanked. The man gasped, and then panted in agony, tears rising in his eyes. The lump vanished from the calf and didn't slide back out when he released the leg. Skye cut the long fringes from the warrior's leggin and made a crude splint of the blood-blackened leather while the warrior watched with eyes that radiated rank hatred.

He heard Victoria, and watched her slide downslope. She was leading two captured ponies, a dun and a black.

She stared, angrily. "You crazy sonofabitch. Them no-good devils want to butcher you. That's all they got in their heads, is putting an arrow or bullet through you, or torturing us both until we're out of our heads. You crazy?"

"Let's go, Victoria."

"You're crazy, white man!"

"I do what I have to," he muttered. *White man* was her ultimate insult.

She found the bonnet-bearer who had manhandled her, slid out her knife, grabbed the scalplock, and sliced a circle in the scalp. She pressed her moccasin on his neck to pin his head to the earth and yanked. The scalp didn't pop loose, so she tugged violently, muttering imprecations. That time it ripped free, leaving a circle of tan bone. She held it up, triumphantly, watching the juices drip from it, and howled like a lobo wolf. Then she tied it to her saddle.

The third one lay quietly, his unblinking gaze on Skye.

"Let him go," Skye said to her.

"He'll try to kill you. It's bad. You'll shame him. He'll hate you for not killing him."

"Then he can live with his shame."

"That's worse than killing him. You make him feel bad now."

"Maybe that's the way to stop Comanches from killing, Victoria. Make 'em feel bad about war."

"It'd be easier to stop a wolf from hunting meat."

Heavily, he clambered into his saddle. She mounted her mare, and they left, leading her two prizes.

At the nearest rise, she broke ahead, circled around, and rode up the rear until she could peek over its ridge without being seen. Then she rode down and met Skye again.

"They're coming," she said. She eyed him, and spat. "And they don't have no white man's weaknesses, either."

He saw tears on her weathered cheeks, and knew she felt as bad about the carnage as he did. They had saved their own lives and kept the wolves away from the wagons, but neither rejoiced.

Chapter 49

Mutiny. Hyacinth Zephyr Peachtree seethed with resentment. He could threaten Hercules and Concorde with instant dismissal but it would do no good. They were going to obey the squaw, even if she led them all to their doom. How that Shoshone woman wielded power over his men he couldn't imagine.

She called a halt at the foot of the Wagon Mound, that bread-shaped landmark that looked just like the sheeting on a prairie schooner to travelers on the Santa Fe Trail.

"We will rest them," she said, pointing to the weary mule teams.

"Madam, perhaps it hasn't occurred to you that Comanches are bearing down upon us this very instant. Those are the words of your husband."

She ignored him. "We will rest them," she said. "They look tired."

"They're not so bad. They'll get us to the Army. They know my whip. I'm not of a mind to be captured, tortured, and scalped. That may be just your cup of tea, but it's not to my taste."

She ignored him, much to his annoyance. He reminded himself that he had sacked the Skyes several times over— which made her domination of the outfit all the more galling.

He watched Hercules unhook the five-mule team of the second wagon and lead it to verdant grass that miraculously carpeted the whole flat.

"I'll have your hide, you jackanape," he said. "We'll have a reckoning in Santa Fe if we aren't tortured and mutilated first."

But Hercules ignored him. Carmody unburdened and picketed his mule. Carlotta slid off her pony and gave it to Mary, who put it on grass along with her horses.

"How long do you plan to sit here and let the Comanches catch up?" he asked. "You'll invite them to supper, I suppose."

"A while. I will go see."

"In a while it'll be dark; then what? Camp here and twiddle our thumbs until they ride in and butcher us."

She adjusted her cradleboard until it rested easier and then padded toward the flank of the huge rock that erupted perhaps five hundred feet above them. When he saw that she was going to reconnoiter, he followed. She hastened toward the northeastern slope and climbed it, leaving him puffing behind. She obviously wasn't going to try for the top, just for enough height to give her a grand view.

By the time he caught up with her, wheezing air, she was turning to come back down.

"What did you see?" he asked.

She pointed at a small knot of horses. "My man and Victoria," she said.

"But that's several horses."

"It is my man."

"Are you sure?"

She smiled. "They have two captured horses. That is good."

He didn't see what she saw, but he took her word for it. "What else?" he asked.

"There. Like a cloud shadow passing over the land."

He followed the vector of her finger, and saw a sight so terrifying he wanted to scramble into the nearest hole. There on the horizon, but much closer than before, a vast migration crawled southward, a gigantic snake composed of thousands of people and animals.

"What do you make of it?"

She shrugged. "Big Comanche village. Many horses. Too many to count. See there." She pointed to a closer flat, and he saw another moving mass, this time distinguishable as an army of horsemen jostling southward. More than he could count. And closing in.

"My God," he muttered. "Let's get out of here!"

"We will rest the mules," she said, turning down the slope.

"Whose side are you on?" he cried.

She turned and stared into his eyes. "The night is a friend," she said.

Minutes later Skye and Victoria rode in, leading a dun and a black. The guide stared at the grazing mules and horses and into the frightened faces around him.

"We bought a little time," he said. "But it won't make 'em friendlier. How long have you been here?"

"Just a little," Mary said.

"Too long, Skye. They're rested now. We'll be butchered if we stay here," Peachtree said.

Skye squinted into the western heavens. "Sundown in half an hour. Dark in an hour," he said. "Let 'em rest."

"But my God, Skye . . ."

Skye dismounted from Jawbone and let the sweat-caked horse wander free. "You're right, mate. It's hard to call this one," he said. "We could run. Your stock'd last a few miles—maybe less. Then you'd be tugging harness off the dead and dying. After that you'd be on foot. You can do that—or we can walk them through the night, with plenty of rests."

"Comanches won't attack us?"

"I didn't say that. There'll be eager ones, warriors looking for horses and coups, gnawing on our flanks all night. But a concerted attack? Moon's coming up after midnight; that'll be when the trouble starts."

"We're going to walk all night?"

"You got any better idea? Starlight's all we got, but it's some. Night's the great blessing of the outnumbered, Peachtree. It's a merciful blanket."

"Can you find the trail?"

He gazed south. "Yonder's where the mountain branch and the main trail meet up. Lot of traffic over that piece, clear to Santa Fe. Victoria'll read it, even by starlight."

"How far to the Army?"

"I don't rightly know. The Mora River's maybe twenty, twenty-five miles. I don't know where the post is. Could be south of the river."

"We saw two bunches of the devils; the village off on the horizon and a war party. How far's the war party from us?"

"I don't rightly know. I'm thinking an hour and a half, unless they want to run their ponies. Comanches always have plenty of fresh ponies along. If they pushed, they could bloody well be here before dark."

"An hour! We've got to fort up!"

"I'm guessing they're not going to try. We're just sport. A couple of wagons, a few horses. They'll try to pin us down, get south of us to block the road, and have their fun in the moonlight."

"What if you're wrong? Skye, you've got human lives in your hands. One miscalculation and we're all dead."

"That's been going through my mind, mate."

"Where'd those two horses come from?"

"Dead Comanche scouts."

"They'll help. We can harness one—"

Skye shook his head. "They're plumb scared of white men. They'd go crazy in harness." He turned to Carmody. "See if you can ride one."

Elisha Carmody nodded. He clambered aboard the black, into a rawhide Comanche saddle. The black stood rigidly, its ears laid back. Victoria handed Carmody the rein, which ran to a cord knotted around the horse's jaw and tongue.

The horse pitched. Carmody yanked its head up. The horse sidled. Carmody turned it in a tight circle. The black gathered its muscles to leap; Carmody pulled its head clear around to his boot. Then the horse settled into a shivering walk.

"All right, mate, he's yours." Skye turned to the roustabout. "Hercules, the other's yours if you want it. Take some weight off that second wagon."

"Good idea, Skye," Hercules said. "Always wanted a Comanch pony. They run like the devil."

"But Skye—their shotguns are on the wagon," Peachtree said. "I want him up there, defending us."

"He can carry his shotgun, Professor." He turned to Carlotta. "You want to ride or sit a wagon?"

"Just kill me before they come," she said.

Skye walked to her and enfolded a small pale hand in his massive ones. "Carlotta. You're one of the bravest women I've ever known. We'll get you through."

But tears welled in her eyes, making Peachtree wonder once again what had happened back there.

Peachtree had enough. Hundreds of Comanches an hour away, and here they all sat. He hurried out to his team intending to hook it to the doubletree of his wagon. Let them sit around for the torturing; he would be far gone.

But Concorde reached the mules ahead of him. "Boss, they hardly done got a chance to rest."

"Get out of my way."

"Boss—there's no sense in running 'em to death."

"I'm not going to run them; we're going to trot, and I'll be five miles south by the time they reach you. Far enough not to hear your screaming when the red devils cut off your privates."

Skye loomed up. "All right, Peachtree. You take one of thóse Comanche ponies. He's fresh enough. Go if you must. We'll follow along with your wagons. Go find the post and bring help."

"Are you sure there's a post to find?"

"Bent told me they're starting a post. That's all I know."

"Will I dodge Comanches?"

"Looks that way, mate. Some'll be out ahead of the rest to cut us off."

The decision paralyzed Hyacinth Z. Peachtree.

Skye's steady calm pooled around the guide, making him seem like a fortress.

"Mister Skye," he said, wearily, "I am in your hands."

"Not my hands, mate," Skye said softly. "We're in the hands of God. I'm just as afraid as you."

Chapter 50

In all his years, Elisha Carmody had never hungered for night as he did now. He could barely endure the waiting. He fully expected silent savages to pounce out of the thickening dusk and butcher them. The only mercy was that Victoria had posted herself up the slope of the Wagon Mound, where she studied the quiet prairies with her sharp eyes and Skye's telescope.

November might be cold, but now it offered the mercy of an early nightfall. All of them, including the Skyes, had been strung as taut as a fiddle string. Skye paced restlessly. Hyacinth Peachtree had sunk into silent hysteria. Mary Skye studied the murky distances and fondled her fussing child, who sensed his mother's fears. And poor Carlotta Krafft-Ebing had simply curled up into a ball, her arms clasping her own body, as if awaiting the executioner.

All of this waiting, he knew, was to rest the mules and horses. These trail-worn critters were going to pull the wagons and carry their loads through the entire night after a long day of hauling, and months of body-wasting toil. The Skyes were giving the animals—and themselves—the only chance.

To help endure the wait, he worked with the black Comanche pony again. He mounted and dismounted. He scrubbed off the white handprints on its rump and the white chevrons from its withers. They had been some warrior's horse medicine for battle. He discovered that no saddle blanket lay under the rawhide saddle; that the horse's back had been scarred and galled. He folded his bedroll blanket into quarters and cinched the Comanche saddle over it.

He saw Victoria hastening down the slope, and fear flooded him, halting in his chest like a stalled heart.

"We go now," she said quietly.

"Where are they?" asked Skye.

"One scout pretty damn close, getting ahead of us. The rest come quick."

With that, the whole party exploded into action. In a minute the mules were hitched and everyone horsed or seated. With a wave of his hand, Skye led them south into a deepening blackness that Carmody felt embrace him like a lover. He could see only the palest fringe of gray over the brooding Sangre de Cristos in the west. The figures around him were dissolving in blurs, and finally into presences known more by ear than sight.

The darkness did not reassure him. The soft beat of his pony's hooves marked his passage. The squeak and groan of leather eddied around him. The iron tires of the wagons grated over rock ahead of him, sounding like thunder in the thickening silence. He heard the hollow scrape of travois poles behind him, and the occasional snorts and mutterings of the horses. What good was night when their passage was as noisy as a flock of crows? He wanted to glide like an owl, unknown to the world.

The long rest had certainly helped the livestock. He felt his pony walk at a brisk clip; his mule didn't need tugging. The mule teams put shoulder to collar, and pushed. There was something exhilarating about moving ahead; about fleeing from mortal danger. Still, he feared that the sharp-eyed Comanches would engulf them, and his last recollection in this life would be the searing jolt of an arrow piercing clear through him.

Then night fell at last like a wall of coal. He didn't even know where he was going; the pony simply followed the rest. A brutal wind laced his back like a hundred arrowpoints, bringing on it the hint of something that animated his pony. He feared the black would wheel and bolt for his own herd and the familiar scents of the Comanche village. The cloudless heavens stabbed pinpricks of light that separated the sky from earth but he could not see even his closest companions.

This was a night passage. He had always supposed that the night hid evil from the world; that night was the hour of murder and lust, torture and greed, while the benevolent sun shone upon mercy, charity, constancy, and work, when no deed was hidden from the assessments of others. But this night he blessed for its mercy. If he lived at dawn, he would remember this darkness kindly for sparing him another minute, another hour.

He dreaded the dawn. If they weren't yet in the safe bosom of the Army, the Comanche hordes would engulf them, even as trembling light would engulf the darkness. But at least for now he had the darkness for a friend, and a final chance to sum up his life and work.

A soft mutter of noise rose out of the gloom to his left, and it alarmed him. His horse stiffened under him. Then the noise receded into the slumbering silences. What was it? He feared the Comanches knew exactly where this little party was, and were circling around for an ambush when the moon rose. He wished he might ask Skye, but Skye led, and Mary and Victoria guarded their rear. He felt alone.

If he died now, he thought, would he have lived in vain? He knew his greatest work lay before him. With only the power of his rhetoric he hoped to free men from their private prisons, and give them the tools of joy. That enterprise might die tonight on the trackless wastes of this southern plain, and the world would never receive what he wanted to give it. The thought of dying now, his true calling scarcely begun, filled him with melancholy. He couldn't change the world, but if he were given time enough to win a few followers who could take his message of self-mastery and sovereignty to others, he would give his fellow Americans something precious. He wished suddenly that he had put his ideas into essays and published some tracts. Nothing troubled him more, in this dark hour of peril, than the thought that everything he believed in might die with him.

But not all of him would perish. He had given the world sons. He had helped his constituents. He had known love unbounded, sweet as rose petals, and the bosom of Deborah, the woman he would love beyond the grave. Those things could not be taken from him by a Comanche arrow. He dreaded torture, but if it came to him and his body didn't betray him, he would concentrate upon his memories, upon those hours, also in the tender dark, when he had held his beloved in his arms.

He felt himself riding up to someone, and it proved to be Skye.

"We'll rest 'em a few minutes," Skye said.

"But we've ridden only an hour."

"We'll save 'em for the moonlight," Skye said. "Some Comanche are sliding around us. A few scouts anyway, out in front of the rest. They're using owl talk. I've known it from Jawbone. He tells me things."

"Won't they put an arrow into us if we stop?"

"If you can't see them, they can't see us. And Victoria has ways, mate."

"If it weren't for you, Mister Skye, I'd go to pieces."

Skye laughed quietly. "If it weren't for Jawbone, Victoria and Mary, I'd join you."

"What are our chances?"

Skye lifted his topper. "If I measured odds, I'd be under

the sod—long ago. There's only one rule: make the best of it even if it's a bad hand. Never quit. Never give up."

"That's a comfort, sir."

"I'll go look after Carlotta, mate. She's the one I worry about."

He vanished into the stillness. Off a way, a coyote barked. He lifted the collar of his coat against a biting northwind that numbed his neck and hands and robbed his feet of sensation. Then, imperceptibly, the entourage started up again. The iron tires crunched gravel; horses snuffled. He heeled the pony and yanked his packmule along. They moved through an engulfing blackness. He felt almost safe as long as they were moving.

He heard faint papery noises out upon the blackness, and his horse did too. They struck cold terror in him. He wondered whether he was silhouetted against the starlight; whether some savage would spring out of the night and bash his head open with a single blow of a warclub.

But it was no good to entertain terrors. The thing to think about was not a warrior leaping at him, but how he might dispatch some warrior stalking him. He wished he had his carbine in hand; it hung from a sheath on his packmule. He lacked so much as a stick with which to defend himself.

He realized that for every terror he entertained, Carlotta Krafft-Ebing must be feeling a hundred. He could comfort her. That would be a worthy service. He reined up and let the soft shuffling sounds pass him by until he thought she approached.

"Carlotta?"

He received no answer.

"Carlotta, it's Elisha."

A ridden horse edged closer.

"Is it Hercules? Mary?"

The horse slid toward him. He could hear it ten or fifteen feet off.

"Who are you?" he whispered, and knew by a faint smoky

smell borne by the north wind even before his eyes confirmed it. He kicked his pony hard and it spurted ahead. But he knew it was too late. The Horseman of the Apocalypse plunged after him. An instant later the footlong point of a lance pierced his back. He felt the iron stab through his own muscle and gut, a white explosion, even as he felt himself catapulted clear out of the saddle, skewered by a giant shaft. He tumbled over his pony's ears toward the onrushing earth, and knew he was dead.

Chapter 51

The sound of scuffle and a single groan froze Skye. He had known the sound of muffled violence for as long as he had been in the mountains. He peered about sharply, expecting a war-ax to cleave his skull, but saw nothing in the inky foreground. Under him Jawbone trembled, ready for mayhem.

He waited for Peachtree's team to shuffle by.

"Whoa up, Hyacinth," he said softly. "There's trouble."

"Here? Are you sure?"

"Stop the wagons, and don't shoot at shadows." He addressed the blackness behind him. "This is Skye. I'm calling roll. Give me your names now," he said in a voice intended to carry no farther than the end of the column.

"Peachtree."

"Parsons."

From farther back, "Concorde heah, boss."

"Hercules, riding beside Concorde."

Silence.

"Victoria, who's back there?" Skye asked, filled with dread.

"Dammit, how should I know?" she replied.

"I am here, Mister Skye," Mary said.

"Is Carlotta with you?"

"Yes," came a woman's voice.

"Elisha?"

Silence.

"Elisha, where are you?"

From the darkness on the right rose the faint drum of hooves, slowly fading.

"Elisha Carmody, answer if it's safe to do so."

Skye sighed. He would have to ride back for a look. "I'm going back for Elisha," he said in a voice meant to carry. "Don't shoot me. This is Skye. Don't shoot me. Concorde and Hercules, do you understand that?"

He heard some muffled yesses. He turned Jawbone back and rode, humming a tuneless song, his revolver clamped in his hand.

"Elisha, speak to me," he said. "We're missing you. Elisha, where are you? Whistle once."

He tunneled back through the mineshaft of night, passing the second wagon.

"Ah'm here, Skye." Concorde's voice.

"I'm beside the wagon, Skye." Hercules's voice.

"All right."

A dread of what lay ahead filled Skye. Jawbone minced like this around death and blood.

He found himself among the pack animals and travois ponies.

"Dammit, Skye, we're here."

"Who, Victoria?"

"Me and Mary and Dirk, and the Potawatomi lady."

"We're missing Carmody."

"The sonofabitch is dead. I heard it."

He heard weeping. "Carlotta, my women are right beside you."

He turned back, sensing Jawbone detour around a place. "Elisha, Elisha," he whispered. Then he straightened. "I'm getting off Jawbone and looking around. Hold your fire."

"Carmody's missing?" Peachtree's voice.

"He's not answering."

"Skye, is it possible?"

Skye didn't answer. He felt around in the darkness, dreading what he might find. But only silence rose up at him.

He finally drifted back to Jawbone. "Nothing," Skye announced. His voice would carry as far as it must.

"The man got took away by the redskins," Concorde said. "Lordamighty."

Peachtree said, "There's nothing we can do, Skye. Let's go."

"We've got to know," Skye said. That was the law of the mountains. Every man helped another no matter what the risk. He remembered the time Jim Bridger was just a lad, and had been appointed to watch over old Hugh Glass, who had been mauled almost to death by a grizzly. The brigade couldn't wait for Glass to die, but neither would they desert him. Bridger was supposed to stay and bury him, but didn't. Glass survived, and somehow crawled miles for help, dragging a broken leg. Old Gabe had never lived it down. Skye would never violate the iron law; if Elisha Carmody could be saved, Skye would save him.

"Peachtree, have you a lantern?" Skye asked.

"Good God, Skye, they'll put an arrow through you."

"I want a lantern, mate."

"They'll put arrows in us. If Carmody's gone, he's gone."

"Give me a lantern, mate."

"Sonofabitch, Skye." Victoria's voice brimmed with anger.

They were all afraid, none more than himself. He groped his way up to the medicine wagon and found Peachtree fumbling around his cabinet. "It's a candle lantern, and here are two lucifers, you crazy idiot. Don't light it until I get out of here," Peachtree said.

Skye took the lantern and the matches and walked back to the area behind the second wagon where Jawbone had minced. He listened quietly, his ears and eyes straining for sight and sound, but he sensed nothing. He opened the lantern gate, and felt the candle within. Then he struck a lucifer on his boot. It flared blindingly, and he held the match to the wick until the candle lit. He heard a rustle out there and crabbed back to shadow. But nothing happened. Gingerly, he edged back to the lit lantern and lifted it.

"They'll see that miles away, Skye," Hercules said.

"It can't be helped."

Swiftly Skye walked down the entourage, working back to the women, whose unblinking eyes shone back at him. He turned around and hunted again, finding nothing. The Comanches had Carmody.

He tried one last sweep, hating the light, his flesh prickling against the arrows he expected. This time he roamed wider and found Carmody, scarcely ten yards from the women.

The lecturer lay on his stomach with a bloody black hole cratering his back. Skye lifted the lantern toward Carmody's head. A six-inch circle of naked scalp glowed yellowly.

"Elisha, Elisha," Skye cried, kneeling.

He found no life in the warm body. He peered around the darkness, finding no packmule or pony. He didn't need light anymore, and blew the candle out.

"Dammit," said Victoria, sliding beside Skye. "He's hurt?"

"Dead."

Peachtree called. "What is it, Skye?"

Skye stood, aching in his soul. "Elisha Carmody." He handed the snuffed lantern to Victoria, reached down, and lifted the man. Carmody had been a heavy man; weighty of body and mind. "I'm coming; don't shoot," he said, carrying Elisha toward the supply wagon.

"What is it?" That was Hercules's voice.

"We've lost Elisha."

He heard weeping somewhere behind, and silence ahead.

"We shouldn't have waited," Peachtree said. "You let them catch up." The accusation hung in the night.

Skye thought about it while he carried Elisha. The man lay so heavy in his arms. He had never carried a man so heavy. Had he doomed a good and noble man who was giving himself to the world? Skye thought of the road ahead, the exhausted livestock, the coming moonrise, and knew he could have done nothing else. A lone Comanche scout had tried for a coup and succeeded. They were still going to have to run when the Comanche Moon rose.

Skye didn't answer. Let them think it. If they lived through this night they might change their minds.

He laid Carmody upon an indentation in the tarpaulin of the wagon, daring Peachtree to complain. Carmody would ride safely there until they could bury him. It would add to the load on the five-mule team.

"You wanna drive, Hercules?" asked Concorde.

"What're you afraid of?" Hercules asked.

But Concorde clambered to the ground. "Ah guess Ah'll ride that pony," he said. It wasn't a question.

Skye could hear Hercules clamber to the seat, and Concorde pull himself into the Comanche saddle.

Skye found Jawbone and mounted. The night was filled with unspoken accusations that flew by him like arrows. He rode slowly back to the women and found them huddled together on horseback.

"Miss Krafft-Ebing, I'd like you to ride with Hercules."

"But . . . but . . ." She was trying to say something but was so rattled she couldn't.

"It's safer up there beside him." He didn't want her back with his wives. Mary and Victoria might have their hands full against Comanches and wouldn't have time to protect Carlotta. He didn't want her in the middle of the train somewhere, to be picked off the way Elisha had been.

She let him take the reins and lead her pony up to the wagon. Mutely she dismounted and then clambered up to the bench.

"Lot more weight now, Skye," Hercules said.

"It can't be helped. You guard her. And make sure what you're shooting at. I reckon moonrise is an hour away. I think you'll be doing a bloody bunch of shooting. Give her the lines and defend her with your fowling piece."

"What's the delay, Skye?" Peachtree's voice.

"Start 'em rolling, mate," Skye said tautly.

He watched the wagons lumber ahead as heavy as mastodons in the night. The teams required whipping, and didn't want to move. Skye sat Jawbone, feeling heartsick. Dead, dead. Elisha Carmody, a man with courage of mind and a vision of goodness.

His silent troupe rode by and he fell in beside Mary and Victoria. The blackness didn't conceal their tears from him.

"I don't know if we'll make it," he whispered to them. "I'm doing the best I know how, and it seems like nothing at all."

Victoria steered her mare close beside him, and he felt her hard little hand clamp over his. In the midst of their terror she was giving him love.

Chapter 52

Carlotta huddled next to Hercules, feeling the night wind numb her feet. The weary team stumbled along, not far from collapse. Hercules occasionally cracked the whip to remind the mules of duty. She could barely make out the medicine wagon ahead of them. Concorde was riding beside Skye's women, as far from Carmody's body as he could get.

She turned but could scarcely see Carmody's form behind her on the tarpaulin. The oddest sensation overtook her. It was as if, in leaving life, he had bequeathed his treasure to her and now it rested in her soul like gold coins. She had ceased being afraid. She had simply run out of her supply of terror. She peered alertly into the murk, listening for rhythms unlike those of the shuffling mules and sullen groan of the wagon. Her fear had transmuted into resolve. She might die this very night but she would die a transformed woman.

Elisha Carmody had shown by his own example what private discipline might achieve, not only for his own contentment but for the sake of others. She yearned suddenly to be like Elisha, the martyred apostle of self-dominion, the victim of a noble savage.

This was the New World! She felt herself a traitor to everything she had stood for. But she also felt stronger than she had ever been. She felt the stirrings of dominion over her ungovernable temper, dominion over her lusts, and dominion over her terrors. She was just as afraid now as she had been before Carmody's death, and yet something was different: she had triumphed over her emotions.

"Hercules," she whispered, "this good man behind us, he was a great citizen of your Republic."

"Shhh, Carlotta. We've got to listen for trouble."

"He set me free, Hercules. I am forever indebted to this American saint."

Hercules elbowed her.

"We must not be afraid," she said.

"I'm so scared I can't swallow," he replied.

"Be like Elisha Carmody, in command of his heart. Don't let anythink rule you."

He grunted and clapped lines over the croups of his mules.

She slid into silence. It would invite an arrow to talk. The hard seat wearied her, but she endured it. She spotted in the east the first sign of the rising moon, a faint glow over a distant horizon; the opening jaws of hell. Maybe she would die. She suddenly felt gladness that on the eve of her death she had found something better than tantrums, something finer than surrendering to her volcanic whims.

The medicine wagon ahead stopped, and Hercules tugged the reins. His mules quit at once.

Hyacinth's voice drifted back to her. "But Skye, if we just keep going we'll outrun them. The teams are all right."

Hercules grunted his disagreement.

Skye and Jawbone ghosted close. Already the dim glow on the horizon ruined the peace. "We'll rest as long as we can. We may have to run if the Comanches use the moonlight."

"How do you know they're out there?" Hercules asked. "We haven't been troubled for hours."

"I don't," Skye said simply.

"These mules are done in, Skye."

He sighed. "All the more reason to rest 'em, mate. Five minutes' rest now might save our lives."

"How far are we from the soldiers?"

"I wish I knew, Hercules."

"What if the Army ain't there?"

"There's likely some Mexican *placitas* on the Mora." Skye studied her. "How are you doing, Miss Krafft-Ebing?"

"Mister Skye, I have somethink to say to you: maybe if we die now it will never be said. You are a good man. You and your good wives. Elisha Carmody was a good man. He gave me the gift of life. His words come to me now. I will go from weakness to strength. Because of him I have courage. Because of you I have hope."

Quite distinctly in the thickening light she saw him lift his topper and settle it again. "Miss Krafft-Ebing," he said. "You're a brave woman. We'll do our best. And if we fail, I'll take your kind words with me into hell."

A sudden anguish clutched her throat. "Come," she said, reaching out to him. He edged Jawbone closer until she could smell the moist breath of that terrible horse. Then she caught Skye's rough hand and pressed it between her own. She kissed his cheek.

"Well, now, Miss Krafft-Ebing."

"Whatever happens now, Mister Skye, you know of my love and respect."

"I, ah, thank you. Yes. Ah . . ."

Ten minutes later the moon sat on the prairie like a distant fire. It was pared on one side, radiating orange light that drove away the murkiness and made everything plain.

"Is that a Comanche Moon, Mister Skye?" Hercules asked.

"That's a Comanche Moon, mate. It was full two nights ago. They love to raid when the moon's just past full. They wait for these nights like a child waits for Christmas. They own the whole night when they have a moon like this one."

The Comanche Moon illumined the world with a ghastly glow that whispered of scalpings and arrows and murder.

A coyote barked at the moon from a knoll to the north. Skye listened intently, saying nothing. Another coyote answered, far to the south.

"Comanches believe the coyotes are their brothers. So do the Snakes, Mary's people," he said softly. "Time to move along."

The wagons rolled again while mules coughed and muttered. Carlotta looked behind her. Mary and Victoria rode at the rear, behind a mass of horses; and Concorde rode with them. The heads and shoulders of Peachtree and old Parsons poked above the medicine wagon, as clear as a tintype. And sometimes she could see Skye, out in front. Flat grassland lay silvered and solemn about her, brooding with unseen menace. At least she could see several arrow-flights to either side, and that was a comfort. She could watch her death coming. Elisha Carmody hadn't been given that small blessing.

The fat perfidious moon vaulted whitely upward, painting the plains with a white glare. She felt naked before the world.

"You ever fire a revolver?" Hercules asked.

"No."

He reached to the floorboards and handed her a holstered revolver on a belt. "Well, I'm going to give you one. You hold it with both hands. You gotta cock it, pull the hammer back. Then you sight down the barrel and squeeze. Don't jerk; just squeeze. It'll surprise you, shove your hands right into the air. That's recoil. Just level it again and do the same. Every barrel's loaded. Look at them caps there on the nipples. Another thing: you jist wait your turn. Don't you go firing it at some shadow far out there. These here Colts are for close work. Sort of a last resort."

She felt the cold power of the weapon in her hands and

knew she could use it. Only a few hours ago she would have emptied all six chambers without effect. But not now. Elisha's soul had handed her courage as it departed. She felt sure of it.

"I think maybe I am good with this."

"Might save our lives, Carlotta. I've got the scattergun but that's it. Won't be time to reload, I reckon."

"No, I don't suppose so," she said. She lifted it, cocked it, let the hammer down slowly, and studied the vague distance where the light swam strangely.

Where faint movement paralleled the Peachtree entourage. It galvanized her. She looked to the other side and saw commotion there as well. Comanches on both sides, barely in sight.

"Oh!" she exclaimed.

Hercules sighed. "Skye was right. I'm glad we rested these critters. They're going to run until they drop, Carlotta."

She looked around her. To the rear, Victoria and Mary were steering their ponies in between the packhorses and travois horses for protection. Concorde was holding his shotgun ready. Ahead, Skye was putting Jawbone into a trot. The wagon teams lurched forward under the crack of whips.

"Wish we had rifles," Hercules muttered. "We could keep 'em out there, I think."

"Hercules, look at them."

The moonlight shot white embers off of scores of shadowy horsemen, dazzled from lance points, shivered the air like ghosts. The silver-brushed Comanches flowed on either side like a distant river of horses and riders. She knew she was seeing the entire warrior contingent of that village.

"I reckon we're at their mercy unless that fort pops up mighty fast," he said, something desolate in his voice. "May as well say *adiós* now, Carlotta. I thought I had fifty years left, instead of five minutes. Shows you what a fool I've been."

"Don't, Hercules."

So she would die after all, just like Elisha. She decided she would die a good death for Elisha Carmody. Maybe they would meet on some hazy shore across a black ocean and she could tell him that even for the minutes left to her, his vision had transformed her. She found comfort in the thought.

Chapter 53

Peachtree's tasseled whip snapped over the croups of the mules, blooding them into a sluggish trot. He cracked it again and again, until the weary team broke into a slow gallop. Somewhere ahead was the fort. He would drive them to it even if it killed them. But the instant he stopped the whipping, they slackened.

Around him, ghostly armies slid through the night, little more than tricks of light. But the Comanches weren't apparitions. He eyed Pontius irritably, feeling an impulse to throw the old man off and lighten the load by a hundred fifty pounds.

Skye and Jawbone blocked the path. The miserable guide was going to stop him again. White heat exploded through Peachtree. If it weren't for that wretch he'd be safe now. He thought to swerve around Skye but thought better of it. Instead, he tugged the lines. The mules quit instantly.

"Don't you preach to me about the teams, Skye," he said. "We're running for the fort."

"Rest them, Professor."

"Rest them! Are you mad?"

"We've got miles to go. You can't outrun Comanche. All you'll do is kill your mules. Rest a minute. Then just keep 'em moving. A moving target's hard to hit."

"But Skye—there must be a hundred of those devils."

"You'll waste lead shooting from a bouncing wagon."

"Skye, they'll pull ahead. They want to get between us and the fort."

Skye stared. "And you think you can outrun 'em."

Peachtree had no answer to that. He slumped in the seat, defeated. The teams had been hauling that wagon since the previous dawn. It was a miracle they could even walk.

"Give 'em a minute, mate. We're safe enough. We've a good field of fire; not a hill or a gulch in any direction. Then, with luck, we'll trot 'em to the fort. If not, we'll make a stand."

"But Skye—"

The guide eyed him gently. "You have a better idea?"

"We're all going to perish," Peachtree said. He eyed the slumping mules, which stood with heads low and legs braced. Their flanks heaved as they sucked the thin air. The truth of it was, the mules were about finished.

"I'm going back and check the others. Keep an eye out. There's always a few that'll sneak in."

"Do you think I haven't been watching? Do you think I'm some greenhorn?" Peachtree asked hotly.

Skye didn't reply, and the silence galled Peachtree.

The guide walked Jawbone to the rear, carrying his big Hawken. Reluctantly, Peachtree clambered down and began to rub his mules one by one, hoping that it would help them. Their tongues hung out; they hadn't been watered.

"Keep an eye peeled, Pontius," he said.

"I'd help you if I wasn't so stove up."

"Just watch."

"There's nothing out there but bloodthirsty savages meaning to stop my clock," Parsons said. "Just a few bushels and pecks of 'em. No match for three, four white men. I always hankered to check out right after the last curtain call, with the applause in my ears, sweet as honey. Just get back to the Green Room and sail away. Doesn't look like it'll happen. No boards to tread around here, is there? I have to admit, Hyacinth, this isn't the end I had in mind. I'd take it kindly if you saved a round for me if they swarm in. It'd be a little easier."

"Just watch, would you?"

"Well, I'm watching. This moonlight's pretty good and Skye's got us parked in plain sight, with bull's-eyes painted on us. That bunch, they're getting fractious out there; look at 'em. Say, Hyacinth, I'm aching worse than ever. You mind if I have a nip?"

"Yes, I mind. I want you alert."

"I reckon I could walk some with that Nepenthe in me. If we're going to have to walk, Hyacinth . . ."

"Oh, why not? You might as well croak painlessly." He abandoned his mule rubbing, extracted one of the last bottles of Nepenthe, and handed it to Parsons.

"Ah, heaven ten minutes before my arrival there," Parsons said, twisting the cork free.

Peachtree left the old man to his rambling and walked back to the second wagon, where Concorde was rubbing down that team. Hercules sat above, his fowling piece at the ready.

"They're done in, Professor," Concorde said. "They're plumb ground down. Dry as a temperance meeting. Maybe we can get another mile or two from them. It don't matter much. We can croak heah, or we can croak up ahead."

"They weren't heeding my whip none," said Hercules. "That's a sure sign. Maybe we should just fort up here."

"We're at the mercy of Skye. Whatever that oaf decides, that's our fate," Peachtree said. "I rue the day we met him."

Jawbone squealed. Skye came running.

"All right, start 'em walking. Keep 'em walking if they're up to it. Hold your fire. You're not going to see a live Co-

manche. They've a way of riding on the far side, shooting
from under the horse's neck. Best cavalry in the world."

"But Skye, if we don't shoot—"

"Keep your scatterguns for the last. Rifles count now. I'll
be shooting. So will Mary and Victoria. We're going to try to
keep them out a way, kill their horses. All right. Start 'em up.
If one's hit, cut him out fast and keep walking."

With that, Skye rode out front again. When Hyacinth
reached his wagon seat, the view from both sides filled him
with dread. Mounted Comanches rode slowly by, just beyond
rifle range, their circle steadily narrowing like a noose tightening around a neck.

He whipped the mules to action, and the caravan lumbered
ahead, so sluggish and worn out that he knew they wouldn't
go a mile.

He heard a shot from behind. Victoria sat on her unmoving
pony, swiftly reloading. Far to the rear, a Comanche horse
stumbled and collapsed. Another warrior plucked up its rider.

Ahead, Skye's fifty-caliber Hawken boomed. He too had
fired from a standing horse. At an awesome distance, a horse
collapsed. Its rider ran off while Skye reloaded.

For a while the Comanches kept their distance, and the terror that had constricted Peachtree's throat eased. Maybe the
Skyes could keep the Comanches off.

Skye shot again at a black blur with no visible effect. That
dark horse raced through the silvered night while Skye quietly poured a measure of Dupont down the barrel and
rammed a patched ball home with his wiping stick. He didn't
seem to be in a hurry, and Peachtree marveled at his calm.
His own pulse raced out of control.

The mules lagged. One staggered. Others stumbled. He
cracked a whip over them with little effect. He snarled at
them but they ignored him. They were so played out that not
even the flesh-cutting lash of his tassel could hasten them.

"Come on, come on, move," he muttered.

"They're as dead as we are," said Pontius. He lifted his

bottle again. "Say, Hyacinth, this stuff's a little frisky. It's raising a sweat."

"Pontius—cork that bottle and drive. I'm getting down. I'm going to grab a bridle and drag them, if that's what it takes."

Pontius plugged the cork and pocketed the bottle. "Well, I'll save the rest of this juice for the torturing," he said, taking the lines.

Two of the Skyes' rifles cracked, and two ghostly horses staggered out there, still beyond arrow range. The Skyes' deadly accuracy awed Peachtree. Skye had dismounted and was using Jawbone's saddle as a bench rest, firing with methodology.

Peachtree grabbed a bridle and tugged violently. The lead mules came along, and slowly the wagons lumbered through the night. He wished he could see, but on the ground he could catch only glimpses of the tightening noose.

Then an arrow snaked across the grass ten feet in front of Peachtree. He jumped. The Comanches had edged into range. Skye's rifle boomed. The nearest horse stumbled, pitched a rider, and staggered off. The warrior didn't retreat. He rained arrows on the caravan. One slapped into the medicine wagon. A horse screeched.

A rifle cracked. The warrior tumbled backward and slid to his knees. The wagons creaked on. Peachtree saw Hercules dragging his mules too. At least the wagons were rolling. Some of the packhorses were catching up, passing the wagons. He heard Victoria cursing.

He saw Mary stop her pony, patiently aim her rifle, and fire at a Comanche pony racing obliquely toward them. The horse staggered but kept on, shrieking its pain. Its rider swiftly loosed an arrow that snapped past Peachtree. Concorde fired his revolver at the closing horse; and again. The Comanche horseman raced by only rods away, his horse gouting blood but not down.

Mary shouted something in her Shoshone tongue at the Comanche. What good were savage curses? Peachtree wondered. On both sides the Comanches whooped bloodcurdling howls in the night. Scores of them swung to attack en masse, vanishing behind the ponies' bodies, closing in for the kill. Peachtree let go of the bridles and raced for his fowling piece. The Comanche Moon shown brightly upon the empty plain.

Chapter 54

Mary wept for her son, whose cradleboard she had lashed firmly to a travois. She would never see the infant again, but at least the child would survive. The Comanches would adopt the boy and he would grow up one of their own. They would never know that he was of their blood also.

The Plains sign language for both tribes was the Snakes, made by placing the right palm downward, forearm across chest, with a wriggling motion. They were almost one people. These warriors shouted words she knew. Maybe, she thought, she would shout back at them when they rode close.

Ahead, the pale-fleshed people had driven the wagons side by side and were herding the mule teams and packhorses between them, making a fort. All of Mister Skye's cautions had been for naught: the mules had played out and would not move. They would die right here because of Peachtree's haste.

But she had no time to think about that. The warriors were whirling out of the silvery night to butcher them. She lifted her thirty-six-caliber converted long rifle, aimed carefully at the closest horse, and fired. The butt smacked her shoulder even as the powder flashed. The racing horse staggered and kept on. She ducked as arrows followed the flash. She set the rifle on the ground; loading it took too long. She nocked an arrow and crouched behind her restless mare, waiting for the Comanche vanguard to come. When one horse veered straight toward her, she pulled her bowstring, feeling the power of the compound bow in her muscles, and loosed an arrow at the shadowed warrior hanging under the horse's neck.

"Why do you kill your friends?" she cried in their tongue. "You eat dogs!"

It was a deadly insult. No Comanche or Shoshone ate dogs. The coyote was their brother, the friend of the People. A Comanche band hosted packs of valued dogs.

She heard the punch of rifles and the shouting of the warriors. She understood what they were saying: "A-hee! We will kill these pale devils. A-hee! We will take scalps tonight."

"You won't take my scalp," she cried at them in her Shoshone tongue, as she loosed another arrow. That one pierced the heart of a horse. It screeched and died instantly, tumbling its rider, who sprang behind his war shield and began edging closer. She drove an arrow into the warrior's thigh just under his shield. "Why do you kill the People?" she cried. "You are worse than Arapaho dog-eaters."

The warrior screamed, fell to earth, and an instant later was rescued by two warriors, who lifted him up and dragged him away. She loosed an arrow at one's horse and it staggered.

"You are worse than *piamempits*, the Big Cannibal Owl," she howled after that one.

An arrow seared by, catching her hair and terrifying her. But she heard them talking to each other about her: Someone with the pale devils spoke the tongue of the People, they shouted.

"The *nunapi* protect us!" she yelled at them. Those were the Little People, feared by Comanche and Shoshone alike.

One of them turned and stared.

But they came and came, alone, by twos, by fives and tens, thundering by, loosing lethal arrows that thumped into pack-horses and clattered off the wagons. She heard screams, the sobbing of horses, the braying terror of mules. She glanced quickly at her son, still safe in the middle of the pack herd. Soon he would have no mother. A sob caught her throat.

The hollow booms of scatterguns reached her, along with the screams of horses and men. Revolvers crackled like burning fat, and Mister Skye's Hawken thundered regularly, like slow heartbeats. Her man lived. The warriors streaked by, barely visible behind their shields of horseflesh, so many she dared not lift her head.

"*Nemenuh,*" she cried. "I am of the People."

That time a warrior popped up, stared sharply, and raced off. She let him race by unscathed, a messenger carrying her word.

"*Nemenuh!*" she yelled after him.

She heard the mad bark of coyotes, a favorite war cry of her Shoshones and their southern cousins. Mister Skye's deep-throated Hawken boomed again and a horse tumbled. Her tears blurred her vision a moment; she wiped her eyes. Nine arrows left, and she would find nine targets for them before they took her scalp.

"*Nemenuh,*" one of them shouted to others. "*Nemenuh.*"

She wondered about Jawbone and spotted him back among the mules, angrily herding them in circles. Mister Skye hadn't let him out; the white men would shoot him. The last two warriors raced by but farther out, and a sudden hush caught her. She could see nothing but dead horses scattered out on the grass, meat for the coyotes and wolves. She lifted her long rifle, charged the barrel with a careful measure of powder from her horn, and drove a patched ball home with the stick. She slid a cap over its nipple to arm it. When they came again she would greet them with nine arrows, a charged long rifle, and her skinning knife.

Dirk whimpered. She rushed to the cradleboard, afraid. Nothing had harmed her son; the noise and agony had disturbed the little boy. "You are my son; you are Mister Skye's son," she crooned.

Victoria padded up to her. "What did you tell those dogs?"

"I told them they were worse than dog-eating Arapaho. The Little People, *nunapi*, protected us. Things like that. How are we hurt?"

"We all live. Two mules are dead; a packhorse also, the gray with the bad hoof. Hercules's arm bleeds like a river, but they stopped the blood. What else did you say to them, Mary?"

"*Nemenuh*. I am of the People. It was to confuse them."

Victoria spat, something angry in her hawking. She liked a good clean fight, not trickery. "You say anything else?"

"I told one he was worse than the Big Cannibal Owl—a creature they fear much."

Victoria's weathered face cracked into a weary smile. "Big Cannibal Owl," she said. "You ain't ever told me about him."

"He comes in the night to eat Snake children."

Victoria cackled.

Mister Skye came to her, holding his hot-barreled Hawken gingerly by the stock. He smelled of burned powder and sweat. "Something happened," he said. "They're gone. We beat 'em off. This child thought he'd go under for sure."

"Gone?" Mary was amazed.

"Not a lick of 'em in sight. They're not nerving themselves up for another try out there. We'd hear 'em singing and drumming. You got some kind of medicine I don't know about?"

"But Mister Skye—they're just getting ready again."

He sighed. "I don't feel it. They took a lick at us and something made 'em quit."

"She was yellin' at 'em in Snake," Victoria said. "She's

got a mean tongue. Sonofabitch!" Victoria cackled like a deranged hen, hoohawing around.

Mister Skye lifted his topper. He looked haggard, Mary thought. None of them had slept for a long time. That afternoon he and Victoria had fought the scouts. Then he had dealt with the crazy white men all night, and fought the Comanches. "You saved us, Mary," he said, gently.

Mary didn't like the honor he bestowed upon her. It had been wrenching to fight warriors who spoke her tongue, even if they were devils. She turned away, not wanting Mister Skye to see her face. She would tend to Dirk, who had suffered inside his little prison all night and needed to be cleaned.

But Victoria's arm found her. "Sonofabitch!" the old woman said, hugging Mary. "Them Snake words saved us."

Mary pushed back her impulse to weep. It had been like fighting her own Shoshones.

She cleaned Dirk, oblivious of the frantic men around her. The boy had messed himself. She wiped the leather with bunches of grass and then cleaned him with it. She was thirsty, but they had no water. She sat on a travois and took the child to her breast. He sucked greedily. Off a way the white woman huddled silently on a wagon seat. Hercules and Concorde pulled harness off two dead mules and then unharnessed an injured one and haltered it. Mister Skye led Jawbone out to sweet grass.

She saw no warriors out on the moonlit plains, but many dead horses, most of them shot by her man. He had saved the troupe with his big rifle, she thought. His bullets went true, for he was the greatest of all warriors. It hadn't been her Snake words. Somehow, it seemed terribly important to her to believe her Snake words hadn't turned back the tide. She shifted her son to her other breast, and sat contentedly. The pale men had all been saved. Her family had survived.

Chapter 55

Hyacinth Zephyr Peachtree surveyed the wreckage with mounting indignation. Two big mules dead of arrow wounds; another injured in the stifle and limping. Arrows poking out of his lacquered green wagon like porcupine quills. More arrows poking out of his supply wagon. The waterproof tarpaulin over its top had been perforated in a dozen places and would no longer protect his goods. And, terrible to behold, two arrows poking from the body of Elisha Carmody, lying on the tarp.

The Skyes had got him into it, of course. They had hung on like ticks, slowing him down, undermining his command of the Peachtree Medicine Show. But for the Skyes, he would be in Santa Fe by now instead of halted on a Comanche-infested plain.

Skye approached him. "You'll want to hobble them tonight, mate," he said. "There may be a few Comanches looking for a prize or two."

"Skye, we've managed to get along just fine without your advice."

"It's Mister Skye, sir."

"Skye, does it occur to you that you owe me three mules and repairs, at the very least?"

"No, I can't say that it does."

"Skye: if you hadn't slowed me down, we wouldn't even be here pulling arrows out of our equipment."

"You're right, Professor; you wouldn't be here. You'd be back a hundred miles with a lame, wind-broke team and no way to move."

"I'm glad you agree with me, Skye. If you hadn't set the snail's pace, I wouldn't be here. I wouldn't be suffering these losses. May I remind you that I sacked you, and your presence subverts my authority. I lay the blame for this fix entirely on you." Skye didn't reply to that; the man couldn't, after all. The logic of it was beyond cavil. "I'll want a full refund, Skye. That'll buy good mules and repair my wagons."

"We'll talk about it in the morning, mate. I'm going for water at dawn. That post can't be too far ahead."

"Well, Skye, at least we agree. You've harmed me, and I want to be recompensed."

"We'll see," Skye said wearily. "I'm too tired to think tonight. Meanwhile, you might want to post a guard."

"You have Jawbone; he's sentry enough."

Skye laughed, annoying Peachtree all the more, and headed for his lodge, which his women had raised well away from the Peachtree equipment. Peachtree's men were spreading their bedrolls under the wagons. They all were parched, but thanks to Skye's bungling they were miles from water.

Peachtree didn't sleep a wink. The terror haunted him. Every shift in the wind, every change of the rhythm of the night, brought him up, and sometimes the others, too. The hardpan rose up to devil his hips and shoulders. He had never known so rotten a night, lacking even fitful sleep. Not even his loaded fowling piece offered solace.

The fat moon still shone when a surly gray dawn overtook the dark. He felt half frozen. They would lack even the solace of hot tea. The more Peachtree brooded, the more he resented Skye. All his misfortunes could be laid at the feet of that bungler and his savage women. He rose and walked, trying to drive the ache from his bones, but his flesh protested. The others got up at the same time, as miserable as he. The sight of Skye's lodge enraged Peachtree. The man always slept warm.

"Harness the mules. Put the seven good ones on the medicine wagon and hook the supply wagon to it," he said. "Tie the injured mule behind. Let's hope we don't meet a hill."

"Ah could sure use some coffee," Concorde said.

"You'll have some when we find water and wood. Let's get there, wherever it is."

But before they completed their harnessing, an apparition marched out of the south. A double column of mounted soldiers materialized in the predawn haze, twenty blue-clad men led by a mustached captain who surveyed the wagons, the arrows, Carmody's body, and finally Skye's lodge before turning to Peachtree.

Jawbone squealed. The officer stared at the blue roan a long moment.

"You've had trouble. We heard something last night."

"Well, that's the Army. You didn't come when you heard shooting; you waited until you could make a picnic of it."

The captain's cheek ticked. "It was debatable. I'm Walker McCord, First Dragoons," he said. "It says Peachtree on the wagon. That you?"

"That's me, sir. We're hard put for water—"

"Sergeant Seidman," McCord said.

A beet-red three-striper instantly offered a canteen. Other soldiers offered theirs. Peachtree guzzled gratefully, lifting the canteen over and over until his thirst abated.

"All right. Whose lodge is that? And what happened?"

"That's a lout of a guide named Skye, and his squaws, and a performing woman we had with us."

"Skye? Of Fort Laramie? Is that Jawbone?"

"Yes, sir. You know him?"

"You're a lucky man, Mister Peachtree. The luckiest man alive. Who's the deceased?"

"His name's Carmody. Elisha Carmody. He called himself a former congressman. He was with the Skyes, not us."

"Carmody. Haven't heard of him. I'm very sorry. We'll bury him and notify his relatives if you have an address. What happened, Peachtree?"

"Comanches, sir. More than you can imagine."

"What band? Do you know?"

"They all look alike, Captain."

"You put up a good stand."

"We did, sir. Against three hundred of the devils, anyway. How far are we from your post?"

"Maybe three miles. Not far."

"That close? We were that close? And the Mora's there?"

"No, the Mora's about seven miles. Fort Union's on Wolf Creek, a tributary of the Mora."

"My team's in a bad way, sir. We need water."

"We'll escort you. If your team can't make it, we'll drag your wagons. I want to talk to Skye and then we'll be off. Sergeant, break out some hardtack for these people."

Peachtree walked beside McCord's chestnut to Skye's lodge, wanting to make sure that oaf got the story straight. Skye was waiting for them, beside his wives.

"Walker McCord!" roared the guide. His wives stared uncertainly. Jawbone snorted.

"You look the worse for wear, Mister Skye. There's a new hole in your hat." Captain McCord was grinning. "Took on a few Comanches, did you?"

"More'n I want to think about."

McCord tossed his canteen at Skye, who handed it to Mary. She drank greedily, and passed it to Victoria.

"We're three miles from the post. Can you make it?"

"This child usually does."

McCord laughed. "Let's hear it, you old coon."

"He prefers to be addressed formally," Peachtree said.

"They jumped us after moonrise, Captain. Big village out on the Canadian. Mary says they're the Antelopes. We'd dealt with a few of their scouts earlier—Victoria and me. Had to keep them off these folks. But one slid in before moonrise and got our friend Elisha Carmody. He was some man. One to ride with, I'll say. He left a big hole around here, Walker."

"We heard something or other. Night sergeant reported it this morning. We'll take you in, Barnaby. These folks are in tough shape—you're not much better off."

"That'd be mighty kind, Captain. How's the missus?"

"Kate's back in Ohio. We haven't got enough of a post for women yet. Next year, maybe. How are your ladies?" he asked, surveying Mary and Victoria.

"Vexed by the bloody Comanche, but we didn't go under."

McCord turned to Peachtree. "Well, sir, let's go. I can tell you one thing the Army knows: you wouldn't be talking to me right now if you didn't have the Skyes guiding you."

"Well, I didn't. I sacked them. They're responsible for these losses, this disaster—"

Captain McCord laughed dismissively, which annoyed Hyacinth Z. Peachtree. He decided to hush up for the moment but one way or another he was going to get a refund from Skye.

It took the sluggish mules an hour to toil their way to Fort Union, a huddle of raw log buildings on a flat below a beetling gray mesa. The red, white, and blue flapped lazily from a pole at the center of the parade.

"Take care of all this stock," McCord said to his sergeant.

Much to Peachtree's joy, the United States First Dragoons swiftly watered the mules and rationed out oats and hay, while a ferrier sergeant saw to the wounds.

"You're very kind, sir," Peachtree said to the sergeant.

"Anything for Barnaby Skye, sir."

Peachtree throttled back a retort.

"Mister Peachtree, we'll go report now," McCord said. "Our commander's Lieutenant Colonel Sumner, Edwin Vose Sumner, and he'll want every detail. We may go after that village."

"I suppose he's a friend of Skye, too."

"The whole Army of the West is a friend of Barnaby Skye, sir. There's no better man on the borders."

"Well, that's debatable—"

"No, Peachtree—that's not debatable. You obviously owe him everything. Your medicine troupe didn't lose a life. Those twenty-seven dead horses I counted out there beyond your camp—I'll warrant none of them were shot with your scatterguns. You've got eight live mules and two wagons, and your lives. I'd say you owe him more than you'll ever be able to pay. What price is your life, sir?"

Hyacinth Z. Peachtree decided that silence was politic. He would take it up with Skye later.

Chapter 56

The scene Hyacinth Z. Peachtree was witnessing on a wind-harrowed plain well away from Fort Union stirred something in him. The United States Army was burying Elisha Carmody.

The relentless wind stirred the Stars and Stripes that lay upon the pine box beside the newly opened sod. Around this desolate place stood the United States Dragoons in dress blues with maroon stripes down their trousers, gold thread on their tunics. Peachtree had donned his best clawhammer coat and silk top hat, while Carlotta wore a borrowed black shawl. Pontius P. Parsons, Hercules, and Concorde all gathered at graveside, along with Skye in his buckskins, looking like Nature's Child. Skye's wives wore their finest beaded festival clothes. Six pallbearers, each a noncommissioned officer wearing dress blues and white gloves, stood at attention.

Lieutenant Colonel Sumner waited patiently at the head of the grave until all was ready, lifted his pince-nez, and began.

"I regret that this half-built post has no chaplain to bury a fine American citizen, but I consider it an honor to fill that office," he began. "This is the first burial in our post cemetery. It is our sad duty to bury a former United States congressman. I've talked at length with Mister Skye and Professor Peachtree and others here, learning what I could about this gentleman from Ohio, Elisha Carmody. And the more I learned, the more amazed I was by this extraordinary American."

Everything about Sumner pleased H.Z. Peachtree. The commanding officer had spent two hours closeted with Peachtree and Skye, asking intelligent questions not only about the trip south, but also about Elisha Carmody, the condition of the Indian country, its tribes, and the state of the Western Army. He had treated Peachtree with the utmost respect.

He had instantly sent two troops out to make sure the Comanches didn't harass travelers on the Santa Fe Trail, but stopped short of a punitive strike because he was shorthanded and the post was largely staffed by engineers and construction workers.

"I understand that Elisha Carmody, after serving two terms as a Whig congressman, retired from that high office to pursue a vision that he had refined during his years in office. He took his insights about the human condition to his former constituents and then to the larger world, and died here on these lonely wastes a martyr to the ideal that inspired him. It will benefit us now, and honor this distinguished American, to recount briefly what Elisha Carmody saw as the hope for fallen mankind."

Peachtree felt a certain envy. Here was Carmody being praised to the skies for his devotion to the blessedness of mankind, while the world scarcely recognized Hyacinth's even more profound devotion to the comfort of his fellow mortals. Let a man pass the hat to support his idealistic lectures and he was a saint. Let a man charge for his skills, and he was merely a huckster. But Hyacinth set aside his annoyance for the duration of the service. He could enjoy a lofty moment as well as the next man.

"Elisha Carmody found that politics fell short," Sumner was saying. "So did law, government, and all social institutions that we look to for our salvation. He turned instead to the ultimate resource of each mortal, one's internal strengths, and found there the keys to personal happiness and freedom. As I understand it, Carmody was bringing to the world a vision of self-discipline as the means for each of us to overcome our slavery to the vices that overwhelm many a mortal. Let law and order reside in the soul, not in government or politics, he proclaimed. And whoever imposed law and order on himself would, by some remarkable paradox, be set free to pursue happiness. That, dear friends, was radical doctrine. It was also rooted in the vision of our founding fathers, as I interpret them."

Colonel Sumner dwelled a while more on Elisha Carmody's moral vision, and then the man himself: "We bury a great American here. This man abandoned high office and devoted his every cent to propagating his vision for a happier world. He scorned even a saddlehorse, electing to walk to California so that he might have that much more money to devote to lecturing.

"Let us remember him with esteem. The United States Army honors him. The flag that now covers his coffin will be sent to his children, along with an account of his final days. Now, if you would, let me offer a prayer to the Almighty Father for the repose of this man's great and generous soul."

Peachtree lifted his silk top hat from his shining locks, and held it to his breast as Colonel Sumner read a burial prayer and led them in the Twenty-third Psalm. Two sergeants lifted the American flag and folded it into a compact triangle. The six pallbearers, each handling a canvas strap, slowly lowered the plain pine box into the lonely prairie. A Dragoon squad fired three volleys honoring the dead, each spaced by a lonely silence. Colonel Sumner read a benediction.

They paused in the wind, each paying homage to a rare man. Peachtree did his best to remember Carmody with esteem. The lecturer was certainly a likable sort, and he'd contributed steadily to the well-being of the entourage, gathering firewood, helping Skye's women with their tasks. He had always been on hand when Concorde or Hercules was assembling harness and throwing it over the backs of a dozen fractious mules. Peachtree could grant Carmody that, even if the man's ideas were crackbrained. How could any mortal govern his passions? Why, the conduct of Barnaby Skye was enough to disprove the man's notions.

They walked quietly back to the post through an aching noon, and Sumner fell in beside Peachtree. "Did I do the man justice?" he asked. "I wanted to."

"Colonel, you gave him his due."

"Why, Mister Peachtree, I simply wanted to honor the man. Now what are your plans?"

"A little at sea, Colonel. We'll be going on to Santa Fe as soon as my mules recruit. We're in a bad way after that trouble with the savages. Our destination is California."

"What about Skye?"

"He can do whatever he wishes. I've discharged him. Now I know what you people think of him, but I must say, sir, he got us into that mess. He slowed us down. We should have been through here a week ago. And now I'm short some mules."

"Your mules . . . that reminds me. My quartermaster's been eyeing them. They're badly gaunted but sound enough, and they'll recruit with good care. It happens we've about twenty mules we're pensioning. Most of them are saddle-galled. We had a corporal here who wasn't using blankets under pack-saddles. They're useless to the Army, but perfectly sound and in good flesh. Do you suppose you'd consider a trade? A dozen galled mules, perfectly fit for harness, for your eight? Eight sound mules are worth more to the Army than a dozen we can't use."

"Saddle-galled mules? Fresh and fat?"

"All just fine except for some galling on the withers. Healed over but too scarred to use again. They'll be fine for harness. They aren't harness-broke, but the Dragoons aren't without some ability in that area. I'd say that by tomorrow we could turn over a dozen mules that've tasted life in a collar."

Ecstasy bloomed in H.Z. Peachtree. "Well, if it's a square proposition, you have a deal, Colonel."

"I thought you might like it, Peachtree," the colonel said. "You wouldn't get anything but a square deal from me."

In short order bills of sale were exchanged and Peachtree found himself the owner of a dozen Army mules, each with a U.S. brand on its shoulder. Even before the exchange, Army muleskinners had harnessed the mules and now were driving them in great circles with whips in hand. Peachtree watched contentedly, seeing military skills transform the mules into reliable teams. They'd be rambunctious a few days, but nothing he and a tassled whip couldn't handle. He plumbed cunning mule minds better than mules knew themselves.

He found Skye watching the training and thought to get rid of the man once and for all. "We're leaving in the morning, Skye, and I'll thank you not to join us."

The guide smiled. "I imagine we'll be coming along. You paid me to get you to Santa Fe."

"Well don't feel obligated. In fact, I still want a refund. You cost me a fortune."

"Well, mate, you've traded for fresh mules, and aren't hurting. I put that idea in the colonel's ear. I thought it'd solve your problems for you."

"You seem to have magical powers over the Army."

The guide shrugged. "You hired me to get you to Santa Fe so you're stuck with me until I get you there. I'm always looking for ways to help clients. When I saw their galled mules, I thought of a trade."

The man was maddening. The frontier oaf thought he was

a guardian angel. Hyacinth Z. Peachtree scarcely knew how to reply. "What's Carlotta going to do?" he said.

"We'll take her there. My wives and I, we thought maybe if you don't want her, we'd spare her enough to get by for a time. She wants to talk to you, by the way."

"She wants to hire on. I know her better than I know myself."

"No, she said she wants to give you a gift."

"A gift?"

"That's what she said."

"Skye, she's never given a gift in her life. She takes gifts; she doesn't give them. She's incapable of giving another mortal a gift. This is obviously some sort of hoax."

"No, she's serious. She wants to sing one last time with your troupe in Santa Fe—help you get some cash together. She said she owes it to you."

"You'll have your little jest, Skye."

"It's Mister Skye, sir, and we'll be ready to escort you to Santa Fe whenever you are."

"My God, Skye, what a pest you are."

Skye stood there grinning, a stubble-jawed, craggy-faced, smelly ruffian with an absurd hat.

Chapter 57

Santa Fe! H.Z. Peachtree exulted. This very night he would recoup his fortunes in the famous old plaza at the end of the trail. He still hoarded thirty fleeces garnered at Pueblo, money of a sort in cashless Santa Fe. These he would trade for Dover's Powder and other delightful chemicals at the nearest apothecary. Tray upon tray of green bottles still rattled in the cabinets behind him. His cask of pure grain spirits had been recovered from the Skyes. He possessed various berries, leaves, and stems to produce more elixirs.

The next Nepenthe would be different, of course: there would be an amiable dose of opium in a tincture of grain spirits, plus a little tobacco leaf and resinous flavorings. He would end up with lip-smacking laudanum. Before nightfall he'd have the elixir brewed and corked.

Ahead of him, Skye still plodded along on that vile horse, and behind, his wretched squaws still herded their misbegotten travois ponies. It didn't matter. In an hour he'd be rid of them once and for all. Tomorrow, he'd outfit for California with this night's take. In a week, he'd be on the road again, with a fat purse.

They traversed a road cut into piñon pine slopes that formed the pedestal of a snow-burdened mountain clapped with gray clouds. On the flats below him he saw little adobes surrounded by fallow garden plots. They entered a narrow clay street hemmed by low houses of mud brick, much eroded by the elements. This thoroughfare bustled with life: seamed old women in black, tawny children, raven-haired ladies wrapped in *rebozos*, swart men leading mules harnessed to *carretas*, and an occasional giant freight wagon and ox team, driven by profane Yankee teamsters.

They rolled past an ancient church of adobe bricks, descended a rutted slope to a creek bottom, and followed the twisting, stinking passage, not much wider than an alley, toward the plaza, the heart of this strange city the Mexicans called Holy Faith. No one paid attention to Peachtree's entourage. This city had seen all manner of mortals, and was not excited by a mountain man in buckskins and a battered top hat, or even by the squaws driving the travois ponies.

Elation overtook him. "Well, Pontius, we made it, no thanks to that dunce ahead," he said.

"Mudpie town, that's what it is. You'd think they'd prefer honest red brick," Parsons said. "But then, these sorts never do anything right. Give me brick and I'll show you civilization."

"Tonight, my old friend, you'll have a dose of laudanum for your aches and pains—the real thing."

"Ah, the genuine stuff. And none too soon, H.Z. These battered bones protest every time this springless contraption of yours kisses a pothole. Which is to say, every three seconds. Get me the juice, or I'll retire. I'm no good without it."

"Why, it's at the top of my list, Pontius. You deserve a jug of it. By the way, I'll be calling it Nepenthe tonight, not Pain Extractor. The name has great possibilities."

"Whatever it is, don't keep me waiting."

They rolled past a one-story hotel billed as the Exchange, and burst upon a large plaza bustling with polyglot crowds. Its vitality astonished him. Here stood wagons cheek by jowl, Yankee traders, pilgrims bound for the gold fields, caramel-colored ladies in woolen coats, blanketed Pueblo Indians, several squealing hogs in a *carreta*, a pack of varicolored mutts decorating wagon wheels, bearded hucksters shouting at the mobs, and braying mules by the dozen. Soldiers from Fort Marcy up the hill dappled the mob with blue.

He saw more Anglos than Mexicans, many of them with wagons destined for the California gold fields. A great joy suffused him. He had fretted that there might not be any English-speaking people around to sell to. He knew how to huckster bonehead Yankees. But these superstitious greasers were another matter. In every *placita* along the way, he'd passed little adobe niches that protected images of the saints and the Virgin. He knew he couldn't compete with saints and miracles, priests and holy water, when it came to corporal needs.

But here in this fine brawling square were scores, maybe a hundred, of Kentuckians, Illinoisans, Virginians, and New Englanders, every one of them needful of Nepenthe, even if they didn't know it yet. Old Parsons would be in his element.

Skye reined up before a porticoed adobe building stretching across the entire north side of the plaza. H.Z. knew it was the Palace of the Governors. Off to the east Peachtree could see the massive towers of an adobe church he knew was *La Parroquia*. Squat shops lined the bustling plaza like yellow incisors, each of them promising delights unheard of. Peachtree halted the lively mules and helped Pontius down.

"We're here, my friend," he said expansively, feeling a vast pleasure that was scarcely diminished by the sight of Skye clambering off that devil-eyed horse, or of his sullen squaws and their savage travois, or even of moody Carlotta, slowly dismounting and brushing her hiked skirts down.

Peachtree approached a clerkish-looking bearded Yank in a black suit, whom he suspected to be a Santa Fe trader.

"Sir, a word, if I may. Are you acquainted with this ancient metropolis of the Spaniards, perchance?"

The man nodded, surveying Peachtree's wrinkled clawhammer coat, grimy collar and cuffs.

"Ah, good. I'm looking for a first-rate apothecary with a good inventory."

"I see by your wagon the nature of your calling," the man said. "Why, we have several. Right out there, on Palace, is one, a transplanted Scot. A sharp dealer, though. He'll gouge you."

"Well, will he trade? I'm shy of cash, but have valuable commodities."

"Anyone in Santa Fe'll trade, sir. You'll have to haggle, that's all. Now, off the plaza yonder, on Mule Alley, there's a *curandera* who runs an herbal shop. Properly, she's a *yerbera*. The shingle at her door says *Yerbas y Remedios*, eh? Now, mind you, she doesn't talk English, and you'll not find her there before noon."

"Oh, that's capital, capital. I'll restock my simples, sir. I'm H.Z. Peachtree, as you must have gathered, and if you'll come around here late in the afternoon, my troupe will be entertaining with bright airs and cheerful marches. I offer painless salvation, and I trust you'll—"

"It's nothing." The stranger bowed slightly, and wandered off.

Peachtree exulted. Simples and powders within a block or two. A little time in his cabinet laboratory brewing and bottling, and he'd be in business.

He turned to find Carlotta standing beside him, looking solemn. "I suppose you want a job again."

"No, but I'll sing for you tonight."

"Well, that's fine. I always liked the ring of it: H.Z. Peachtree and the Potawatomi Princess. It has a certain cachet."

"Hyacinth?"

He had been flippant, but he saw a seriousness in her that gave him pause. "You're going to say goodbye?"

"No, not really. I'm goink to say I'm sorry. I am all this time quittink. All this time I think I am too good for this travelink show. I have a good voice so I quit just to let you know. I quit every opera house in the world. I was wrong. I make life hard for you and for all the others." She looked as if she wanted to say a lot more, but her brave moment faded and she stood silently on the brink of tears.

Ah, female wiles. What man can resist a lady's tears? "You want a job," he said. "That's what all this is, my little canary."

"No, I wouldn't take a job even if you offered me one."

"Well that's fine; I wouldn't offer you one even if you asked me. What are you going to do now?"

"I don't know," she said, a quaver in her voice.

He contemplated the matter, his eye roving down her lush figure. "Well, there's only one thing to do, Carlotta. Get married."

"Married? To you, Peachtree?"

"Who else?"

"Do you love me?"

"Of course not. Neither do you love me."

"Then why do you propose this mad idea?"

"Lust and greed, mine and yours."

"Yes, those would be your reasons. I'm sorry, Peachtree. I'm goink to start over. But not with you. I'm not the same woman I was. Tonight will be the last act."

He saw she meant it. "It's a mistake, Carlotta," he said.

"We must overcome our mistakes. Goodbye, Peachtree."

"Carlotta—I'll pay you your back wages as soon as we're out of Santa Fe."

She stood in the dust, paralyzed, and he knew he had her.

"Goodbye, Peachtree," she said, and walked away.

Chapter 58

Dread gripped Carlotta as she approached the Skyes. She had nothing but her trunk and a few clothes salvaged from the Comanches. She stared around the alien plaza, seeing no hope anywhere, no honorable way to make a new life.

Peachtree, Concorde, Hercules, and Parsons all stared at her, not really believing. It would be so easy to run back to them. They were all the family she had and the only hope of a roof and food. But she resisted that temptation with what little courage she could muster, and walked steadily to the Skyes.

They were standing there uneasily, their gazes question marks. She loved each of them, and this moment of parting filled her with such anguish she couldn't contain her tears.

"I have left the show for good," she said to Skye.

Skye studied her a moment. "What're you going to do, Carlotta?"

"I don't know. I find somethink, yes?" She knew her false cheer didn't ring true.

"Dammit," said Victoria.

"Maybe I sing on the street corner, and pass the hat," she said. "I have a voice, yes?"

"You have a lyrical voice, Carlotta," Skye said.

"I will sing, then. I will sing in Spanish and maybe they will slip me a few *pesos*—or is it pennies now? Then I'll buy bread."

"You'll hear offers you won't like," Skye said grimly. "They may take you for a vagrant. Unescorted woman in a Mexican town—"

"Dammit, Mister Skye, give her the horse."

Skye looked uncomfortable. "Miss Krafft-Ebing, my wives and I, we've been troubling about you some. This horse—the one we got when . . . you know. It's yours."

"For me?" She fought a great upwelling of tears. "Why for me?"

"We thought you might want to go east. Go to Kansas City. Sing there. Start life over. The horse'd be a start. With that and some cash you could join an eastbound wagon train."

The horse would be a beginning. She couldn't afford to stable it but she might trade it. "You are so good," she said, pushing back the pain in her heart.

"Mary and Victoria, they thought maybe you'd need some cash. We've some extra this time. We'd like to give you a stake. Enough to get you some chow and a bedroll. Fetch you a room tonight."

"Oh, Skye."

"I prefer Mister Skye," he said, his blue eyes merry. He extracted a leather bag from under his belt and peered about sharply, but no one was watching. Then he handed her five double eagles that shattered sunlight in her palm.

"Oh, Skye. I—can't take this!"

"It's for you, Carlotta. If you'd like, we'll get you outfitted, put your pony in a livery barn."

"But you need it."

"We've enough to winter in Taos. And ways of getting by if we don't have enough."

"Dammit, take it," Victoria said.

She stared at the bright twenty-dollar gold pieces with the American eagles on them. She could rent a hall, have a poster put up, hire a guitarist, sing in concert, charge admission, get ahead. She could sleep in rooms tonight, buy a supper, buy food for the trail, feed her horse, go east with the next wagon train.

"You'll want to hide that," Skye said.

"Oh, Skye," she cried, "Thank you." The tears came up, and she couldn't stop them for a long while.

The big guide found a room for her at the Exchange, stowed her trunk in it, put her horse in a livery barn behind the hotel, converted one of her double eagles into small change. He introduced her to the clerks in the Palace of the Governors and charged them with her well-being. After that she and the Skyes stood in the solemn plaza, unable to delay the moment any longer.

"Time for us to mosey along, Carlotta," Skye said roughly.

"Oh, Skye," she said, the tears rising again. "Oh, my darlinks."

She clasped the big guide to her and wept into his buckskin shirt, and then she held Victoria and wept, and then Mary. She loved these people who had loved her, helped her, and shepherded her to the end of the trail.

"I cannot repay you," she said at last, rubbing tears from her cheeks.

"Just seeing you starting a new life is a greater reward than you'll ever know," Skye said. "It's Elisha Carmody we can never pay."

"I will try," she whispered. "He showed me the way. I will master myself. He gave his life for me and I'll never let him down."

Chapter 59

Barnaby Skye itched to get out of Santa Fe. Jawbone trembled, ready to massacre every living thing in sight. His wives stared at the first city they had ever seen. Their travois horses occupied too much space in the plaza, and occasioned squinty stares from Yanks who preferred dead Indians to live ones. Skye eyed the hubbub sourly and resolved to get out before trouble started.

"We'll go right on to Taos," he said to Victoria.

"Sonofabitch, I never seen so many white men. This whole city's knee-deep in horse apples."

"Are there stores in Taos too?" asked Mary.

"A few. It's just a little place, with a plaza like this, Mary. Very quiet. You'll be right at home."

"Well I want to see everything."

"White men stink," Victoria said, eyeing Skye maliciously.

He retreated, intending to settle anything that needed settling with Peachtree, who had parked on the south side of the plaza and was examining the contents of his cabinets.

"Well, Professor, we got you here safe and sound," Skye said to his back.

Hyacinth Z. Peachtree turned slowly to face Skye, his face a thunderclap. "I suppose you'd like to think so," he said. "The fact is, Skye, you delayed us, cost me a young fortune, and nearly destroyed the Peachtree Medicine Show. You let on that we would need a guide to cross a trackless waste—but there were lodgetrails the whole way. Fraud's what I call it."

"Well, mate—"

"And another thing, Skye. If you hadn't held me back, we never would have met those Comanches. As a direct result of that you cost me two dead mules, a wounded mule, and a wagon so pocked with arrow holes that I'm forced to have it rebuilt and relacquered. Look at it! I'm a practitioner of apothecary arts; I can't be seen with a shabby vehicle of the sort used by any common huckster. Just as bad, sir, you cost me my simples. You undermined my authority, causing division in my company. That crackpot fellow you insisted on bringing along cost me the Potawatomi Princess and wrecked my show."

"Professor, it wasn't exactly like that."

"Wasn't like that?" Peachtree glared. "Skye, this outfit has more seasoning than any beaver-trapping oaf could get in two lifetimes. We didn't need you to deal with savages; we did it better. I rue the day we scrambled around to meet your inflated price."

"It's Mister Skye, mate."

"Well, Mister Skye, here's a bill."

Peachtree thrust a paper at Skye. In a fine copperplate hand was an accounting:

Arrow damage to H.Z. Peachtree wagon $100.00
Death of two mules...$200.00
Injury of one mule $50.00
Failure to supply meat, per agreement $50.00
Total...$400.00

Skye read it, not surprised. The amount was about what he had charged to guide them. "Well, mate, you've twelve fine Army mules in good flesh right now because of a trade I suggested to Colonel Sumner."

"Twelve mules with saddle galls, Skye. Their sale value's far below the twelve flawless mules I drove into Fort Laramie."

"You worked one to death yourself, mate."

"Why, trying to make up the time you cost me. Every day's delay cheats me out of income I'd be earning in California."

Skye didn't argue. Taos beckoned. "All right, send it to my agent, Colonel Bullock, Professor."

"No, I want it settled here."

Skye laughed. A wild joy built in him, the joy he had known roving the sweet windswept meadows, the trackless prairies, the valleys of rushing creeks. The joy he'd felt when he carried Victoria for the first time into the honeymoon lodge, and again when tender Mary bonded herself to him. And still again when he beheld the wonder of his infant son. He laughed, remembering the day when Jawbone was born and how the little devil scampered with the sheer delight of being alive in a whole world without fences.

"Send it to Bullock, Peachtree," he said. "He'll know what to do with it."

"I'll have you in court, Skye."

"You do that, mate."

"The least you can do is give me that Comanche pony."

"I've given it to Carlotta. She can go east with any trading company now."

"Yes, with my horse."

"Peachtree, up that slope's Fort Marcy. I told her that if you try to take anything from her, to go there. I've already talked to the clerks in the governors' palace. They'll have a good stout brig. Understand?"

Something seeped out of Peachtree, like a teakettle surrendering steam. He stared, then nodded. "Say, Skye, what happened to her that time she quit?"

"That's for her to tell you."

"Where are you going, Skye? I want to know."

"It's Mister Skye, mate."

Peachtree grimaced, and turned to his labors. He was concocting elixirs.

Skye hurried his little family north on the Taos Road, and left the city of Holy Faith none too soon for his tastes. Ahead lay three days of travel along a twisting trail that would take them through *placitas* and along creeks tumbling out of the Sangre de Cristo mountains.

At the end they would enter San Fernando de Taos, a Mexican village snugged against the backbone of the Rockies, where the winters were mild and sunny. It had been a favorite resort of the mountain men for years. The hospitable Mexicans had welcomed them and sold them Taos Lightning, a lethal whiskey they called *aguardiente*. There had always been *bailes* and flirting with the bright-eyed *señoritas*; lazy, happy days mending gear, telling tall tales, and sleeping late under warm buffler robes with a silky woman.

It would be the same as the old bachelor days, only better. This time he would have his family with him. This time, too, he and an old friend would while away the hours with good palaver and memories of the doin's in the mountains. It had been a heap of winters since he'd seen Christopher Carson. He'd never met beautiful little Josefa or Kit's children, and he was looking forward to it. Old Kit had built himself a 'dobe house east of the Taos Plaza, and Skye would be spending much of the winter at its hearth. Off a way was a fine stand of cottonwoods, about right for a winter lodge, with plenty of feed for Jawbone and the rest of the horses.

Victoria reined up beside him. "Is it true that Christopher Carson has a wife, Mister Skye?"

"A beautiful young Mexican wife, Josefa Jarimillo, and children now, Victoria."

"Who would have thought it?" she said. "It is said among us that he shared his blanket with every Absaroka girl—and every Snake girl too, when he was in the North."

"Well, that's a legend, Victoria."

"No, it's true. The Kicked-in-the-Bellies call him Blanket Kit."

"It's not true, but don't take notions."

"I won't, Blanket Barnaby."

Barnaby Skye reared back his head and roared at the blue heavens, until Jawbone got cross and bucked.

Author's Note

The traveling medicine show was a colorful American institution through much of the nineteenth century. It reached its zenith late in the century, when the larger shows rented theaters and halls for their performances, or used large tents. The medicine show waned with the enactment of food and drug laws, and with the advances of scientific medicine.

The shows hawked every imaginable curative, from the ineffectual and harmless to the powerful and harmful. Typically the product was diluted alcohol with strong flavoring added. Many shows featured Indian remedies, exploiting the public's correct perception that tribal healers had effective medicines not employed by white doctors. Some used various opiates such as morphine, codeine, laudanum, paregoric, and Dover's Powder. Others employed herbal remedies. As cures, most were worthless.

The active ingredients in H.Z. Peachtree's herbal concoctions include scopolamine, atropine, and hyoscyamine. These alkaloids are found in jimson weed and henbane, and comprise the active ingredients of belladonna, or deadly night-shade, a drug used from ancient times as a sedative and poison. Peachtree also employed nicotine, a nervous-system depressant so powerful that only fifty milligrams, one-twentieth of a gram, is considered lethal. Some of these alkaloids are also hallucinogenic. All can be fatal in overdose. Henbane, while not native to the Rockies, colonized itself and is now commonplace there.

For an amusing look at patent medicines and medicine shows, see *One for a Man, Two for a Horse: A Pictorial History, Grave and Comic, of Patent Medicines*, by Gerald Carson, Bramhall House.

—RSW

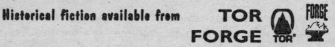